Savage Ransom

OTHER BOOKS BY DAVID LIPPINCOTT

The Blood of October

Tremor Violet

The Voice of Armageddon

E Pluribus Bang!

Savage
Ransom

David Lippincott

RAWSON ASSOCIATES PUBLISHERS, INC.
NEW YORK

Library of Congress Cataloging in Publication Data

Lippincott, David.
Savage ransom.

I. Title.
PZ4.L767Saw   [PS3562.I58]−813′.5′4−78-3114
ISBN 0-89256-061-4

Copyright © 1978 by David Lippincott
All rights reserved
Published simultaneously in Canada by
McClelland and Stewart, Ltd.
Manufactured in the United States of America
by Fairfield Graphics, Fairfield, Pennsylvania
Designed by Julian Hamer
First Edition

For D.B.W.

Savage Ransom

When the children in Greenport first began
disappearing, people right off assumed they'd
been kidnapped and started wondering how
much it would cost to get them back. They
made it sound like a business deal, so much
money down and back comes your kid. Well,
there was going to be a ransom, all right, but
something that would cost a lot more than
money.

I'm trying to make a point, you see, and to do
that right, I have to demand a sort of ultimate
ransom. One that will really test people. The
ultimate ransom for the ultimate kidnapping.

Tough on the kids, of course, but if I can
prove my point, the plan will leave children
everywhere a little better off, so I guess it'll be
worth it.

Hell, I only wish somebody a long time ago
had done as much for me.

—TAPE-LOG OF THE PIPER,
ENTRY DATED MAY 17.

Prologue

It looked out of place, and was. Most of the cars and pickup trucks on Havmeyer Street in Greenport had a new, polished look to them; the black Volks van had been recently refinished, but with an uneven coat of paint that only accentuated how old it was. Inside, the Volks looked even more dilapidated. The floor in the van's rear was of stained, slatted wood, and running around both of its sides at about eye-level were rows of rusted meat-hooks. This unpromising area was separated from the driver's compartment by a thick wall pierced by a small sliding door on the right-hand side, a reminder that at one time the truck had been refrigerated. The van, when its paint was new and its original owner hopeful, had apparently been used to deliver large cuts of meat.

For a long time, the Volks sat parked, both front and rear right wheels against the curb, while its driver alternately stared off into space or looked up the street to where the garish blue-white light of a small delicatessen threw a patchwork of shadows onto the evening pavement.

At 8:17, the driver's head snapped up; one of his hands rapped against the sliding door to the rear compartment. The door opened slightly and the dim shadow of a face appeared, its eyes following the driver's. Fifteen-year-old Angel Sanchez, his shift at the family delicatessen done for another day, walked briskly out of the store. Through the large plate-glass window, he saw his mother waving to him and returned the gesture, then turned to start up the hill, beginning the long walk to his home in the town's poorer section.

After watching for a few moments, a grunt from the rear compartment of the van set the driver in motion; the Volks' motor started, and as Angel got halfway up the hill, the van pulled away from the curb and began slowly moving up the

street, carefully keeping some distance behind Angel. Its headlights remained unlit.

Perhaps half a mile further on, Angel reached the skeleton
of steel and concrete which marked the site of a new office
building under construction, the wheelbarrows and scaffolding
abandoned now for the day. The opposite side of the street
was equally deserted, with a vacant lot waiting its turn to be
built upon. The dim face in the rear compartment of the van
nodded at the driver, and the door slid closed. Stopping for a
moment, the driver turned off the engine, then started it up
again, switching on the headlights at the same time. With a
noisy shifting of gears, the Volks drove up the hill, its
squealing brakes halting it directly beside Angel.

A lift was offered. Angel sighed. It had been a long day:
school, the lengthy trip to the family store, his stint there, and
now, the hard walk home. Still ahead lay several hours of
homework. Gratefully, Angel accepted, pulling open the door
and sliding in beside the driver. The van began moving. Twice
Angel attempted conversation, but it was not returned. Angel
shrugged and studied the driver's compartment listlessly; the
inside handle of the door beside him was missing, but the van
was old and it didn't strike him as peculiar.

Angel's first real premonition of danger was a chill breeze
on the back of his neck. Automatically, he began to turn in his
seat. He never got very far. The driver suddenly slammed on
the brakes and shouted, "Now!" Almost simultaneously, he
lunged at Angel and pinned his legs and lower body to the
seat.

What happened then all took place so fast that Angel only
had fleeting impressions of it, a dizzying succession of pictures
and sensations as if watching a slide projector out of control;
a slamming sound as something behind him slid fully open; a
pair of hands that appeared suddenly in front of his face,
holding a thin piece of rope or wire which the hands yanked
tightly around his neck; one of the hands grabbing him by the
hair and forcing his head backward across the top of the seat;
the wire tightening; his own hands groping for the door
handle, not remembering it wasn't there; his legs thrashing
against the dashboard until the driver pinned him tighter by
sitting astride his body; a sudden, damp moistness in his

trousers; a feeling that he was starting to lose consciousness; the hand that had hold of his hair pulling his head so far backward over the seat that for a second he got an upside-down view of the face behind him; a cracking, snapping sound he realized was coming from his own neck. And then, nothingness.

For a few moments after his neck was broken, Angel's autonomic nervous system continued to function. His back arched repeatedly, straining against something Angel could no longer see or feel. In spite of the driver sitting astride his body, his legs thrashed convulsively, the feet beating a frantic tattoo on the van's floor, as if trying to tap-dance their way to safety. A series of spasms shook his entire body, rolling his head against the back of the seat in great circles. From somewhere inside him there came a bubbling moan, while a small stream of saliva dribbled down his chin. At 8:46 the slight twitching of the fingers on his right hand stopped; Angel Sanchez was visibly, as well as medically, dead.

Quickly, the driver and the still-dim face behind the panel passed Angel's body through the opening of the sliding door into the rear compartment. The driver had just slid over behind the wheel again when the face reappeared at the opening. For a moment, the two of them sat mute, panting slightly, partly from exertion, partly from excitement. Finally, the driver turned and spoke. "Well, we can do it."

The face appeared to shake itself before answering in a soft voice. "Now it begins. . . ."

The driver came to life and slammed the Volks into gear. Slowly, it disappeared up the long hill and vanished into the darkness, Angel Sanchez's body banging mournfully against the side of the van from where it hung suspended by one of the butcher's hooks.

Chapter 1 _____

They're never going to put up a statue of me at the Central Park Children's Zoo, or give me a moving wax dummy with my face at Disneyland, but that's because no one can see what I'm trying to do.

Most people will probably just say I'm nuts. Or, worse, that it was done for kicks. But if I can get my point across, in the end, what they say about me is unimportant.

Besides, in Central Park, a statue's just a place for pigeons to sit.

—TAPE-LOG OF THE PIPER,
ENTRY DATED MAY 10.

That day, May 12th, the morning after Angel Sanchez disappeared, the sun, at latitude 73 degrees 40 minutes West, longitude 39 degrees 50 minutes North, did not pull itself out of the grayness of the Atlantic until 6:13 A.M. Its first tentative rays raced across the water, striking the southern shore of Long Beach by 6:14, then picked their way across Long Island, from Baldwin on the South Shore to Bayville on the North, before sprinting across Long Island Sound at 6:16. Almost across, the shafts of sunlight touched briefly on Great Reef and Little Reef Islands before plunging into the welter of inlets and bays flanking the town. There, the sun first bounced off the masts of the larger yachts lying in the outer harbor, then made its way across the still-damp decks of the smaller craft lying closer to shore, finally bursting against the polished brass cannon of the Leafpoint Harbor Yacht Club at precisely 6:19.

The sun, although uninvited, had arrived in Greenport, Connecticut. Located midway between Rye and Greenwich, Greenport was the archetype of the golden suburb. Further inland, washed by the same early morning sun, lay the township itself, a vast area comprising some 75 square miles. Greenport was the ultimate product of the peculiarly American penchant for living handsomely in idyllic, countrylike surroundings while growing rich in the violent squalor of some nearby city. In the case of Greenport, this penchant did not come cheaply; it had the highest per capita income of any township in the highest per capita county (Fairfield) in the highest per capita state (Connecticut) of mainland America. And, with the exception of a few second-generation entrepreneurs, Greenport's per capita income was largely self-made—by the Chairmen, Vice-Chairmen, Presidents, Executive and Senior Vice-Presidents of some of the country's largest corporations. These men huddled together here, in an area they felt appropriate to their dearly bought status: the land was lush, the houses impressive, the clubs lavish, the Sound serene, and the atmosphere protected and tranquil. It represented the perfect escape from the violence and visible poverty of the city that allowed them to live in so affluent a setting; violence here was so rare as to be unknown, and if there *were* poor in Greenport, they had the good taste to stay out of sight.

In general, the larger estates tended to be further inland, growing in size as they followed the land across the Connecticut Turnpike, the Merritt Parkway, and the entire distance of 87 miles to the New York border. There was one notable exception. Close to the Sound, slightly to the east of Leafpoint Harbor, still pale in the early morning May sunlight, a serrated point of land sloped down to merge with the water. This was the Long's Bay area of Greenport, and behind its guarded gates lay some of the most expensive property in a town where all land sells dearly. On the second floor of one of its larger houses—pretentious by the studiedly underplayed local standards—the sun breached the slats of a venetian blind and fell upon the sleeping eyes of Kip Grolier. His handsome teenaged face contorted in its sleep against this intrusion, as the boy mumbled some incoherent incantation and turned over, burrowing deeper into the pillows to shut out the light. If Greenport was the golden suburb, Kip was its golden boy.

Almost painfully handsome, Kip (for Christopher, Jr.) was mature for his seventeen and a half years, gifted with a warm smile that made him instantly likable. But appearance was only a beginning. Kip Grolier was President of the Student

Body at Greenport Country Day, the cornerstone of the De-
bating Society, at the top of the Honor Roll, captain and star
performer of the swimming team, and probably the best-liked
and most respected boy in the entire school. He was the model
suburb's model teen-ager, the affluent father's ideal son, an
Eastern achiever's proudest possession. The golden boy.

The morning of May 12th, however, began as less than
golden for Kip. To start with, he had not slept well, his mind
too crowded with thoughts and expansive plans for the future.
Besides this, the day became quickly filled with petty annoy-
ances and irritations. The irritations began when the sun
struck him through the venetian blind; no amount of twisting
or turning provided escape. And when he had stamped over
angrily to adjust the blind, the early brilliance of the sun
bouncing off the waters of Long Island Sound beneath his
window brought him fully awake. For a while, back in bed,
Kip thrashed and tossed, trying to recapture sleep. Finally, at
seven, he gave up and took a shower.

The luxuriant torrent of hot water streaming smoothly
down his body made Kip feel a little better; abruptly, the
shower-stall door was yanked open and his brother Carey, a
bright but moody 12, appeared unannounced to tell him that
Mrs. Braun, the housekeeper, wanted to know why he wasn't
downstairs at breakfast with the rest of the family. She didn't,
Carey added, plan to cook several separate breakfasts.

The disquiet in Kip grew. Mrs. Braun was a sore spot with
Kip. He disliked her, had always disliked her, and was sure he
always would. Five years earlier, when his mother had withdrawn into herself, moving into two third-floor rooms which
she rarely left, she had abandoned her family to Mrs. Braun.
Upstairs, in these rooms, his mother remained hidden, reading
books, listening to records, and occasionally sitting down at
her piano to repeat the same passage from Chopin over and
over again. Doctors were called in, but soon abandoned; his
mother would not budge.

At the time, Kip had felt cheated by his mother's sudden
self-banishment. His father, gentle and understanding as always, tried to explain it to Kip, but couldn't; Kip tried to understand it but couldn't. The truth was that neither of them
could explain it because neither of them understood it. Sometimes, lying awake, Kip tried to blame the situation on himself,

which he knew was absurd; sometimes he tried to blame it on Mrs. Braun, which was even more absurd. But absurd or not, Kip had never been able to rid himself of his resentment of Mrs. Braun.

Downstairs, they were all there: his father, smiling and amiable; his 15-year-old sister, Dee, a little surly but trying to be pleasant; and Carey, sulking as he ate his grapefruit, apparently still smarting because the shower door had been slammed in his face.

Dee and Carey started some sort of complicated argument, only half-serious, and his father skillfully inserted himself between the opposing positions; Kip's natural high spirits returned. For a moment, the whole table seemed to be laughing and talking. But it all came to a sudden end. From upstairs, clear and penetrating and painful, the passage from Chopin began echoing through the house. His father hid behind his newspaper. Carey and Dee looked annoyed, and Dee turned toward Kip to ask if he would give her a lift to Seven Hills if he was going anywhere near the club. Kip squirmed. Dee was still too young to drive, and needed someone to get her to Seven Hills or she couldn't go. But today, for once, it couldn't be him. Painfully, Kip lied, saying he was waiting for someone who was going to meet him here; his eyes avoided his sister's when he spoke, wondering if she saw through such a transparent lie. His father looked at him curiously, then told Dee he would drive her over himself.

From upstairs, falteringly, the phrase from Chopin began again. They all busied themselves with their plates, trying to pretend the sound didn't exist. To admit that it did would be too painful.

The family of Angel Sanchez was experiencing its own kind of pain. Angel's mother and father sat, fat and uncomfortable, in two wooden chairs in Police Chief Hamish Hamilton's stark office; beside them stood their young niece, Rosa, whom they had brought along to help if their English failed.

Hamish stretched out his incredibly long legs and studied them; the Sanchez family had seemed to shrink when he stood up to greet them. It was not an unusual occurrence; Hamish was six feet four, with a craggily handsome face and a Wyoming drawl, deep-pitched but soft enough to reassure anyone.

Yet, his height almost always intimidated outsiders to the closed society of Greenport, such as the Sanchezes.

"And Mr. Whitemore, he say that Angel run away." Rosa was quoting the Town Manager, who had sent the Sanchezes over to Hamish's office. "He say that he is runaway delinquent and there is nothing he can do."

Hamish sighed. Alan Whitemore was two-thirds public relations man, but he reserved his expertise for the press and for the town's wealthier citizens. In dealing with people like the Sanchezes, his touch was heavy-handed. "How long has this boy been gone?"

A hurried conference between the Sanchezes and their niece took place. Rosa turned back toward Hamish. "Since last night. It does not seem long, I know. Mr. Whitemore say that already. But Angel is not kind of boy who run away. You know him, Mr. Hamilton. And he left the store and waved at Mama Sanchez and said he was going home to do his homework. He never arrived there, his younger sister Carmen say. He took no clothes. He had an exam at school Monday. He was very proud, Angel, of his marks; he work all night, all day, to get ready for that. No, Angel not run away, Mr. Hamilton."

Inside, Hamish agreed. He knew Angel—the boy did his lawn, and last summer had put together a bunch of other boys to vacuum people's pools. He had a scholarship at Country Day, of which not only he, but the whole small Puerto Rican community in Greenport, was extraordinarily proud. No, Angel would not run away. But only fourteen hours . . . well. "I sort of agree with you. Only"—rapidly Rosa translated for Mr. and Mrs. Sanchez—"only it's like this: fourteen hours is just not enough to take action on. Even longer, without suspicion of violence, hell, doesn't give us anything to work with either. See, the runaway kid problem doesn't hit us much here, but the rate across the country—"

Rosa exploded. "He maybe dead. A car. A hit-and-run driver. A sick man who goes after boys. Anything. *Madre Dios.* You are no better than Mr. Whitemore. You know Angel and you say too he would not run away, but you do nothing. He say Angel right age and 'ethnic background' "—she spat out those last two words—"to be runaway. **Mr.** Whitemore and you—both of you make me sick."

The older Sanchezes shrank at their niece's explosion; they were not comfortable with such a tone used on officialdom. As Hamish rose to his feet, he saw them shrink even further. "I said I didn't believe Angel ran away and I meant it, Miss Sanchez. Thing is, I can't do anything yet, officially. Unofficially, I'll put out the word to my men and the patrol cars. Then, if he still hasn't shown up, we'll start sniffing around other possibilities. We have to let a little time go by. Until then, I'm afraid . . ."

Rosa Sanchez did not wait to find out what Hamish was afraid of. She swept the elder Sanchezes out the door, pausing to turn and stare at Hamish with contempt. Then, after a sad shake of her head, she was gone, pulling the door shut with a slam. For a moment, Hamish sat down behind his desk, trying to make sense of Angel Sanchez's disappearance. It was probably nothing, Hamish told himself. Angel had stayed with a friend, forgotten to call home, and then overslept. Not like him, but possible. Or maybe he was afraid to take Monday's exam—no, Angel was too good a student, too proud of his work for that. Perhaps he had had a fight with his family, so he—no. None of it made sense. Hamish Hamilton shook his head. Kids.

Chapter 2 _____

Angel Sanchez was just a test run. To make sure. I picked Angel because his family's so poor there's nobody who can raise a big fuss over his disappearance.

Of course, this meant I had to plant him where his body would never turn up. Just down the street from his family's store there's a lot of building going on, and I found a deep concrete form due to be filled this morning. By now, little Angel's under a couple of tons of cement.

It's a nice touch, putting him so close to his family. Maybe they can wave back and forth to each other.

—TAPE-LOG OF THE PIPER,
ENTRY DATED MAY 12.

Hamish Hamilton watched his office door open and saw Jenny Cobb come through the doorway into his office. He hoped his surprise was not visible. When Alan Whitemore had called him and said that he was sending over a lady psychiatrist from the Demings Institute—she would be spending several weeks in town doing "in-depth interviews" for a survey, Whitemore said—Hamish fully expected the lady to wear flat heels and thick glasses. The fact was that Jenny Cobb could have worn just about anything—or nothing—and still been a knockout. She had the radiant face and the bright scrubbed look of a little girl, but her elfin green eyes whispered of something sensual, something that merrily challenged you to come explore her. Small, trim, exuberant with energy, Jenny wore her honey-blonde hair in the longer style of twenty years ago; sometimes when she moved her head, she would have to toss it back or move it away from her face with her hand so that she could see. The gesture reminded Hamish of an impatient little girl.

Even at 34, it was this little-girl freshness about Jenny that kept men guessing her age a good seven or eight years below what it actually was. When she was younger this had irritated her; now she welcomed it. Hamish stared at Jenny openly, simultaneously knowing he shouldn't. He was not the first man to be so affected. For, on top of her looks, Jenny was blessed with an easy laugh, a sharp wit, and the faintly erotic sense of humor so many people whose lives are devoted to psychiatry seem to have.

Hamish continued to stare at Jenny, struck mute. The hand readied to shake hers remained lifeless in his lap. Startled at the erotic fantasies he was allowing to intrude into his thoughts, Hamish finally uncoiled himself from his chair and rose to greet her. She seemed to stare at him with just the faintest suspicion of disbelief.

"Six feet four," he said before she could ask. "In Wyoming, see, that's short."

Jenny tilted her head slightly and smiled, then straightened it again to lock her eyes with his. "I thought perhaps it was so you could look down on all the rich honchos that live around here."

He smiled, but the smile faded quickly, overcome by a return of his uncomfortable feeling about Angel Sanchez. He sighed. "Everybody around here isn't rich." Struck with a sudden fit of shyness, Hamish averted his eyes so she couldn't see his stare. For Jenny, it didn't require seeing his eyes to figure out exactly what he was thinking; the fact amused her. There was an awkward silence. Finally, Hamish gestured roughly toward a chair for her, and sat down himself.

"Alan Whitemore said something about you're a psychiatrist or something." Hamish listened to his own sentence and realized it was terrible and didn't make too much sense. He was about to clarify it when Jenny began talking herself.

"Master's from Johns Hopkins. Doctorate from Columbia. Residency at New York Hospital. I guess that adds up to a psychiatrist or something."

"I didn't mean it that way. Only somehow, I've never met a lady shrink before."

In spite of herself, Jenny was unable to stifle a bubbling

laugh. "Well, they let us fly airplanes and drive trucks—there's
even a brain surgeon. A blunter but more direct route to the
mind than mine. A lady shrink—as you put it—can't do too
much damage compared to that."

Hamish was baffled, and again found himself on the defensive. "I didn't mean that either. What Alan said was that you
were in Greenport to do"—he referred to a slip of paper on
his desk—"do in-depth interviews."

Jenny laughed. "You really mean, what's a nice girl like
you doing in *et cetera, et cetera*, don't you? Okay. When I got
through all the learning stuff, I worked at a hospital for disturbed children—St. Albans—not far from Rochester." Jenny
shuddered so visibly even Hamish noticed it. "It tore me up. I
couldn't take it after a while, because I'd get too emotionally
involved with their problems. Very bad for a psychiatrist. So I
took this job with the Demings Institute. They're doing a survey on the American suburb, and my job is the in-depth interviews. Why they picked Greenport is obvious. It's probably
a waste of a lot of education, but that's why I'm here."

"I don't want to appear stupid, but this in-depth interview
thing . . ."

"I probe. You see, most people, if you ask them questions
about something like why they live in Greenport, will tell you
what they think you want to hear, or what they think they
ought to answer. They may not know the real reason themselves. So in an in-depth interview, you poke around under the
surface and find the hidden reasons, their real attitudes, their
secret motivations—frequently sexual, although certainly not
in an overt way."

"You've come to the right place."

"Here. Wide open?"

"Not so's you notice. But like any place with a lot of
money, there's women with too much time on their hands. A
lot of booze. A lot of guys desperate not to grow old. After a
while, low golf scores don't do the job. Somebody else's wife
does."

"That's not just Greenport. That's anyplace outside of the
ghetto."

"Maybe."

The way Hamish said "maybe" was perilously close to Gary
Cooper in a Western. Jenny stared at him, although unlike

Hamish's, her stare was free of sexual overtones. It was one of simple curiosity. For Jenny sensed that behind the creased, angular face—with its Indian nose and the determined set of its jaw, placing it somewhere between Burt Reynolds and Clint Eastwood—lay a highly vulnerable personality. One so battered by events it had withdrawn inside a laconic shell in self-protection. This kind of personality never failed to fascinate Jenny, if only by challenging her to unravel the reasons behind it.

Up to this point, Hamish as a sexual partner hadn't even occurred to Jenny, something that in itself was unusual. Jenny Cobb was neither virgin nor whore; she loved sex, she enjoyed it freely and frequently, and the subject was rarely very far from her mind. Fleetingly, as she studied him, the usual array of sensual considerations crept into her consciousness, but were dismissed. Too many prejudices. A small-town cop, for Christ's sake. Six feet and more of him. And even if he did wear a tweed jacket and gray flannels instead of a uniform, he was still a cop. An innate resistance, she supposed. Hamish. Sometime perhaps, somewhere. Not now.

They talked for perhaps half an hour, sparring for position. Hamish was amazed that so much knowledge could be crammed inside so attractive a head. For herself, Jenny wanted to ask him why someone as natively bright as he was would settle for the job of handling a 110-man police force, but kept herself in check. When they were back talking about her doctorate, Hamish deepened the mystery further.

"I don't have all those degrees like you, of course. Just a B.A., and a year up on a Master's from the University of Wyoming. Never finished it. But it doesn't really matter in a job like this." This time Jenny did start to probe, but was thrown off the track when Hamish answered his phone; they never got back to it.

"Whitemore again. He's a little nervous about you."

"He's a little nervous about everything. That's the impression I got. And very hostile underneath the phony charm." Jenny stopped, wondering if this was a very bright thing to be saying about the Town Manager and Hamish's boss. "Of course, I don't know him really. If he's a friend of yours, I'm sorry."

"He's not. Alan Whitemore's a jerk. I don't mind jerks, but he's a *pompous* jerk."

A mischievous look crossed Jenny's face. "Probably doesn't believe women should dabble in psychiatry, either."

"Oh, Christ," sighed Hamish.

When Jenny Cobb arrived in Hamish Hamilton's office, she had only one interview scheduled for the day, one set up a month before by mail; when she left, she had an additional one, set up for her by Hamish Hamilton. And from that suddenly improvised additional interview—Hamish grabbed at the first name that occurred to him—Jenny was to learn that there was a lot more to Greenport than merely being tall or short, rich or poor.

It was one of the few times anyone in the Greenport Police Department could remember not being able to find Hamish Hamilton. Usually, he left word where he was going, or at least, that he could be reached by the radio in his car. This afternoon, though, he seemed to have simply disappeared. The best information anyone could supply was that a sudden phone call had come from Alan Whitemore, and that Hamish left immediately afterward. Alan Whitemore was of no help, since he was also missing, and no one in his office seemed to know where he was, either.

Actually, Hamish and Whitemore were together at the Axminster place in Long's Bay, sitting on an uncomfortable couch while Gilly's mother and father dodged and weaved around the subject that was torturing them. Gilly, they said, left the house at 8:30 this morning and, well, simply disappeared. He had never done anything like that before; something had happened.

Alan Whitemore looked puzzled. "Kids, oh well, you know. It's only been a few hours. He could be anywhere."

Crossing and uncrossing his long legs, Hamish sensed some vital part was being withheld from them. "Does sound like you're jumping to conclusions," he added finally. "Have you tried his friends? Maybe . . ."

Hamish felt an uncomfortable sense of *déjà vu;* he seemed to have just finished saying the same sort of thing to Rosa, Mrs. Sanchez's niece. He shifted himself on the hard Louis Quinze sofa again. Regardless of the difference in backgrounds, that two boys of not too-different ages should both apparently vanish from the face of the earth the same day was pushing coincidence too far. "He'll turn up, Mr. Axminster," Hamish said, with a total lack of conviction. "Probably some perfectly simple explanation."

It was Mr. Axminster's turn to look uncomfortable. He gave a long sigh, as if something he didn't care to do had suddenly become necessary. "There's a few things that make it a little less than simple," he explained. "You see, recently there's been a lot of play given me in both the *Times* and *Town & Country*." He produced some clippings, including pictures not only of himself but of his home, his boat, and his son. "I suppose it was stupid to allow this sort of stuff to appear; it's an open invitation. Anyway, we think Gilly's been kidnapped."

Simultaneously, both Hamish and Alan Whitemore attacked this premise. To reach such a conclusion on the basis of so short a time was ridiculous. Gilly was with friends somewhere, he would turn up, they were worrying unnecessarily, Gilly was . . .

Abruptly, Mr. Axminster went over to the desk and returned carrying a small reel of tape. Carefully, he fitted it onto a thin, leather-encased tape machine, a piece of sleek, satin-chromium equipment that looked out of place in this elegant room filled with antiques. "This morning," he said, "just after twelve o'clock, someone called my office. I'm not usually there on Saturdays, but I had some things to do. I don't remember the words exactly, but whoever it was on the other end asked me if I was worried about Gilly yet. Then they gave me a number to call and hung up." From his pocket, he withdrew a piece of paper on which a telephone number had been hastily jotted down. "I thought it was some nut," Axminster said, "but I called the house and found out Gilly hadn't come home for lunch. So just to be on the safe side, I turned on the phone recorder in my office and called the number." Grimly, he threw a switch on the machine.

The voice was hollow and echoing, with a desperate sound to it. "Please, Daddy, do whatever they want. It's Gilly, Daddy. Please, Daddy, help me . . . do something, for Christ's sake do—" The voice on the tape stopped suddenly, replaced by a long, loud buzzing.

For a moment all of them sat there, Mrs. Axminster trying

not to cry, Mr. Axminster wearing a look of both anger and helplessness, Whitemore and Hamish stunned. Finally from Hamish: "You're sure that was Gilly's voice?"

"Positive. The inflections, the mispronunciations, even the crazy little swear words. It's Gilly."

Hamish thought for a moment, then asked, "Could I use your phone?"

Axminster nodded and watched as Hamish took the note with the number from him. "You won't get anything," he noted with a sigh.

Pushing each button on the phone carefully to dial the area code of New York City and then the number Axminster had given him, Hamish heard an unusually long progression of clicks over the wire—direct-dialing long distance always produced a certain number of these, but this series seemed interminable. Then he heard the phone suddenly answer in the middle of a ring. "When you hear the signal, Eastern Standard Time will be one forty-ayate and thirty seconds . . ." This was followed by the usual quavering signal of the New York time center. After a pause, the operator's voice began again. "When you hear the signal, Eastern Standard Time will be one forty-ayate and forty seconds . . ." Hamish hung up, turning around toward Mr. Axminster in confusion, to be met by the man's gesture of helplessness.

"I tried calling the number again myself, maybe ten minutes after the first call. I don't understand what's going on."

Hamish copied the number on a slip of paper, folding it and slipping it in his pocket. "I'll get with the phone company. There's something crazy here; kidnappers don't give you their phone numbers."

Impatiently, Alan Whitemore cut in. "Have you called the FBI yet, Mr. Axminster?"

Axminster shook his head. "I talked to my lawyer. He said to hold off a bit. He said kidnappers are a volatile lot and had to be handled carefully. And to make sure you gentlemen arrived separately and unseen. That was the reason for all the secrecy."

"I think you should call them now," said Alan Whitemore firmly. "They have a great deal of experience in these things."

"No."

Hamish's statement was so flat, so firm, so unexpected, both

Whitemore and the Axminsters swung their heads toward him
in surprise. Hamish met their stares head-on. "There's something wrong here. I can't put my finger on it yet, but none of
this adds up. The FBI—well, just now, anyway—would only
add confusion."

Alan Whitemore and Axminster began arguing with each
other, while Hamish threw in his own opinions and comments
from the side. The voices became louder and more insistent
as the three-sided argument gained in momentum.

The voices stopped suddenly as the room filled with a
strange sound. It came from Gilly's mother, her eyes suddenly
filled with tears; she sat rocking back and forth in the chair
with her hands over her ears, trying to shut off the voices of
these men arguing about her son as if he were some prized
piece of property in a business transaction. For a second, no
one moved or spoke. Axminster started across the room
toward her, but she fled, waving him back with one hand as
she disappeared quickly up the stairs.

Hamish winced. Whoever was doing this to the Axminster
family was not, he suspected, doing it for money, but for the
effect he just saw overcome Mrs. Axminster. He was unable to
shake the suspicion there was some connection between Gilly's
and Angel's disappearances. With one big difference: the
Axminsters were rich, while no one could expect to collect
anything from the Sanchezes. The pattern was illogical. The illogical always terrified him. He shuddered. Later, he was to
find that shuddering had become a daily phenomenon.

About half an hour later, Mr. Grolier almost ran into Kip,
climbing into his car near the front door. For a moment, he
considered something, then called to his son. "Kip. Say, by
any chance did you run into Gilly Axminster this morning?"

Kip looked at his father curiously, letting his brows knit in
confusion. "I don't think so. No, I'm sure. Definitely not." The
look of confusion was replaced by one of bafflement. "Why,
Dad? Is something wrong?"

"No. No, of course not. I was just wondering. Forget it."

Both Kip and his father were lying. Mr. Grolier knew there
was plenty wrong, but he also suspected he shouldn't even
have let on as much as he had. Mr. Axminster had been very
positive on this point: tell no one. He came to see Mr. Grolier
immediately after Hamish and Alan Whitemore left his house;

besides being a close friend, Grolier held a lot of Axminster's equities at his brokerage, and the man had to know how quickly he could raise ransom money. In the process, the disappearance of Gilly had had to be revealed. Mr. Grolier had assured him there would be no problem about the money, and that no, of course not, he would tell no one.

Kip's lie had been more direct. But there had been no way of avoiding it. Five hours earlier, in the clearing near the cistern, he had sat in the shadow of a giant spruce, his knees slightly pulled up as he leaned against a tree trunk, waiting. Ahead of him, in the clearing, was the cistern. It rose perhaps three feet off the ground, and the disc-shaped slab of concrete that usually capped it lay leaning against the base. The Grolier home had been built in the twenties for a bootlegger, and there was a wealth of lore attached to the cistern he was staring at. To begin with, it really wasn't a cistern at all; it was merely built to *look* like one. For beneath it, twenty feet straight down, was a deep well. Local stories claimed that this well beneath the cistern was riddled with passages and storerooms where the bootlegger used to store money, bullion, and—occasionally—people. Eight years earlier, when Kip's father bought the place, he had wanted to tear down the cistern and fill in the well as a possible danger to his children, but once Kip had heard the stories, he pleaded with his father. As always, he won; the cistern still stood.

Over the years, Kip had explored it thoroughly. Down one side ran a rusty ladder to nowhere, ending just above the surface of the well water. Across from the ladder was a heavy fixture in the stone wall to which, the old-timers said, had once been attached a rugged, winchlike derrick; it was used, old-timers claimed, to lower heavy crates of the bootlegger's private stock to the hidden storage areas below. And Kip quickly discovered their stories were probably true, for concealed in the stone sides of the well were entrances to several different tunnels, one of which led to storerooms hacked out of the almost solid stone undersurface of the land.

Now, older, Kip still came here to the clearing as he had in childhood, to plan, to fantasize, to dream, listening to the wind pass through the needles of the evergreens with a strange musical sound, as if someone were brushing a feather across the strings of a harp. Lulled half-asleep, Kip turned his head in annoyance at some small sound in the shrubbery behind him, a curious whistling noise, dismissing it with a wave of his hand.

Then, emerging from the woods into the open space, he saw Gilly. Gilly Axminster was 10, and the Axminster family lived on the Long's Bay property that adjoined the Groliers'. Gilly worshipped Kip; he had walked to the clearing knowing he could frequently find Kip there. As soon as he saw the older boy, Gilly's face brightened and, running over, he tossed a tennis ball directly at Kip so that he would be forced to catch it. Kip grabbed it and, getting to his feet, threw it back. Suddenly, Gilly stopped, his eyes riveted on the cistern. "Somebody left the cover off."

"Oh, another guy and I were hacking around. When he left, I forgot to make him help me with it."

Gilly couldn't hide a faint look of disapproval. "K.K.?"

"Yes, K.K."

The look of disapproval widened, but Gilly said nothing. K.K. was not Gilly's favorite person—not anyone else's for that matter—and Gilly was one of the few people who even knew he was a friend of Kip's. K.K. was the complete opposite of Kip: pasty, frail, and thoroughly unpopular. Although a classmate at Country Day, he was deliberately left out of everything. Even his nickname was an insult. (K.K. was short for "King Kong," a name cruelly ridiculous for someone so slight.)

For a moment, Gilly avoided Kip's eyes, still depressed by even the thought of K.K. Then his eyes returned to the cistern and his face lit up. "Can I look down inside again? Like we did last year? Will you hold on to me?"

Kip shifted uncomfortably; somehow it was the last thing he'd expected Gilly to suggest. "Oh, I don't know. It's kind of dangerous and—"

"Please, Kip. *Please?*"

Kip took a playful swing at Gilly and surrendered. "Oh, damn it. Okay. But no messing around, understand?"

Gilly nodded. With a grunt, Kip gently lifted Gilly up onto the wide cement edge of the cistern, carefully steadying him with both hands. From his pocket, Gilly drew some pebbles he'd scooped up on the way over and dropped them down inside, listening to the hollow splash they made as they fell into the dark water below. With one of his hands, Kip brushed away a gnat biting his neck and swore loudly; Gilly was so fascinated by the pebbles, he barely turned his head. Suddenly, Kip drew back his free hand and hit Gilly behind the knees as hard as he could; Gilly's legs buckled and he plunged head-first into the cistern. Falling almost gracefully, he didn't even hit the sides of the well on his way down into the water. Staring, Kip listened to the frantic yelling and thrashing. Gradually, as the shock of the fall wore off, Gilly regained enough breath to move and form words. Kip's stare was so fixed, he did not even acknowledge the figure that emerged from the undergrowth around the clearing and joined him at the edge of the cistern.

"Christ," said the figure. "He came just like you said but, my God, I didn't expect him to practically do it *for* you."

Kip shrugged and pulled something from his pocket, which he began carefully attaching to a long piece of string. The other figure watched, fascinated, wanting to ask about it, but stopped by something in Kip's expression.

To Gilly, the whole thing happened so fast it was hard to believe any of it. The water was cold—freezing, in fact—and he was too busy trying to keep his head above water, flailing and yelling, to think too much about it anyway. He saw Kip's head appear over the rim of the cistern, staring down at him, and supposed that at any moment, Kip would be hauling himself over the edge and climbing down to pull him out. The whole thing had been one of Kip's jokes, he told himself. But the joke was not a very funny one, because his mother would give him hell when he came home with his clothes sopping wet. A sudden anger swept Gilly and he looked up again, wanting to tell Kip how bad a joke it was.

Gilly was surprised to see that there were now two heads staring down at him—Kip's and K.K.'s. That's whose fault it was, then: K.K.'s. He saw Kip lower something on the end of a string, a small black object that spun around as it came down. Neither of the boys above seemed to be making any effort to come down after him, and Gilly's voice carried a new note of panic. "Get me out of here, dammit, Kip, get me *out of here.*"

"Be right down, Gilly, just keep steady." Gilly could see no smile on Kip's face about his lousy joke; in fact, the expression was completely cold. "Look," Kip called down. "I'm pulling a joke on your father. On the end of the string is a little tape recorder. And I'll be right down as soon as you say what I tell you to. Just say—"

"Kip. Please, Kip. Get me out of here, Kip. *Please.*"

Kip's voice stayed sounding infuriatingly calm. "Right, Gilly, right. Coming down in a sec. But first, say . . . let's see . . . something like . . . well . . . 'Do whatever they tell you, Daddy. It's me, Daddy, it's Gilly. Please. Do whatever they want.' Got it, Gilly?"

From Gilly came a high-pitched howl. He couldn't understand what was happening to him, how Kip, his idol, could be talking about a gag on his father at a moment like this. The cold was numbing his arms and his flailing was growing weaker. From above him, the voice kept sounding incredibly calm. "Say it, Gilly: 'Do whatever they tell you, Daddy. It's me, Daddy, it's Gilly. Please do whatever they want.' Come on, Gilly. Say it, and we'll have you out of there in no time."

Sputtering and coughing, his mouth half filled with water, not believing what was happening or how it could be happening, Gilly said the words desperately. "Please, Daddy. It's me, Gilly. Do whatever they want. It's Gilly. Please, Daddy. Oh, God, somebody help me. Do something, for Christ's sake, Kip, do something!"

"Very good, Gilly." Gilly looked up and watched in confusion as the string was pulled up and the little black machine was pulled out of sight over the cistern's edge. Then the two heads disappeared. For a second, Gilly panicked again, thinking they were going off to leave him to try to get out on his own. No, Kip wouldn't do something like that. Not even K.K. would. The faces suddenly reappeared, the muscles in Kip's neck straining. Gilly almost forgot to tread water as the terror of full realization swept over him. Slowly they were pushing the heavy cover of the cistern back across its top, rocking it, edging it forward, so that little by little the concrete disc began to shut off the light.

Frantically, Gilly looked around him. Slightly above his arm's reach was the bottom rung of the iron ladder. Kicking his hardest, he could almost rise far enough in the water to reach it. Once Gilly thought he felt the rough metal of the ladder as his fingers brushed the bottom rung. With his left hand, he tried desperately to get a hold on the rough stone sides of the well, but years of persistent dampness had left the stones covered with a slime that gave his fingers no purchase. One final lunge toward the bottom of the ladder failed and, exhausted, Gilly sank back into the water.

As loudly as Gilly screamed and pleaded, only his voice came echoing back off the steep walls of the well. Abruptly, his screams became shrieks as he saw the cover slide over until it lay across almost the entire top of the cistern. For a moment, a single, narrow shaft of light remained, but after one final shove, even this disappeared. Gilly was left in total darkness.

Little by little, his frenzied crying and splashing grew more muted as the coldness of the water began to take full effect; Gilly found his mouth more frequently filled with gulps of water, making his calls for help as difficult as they were useless. After a while, the only sound in the cistern was the increasingly slow rhythm of his splashing and a sudden, soft sobbing; eventually even this stopped, replaced by a curious, bubbling sigh as Gilly's exhausted body surrendered itself to the water, unseen, unheard, alone.

Above, in the brilliant sunlight, Kip and K.K. panted from the exertion of struggling with the top. Exhausted, K.K. supported himself by leaning on the cistern with one shaking arm. He looked at the pocket tape recorder Kip held, one hand gripping it firmly, the other struggling to untie the string he had used to lower it to Gilly.

"I don't get what that thing's for," K.K. said, still staring at the machine.

"You're not supposed to."

K.K. ignored the rebuff and picked up the tennis ball off the ground where Gilly had dropped it. As Kip stuffed the tape recorder back in his pocket, K.K. tossed the ball to him with a mumbled, "Catch."

For a moment, Kip looked at the fuzzy yellow ball, then pulled his arm back and threw the ball so hard it sailed out of the clearing. It vanished through the treetops, possibly going far enough to drop into the Sound, a few dozen yards beyond. His mouth wore a tight, grim look as he pronounced his benediction: "Mr. Grolier: Game. Set. Match."

"You sure the police send you?" demanded Rosa, her eyes narrowing as she studied Jenny Cobb. This meeting was the hastily improvised one that Hamish Hamilton had set up in his office while Jenny was still there, and its beginning was not an auspicious one. For when Hamish had called to arrange it, Mrs. Sanchez, in spite of all of Hamish's explanations and disclaimers, kept expecting that Miss Jenny Cobb would arrive with some sort of news about Angel. Rosa was sent for. But instead of giving them news, this pretty young lady with the golden skin sitting opposite Rosa and herself kept asking *them* questions. Questions about life in the small Puerto Rican community in Greenport, about how they were treated, about how they felt about almost everything, it seemed, except anything to do with Angel. Rosa became irritated. Why such questions at a time like this? Hamish should have foreseen—but hadn't—Rosa's reaction. By the end of his first meeting with Jenny, he was behind schedule and had grabbed a name weighing on his mind at the time, perhaps also hoping that the Sanchez family would help get Jenny over her idea that everybody in Greenport was so damned rich. The choice was stupid.

As soon as it finally dawned on Mrs. Sanchez that there was nothing to be learned from Jenny, she lost interest, answering the questions listlessly, doing little odd jobs as she sat in her chair, things that wouldn't make her appear too rude. Mostly, though, she thought about Angel, torturing herself with the possibilities of what might have happened to him.

The session was interrupted only once. Around two o'clock, the mail arrived. Mrs. Sanchez held it in her lap—two pieces of junk mail and a small package wrapped in cheap brown paper—as she tried to answer Jenny's question about the difficulties of making ends meet in an area of so much wealth.

The question was a complicated one, and Rosa had difficulty both in translating and trying to explain it. Mrs. Sanchez listened, nodding her head slowly while she took the two pieces of junk mail, slit them neatly open, and discarded them. Absently, she took her scissors and began cutting the string on the package.

Jenny was leaning forward, talking to Rosa, when the sound first hit her. It was not a scream exactly, but a sound that began somewhere deep inside Mrs. Sanchez and rose from her mouth in an explosion of noise, a shriek that had no beginning nor end, no top nor bottom, a cry of human anguish, a scream that rattled the windows and assaulted the ears. Wordlessly, the now open box was extended toward Jenny. Inside was a human hand, the small fingers partly curved upward. In the center of the upturned palm was taped an inexpensive gold ring with an opaline stone set in its center. Three years before, it had been a twelfth birthday present from the proud father of Angel Sanchez.

When Jenny Cobb called the Greenport Police Department at 2:14, three minutes after the package had been opened, she asked for Hamish Hamilton. He was not there, she was told, nor was there any way of reaching him. Almost incoherently, she told her story to a desk sergeant. By 2:19, the modest little home of the Sanchez family was engulfed by police.

At first, there was understandable skepticism that the hand could be that of Angel's; a note in Hamish's office indicated the boy disappeared only the night before. So it would be impossible, the sergeant said, for a package containing his hand to arrive in today's mail. In the middle of this discussion, while Mrs. Sanchez fingered her rosary and prayed to her God that the police sergeant who made this announcement was right, Hamish arrived. His examination of the wrapper in which the package came revealed that no amount of praying to anyone's God would change one fact: the cancellation mark across the stamp was a phony, drawn in black, indelible ink. The package had not been mailed, then, but dropped into the mailman's rolling mailbag somewhere along his route this morning, probably when he was in the doorway of one of the small stores that lined these blocks, getting signatures for insured packages. The post office was called and the mailman sent for, but little was learned. Acting on Hamish's orders, fingerprints from the hand were quickly compared with fingerprints in Angel's room, on his bicycle, on his toothbrush. No room for any further doubt remained. The hand in the box was Angel's.

By three o'clock, practically everyone in Greenport knew about the Sanchezes' grisly package, although just about no one in Greenport had the faintest idea of who Angel Sanchez was. His classmates at Greenport Country Day, where Angel, as a scholarship student, was considered very much outside of the mainstream, had neither liked nor disliked him; more realistically, the difference in backgrounds and lifestyles meant most of the other students never bothered to know him.

No immediate wave of fear swept the town; the Sanchez family was, well, *those* people. Of a kind where personal vendettas and family violence were a common occurrence. No one except Hamish and Alan Whitemore knew yet about Gilly, and how quickly the violence was moving toward all of them.

Chapter 3 _____

One thing that really gets me is how the whole family tries to pretend Mom doesn't exist. Christ, all of them—Dad, Dee, even Carey—certainly know she's there: they see the food go up, they see the empty plates come down; they hear her piano, and they hear that tired snatch of Chopin.

Well, in a way, I can understand why they act like that. I was the closest to her, and I can still remember how confused and hurt I was when she first went to hide in those two rooms of hers. Like I'd been cheated, or robbed. And it wasn't until I accidently discovered what the scoop was—until I found out what really goes on up there and why she's hiding—that I understood myself.

But, Jesus, I wish she'd find something besides that crazy Chopin.

> —TAPE-LOG OF THE PIPER,
> ENTRY DATED MAY 19.

Kip Grolier sat motionless, staring at the gray blankness of the cistern. He knew he had a lot to do and shouldn't be wasting his time here, but so frequently his best ideas were crystallized in this private little area of his that he had decided the visit was necessary. Downtown, there were things he had to buy, which meant getting to the Greenport Savings Bank before it closed. At 5:30 there was that appointment Country Day had set up which he had promised to appear for; his availability had been double-checked only yesterday. Earlier, he had learned of the package being sent to Angel Sanchez's family, and was livid with K.K. for having done something like that without consulting him. The ultimate ransom was supposed to be extracted from the wealthy, people who could afford to pay anything but who would discover money was not enough to buy back their children. Angel Sanchez was poor, and had been selected for precisely that reason; he was to be nothing more than a test, a trial run, to see if Kip and K.K. had the nerve to go through with the plan Kip proposed. They did. But by mailing that damned hand, K.K. shoved Angel very much to the center of things; inevitably, as other children began disappearing, the hand would be recalled and assumed to be part of the same plot, blurring the whole point Kip was trying to make. Swearing at K.K., Kip picked up a pebble and threw it hard against the cement cylinder of the cistern. Sometime today he would have to work in a visit to K.K. to tell him what he thought; he didn't know how or when K.K. removed the hand, but by now some damned State pathologist had probably examined it and told people Angel was dead before the hand was removed. No oxygen in the blood or something, Kip supposed. And if people should decide this was going to be the case with all the kidnapped children, Kip told himself, his plan would fall apart.

But as he tortured himself with this thought, he realized that part of the ultimate ransom should be that the children's families paid in spite of the logical assumption their child was already dead. Things like knowing some of the other children were already dead would heighten the illogic of their payments.

The idea exploded in Kip's head. Without realizing it, K.K.'s mailing of the hand could actually help Kip's plan. Taking the miniature tape recorder out of his pocket, Kip quickly dictated more items he would need to buy downtown. The afternoon's ration of time was growing tighter. K.K. still had to be chastized—now not because he'd botched things up by his mail delivery, but for not checking with him first. Chastizing K.K. always gave Kip a certain pleasure anyway. It was that damned interview the school had arranged for him that was really going to screw things up; it was an honor, they said. Kip again considered simply not showing up, but then decided he had no choice. With a sigh, he stuck the recording machine back in his pocket.

For a moment, he stood and stared at the cistern, wondering if they shouldn't get rid of Gilly's body. After all, the place should be tidied up if it were to receive new visitors as

soon as Kip planned. Whistling, he trotted back to the house
to get his car.

The shopping took Kip so much longer than he expected
that he had to put off his confrontation with K.K. until after
the interview. In Greenport, his first stop was at the bank,
where he withdrew six hundred dollars. There was nothing
about this that should have bothered him; it was his own
money, and there was still plenty left. But nevertheless,
the act of taking money out gave him a strange feeling. For a
moment, he had stood at the teller's window, staring ruefully
at the balance in his bank book, as if he had just committed
an act of treason; then he shrugged, slipped the money into his
wallet, and left. Still in Greenport, he went to Hannel's, an
electric supply store, and bought three additional cassettes
for his pocket recorder; while there, he spotted a used, full-
sized Panasonic tape machine and bought that as well. This
was all he thought it wise to buy in Greenport itself, particularly in stores where he was known, so he drove over to
Stamford, a larger and more anonymous place. At Malley's,
one of the bigger hardware stores in this part of the state, he
bought four double-strength padlocks, tamper-proof and of
extremely heavy gauge. Also at Malley's, he bought a metal
drill, two large extra-strength hasps, and a variety of nuts and
bolts. Three six-foot lengths of heavy chain, an extra air tank
and mouthpiece for his wet-suit, a stone drill, and six stainless
steel pitons completed his purchases there.

Outdoors again, he blinked in the sunlight, dumped the
awkward package into the back of the Porsche, and walked
two blocks further down the street. Purposefully, he strode
into Apollo Palaestron's House of Magic.

The place had always held a fascination for Kip. In some
earlier day, Apollo Palaestron had been a successful magician;
an old man now, he was in the business of supplying profes-
sional-caliber equipment to talented amateurs. You could buy
devices that allowed you to saw a lady in half, make people
disappear (Kip only wished it was that easy), or cause a
shredded pile of newspapers to blossom into a stalk of flowers.
In fact, if you walked around the dusty, ill-lighted little place
on State long enough, you could find just about anything.
Casually, as if he'd just come across the idea, Kip asked the

old lady who acted as salesman if she had any handcuffs—he was doing a play, he said, that required them. They would have to be strong, Kip added, because the script required that people be suspended from them.

With a slap, the old woman laid a pair of handcuffs on the glass countertop. "Nothing tricky about these, young man. You could hoist an elephant from 'em. They're the real thing. We got 'em surplus from the State cops."

"Great," announced Kip after examining the cuffs. "They'll do just fine." Glancing at his watch, Kip swore softly; Bridgeport was still unvisited, K.K. as yet unchastized, but he had no more time if he was to get back to downtown Greenport for the damned interview. He drove at top speed, pulling up on Greenport Avenue a bare four minutes before he was due.

Kip Grolier was annoyed. There was no one there when he arrived—just a note on the door, apologizing, asking him to wait a minute or two, and telling him to make himself comfortable. Angrily, he sat down on a hard wooden chair, his incandescently blue eyes following a tiny hairline crack running down one wall of the miniscule office. The crack began where the wall joined the ceiling and grew branches as it went, finally ending at the baseboard in a filigree of tiny lines as complex as a diagram of the human circulatory system. With so much left to do today, Kip shouldn't be wasting his time sitting here, and he wondered if he shouldn't just leave; only the note on the door, addressed to him by name, stopped him. Suddenly, the door flew open and she walked in. "I'm sorry," said Jenny Cobb. "But it's been quite a day. A terrible day."

Kip looked at her with amazement. When Greenport Country Day asked if he would be interviewed by a lady shrink from the Demings Institute, he had mentally pictured Miss Cobb as middle-aged or older, academically dry, and probably ugly. Simultaneously, Jenny was studying Kip. To Jenny, the most amazing thing about Kip was his frankly sensual appeal, rare in someone that young. It came from the staggering blaze of his smile, from the piercing yet questioning blue of his eyes, eyes that seemed far too large for his face, shining out from dark, golden skin. And it came from the high cheek-boned face, topped by almost tow-headed blond hair. Looking at Kip again, Jenny felt something inside herself twist, and reproached herself; Greenport's model teen-ager probably acted as well as looked the part. To begin fantasizing about him was absurd.

Struggling to remain professionally objective, Jenny put down her papers and seated herself behind the desk, waving Kip to a chair directly in front of it. "Again, Kip, I have to apologize for being late. I was doing an interview over at the Sanchez home when that dreadful package arrived. . . . It was, well . . . terrible."

"How did they take it?"

The question startled Jenny; to her, the reaction seemed strangely low-keyed. She tried to strike the same casual tone. "Oh, about the way you'd expect, I guess. It must have come as an absolutely unbelievable shock."

Kip shrugged. Spreading a pile of papers in front of her—sent to Jenny by Country Day before she even arrived in town—she forced herself into the routine of the in-depth interview. Usually, Jenny spent a little time putting the respondent at ease; with Kip, she short-cut the process. "Chair all right for you, Kip?"

"Fine. Everything's fine, Miss Cobb."

"Jenny. Just call me Jenny, why don't you?"

"Okay."

"Cigarette?"

"Don't smoke." Kip watched as she made some small mark—an action Jenny apparently thought would be unnoticed—on a long piece of paper. "Anyway, I'd already guessed you'd find some indirect way of getting at it."

Although a little put off, Jenny laughed. "Well, it does avoid asking the question directly. Some people put up barriers, you see." She laughed again—husky, throaty, yet totally feminine. It was a kind of laugh Kip had never heard before, and the sound of it affected him strongly.

The laugh faded away as Jenny continued: "Now, as they probably told you at Country Day, I'm here doing a sociological/psychological study for the Demings Institute. We're trying to find out what makes the American suburb tick. And I'm in Greenport because many people consider it to be the model suburb. That made it an obvious choice for some of our interviews."

"I see." Kip not only saw, he could guess what was coming

next. Jenny Cobb did not disappoint him. "*And,* since the school described you as the model teen-ager, you, Kip, were an obvious choice, too."

"I don't know what to say."

"Your record says it for you." As Jenny rattled off his ac-complishments, from President of the Student Body to his latest appointment, Valedictorian of the graduating class, Kip found his mind wandering. He couldn't pretend he didn't en-joy hearing so glowing a recital about himself, but he also couldn't help, with a touch of grim humor, wondering how Jenny Cobb would feel if she knew a little more about him. Or about the details of the plan which kept intruding into his thoughts. He'd have to go to the Radio Shack in Stamford, it suddenly occurred to him, and pick up some things there; that meant another trip to the bank, which meant Monday after school was already shot.

For herself, Jenny was having considerable trouble keeping her own mind on the questionnaire. When she had first come into the room, she was struck not only by his almost sensuous good looks, but by the animal way his body moved, the grace of his stance, and the effortless ease of his gestures. Now, an additional sensation hit her. He was sitting in the chair with his legs splayed in front of him; in anyone else, it would have seemed a display of bad manners, but in Kip, it seemed a pose of unwitting eroticism. For a moment, Jenny struggled to pin-point why. The explanation was an obvious one, but one which made her uncomfortable: his khaki trousers were too tight—she remembered noticing it when he walked over to her—the product, probably, of an overzealous laundry. The result was a subtle but undeniable khaki bulge, and in spite of herself, Jenny had trouble pulling her eyes away.

Clearing her throat, Jenny forced her eyes back onto the papers on her desk. My God, she reprimanded herself, she was sick. He was little more than a child. She found herself blush-ing, wondering if Kip had noticed.

He had. The stare was not new to him. Usually, when he encountered it, the stare came from certain anonymous older men, frank crotch-watchers. Sometimes, though, Kip also de-tected it in women—staid, older matrons, probably not even aware of what they were doing. With Jenny, he was pretty sure she knew exactly what she was doing, and that she was embarrassed by the fact. This thought in itself excited him further. Jenny's eyes, however, were now riveted on her papers.

The interview, suddenly turned lifeless by Jenny's grim determination to stick to business, plodded forward. Yes, Kip had lived all his life in Greenport. No, his father had originally come from Milwaukee, then moved to New York City. He'd taken *his* father's municipal bond business and expanded it there. Yes, his father had moved his family to Greenport because they didn't want to raise children in the city.

For the first time in some minutes, Jenny allowed her gaze to rise from her interview sheet, the stare carefully avoiding anything but Kip's eyes. "And would you raise *your* children here, too, Kip?"

"Of course."

"Why?"

Kip was thrown. The way things were, all this talk of children, of children growing up, of whether he would raise his own children here, was deeply unsettling, as if Jenny Cobb knew something she obviously didn't.

Kip saw a small frown on her face as he floundered with an answer to her very simple question. "Well, I'd bring up my own children here because . . . because . . . that is . . . because, well, it's a great place for a kid to grow up, that's why." Jenny appeared to study him for a moment, seemingly confused by his circular answer. Then, referring back to the interview sheet, she moved on to other areas.

Kip's feelings about morality in Greenport were explored, with Kip somewhat defensively insisting the town was probably no better or worse than any other community. Yes, the drinking was heavy, he supposed, but wasn't that true anywhere? No, he knew of no hard drug usage among his age group. Grass? Well, of course. Was money overemphasized here? Well, money was money. Only people who didn't have enough ever considered it overemphasized. No, Kip didn't think that parents in Greenport considered their children as mere possessions, not more than anyplace else, he guessed. But the question had struck at the root of something deep inside Kip, and in an effort to conceal this, he burst out laughing. "You're trying to crucify us, Miss Cobb. Greenport is really a great town."

He noticed that her answering smile had a certain grimness

to it. "I'm sorry, Kip. We're deliberately a little abrasive in these interviews. Sometimes it makes people blurt out things. All we really want is an accurate picture . . ."

"Some picture." Kip said it with enough of a good-natured smile that they were both able to laugh. This was the basic pattern that held for the remaining half-hour of the interview, Kip stoutly defending Greenport, his answers laced with wry humor.

When Kip left, he felt drained. Jenny's constant questions about children and their relationships with their parents were, in a way, what Kip's plan was all about; some of her comments seemed almost to be accusations. The process made him uneasy, leaving Kip with a sense of danger that was thrilling and terrifying at the same time. Or was it her appearance and visible physical attraction to him that provided the thrill and the excitement? Somehow, Kip knew, he was going to have to see Jenny Cobb again.

Jenny herself wasn't half as clear in her analysis of what had troubled *her*. Something was wrong, but she could not put her finger on it. For no reason, after Kip left, she found herself picking up a red felt-tipped pen and marking his folder "Respondent Uncooperative." Jenny made a sour face. From nowhere, a memory of the too-tight khaki trousers had flashed across her brain. *What*, precisely, was she accusing the respondent of being uncooperative about?

"It looks dead to me." Kip Grolier was staring fixedly at the white rat lying at the bottom of one of K.K.'s cages. His friend's lab was a place to which Kip came as rarely as possible, but today, besides preparations to make for the next stage of his plan, he had a score to settle with K.K. The lab consisted of three rooms over the garage of the family's home; outside, the rolling lawn sloped gently up to the main house where K.K. and his mother lived. His father had died when he was a baby.

"Pick it up," suggested K.K. Kip looked at the rat suspiciously. Its four legs were raised stiffly in the air, its eyes open but unseeing. Those damned white rat experiments of K.K.'s always left him cold, but K.K. insisted they were a necessary part of his experiments in behavioral science. "You're as crazy as your animals, K.K.; I'm not going to handle any damned dead rat."

K.K. sighed. He knew that Kip had some other reason for being here than to talk about the experiments, yet he couldn't help but be pleased by Kip's interest, affected or genuine. "It's not dead. Catatonic trance. I drove it crazy."

"Big deal. Are you sure it didn't drive *you* crazy?"

K.K. managed a laugh, but not a very convincing one. "It was a subject in the circle-oval experiment, originally perfected by Dr. Burnside. What happens is . . ."

"Shit." Kip looked around the main room of the lab again. It was filled with long rows of cages, each cage perhaps a foot square. Inside, sometimes in pairs, more frequently in isolation, were the rats. Some poked their noses against the wire mesh; some ran in endless circles across the shredded paper lining the floor, occasionally hurling themselves against the sides of the cage, their small pink feet clutching the woven wire in a sort of frenzy. Others huddled in the corners, waiting numbly for what might turn out to be either a food pellet or another electric shock—whatever the experiment called for. The smell of the room always got to Kip, with its sour, cloying odor of urine-dampened paper. To all of this, K.K. appeared oblivious. Wearing a T-shirt and denim shorts to stay comfortable, he moved from cage to cage, whistling softly, making notes on a pad. As Kip studied him, he wondered if K.K.'s interest in his experiments wasn't really because here in the lab, as no place else, K.K. was the master, the maker of decisions.

Carefully, Kip began laying the groundwork for putting K.K. back in his place. "I thought you were going to get rid of these," he said, stopping in front of the largest cage. It was filled with white rats so contrary that K.K. was unable to use them in his experiments. Unpredictable and vicious, they stared out through the wire of their cage, their sore, red eyes filled with hatred for the creatures who had imprisoned them.

"I'll get rid of them someday, I guess. But they're so mean, watching them is kind of fun. Maybe I can breed a line of genetically vicious rats that—"

K.K. stopped in mid-sentence, watching Kip nervously. Each cage was equipped with a cleaning door on top, and Kip had opened it and slipped his hand inside a little. Gingerly, he snapped his fingers at the pack.

"Jesus, Kip! Those damned things will take your fingers right off. Get your hand out of there before—"

K.K. was never able to finish the sentence. Before he could say anything more, Kip had grabbed him and shoved his body hard up against the cage. Quickly, Kip twisted one of K.K.'s arms behind his back. With one finger, Kip flipped back the cleaning door of the cage and jammed K.K.'s hand and arm all the way inside; simultaneously he banged the side of the cage with K K 's body. "Kip, for Christ's sake! Don't! They'll get my hand. Jesus! Let go!"

"Listen, big shot," hissed Kip, "you're a very big man with hands. You send them to people. You send them without telling me you're going to. Let's see if your little friends in there want to send *your* hand to anybody or if they just want to enjoy it themselves."

Kip's full weight had K.K. pinned against the side of the cage. K.K. quickly twisted his body around enough so he could see Kip's face and discover whether he was kidding. He wasn't. Kip's eyes had taken on a cold, vacant look, a look K.K. remembered seeing only twice before: when Kip had begun pulling Angel's head back by the hair and again when he had hit Gilly Axminster behind the knees. K.K. tried his best to keep his hand steady inside the cage; any movement would only draw the rats' attention to it. He could see that the banging against the side of the cage already had the rats excited, their backs arched, their noses twitching. One particularly large rat had already begun advancing toward his hand— probably, thought K.K., smelling the sweat on it and recognizing the presence of food.

K.K. pleaded very softly. "Kip, I meant to tell you. I just had the idea and you weren't around, so I sent the damned thing. I'm sorry. Christ, I'm sorry. But, please . . ."

Kip studied the rats and K.K.'s hand. He could see the effort K.K. was making to hold it steady, but by maneuvering K.K.'s arm inside the cage, Kip began forcing K.K.'s hand to move. "Come on, little friends. Lunch. A little anemic, maybe, a little smelly, maybe, because K.K. doesn't like showers too much, but very tasty. C'mon, there. Atta boy." The rat closest to K.K.'s hand had frozen, crouching when Kip began to move K.K.'s hand; now it began advancing again, sniffing, its nose twisting fiercely.

"Please, Kip. I'm sorry, Kip. I mean it. Please don't, Kip." K.K.'s voice was whiny and trembling, but kept deliberately soft. Kip shook K.K.'s arm again, forcing his hand to drag across the shredded paper at the bottom of the cage.

Suddenly, from the center of the huddled pack, another rat shot past the first and opened a nasty rip on the fleshy side of K.K.'s bare arm. K.K.'s small reserve of self-control vanished. The scream that came out of him was shattering, his hand struggling to raise itself off the floor of the cage. The smell of the blood sent the rest of the rats into a frenzy, all of them trembling and waiting. Methodically, the lead rat began moving forward. "Kip! For Christ's sake!"

"No more doing things without telling me?" asked Kip softly.

"Anything. Anything, Kip. Just let go of my arm. Jesus!"

The sudden laugh from Kip startled K.K. His arm was abruptly released, and K.K. quickly slapped a handkerchief over the wound, staring at Kip. "You're crazy."

"No. But you almost scuttled my whole plan with that stupid stunt of yours. You had to be taught a lesson."

"Scuttle! How the hell could I scuttle your plan when I don't even know what it is?"

"By not obeying. Hell, your rats take orders better than you do."

Walking toward the door, Kip carefully flipped open the cleaning door on the top of each cage he passed, banging their wires as he went by to be sure the rats inside would start running around. As he slammed the door to the lab shut behind him, he could hear K.K. frantically running down the aisle of cages, cursing, trying to get the cleaning doors closed before the rats escaped into the lab.

For a day or two, he knew, K.K. would sulk. Then the loneliness would get to him and he would come crawling. He always did.

Chapter 4 _____

> *There's talk at school about some sort of serv-*
> *ice for Angel Sanchez. That raises some prob-*
> *lems. To have a real funeral, you need a*
> *casket and a body, and with Angel, all they*
> *have is a hand. Do you buy a regular, full-*
> *sized coffin to bury something as small as that,*
> *or do you hold the funeral over a miniature*
> *one—something like a cigarette box? It would*
> *look pretty silly coming down the aisle on the*
> *shoulders of six pallbearers.*
>
> > *Because I'm president of the school, I suppose*
> *they'll put me in charge of the arrangements*
> *for Angel. That's a gas. Maybe I'll suggest*
> *they bury him in installments.*
>
> > —TAPE-LOG OF THE PIPER,
> > ENTRY DATED MAY 22.

Even by Monday, the 22nd of May, the Axminsters still hadn't faced the inevitable and notified the FBI. Twice they consulted with Hamish, but he had felt unwilling to commit himself.

"Look," he told the Axminsters, "if we were up against an ordinary kidnapper, I'd say 'yes.' But we're not. Or we'd have heard something more from him by now. A ransom demand. Hell, I don't know—there's no way even to guess what the guy wants. It sounds crazy, but then, the guy sounds crazy."

A small gasp of horror, quickly muffled, came from Mrs. Axminster. Having her only child kidnapped by someone who might or might not kill him trying to collect ransom was sickening enough. But to have Gilly in the hands of a madman capable of almost anything was beyond bearing.

Mr. Axminster studied his wife briefly to see if she was in control of herself before turning back to Hamish. "So, what you're really advising, Mr. Hamilton, is that we call in the FBI, aren't you? That we have nothing to lose."

"I didn't say that. The FBI's got advantages, sure. But I don't know how effective the Bureau is when it's up against a nut case." Hamish paused and studied the Oriental on the Axminsters' library floor before adding in a small voice, "I don't know how effective *anybody* is. Angel Sanchez, for instance . . ."

Mr. Axminster winced at the mention of the name. His wife stared at Hamish, trying to make sense of it, trying to place the name. The pieces came together with a rush. "That little boy and the hand and *everything* . . . ?" Her voice trailed off in a horrible realization of what Hamish was saying; her hand at her mouth, she stared at him in disbelief.

Hamish nodded helplessly.

"Excuse me." Mrs. Axminster stood up and quickly left the room, half-heartedly waving Hamish back into the chair from which he'd risen when she stood up.

Mr. Axminster watched her go, a slight shaking of his head the only acknowledgment of the pity he felt. He looked Hamish in the eye. "Surely, Mr. Hamilton, you don't believe there's any connection between the Sanchez child and our Gilly?"

"Two boys, more or less the same age, from the same town, even from the same school, within a twenty-four-hour period—it's damned hard to duck the possibility."

Axminster nodded grimly. Hamish's logic was difficult to ignore. "Well, then, I guess the next move is up to me, isn't it? I mean, about the FBI. I'll call you with a decision before ten tonight."

"Good. Because that decision is yours and yours alone. Yours and Mrs. Axminster's. I can't even advise you."

Mr. Axminster shook Hamish's hand on the front steps, turned on his heel, and disappeared quickly back inside the red brick Georgian facade.

Contrary to what both Hamish and Mr. Axminster said that morning, the next move was not up to them; it was to be up to Kip Grolier. That afternoon Kip drove to Bridgeport, irritated and upset, feeling he had to act quickly or lose the initiative.

For one snag was severely interrupting the flow of Kip's plan—silence. This Monday morning, he had expected the town to be buzzing with word of the mysterious disappearance of Gilly Axminster. Nothing about him was even mentioned. The papers, even the New York *Daily News,* as well as television, were still full of Angel Sanchez, but no one seemed to have anything to say about Gilly Axminster. At school, all he had been able to learn from one of Gilly's classmates was that he was home sick with a cold. Gilly was cold, certainly, but definitely not home. As he drove along U.S. 95 toward Bridgeport, the silence about Gilly began to infuriate Kip. He realized there had been no unusual activity at the Axminster place of the sort a missing child would produce: no police cars, no anxious visits by family friends, no running in and out of the house by FBI types. None of it made any sense at all.

In frustration, Kip slapped the steering wheel of his car. Maybe Mr. Axminster had never called the number he'd given him, so his father had never heard Gilly pleading for help. Or perhaps Hamish Hamilton—Kip had never liked the man—was laying a trap to catch the abductor, a trap that used silence as bait. What he really needed, Kip knew, was another disappearance, but one that took place in front of a lot of people so Hamish's plan of silence would be thwarted. He would have to work on that, but it would take time. First, he would have to wait for K.K. to cool down, something which would require a few days in itself.

A tremendous honking brought Kip back to his mission in Bridgeport. Angrily, he stared at the driver of the other car and then pulled into a parking space not too far from the store.

"You don't have the same thing but battery-run?"

The salesman at Radio Shack looked at Kip with incredulity. "With the wattage you want?" He patted the CB transmitter on the counter in front of him almost with affection. "Hell, this thing could pull in Alaska. And send as far as—" he groped for a place— "well, Florida, maybe. The wattage you're asking is illegal, of course, but no battery-run job made can do it."

"But the big trucks. You're always reading how . . ."

"Sure. And those big rigs have a twenty-four-volt electrical system just to run their lights. Not to mention auxiliary generators to run the compressor for air brakes, refrigerating units, the whole *megillah*."

An idea seized Kip. With feigned indifference, he bought the transmitter the man put on the counter, an Ellison-Bardek, 40-watt, guaranteed, five-year warranty, Radio Shack exclusive. With a look of reproach, the salesman removed a proprietary hand from the set and sent to the stockroom for packaging materials. Radio Shack exclusive or not, the price tag was a whopping four hundred dollars.

At about 6:30, Kip slipped into the den of K.K.'s house, after peering carefully through the French windows to make sure Mrs. Blakeslee was not downstairs. He knew the place backwards and forwards. K.K.'s mother was, like her son K.K., a compulsive telephoner, and the house had three lines: one for her, one for K.K., and one for the cook. Kip could see that none of the lights on the phone were lit. He pressed down the button on K.K.'s line and dialed the one reserved for K.K.'s mother. Mrs. Blakeslee's light on the phone went on as she answered, and Kip asked to speak to K.K. Watching, he saw the light on the cook's line go on as Mrs. Blakeslee used the intercom. A few seconds later, he saw the cook puffing her way down toward the lab, shaking her head and muttering to herself. Quickly, Kip put the line he was using on "hold." Slipping back out of the French windows again, Kip waited until he saw the old Irish cook re-emerge from the lab, followed by K.K. He was walking slowly, almost somberly, in deference to the cook; she was in some sort of animated conversation with him. From her expression, Kip knew she was complaining about something—probably having to go all the way to the garage to get K.K.

Waiting until they disappeared behind a screen of small evergreens, Kip barreled down the hill to the lab, smiling at the thought of K.K. picking up the phone only to be greeted by dead silence. Sulky as he was, he'd probably overcome his pride and try phoning Kip at home. In the lab, Kip headed straight for K.K.'s desk and took out the keys to the Volks van, which was parked around in back. It was already fairly dark, but not yet dark enough. Later tonight, Kip would come back and "borrow" the van. Borrow, hell. He'd paid for half of it, hadn't he?

Hamish Hamilton and Jenny Cobb had had a good lobster
dinner at the Seven Points Inn and were now sitting over a
cordial in the bar. It had taken Hamish some courage to ask
her out; she must have known he was married. But if she was
as smart as her credentials proclaimed, she had probably figured out by now that his marriage was an empty and sterile
thing, kept alive only by his two sons, Russell, fourteen, and
Oliver, twelve.

At almost precisely the same time, Kip was switching off
the motor of the Volks, braking himself to a gentle stop. For
the last half-mile, he had driven without headlights, counting
on the light from the night sky to keep him on the narrow dirt
road. The area in which he was now parked was bleak and
deserted, and he wanted no tell-tale lights to draw attention to
him. Stretching himself, Kip closed the door very softly and
looked around him. The dirt road had brought him to a
scrub-growth clearing; from its center rose the steel skeleton
of a tower, topped by a flat concave dish perhaps twenty feet
in diameter. The wind through the tower's gridwork made a
humming sound, not too different, Kip thought, from the wind
through the trees near the cistern.

This tower was the receiving relay antenna for local cable
TV, picking up its signal from the World Trade Center in
Manhattan. Quickly, Kip opened the doors into the rear of the
van and, after he had carefully pulled them shut again,
switched on the light. His equipment was ready. The
Panasonic tape machine was threaded with a reel of tape,
while its output was wired into the input receptacle of the Ellison-Bardek 40-watt transmitter. This transmitter, he knew,
was powerful enough to "bleed" over from its CB frequencies
into the normal broadcast range, with the cable TV tower acting as an unwilling antenna. To power the high-amperage Ellison-Bardek, he used a suggestion unwittingly given him at
Radio Shack. It had come when the salesman mentioned the
auxiliary generators used by heavy trucks for their com-
pressors, refrigeration units, etc. That was all Kip needed to
hear. For the Volks van had once been a refrigerated meat
truck, and while the cooling unit had long ago been removed,
the auxiliary generator that powered it had not. A couple of
hours of work coaxed the generator back into operation, and

it now provided more than enough amperage for Kip's transmitter.

With a glance at his watch, Kip started the generator and threw his switches. By turning the gain controls on the Ellison-Bardek, the impedence meters were adjusted to the right readings. Flipping one last switch, he started the Panasonic. With one eye on the needles, Kip leaned back against the side of the van. He didn't dare stay here for more than about fifteen minutes. Then he would drive—again without headlights—until he returned to the safety of the highway. When he got the van back to K.K.'s house, he would have to explain why he'd stolen the keys. K.K. would be outraged. But the session would give Kip a chance to make amends and bring K.K. back under his control. A look of distaste crossed Kip's face. The thought of any dependence on K.K. bothered him, but, unfortunately, Kip felt he had no choice.

Because the next step, while deceptively simple, was a hard one to imagine pulling off without at least two men. Kip wrinkled his nose, turning over alternatives in his mind. The disappearance of another child, this time from right in front of people's eyes, was something he couldn't do by himself. Which brought him right back to K.K. Kip shuddered.

When Kip checked his watch again, it was time to go. His rationalization about K.K. had already made him feel better, and by the time he slipped behind the wheel of the Volks, Kip was almost smiling.

Absently, he ordered her another cordial, but Jenny told the waiter to make it Scotch on the rocks; a little Cointreau went a long way. Hamish stuck to his cognac. He could feel its comforting warmth spreading through his system, helping him build the courage he would need. All things considered, Hamish had no idea of how Jenny would react to a suggestion they go back to her motel. Certainly, he could assume her to be a sexually liberated woman, one of the new breed, untroubled by hangups, or propriety or convention, but there was always the possibility she might consider him too old. At forty-five, a man begins to worry about things like that.

Jenny, perhaps reading his mind or drawing on some sixth sense, took the matter out of his hands. "Do you like this place? I mean, do you want to stay here—or . . ."

Hamish floundered. "The food's good but the atmosphere's lousy. I don't know . . ." Inside, he began swearing at himself. She was opening doors; he was closing them.

Jenny smiled faintly. The man was shy. She had been surprised when he invited her for dinner; once invited, she was not surprised when he propositioned her. By someplace else she herself had meant another bar; he, in spite of his shyness, obviously meant her motel. For a second she considered. What the hell, why not?

Anyhow, sitting in this bar, where a deafening television set was suspended over the rows of bottles and glassware, was beginning to become off-putting. "We could go back to—" Jenny began, but stopped. Hamish's face had gone deathly pale, his thick eyebrows knotted in a frown as he tried to hear something coming from the direction of the bar. Baffled, she was about to ask him what was happening, but he anticipated her, holding up one hand to stop her before she could speak. The jumble of voices in the room was intruding on whatever it was Hamish was trying to hear.

"Quiet! Right now, dammit. Quiet!" he roared across the bar, rising to his full six-feet-four as he did. Heads spun. In the sudden silence, he heard it again. A small, distant voice, garbled by static and fighting the soundtrack of *Kojak*, but a voice that was unmistakable: Gilly Axminster. Pleading with his father for help. Telling him to do whatever had to be done.

In three loping strides, Hamish was across the room; quickly, he turned the channel selector. The message, repeating itself endlessly, was there, in varying degrees of clarity, on all channels.

"Sorry," he said brusquely to Jenny. "Trouble. I'll call you tomorrow." Money was slapped on the table and Jenny sat openmouthed as Hamish went out through the door into the night, moving as if pursued by some inner devil.

He arrived at the Axminster house at 9:43. Mr. and Mrs. Axminster had not been watching television but talking, torturing themselves with the decision they had promised Hamish Hamilton by ten o'clock, one ear cocked hopefully toward the telephone. They had not *been* watching, but by the time Hamish arrived at their house, they all knew about it and their set was on. Gilly was too unusual a name for their friends not to connect it quickly with Axminster, and the phone, Mr. Axminster told Hamish, had rung so often, they wanted to take it off the hook. But, they were afraid they would miss a call from the kidnappers, or—well, it *could* happen—perhaps from Gilly himself. Safe, and wanting to come home. To sort out the calls, their housekeeper, Miss Lewishon, was now screening them.

"We tried to reach you," began Mr. Axminster, the barest hint of reproach in his tone.

"I came over as soon as I heard."

Mr. Axminster shrugged. "What does it mean? That tape. What do they want?"

"I don't know."

"Is Gilly alive?" asked Mrs. Axminster. "Do you think he's still alive?"

"I don't know that either."

At 10:03, Hamish suggested the one thing he *did* know: that it was time to call the FBI. Secrecy was no longer a weapon; it was an enemy.

Chapter 5_____

Nobody knows about it, of course, but I see Mom just about every day. It started by accident, almost four years ago, and damned near every afternoon, I go to her room and we sit and talk. About everything. It's our secret because even Dad isn't allowed in her room. Only me. Well, I was always her favorite.

It took her a long time to get around to explaining why she's there and what's really going on. Nobody but me knows that either. What Mom's got me doing for her is against the law, sure, but, Christ, somebody had to help.

    —TAPE-LOG OF THE PIPER,
    ENTRY DATED MAY 23.

The usually serene township of Greenport was totally unprepared for the state of shock that engulfed it. Its citizens, especially the men, were, for the most part, high corporate executives. They were accustomed to operating under pressure, accustomed to lives in business that were filled with unpleasant surprises, defeats, grindingly difficult decisions, personal attacks, battles, and disasters. But the difficult and wearing challenges they met in their offices were built upon a sort of uniform logic; they could measure the enemy and weigh their chances, anticipating and accepting the daily battles that battered them.

However, the enemy they faced now was both illogical and invisible, one who sent children's hands through the mail like free samples of toothpaste, who put the voices of his victims on the air, and who arrogantly supplied you with his phone number. He was demanding something, but no one yet knew what.

And because Greenport was Greenport, with so many top figures from business and the professions making their homes there, the bizarre aspects of the disappearing children brought the national media into the picture with a vengeance. It would have been a good story in Chillicothe, Ohio; that it was happening in the golden suburb of Greenport, Connecticut made it compelling, lead-story material.

Disregarding Alan Whitemore's entreaties—"Jesus, more publicity's *all* we need"—Hamish had called in the State Police, who set up shop in the unused top floor of the police station. Due to Mr. Axminster's belated call, the FBI was already in evidence, working out of the basement of the First Baptist Church. And because Connecticut's Junior U.S. Senator, Lloyd Blyden, considered his own children fair game, citing both his position in Washington and his family's inherited fortune, the Federal Crime Bureau had arrived in force, too. This influx of newsmen and criminal experts added to the town's mounting alarm; the streets suddenly seemed filled with purposeful strangers hurrying on unknown missions.

In the midst of all of this, the figure of Kip Grolier stood as a rock. Hamish was impressed as he watched him, late that afternoon, holding forth at a hastily called meeting of students and parents at Country Day. The first, crude efforts at safety measures for the children were being outlined, and Kip, as President of the Student Body, stood behind the lectern—just like the headmaster had—and told the students how they could help. Later, he circulated among the fathers and mothers, consoling, sympathizing with, listening to, and reassuring an endless succession of anxious parents. It was a fluke, Kip said, a one-in-a-million coincidence, a simple kidnapping which the authorities would soon solve. The next day, he even arrived at Hamish's office with a scheme to organize Country Day's older boys into squads to provide tight security for the school's younger students, an offer politely but firmly declined.

Kip was giving the premier performance of his life, one so affecting that the father of his next victim—already chosen— went out of his way to tell Mr. Grolier how wonderful Kip was.

Hamish Hamilton, although impressed by Kip, had little time to think about him. For directly after the meeting at Country Day, he hurried to another meeting on the same subject, this one called together by Alan Whitemore, the Town Manager. On an uncomfortable wooden chair, pulled up to the Board table in the cavernous meeting room of Town Hall, Hamish squirmed and writhed, trying to avoid anyone's eyes as Alan Whitemore addressed the assemblage of crime experts. Clearly, the Town Manager wanted these men to realize that, while others might be panicked, he was not.

"Now, I'm aware," Whitemore said, "that all this national coverage has made the situation here sound a good deal more desperate than it really is. After all, when you really boil it down to hard facts, all we've had is one medically confirmed incidence of murder, and one case of what may or may not turn out to be a kidnapping." Hamish struggled to shake the pictures from his mind of the Sanchez family reacting to this reduction of Angel's brutal death to "one medically confirmed incidence of murder," or the Axminsters agreeing that it "may or may not turn out to be a kidnapping." A restless stirring swept around the table; the gathering of criminal experts was apparently suffering the same discomfort as Hamish.

Even Alan Whitemore realized his words had not come out the way he meant them to; removing his glasses, he polished them with a handkerchief, to buy himself some time. " . . . What I mean, of course, is that while the press may have exaggerated the public reaction here—one paper referred to it as 'panic'—it doesn't in any way mean we can minimize the situation. That's why we are so appreciative that all you experts are here."

Whitemore paused, fingering his bifocals nervously, as if waiting for someone to say something; no one did. "Obviously, our Director of Police, Hamish Hamilton, while pursuing his own avenues of investigation, will also be available to help you in any way he can." The silence, eerie in its intensity, continued. A little desperately, Whitemore tried a new tack. "I suppose the best way to start is to ask if any of you here— you're all experts of one sort or another—has any preliminary theory he would like to advance."

There turned out to be as many preliminary theories as there were experts. "It's only a guess at this stage, naturally," began Chief Investigator Cummins of the State Police, "but it strikes me that it's probably some sort of pedophile, with a mind so twisted that he needs to torture the parents as well as their children. We had a case not too different from that in Torrington a few years back. Greenport is a very close-knit town, and people here would probably know if there was a child molester living around. What I'm getting at, I guess, we probably should be looking for someone outside of Greenport, not a resident." Cummins paused, waiting for a reaction that didn't come. Lamely, he added, "Anyway, that was the case in the Torrington thing."

Finally there was a murmur of mixed assent and disagreement. Whitemore seemed all too happy to accept Cummins' last statement; the picture of the killer-kidnapper as a transient psychopath obviously relieved him. Glancing to his left, Hamish studied Jenny Cobb's expression; her face remained a noncommittal mask, but he could see her head moving back and forth in an almost imperceptible rejection of Cummins' conclusion. She was here at his insistence. In explaining this to a skeptical Whitemore, Hamish cited her credentials in clinical psychology. But there was something in Whitemore's face—a sly, inquisitive look—that made Hamish suspect the Town Manager didn't entirely buy his explanation. Hamish refused to worry about it.

"Mr. Cummins' position, I think, is an interesting one, but we have developed our own hypothesis along quite different lines." Blagden Tyne, Bureau Director for the FBI for the area, was speaking in his flat, circumspect voice, one that managed to express the Bureau's feeling that State and local authorities were necessary, but largely inept, adjuncts to its own expertise. Tyne was a wiry, compact man, dressed in a neutral gray suit that somehow gave the impression—even if it wasn't true—of being double-breasted. He was a trim ghost of the early J. Edgar Hoover, constantly adjusting his necktie or flicking imaginary dust off his highly polished shoes, with the ruddy, bland face of a Rotarian. It would be some time before Hamish would come to realize how intelligent and dedicated a man Tyne really was.

"I can say the Bureau believes the abduction of Gilbert Axminster is a simple case of kidnapping. We feel a ransom demand will be forthcoming shortly. We further feel that the murder of Angel Sanchez was either a coincidence or a diversionary tactic."

Again, Hamish could see the barely visible shake of Jenny Cobb's head—magnified by the gentle swaying of her shining, blonde hair—as Blagden Tyne finished speaking; he could feel the same reaction building inside himself.

"I don't feel we're really in a position to offer any hypothesis at this time." An unwilling Leonard LaCross of the Federal Crime Bureau had been called on by Alan Whitemore, getting to his feet with visible reluctance.

"Hamish," asked Alan Whitemore, his tone making it clear that he was addressing him only out of protocol, "any comments?"

Looking up, Hamish let his eyes travel around the dark-stained walls of the Town Hall meeting room, then up to the platform with the American flag drooping limply on its stand, then to the faces of the men around the table. *"Comments? Just one. Crap."*

Alan Whitemore reddened. From the other men around the table came a wave of uncomfortable stirring and a sudden clearing of throats. Only Jenny Cobb laughed, a sound she stifled hurriedly.

Slapping his bifocals on his head angrily, Whitemore concluded the meeting quickly. He made a special appeal to hold all subjects discussed at the meeting in confidence; a leak could endanger not only the tracking down of the criminal but Gilly Axminster's life as well.

Hamish grimaced inwardly. Both points were valid, and both points probably did weigh on Whitemore's mind. But probably weighing almost as heavily was a more basic concern of the Town Manager: publicity was bad for property values.

The frail, small figure of the old lady stood silhouetted against the fly-specked windows of the dusty apartment, her lips pursed, her age bearing up badly against the harsh light. After she had followed Nate Pilkington, the huge black landlord, into the bathroom, she ran a speculative finger across the old-fashioned washstand, trying not to see herself in the cracked and yellowed mirror of the medicine cabinet. "It don't look like too much, empty like this, lady, but a little paint and curtains and some furniture . . ." Pilkington left the sentence unfinished; it was difficult to work up much enthusiasm about his beat-up collection of small studio and one-bedroom apartments, tenanted mostly by Social Security pensioners and Welfare families with more children than brains.

"Two stories up, you said?" the old lady asked. "I know we came up some stairs, but I get confused easily."

"Two stories. Easy climb."

The old lady laughed. "It would have to be."

Nate Pilkington looked up suddenly, as if he saw something wrong with the naked light bulb hanging from the ceiling; a rat had just scurried from the decrepit kitchen into the bathroom, and he wanted to divert the woman's attention. Old ladies were funny about things like that. Especially white old ladies.

The old lady wandered over to the window, her scuffed, flat-heeled shoes making a soft padding sound as she walked, and looked out. Through the thick glasses that almost disappeared into her white hair, which she wore pulled back in a severe bun, all she could make out was another, almost identical building perhaps ten feet across a narrow valley. Leaning against the window frame to steady herself, she turned toward Pilkington. "I'll take it."

Pilkington shrugged in surprise; most of his tenants were as black as he was. "Three months in advance, lady. On account we don't have leases."

"Of course."

"You got furniture coming?"

"There'll be some things in a week or so. Coming from— New Haven. But there'll be a phone man before then. Just have him put the phone between the windows."

Pilkington was surprised again. Most of his tenants didn't have phones. "Okay, sure."

The old lady caught his confusion. "I always have the phone put in first. In case my heart—well, you understand."

"Sure, sure." Pilkington paused. "The three months in advance?"

The old lady turned her back, fishing around in an old leather handbag before turning back to him, then counting out the exact amount carefully, as if each dollar was a personal wound.

Out on the street, the old lady hurried in the direction of Converse Avenue, the flower in her black straw pillbox flopping loosely with each step. At the corner, she climbed into a parked sports coupe and sank into the leather cushions with a sigh of relief.

"You got one?" asked Kip Grolier, studying his passenger.

"Christ, Kip. Yeah, I got one. But this goddamn getup . . ."

"Works beautifully. Whistler's mother couldn't do better."

There was a certain truth in what Kip said. K.K.'s tiny frame and pinched, sallow face had made the transformation easy. At Apollo Palaestron's House of Magic they'd bought the heavy glasses, made of plain, clear glass but so thick, K.K. felt he was seeing the world through the bottom of a Coke bottle. The white wig, with its molded bun, and a kit of theatrical makeup, also from Apollo's, supplied the finishing touches. The print dress was from Mrs. Braun's wardrobe, and the shawl from Mrs. Blakeslee's cook; the handbag came from the Grolier attic. The flat-heeled shoes were bought in Stamford, then deliberately scuffed to make them look old; K.K. didn't want to have to cope with heels. On top of all this costuming, K.K. was an excellent actor—he had the shuffling walk and high-pitched voice down almost perfectly. But he had found the performance upsetting.

"Dammit," he grumbled at Kip. "*You* ought to try it once."

"Too big. And too pretty. You're so damned ugly, it's safe."

K.K. could feel a small twinge of pain surge through him; Kip knew precisely how to hurt him. K.K. longed to explain what he felt, or to rebel and scream his anguish, but couldn't. Kip was too important in his life. K.K. watched him draw a small, yellow-lined pad from the glove compartment and make a heading, "Bridgeport." "Let's see," he said as he wrote, "the address is One twenty-seven Lederle. Apartment number—?"

"Two-G. If you can call that fleabag an apartment."

"Two-G. Okay, you said you were—"

"Mrs. Elwina Braun. Formerly of New Haven. Widow." K.K. watched the small smile light up Kip's face; he had known using the hated housekeeper's name would please him.

"And you mentioned about the phone."

"Said I always put that in first. Bad heart, I told him."

"Lot of that going around lately. Did he buy it?"

"He looked curious, but yes, he bought it. He's not very smart."

"Lot of that going around too," Kip muttered, and began scanning the Apts-for-Rent section of the *Bridgeport Herald*.

"Here's one. Lovett Avenue. Lousy enough section of town. And another on State."

K.K. groaned. "Aw, c'mon, Kip. *Two* more?"

"Plus a couple in Stamford."

"Christ, this rig's killing me. Maybe you'd better get yourself another old lady."

Kip reached over and squeezed K.K.'s knee. "I like the one I've got," Kip said, turning on his most incredible smile. In spite of himself, K.K. melted.

"Can I take off the damned wig, at least?"

"After we've lined up the other two here and are on the turnpike for Stamford."

K.K. sighed. The disguise he could understand. But this series of tacky apartments, the business about installing the phones, the whole progress of whatever plan it was Kip had tucked away in his mind baffled him. But he knew better than to ask. Kip never liked too many questions.

Chapter 6 _____

I don't know what Jenny Cobb sees in Hamish anyway. For one thing, he's damned near old enough to be her father. Of course, strictly speaking, she actually is old enough to be my mother.

Well, I always was attracted to older women. I suppose a shrink would say that that means I have a buried wish to screw my mother. But if that's true, it also probably follows that Jenny Cobb's unconscious drive is to sleep with her father, not really Hamish.

Oedipus, anyone?

—TAPE-LOG OF THE PIPER,
ENTRY DATED MAY 24.

Seven days after the disappearance of Gilly Axminster—Saturday, May 29th—dawned on Greenport with the promise of summer. While the breeze still had a chill to it, the sun was not hot enough to make anyone uncomfortable.

Since the Long's Bay Beach Club pool wasn't due to open until Memorial Day, some of the younger boys had already braved the Sound and swam to the raft anchored off the club's narrow strip of beach. There, by one o'clock, perhaps ten boys lay, letting their bodies drink in the hot sunshine, oblivious to a sign on the beach proclaiming that no lifeguard would be on duty until the Memorial Day weekend. Although the water was still cold, the raft wasn't very far from the beach, and no one had felt particularly daring about the short swim.

Paige Rathbin, 12, was the youngest of the group—and the most uncomfortable. His aunt had bought him a new bathing suit in Hobe Sound last winter, but this was the first time he'd worn it. It came from France and was made of some sort of knitted material that itched, particularly as the sun made his body moist with sweat. On top of this, the loose weave of the suit made it hard to keep it pulled up as tight as he liked.

Aunts, he decided, should not buy twelve-year-old nephews their clothes.

Paige suddenly scrambled to his feet, yelling to get the attention of the older boys on the raft. "If a shark gets me, somebody send for Quint." Then, with a whoop, Paige did a cannonball and struck out directly away from the raft, using the strong crawl that was the pride of Country Day's swimming coach. The water felt cold but good, and the itching from the damned bathing suit vanished.

Perhaps twenty yards from the raft, something happened that mystified Paige. His left foot felt as if a hand had grabbed it. At first Paige thought he'd hit a submerged net, but whatever it was kept grabbing on tighter to his ankle and began to pull him under. He spun his head toward the raft with a frightened yelp. No one paid any attention; they all knew about Paige and his gags.

For a moment, whatever was holding his foot seemed to disappear. But as Paige turned to swim back toward the raft, it grabbed at him again—this time his whole upper leg—pulling him partly under and making his mouth fill with water. Paige knew sharks pulled people under water—he'd seen *Jaws,* hadn't he?—but he also knew that sharks didn't have hands that grabbed you by the foot and leg and then reached up to grab you by the back of the bathing suit to drag you below the surface. In spite of the water he was swallowing, Paige began to scream in earnest. The boys on the raft looked at him, beginning to feel a little frightened, but unwilling to let their fears show; Paige's parting remark about the shark made any indication of genuine alarm open to the risk of being taken in.

The hand yanked harder. Paige felt the loose-knit bathing suit slide down his body as the hand tried to pull him under by it. The suit quickly became entangled around his feet, making his struggles to keep his head above water that much harder. By now his screams had reached a piercing intensity, and several of the boys on the raft were standing up and watching his thrashing, trying to stifle their growing sense of doubt.

Suddenly Paige felt two hands getting a firm grip on him by the waist; he had time only for one final terrified shriek before he was pulled under completely. In the murky water he could see very little—only what appeared to be the dim shadow of a man in a wet-suit. Paige felt himself pulled along underwater at an increasingly faster clip, his hands beating uselessly against the vague shadow that had taken control of him. Twice he caught sight of a pair of yellow diving flippers. His lungs began to swell against his ribcage, desperately seeking air they could not find. It was if something inside him was about to explode. His mouth opened and closed by reflex, gasping for air, but only taking in more water. From nowhere, a hand suddenly stuffed the end of a rubber diving hose into his mouth, and Paige could feel the sudden rush of oxygen to his lungs. He lost consciousness, surrendering himself to the hands, the shadow, and the terror.

On the raft, there was growing confusion. If it was a trick on them, it had been very well done; they had seen no sign of Paige since his final scream. "Probably hiding under the raft," someone suggested. Heads instantly craned over the edge, and the underside of the raft was examined. There was no sign of anything. Finally, Wayne Ellis, at 17 the oldest of the boys, reached a decision.

"He's been under too long," he said simply, and dove off the raft into the water. In the mottled half-light beneath the surface he could see little, but something floating lazily upward caught his eye. Wayne grabbed it and resurfaced. In his hand he held the French bathing suit. "Christ," he said, and climbed quickly back onto the raft.

The younger boys all began talking at once, a babble of excitement, confusion, and nameless fear. Wayne and two older boys exchanged glances; a vision of Angel's hand and Gilly Axminster's smile had flashed simultaneously through their minds.

"We better go ashore and call the police." Wayne said it with firm authority, and the whole group of them moved to the inland side of the raft. For a second no one said anything, but just stared at the short stretch of suddenly menacing water.

Without comment, they raised their hands to their mouths and began shouting for someone to come rescue them, someone, for Christ's sake, to come get them off that damned raft fast.

On the other side of Belle Haven Point, Kip and K.K.—Kip in his wet-suit—dragged Paige Rathbin out of the water and up onto the beach. The extra air tank Kip had bought in Bridgeport was still strapped to his back, its hose and mouthpiece now flapping loosely around his knees. The two of them stopped as they reached the scrub growth and beach plums that bordered the narrow strip of sand; at the end of a dirt road leading down from the Grolier property to the beach, stood the black Volks.

Almost tenderly, Kip replaced the mouthpiece from the oxygen tank in Paige's mouth. "He looks awful." For a moment, the two of them studied the naked Paige, then saw his eyelids begin fluttering. "He's coming around," Kip said. "We'd better get him into the truck." From far away, Kip heard a concerted shouting. "What the hell—?" he muttered.

Through what seemed a dim, distant haze, Paige, slowly opening his eyes, saw K.K. for the first time. The fact that it was K.K. baffled him. *K.K.* had dragged him underwater and brought him here? No, he wasn't strong enough. Besides, K.K. was wearing dry clothes. But Paige knew that K.K. had to be involved somehow. Oddly, Paige found that this didn't surprise him. He felt himself being lifted up onto some kind of platform and, looking up, saw the ceiling of what he guessed was a panel truck. Outside his range of vision, something strange was happening to his hands. Cold, metallic objects suddenly tightened around his wrists, and when he tried to move his hands, he realized he had been handcuffed. Paige felt tired, very tired, and none of this made any sense. It was like a crazy dream that wakes you and then disappears before you can remember what it was.

Suddenly, Paige heard a familiar voice. "Better get a blanket or something around him. He's shivering. We want him alive."

For a moment, Paige couldn't place the voice. Then came the shock. Standing inside the truck, pulling off the wet-suit and climbing quickly into a pair of chinos and a sports shirt, was Kip Grolier.

Paige saw K.K. look at Kip curiously. "Where are *you* going?"

"To put the icing on the cake. You'll hear about it." Kip started out the door of the truck, then paused to look back at

K.K. "Don't forget the blanket. And then meet me at the place. Don't try getting him inside by yourself."

Although Paige understood nothing of the situation, he could sense K.K.'s mounting hostility toward Kip. "Fat chance," K.K. said.

A few minutes after Kip left, K.K. wrapped Paige tightly in a heavy blanket. Paige was becoming drowsy from the effects of shock and immersion, and the blanket felt warm and good; even in the bright sunlight outside of the truck, his nakedness had seemed cold in the chilling breeze off the water. He wasn't sure how long he lay there, confused and frightened, but accepting the blanket's reassuring warmth. At times, he knew, he drifted off into a semi-doze.

Suddenly Paige came fully awake as the blanket was pulled off him roughly. He looked up to see K.K. standing over him, slipping out of his trousers and shorts. "Listen," K.K. hissed. "If you ever say one word about this to Kip, you'll wish he *had* been a shark."

Thirty seconds later, Paige was already wishing it.

The *Coupon,* used mostly as a launch for Kip's father's yawl, *High Yield,* swept around the tip of Long's Bay Point, going so fast it listed to port like a plane making a tight left turn. There was enough chop on the Sound to make the *Coupon* plane across the water, its bottom slapping against the surface as it rose out of the Sound lightly, then fell heavily back on the water. Once around the Point, Kip could make out the Beach Club raft; he saw the boys on it waving and yelling at his boat.

Turning the wheel with a flourish, Kip steered the *Coupon* directly toward the raft. Coming closer, he throttled back the twin Grays and floated noiselessly up to the raft. "What the hell's going on?" he asked, waving cheerfully at two of the older boys from his own class and smiling a puzzled grin. "I could hear you guys clear around the Point."

Wayne Ellis met the smile with a grim look. "Can you take all of us in one trip?"

"A little tight, but sure." Kip paused, allowing himself to look increasingly puzzled—but slowly, by degrees. "What's up?"

"Come on, kids," commanded Wayne. "Everybody into the

boat. But take it nice and easy. Careful, dammit. There's room for everybody."

Wayne was holding the *Coupon* alongside the raft with a line Kip had thrown to him, and he was the last to climb off the raft into Kip's boat, like the captain leaving a sinking ship. Everybody seemed to be talking at once, except for Wayne and another older boy, Tod Ramsey.

Kip spun around at the wheel. "Sit down, kids, dammit, sit down. Everybody down. And shut up. I can't hear myself think."

Kip's voice was commanding, but his orders had little effect. The boys were too frightened and too full of their experience. They continued to chatter as Kip, the *Coupon's* motor virtually at idle, headed slowly for the narrow strip of sand below the clubhouse. Just before they jumped out and scampered up the beach to head for telephones and clothes and help, they saw Wayne Ellis and Tod Ramsey huddling with Kip, Wayne shaking his head as he explained what had happened. Kip kicked the sand with his foot, using some colorful oaths that even the generally knowing younger boys of Country Day had never heard before.

Inside, Kip was experiencing something else entirely. The stage of his plan that called for a child to disappear from directly beneath the noses of people had been a highly gratifying success.

"Jenny, I don't know, I just don't know." Hamish was aware this was the wrong time to start talking about the disappearing children, but he seemed unable to stop himself. They were lying beside each other in the Soundsight Motel, where Jenny was staying during her assignment for Demings. It was late afternoon of the same Saturday, and Hamish was playing hooky. He knew he should be huddling with the out-of-town experts or following up his own leads, however slim they were, but the tension of the last few days had reached him and he needed relief badly. Besides, he told himself, he'd set this date for lunch with Jenny two days earlier and was damned if he would break it. He'd already done that to Jenny once—the night of the broadcast—and twice might shatter any chance he had with her.

Although it was still bright outside, the venetian blinds and heavy blue drapes shut out most of the light in the room, allowing only scattered splinters of sunlight to break through an occasional crack. The starkly modern decor of the Soundsight was vastly improved by the effect, softened and enhanced by wandering shards of light that bounced back and forth between wall and ceiling.

Hamish sighed in contentment. Sitting halfway up, he propped himself against a pillow and lit two cigarettes—one for himself, one for Jenny (he'd seen Paul Henreid do that once in a movie, and all the women in the audience seemed to love it)—and watched as Jenny got out of bed. God, she was beautiful, standing there wrapped in a towel, tossing back her flowing blonde hair and then combing it with her hand as she disappeared into the bathroom. When he first met her, he had thought his attraction to her was largely physical, but inside himself he could feel something else growing, something that defied containment, as if it had a life of its own.

Not, he thought, that the physical part of it—today was the first time—could be ignored. In bed, Jenny had been wild, an imaginative, sensuous, aggressive animal, exploring, provoking, responding, thrashing, as if sex were her own personal discovery, something she had just invented in the last half-hour. For Hamish the experience was totally different from anything he had ever known; something bottled up inside of him for years came bursting out in an explosion of shuddering ecstasy. Making love to his wife, Martha, had been, almost since he could remember, dull and pedestrian, almost automatic. Poor Martha. Jenny Cobb had ruined him for any woman except herself. Merely thinking about his just-finished encounter with Jenny caused Hamish to feel stirrings inside him all over again.

The sound of a passing police or ambulance siren catapulted him back to earth, and Hamish found his brain crowded with more speculations on the death of Angel, the unseen disappearance of Gilly Axminster, and the frighteningly visible abduction of Paige Rathbin in front of a score of his classmates. In his mind, a decision was reached.

A few seconds later, when Jenny Cobb came through the door, she saw Hamish sitting on the edge of the bed, drawing heavily on his cigarette and frowning. For a man of his age, she thought, his body was still in remarkably trim shape, with a flat stomach and the hard horizontal lines of an athlete running across it.

Hamish raised his head as she came into the room, staring at her. "I'm going to have to do it. I was afraid I would, but thinking about it, there isn't any choice: I have to do it."

Jenny laughed. "I thought we just did."

Hamish ignored the feeble joke. "We've got to drill Country Day's whole damned teaching staff. *And* the janitors, administrators, groundskeepers, the works. It'll blow the town open."

Jenny pulled the towel she had wrapped around herself tighter, sitting on the edge of the bed trying to force her mind into Hamish's suddenly changed frame of reference. With shaking fingers, Jenny lit a cigarette, this time without waiting for any help from him. "You don't really have much to go on, do you? It's a pretty strong sort of accusation."

"Figure it out. Three kids, all about the same age, one poor, two rich. All from the same school. Angel Sanchez's family couldn't scrape together enough to ransom a canary, so you have to say money wasn't the motive."

"Maybe Angel was just to throw people off."

"That's taking a chance for nothing. So was that broadcast stuff of Gilly: dangerous as hell. He took another big chance yanking Paige Rathbin underwater while half a dozen people were standing around who might have jumped in the Sound and stopped him. Bet you two bits, by tonight Paige will be on the air too—just like Gilly. To prove he's alive. Taking another chance. Trying to make us think kidnapping again. . . There has to be a reason."

"I'm a psychiatrist, Hamish, not a detective," Jenny replied. "And right now, a tired psychiatrist. The sudden switch. . ."

Hamish cut her off. Watching his face, Jenny could see that for the moment there was no chance of separating him from his obsession. He began speaking again without even looking at her. "What I am thinking about," Hamish said softly, his expression heavy with concentration, "is assault. Homosexual assault, rape—whatever you want to call it. It all adds up."

Hamish's idea made some sense to Jenny, but was built on some very thin premises. "It's possible," she admitted weakly, "but not very substantiated."

"Look," Hamish argued. "It had to be someone who knew

where to find Gilly on a Saturday morning. Someone who knew where his father worked in New York, and that he'd be in the city that particular Saturday. With Paige, it had to be someone who knew those kids would be out on the raft today. Who better than one of the teachers?"

Listening to him, Jenny was still unable to work up much enthusiasm for Hamish's explanation. Missing was the clear, driving motive a psychopath would have "I'm not all that sure that someone on the faculty is the answer to all the questions you've brought up."

"Neither am I. But every boys' school has a handful of queers on its teaching staff; they're good teachers because they enjoy working with boys."

Jenny winced. In her work, she avoided such stereotypes, and Hamish struck her as too intelligent to be thinking in such terms. Suddenly Jenny felt an unreasoning anger flare inside herself. "I think your plan is lousy. Really lousy. You haven't got one ounce of solid proof. It'll be a witch hunt. It makes me sick."

Abruptly, Hamish's face took on a hurt look. Staring at her, he continued putting his clothes back on automatically. With a quick shake of his head, as if trying to get water out of his ear, he sat down on the other bed, trying to figure out what had happened. "I don't see why you're—"

"Because somebody's got to be, that's why. In the end, all you'll accomplish is to lose some perfectly innocent men their reputations."

"It's better than losing more kids, for Christ's sake."

Shaking her head, Jenny suddenly felt silly standing there dressed only in a towel. At the same time, her psychiatric training began to reach her, and she found herself wondering how much of her indignation came from disagreement with Hamish, and how much from a feeling that she came second to his job. Melting, she turned around to face him. "I'm sorry, Hamish. Okay, I disagree with what you want to do, but I didn't mean to get so shrill about it. All wound up, I guess."

"Forget it. Everybody's wound up." He shrugged and walked to the mirror, picking up his tie from the back of a chair on the way. "The pressure's crazy. They keep calling, wanting to know what I'm doing, what steps I'm taking, scared silly maybe something else will happen before I take the right step. Maybe they're right—I don't know. All I know is, I have to cover every single possibility, however remote, no matter who gets hurt."

Lighting another cigarette, she watched him quickly tie his tie in the mirror. For her, the wonderful moments she'd just spent with him had been diminished by the sudden intrusion of his job into the pleasant unwinding she loved after sex. Sometimes, she thought, this exhausted euphoria, of looking back in a sort of instant replay, was almost as important to her as sex itself. Jenny sighed.

"So long." Hamish leaned over and kissed her lightly on the forehead. A perfunctory peck, like a little boy saying good-bye to his mother. Already his mind was a thousand miles away. "I'll call you tonight. If an old bear like me doesn't bore you too much."

"Some bear."

Unhearing, he slipped out the door with a wave.

As he got into his car, Hamish thought he saw the shadow of something move in the bushes, but paid it little attention. It might have been better if he had. Kip, as soon as he saw the door opening, slid down into the shrubbery, and, with mounting anger, watched Hamish leave. Kip was under no illusion as to what had gone on inside Jenny's motel room, and wasn't entirely sure why he was still hanging around. Spotting Jenny's car in the Soundsight Motel's parking lot, Kip's original idea had been to "accidentally" run into Jenny. He had no definite plan, but the recurring excitement he felt every time he thought of her coming on to him during the interview compelled him to see her again. Then he saw Jenny and Hamish disappear into the motel.

Seething, Kip climbed into his own car and roared off. As a policeman, Hamish Hamilton was a natural enemy. But he had just become Kip's competition.

Kip was not used to competition.

Chapter 7_____

*It was hard for me to buy at first. I suppose it
always is. But two years ago, Mom finally explained the whole thing to me. Some crazy
shrink, she said, got her started on too many
tranquilizers, and from there she got into
barbs and amphets. Downers, uppers, the
whole bit. She lives in a sort of floating haze
all the time; that's why she holed herself up
on the third floor. So nobody'd find out.
Frankly, I'll bet Dad knows, but what the hell.*

*Then the shrink died and there wasn't any
way for her to get the stuff anymore. So she
made* me *her connection. Goddamn, what a
bag of gimmicks we use. Maybe ten different
doctors in ten different towns, all prescribing
pills for her. And if all the prescriptions run
out, well, I use a doctor's pad and forge them.
Sometimes I wonder what Miss Cobb would
think if she knew her model teen-ager was
also the town's dope king. Funny, I think
she'd understand.*

—TAPE-LOG OF THE PIPER,
ENTRY DATED MAY 30.

"One every day, that's the way it has to work from now on.
One a day."

K.K. stared at Kip in disbelief. "You're crazy."

They were standing near the end of one of the tunnels that
ran from the well below the cistern; ahead of them stood the
heavy, rusted iron door that opened into the largest of the
storage chambers, a room hewn out of subsurface stone,
measuring perhaps 12 by 20 feet. In his hands, Kip carried a
tightly wrapped bundle of clothes, and K.K.'s words caused
him to flush and drop the bundle. Moving quickly, he suddenly shoved K.K. against the iron door with a heavy thud.

Kip's reaction was so unexpected, K.K. was totally un-prepared for it. As Kip's elbow and forearm pressed against his neck, K.K.'s eyes bulged. "Listen, you little bastard . . ." Kip's voice came in a hissed whisper, so menacing that K.K.'s breath, already partially cut off by the pressure of Kip's arm on his windpipe, came in even more desperate gasps. "Don't ever pull a word like that on me again. Understand? *You're* the one who's crazy, you little prick. Paige told me about what you did to him. That's why I brought him the clothes. We need him. So don't call me crazy, you fag bastard. You're the guy who's sick."

K.K.'s hands were tearing at Kip's forearm now, trying to push it away so he could breathe. With what little motion was possible, K.K.'s head nodded up and down, his eyes staring at Kip, pleading.

With a snort of disgust, Kip suddenly freed him. K.K. slumped to the floor, coughing and gasping, his hands rubbing his neck as he tried to massage the circulation back into his throat.

Kip retrieved the bundle of clothes from the floor and pulled some keys from his pocket; the double padlocks were unlocked and the heavy bolts slid back to allow the door to open. In the dim light of a single bulb, Paige Rathbin could be seen inside the vaultlike storeroom, wrapped in the blanket, his frightened eyes studying Kip and K.K. As he walked in, Kip paused at the doorway and turned toward K.K., speaking as much for Paige's benefit as his. "Lay a finger on him again, creepo, and *you* wind up in here instead of him. Get me?"

Numbly, K.K. nodded. Still rubbing his neck tenderly, he watched as Kip tossed the bundle of clothes to Paige, then heard him talk to the boy reassuringly. K.K. tried to make sense of this mystery. Paige was the first of the children to be taken prisoner instead of being killed. Twice now, Kip had said "we need him," a statement that held little logic for K.K.

A minor coughing fit seized K.K., a product, he supposed, of Kip's assault on his throat. But the only thing K.K. was really sure of at the moment was that when Kip said from now on it would be one a day, he meant it.

Kip *had* meant it. And as he predicted, each succeeding child who disappeared made abducting the next one that much harder. Because the authorities, from the FBI to the local police, quickly tried to draw a ring of security around any place where the children might be vulnerable. On top of the organized precautions, every parent who became frightened added one more person on the alert for anything unusual, and one more person to watch each child's every move. To match this increasing sense of vigilance, the ways of kidnapping the children had to become increasingly ingenious. To Kip, it was a delicious challenge.

And a challenge Kip couldn't resist taking up in public. The night after they took Paige, directly after the now-familiar taped cries of Gilly Axminster went on the air, Paige Rathbin's voice was heard for the first time. To prove that he—along with the others who would soon be joining him—was still alive, Paige said that each night he would read a summary of the day's ten best-selling stocks, along with their prices. Since there was no way these could be predicted and taped in advance, this would be proof for the parents that their children were still alive.

Then, suddenly Paige introduced a new ingredient that left everyone baffled. "And now," Paige read, "I have an important announcement from the Piper. The Piper wants you to know that from now on, one child a day will disappear. One child a day. Feel free to call in all the police you want, all the FBI agents, all of the Pinkerton men this side of the Mississippi—the Piper is flattered by your attention. You won't get anywhere, anyway. One child a day will *still* disappear. Eventually you, the parents, will be presented with the ultimate ransom. Pay the Piper and they will be set free; don't pay and you will never see them again. Simple enough, fair enough." Abruptly, Paige's voice was cut off the air, replaced by a recording of "The Best Things in Life are Free," and, a little later, by complete silence.

Jenny, Hamish, and Blagden Tyne of the FBI, sitting in Tyne's office in the basement of the First Baptist, exchanged bewildered stares. "One a day?" grunted Hamish. "Son of a bitch, that's impossible." He shifted uncomfortably, wishing he felt as confident as he sounded.

"The 'ultimate ransom' doesn't sound like he meant money, or maybe it does," Jenny noted, rubbing one finger across her forehead.

Tyne shrugged, adjusting the knife crease of one trouser leg. "Maybe he means more money than anyone ever asked for before." He replayed the tape made of what they'd just heard, and turned to the others in confusion. "What's all this stuff about 'the Piper'? What the hell's *that* mean? The 'Pied Piper' seems too damned obvious for this creep."

"Maybe not," said Jenny. "In the story, the Piper was offered money by the town of Hamelin to get rid of the rats. He did. But the town wouldn't pay up, so he swiped the children. I don't know what our Piper has in mind for the rats, but he's sure as hell got plans for the kids. One a day. My God."

"Impossible," repeated Hamish, going back to where he started.

What worried them all was that, impossible or not, the Piper might somehow live up to his promise.

The next day they found out. "Ramsey, your entrance in the E-flat passage is always a hair late," said Mr. Gelby, finding the passage in the score set up on a music stand in front of him. Ramsey Lakewood, a 12-year-old serving in the church choir as an unwilling draftee from Country Day, looked at Mr. Gelby as if to protest, then thought better of it and nodded in silent acceptance.

They were standing in the choir loft of the Church of the Heavenly Redemption, an elegantly somber, cathedral-like building off Greenport Avenue. As the boy soprano soloist, Ramsey stood in the very front; behind him was the rest of the choir, and behind them, the new velvet curtains which Mr. Gelby had had installed to improve the acoustics. After a nod from Mr. Gelby to the organist, the choir began again. Perfectly on cue this time, Ramsey Lakewood's pure soprano rose above the choir, "Oh, for the wings, for the wings of a dove . . ."

A few measures later, Mr. Gelby again brought the singing to a halt. "Your entrance was perfect, Ramsey. But there's something wrong with the sound. Our fault, not yours." Pondering, Mr. Gelby studied the relative positions of the choir and Ramsey. "You're the soloist, of course Ramsey," he mused, "but your voice isn't blending with the choir's. Too much separation. We wouldn't want that, would we?" Then, his fingers waving instructions, Mr. Gelby returned to the arrangement of singers he'd always used. "Try standing on the top riser, Ramsey. That's right—in the back. Coming from behind the choir, we should get a better blend."

Muttering, Ramsey fought his way through the choir to the last riser, one step above and behind the rest of the choir. With a small smile, Mr. Gelby waved his arms and the choir began again. This time when he heard Ramsey's first "Oh, for the wings, for the wings of a dove . , ," his smile widened; the attack had been perfect, and the sound, at last, was a blend, rather than a soloist shouting over a choir.

Even Ramsey could hear the difference, and Mr. Gelby became a less irritating figure to him. Glancing at the music stand, he counted the number of measures until his next solo. Twenty-five. The curtains directly behind him seemed suddenly harder than they should have been, and from one corner of his eye, Ramsey saw something move as the heavy velvet parted and a hand clamped itself over his mouth. Almost immediately, more hands seemed to seize him, and he felt himself yanked through an opening in the curtains. The dim light made it difficult, almost impossible for Ramsey to see, but he knew he was being carried, thrashing and twisting to free himself, down the stairs. His struggles became more difficult as he felt his arms twisted behind him and his wrists handcuffed; simultaneously, he felt his legs handcuffed by the ankles. He continued struggling all the way down the stairs, but the hands holding him were strong; the most Ramsey succeeded in doing was to pull his shirt entirely out of his trousers and rip two buttons off his blazer.

In the loft, Mr. Gelby looked up confidently and stretched one long finger toward Ramsey Lakewood to begin his next solo. His mouth dropped open. All that he could see was the heavy velvet swaying back and forth behind where Ramsey had been standing the last time he looked. The choir was stopped. A quick search failed to produce the boy. Mr. Gelby began yelling. The wings of the dove had been clipped. Permanently.

"But these records don't indicate anything like that," noted Hamish, turning the man's dossier over on his desktop.

"Would you expect them to?" Mr. Adrian's voice hovered somewhere between anger and petulance.

"No, but then we only have your word for what you say."

"Usually that's good enough."

"Usually, perhaps. But this situation isn't usual."

"Oh, Christ."

The sound of Jenny clearing her throat made Hamish turn sideways to look at her. On her face was an expression of either caution or displeasure. The way she kept running her left hand through her hair made him pretty sure it was the latter. These interviews with Country Day's faculty were painful affairs. Jenny would talk to Hamish after each one, grudgingly giving her opinion, but mostly trying to show him the uselessness of what he was attempting. The married teachers hid behind the fact of being married, something which Jenny pointed out proved absolutely nothing. The unmarried teachers—like the young Mr. Adrian facing Hamish across his desk now—tried to make themselves sound as if no girl in the state was safe as long as they were around. Even to Hamish, there was something ridiculous about his own efforts; the intent of the interviews was so obvious it was seen through by the faculty almost immediately, and by the time Hamish got around to them, each teacher's particular defenses were up and ready. Stubbornly, though—and in spite of increasing criticism from Jenny Cobb—Hamish plowed ahead.

When the sessions were finally completed, Jenny and Hamish sat in his empty office while Jenny reluctantly compared her notes with his. They had uncovered two teachers who, under pressure, finally admitted their homosexuality, one with indignant fury at what he considered an invasion of privacy, the other as if the discovery was something he had dreaded but expected for years. Both had alibis. As best he could, Hamish assured them their secret would go no further. Their expressions as they left indicated little gratitude, or even much belief.

Two additional teachers—one married, one single—were on Hamish's final list. But as kidnappers they held little, if any, promise. The married man had been, he said, with his wife, a point which could easily be checked, but one which Jenny was rapidly talking Hamish out of even pursuing. The other "possible" was too old and fragile to be a candidate. With a disgruntled sigh, Hamish slapped the faculty list down on his desk.

"How come you didn't interview Huggins?" Jenny asked him suddenly, looking up from her list.

"Huggins? *Huggins??*" Hamish quickly scanned his papers, running a pencil down the edge, trying to find the name. "I don't have a Huggins."

"Not on this list. She's the school nurse. But, well, with that deep voice of hers, who knows? She could be a guy in drag, Hamish."

For a second, it looked as if Hamish might explode into anger. Jenny, still as a stone, sat staring into his eyes, an innocent expression on her face, the smallest flicker of an impish grin playing around the edges of her mouth. "Dammit, Jenny . . ." The fury drained out of him and the ridiculousness of his project lay in tatters around his feet.

"Jenny," Hamish said again, his face creasing in resignation. "You win."

She smiled back and tossed her glowing blonde hair lightly.

Hamish was still at her motel when the first word of Ramsey Lakewood's abduction reached the police. For the second time in a month, the police were unable to find Hamish when they needed him.

"It's a beautiful day for it," said the launchman from Leafpoint Harbor, swinging the club's little cutter around so that he could pull her alongside the *Skipper*, one of the 28-foot racing sloops that were part of the many Zebra Class boats kept here. The two boys, both members of the Junior Yacht Club and both 16, nodded solemnly, hoisting the canvas bags full of sails onto their shoulders before making the leap aboard the *Skipper*. The launchman waved good-bye cheerfully, and the two boys quickly began pulling the mainsail out of its bag and slipping it onto the tracks of boom and mast.

The launchman had been right. The early afternoon following Ramsey Lakewood's truncated solo was warm and sunny. Both boys were playing hooky from Country Day's sports program, trying to escape the oppressive gloom that was swallowing the school. An afternoon on the water, they convinced themselves, was precisely the tonic they needed. If any of the faculty had known what the boys planned, they probably would have stopped them, but George Lennox and Lyle Pritchard had told only their families. And even to them they lied, saying that they had the school's approval. Spring Cup championship, they explained.

Twenty minutes later, they raised both jib and mainsail; Lyle was at the tiller and George up on the foredeck, holding onto the white can which would mark their mooring after they sailed off.

"Cast off!" yelled Lyle, firmly and loudly, as a succession of sailing instructors, fathers, and older boys had trained him. In the brisk but warm breeze of early afternoon, the *Skipper* made swiftly away from the Yacht Club and headed out toward the open water, heeling slightly as the breeze got a firm grip on the mainsail and dipped the boat's starboard gunwales into the bright blue Sound. As they left the harbor, the professional captain aboard the large cabin cruiser *Dexterity* eyed them carefully, making sure they were going to clear his stern with plenty of leeway. Once that he saw they would, he waved to them cheerfully, then returned to polishing the brightwork on the flying bridge.

He was the last man to set eyes on either of them. The *Skipper,* Zebra Class Number 20, became the object of a Sound-wide search by seven that night, when the boys' suddenly anxious parents checked with Country Day's headmaster and discovered no permission for an afternoon on the water had been—or would have been—given.

The boat was finally discovered the next morning, empty but undamaged, clear across the Sound, close to Long Island. Boarding her, the Coast Guard announced she had not been sailed there, but must have drifted over on the outgoing tide, for she was found with sheets loose, her sails flapping forlornly in the morning wind. At first, the Coast Guard clung to the theory that both boys had somehow gone overboard, and mounted a helicopter "man overboard" search of the waters. But by nine P.M. that night, the voices of Lyle Pritchard and George Lennox joined the nightly parade of children pleading with their parents to "do whatever they tell you, *please.*" The boys' little game of hooky had proved expensive.

"We can't ever get a fix on them. They're not on very long, and by the time we begin to get our vectors zeroed in, they're gone." The man talking was Brook Fleming, section chief of the FCC's area field unit. He stood facing Hamish, Town

Manager Alan Whitemore, and Blagden Tyne of the FBI.
Fleming's expression was unhappy; for three nights his traveling trucks, crammed with electronic gear for pinpointing illegal broadcasters, had roamed the area. Each time, the trucks,
their highly sensitive loop antennae whirling on their shielded
metal roofs, came up with nothing.

Fleming felt his professional expertise was at stake. "But I
can tell you this much," he said defensively, "whoever is
broadcasting those tapes has some sort of highly mobile transmitter. So mobile that not one of our fixes has come even
close to another. And since the kind of power he's using re-
quires a high-wattage generator, he's operating out of something big—something at least the size of a small trailer truck."

"Would more mobile units help you?" the FBI's Blagden
Tyne asked the question, suspecting he already knew the answer. "I could call Washington—"

Fleming threw up his hands with an elaborate shrug of his
shoulders. "There's a law of diminishing returns in these
things. Three vectors and we have a fix. Three trucks, three
vectors. In theory, that's all we need."

"Goddammit," roared Alan Whitemore, trying to bluster his
way into the conversation. "If more trucks will be even a little
more help, let's call Washington and—"

The FCC expert turned to him, fascinated by his own re-
flection in the Town Manager's thick bifocals. "Mr.
Whitemore, three trucks is all we can possibly use. It's simple
trianulation"—Fleming started to sketch a diagram on a piece
of paper for Whitemore, but the Town Manager brushed the
paper aside with his hand and faced Tyne squarely.

"For the last two days, one child a day. It's monstrous.
There's vigilante groups being formed . . . men patroling the
back and main roads to keep an eye on the children . . . people
buying guns left and right . . . the town's going crazy . . ."

The town might be on the edge of panic, but it was clear to
Hamish that the person closest to it was Alan Whitemore. He
pulled a yellow pad out from under his arm, sat down, and
calmly began making notes. "Let's see what we really have on
this Piper guy. We know he's athletic, a good swimmer,
strong, and probably young. He's a resident of Greenport.
And in some way, he's connected with Greenport Country
Day; hell, he knows the boys' habits, and where they will be

most of the time. It could be a parent, I suppose. Or some non-parent closely tied to the school could fit, I suppose. Dr. Cobb and I have screened the faculty and found no homosexuals—none we could uncover anyway—who didn't either have an alibi or weren't too old or frail to pull off the Piper's kind of stuff. Then, we can—"

Alan Whitemore had listened to this last sentence of Hamish's recap with his mouth open. He finally found his voice. "Do you mean to tell me that you've discovered homosexuals on the staff of Country Day and all you can say is that either they weren't strong enough or that they had alibis?"

"What more do you want?"

"Does the headmaster know who they are? Have you reported their names to the Board of Trustees? The State Licensing Board? Good God, Hamish, who the hell do you think you are?"

"I interviewed the faculty in confidence. I made promises. Hell, I'm not going to throw those men to the wolves."

Whitemore turned to Blagden for help. The FBI man looked uncomfortable, adjusting the knot of his tie and studying some papers to keep himself out of the argument.

Addressing him by name to force Tyne's head out of the suddenly produced sheaf of notes, Whitemore became more insistent. "Mr. Tyne, certainly the FBI should be checking the alibis, too. You have more resources. . ."

"Well, there could be. . ." Blagden Tyne let his voice trail away to nothingness. He knew what Hamish was trying to avoid, and some inner part of him agreed with him. Still . . .

"Good. Thank you." Whitemore's head spun toward Hamish. "Hamish, turn over the list of possible faculty homosexuals to Mr. Tyne. With all the pertinent facts and information that you and your—" Whitemore paused just long enough to make the point effective—"psychiatrist friend have gathered."

"The names are locked in my desk. And that's where they stay."

"Hamish, as Town Manager, I'm giving you a direct order. Turn over the names and the information."

"As Director of Police, I'm telling you the information is confidential."

"We'll see how long you can make that position stick, Hamish."

Blagden Tyne, determined to halt the argument before it escalated any further, interceded and took Hamish back to where he had been. "Those were interesting hypotheses on the Piper you started listing, Hamish. I was wondering where you came out next."

Relieved, Hamish glanced at his notes and began again; Alan Whitemore sat in his chair, polishing his glasses and fuming like a sulky little boy.

"Let's see," mused Hamish, trying to reconstruct where he'd been. "Youngish, athletic, strong, and connected—either directly or indirectly—with Country Day. Add to that he has scuba gear. And a boat—those two kids weren't yanked off the *Skipper* in a charter job. It all dovetails: the scuba equipment, the know-how, a boat to dive from, and the fact that a boat was also used to kidnap Lyle Pritchard and George Lennox." A sudden thought hit Hamish. With a pursing of his lips, he turned toward Brook Fleming. "Could the generator the man is using for his broadcasts be aboard a boat instead of a truck, can you tell?"

For a second the FCC expert ran the vectors through his head. "I don't believe so. No, definitely not."

"Okay. So this Piper guy has a truck—a large one—and knows how to drive it. If it's big enough, that means air brakes, double-clutching, the whole business . . ." Hamish's mouth suddenly dropped open; he was startled by an idea which hit him as he spoke. For a second he stood silent and still, only his face working as his own statement rolled over in his head. Both Tyne and Whitemore studied him, fascinated. Finally, very slowly, Hamish twisted his body so that his eyes could meet those of a bewildered Whitemore. "Does Henry Parker have a boat?"

Whitemore exploded. "Parker! What the hell are you getting at, Hamish?" The trouble was, the Town Manager knew precisely what Hamish was getting at. Parker was one of the wealthier residents of Greenport—and a firm political supporter of Whitemore's. Parker had started out at the age of 18 as a truck driver and wound up owning—by a series of maneuvers rumored to be not entirely scrupulous—the trucking company. By the time he moved to Greenport, he con-

SAVAGE RANSOM   75

trolled a complex of trucking and warehouse companies that rivaled anything in the country.

"Well," said Hamish slowly, "he has been one of Country Day's heaviest contributors. In spite of not having any sons. Maybe he's snapped and is kidnapping and killing other people's sons to make up for that. Older than I had in mind, but in good shape, strong as an ox, plus he's familiar with most of the school's students. And not only does he know how to drive a truck, he can lay his hands on hundreds of them."

Alan Whitemore was becoming red with anger. He stood up and planted himself directly in front of Hamish. "That's the craziest thing I ever heard of. Henry wouldn't hurt a fly, and you know it. You're just pissed off because—"

"Does he own a boat or doesn't he?"

Hamish's icy calm caused Whitemore to redden further. "Yes, dammit, of course he has a boat. But to claim—"

"Parker. Henry Parker. Lives way out on Seven Hills, maybe half a mile past the Seven Hills Club." Hamish watched as the FBI's Tyne wrote down the information in a small leatherette notebook he'd pulled from his rear trouser pocket.

"Just going to see him will ruin the man," argued Whitemore hotly.

"We'll be discreet, Mr. Whitemore. *Very* discreet." Tyne's notebook was slapped shut with a final sound; the matter was wordlessly pronounced closed to further discussion.

Blagden Tyne nodded to both Hamish and Alan Whitemore, then left. Whitemore, with a final furious glance at Hamish, followed him out by a few seconds, slamming the door behind him hard.

Had Kip Grolier been privy to the argument, he probably would have laughed at the sudden wild goose chase Hamish and the FBI had just sent themselves on. Henry Parker was as harmless as Kip looked. Hamish, talking later with Jenny, *did* laugh.

But the laughter of each was to be short-lived. The next morning Hamish discovered the desk drawer in his office had been jimmied open. The lists, the information sheets, and

Jenny Cobb's evaluations of Country Day's "possibles" were gone.

By noontime, all Greenport knew the names on the list. They also knew that Henry Parker had been "talked to"; Tyne's attempt to be discreet had failed as badly as Hamish's. The smile Kip was wearing after he heard about Henry Parker vanished the moment he learned of the faculty interviews and the list of possibles.

His whole plan, Kip felt, was once again endangered, to be written off by the world as an act of perversion. At this point, Kip wasn't sure what had to be done, only that some action was required. Muttering, he set off to find K.K.

Chapter 8 _____

> *That corny poem about how little things add*
> *up—you know the one. "For want of a nail*
> *the shoe was lost," etc., etc.—may not have*
> *been so far from wrong after all. I had one*
> *objective: to make a point. But look at what's*
> *happened.*
>
> *First K.K. sends that damned hand of Angel's*
> *to the Sanchez family. Right there, the point*
> *began to get blurred.*
>
> *Then Hamish and Jenny Cobb get together. I*
> *hadn't expected that. Those cold, Western*
> *cop's eyes of his, working together with her*
> *brain, spell trouble.*
>
> *Next, Hamish starts grilling the Country Day*
> *faculty. And pretty soon the story's out that*
> *this isn't the work of a kidnapper, but of a*
> *queer. Point blurred again.*
>
> *Taken in themselves, not much. But in the ag-*
> *gregate, real trouble. Nobody's going to pay*
> *the ultimate ransom if they think the disap-*
> *pearance was stage-managed by a killer-fag*
> *and that their kid's already dead.*
>
> *For want of a nail, hell.*
>
> —TAPE-LOG OF THE PIPER,
> ENTRY DATED JUNE 2ND.

On Wednesday, June 2nd, the onslaught continued. Raymond Pierce was the Piper's victim of the day, snatched from what would seem to be about the safest place in town. That afternoon, Raymond and his mother sat in the waiting room of Dr. Denton Sayre, the Pierces' pediatrician. It was time for the annual checkup that would pronounce young Pierce free enough from blights and diseases to attend summer camp. Several times, his mother tried to persuade her 14-year-old of

something, and as many times, she was glared back into sub-
mission.

When Dr. Sayre's nurse told Raymond to go into examining
room "A," and the doctor would be with him in a few
minutes, a sudden expression of pain crossed his mother's
face. It would be the first year she hadn't gone inside with
him, and that fact suddenly made her feel old. "Are you sure,
Ray, you don't want me to?"

"No. You promised. The agreement. You promised."

Mrs. Pierce sighed. It was a battle she had known she
would lose.

"Doctor's with someone in 'B,' Raymond," said the nurse,
"but just take off everything and lie down on the table." The
nurse saw the uncomfortable look in the boy's eyes. "There's a
towel on the table. Doctor will be right in."

Mrs. Pierce settled herself uncomfortably in the waiting
room, picking up a copy of *Town & Country* and flipping listlessly through the pages, lulled into a semi-doze by the hum of
the air-conditioner battling the prematurely hot weather outside the window. A few minutes later, her eyes opened again
as Dr. Sayre came out of examining room "B" and paused to
eye her quizzically. "Raymond's in 'A,' " the nurse said.

"Good." Sayre forced a smile for Mrs. Pierce's benefit. Mrs.
Pierce didn't even try to return the smile, but watched grimly
as the doctor said something to his nurse and disappeared
through the door into "A." Almost immediately the door
opened again, and the doctor stepped back into the waiting
room, wearing a puzzled expression. "I thought you said Ray
was in 'A.' "

"He is."

"Not in *my* examining room 'A,' he's not." He threw the
door wide open.

A gasp came from Mrs. Pierce as she raced to the door and
took in the room. The table was empty, its sheeted pad still
showing the impression of where someone had recently lain
upon it. When she touched the sheet, it was still warm. On the
floor was a rumpled towel, one which earlier had been neatly
folded and placed on the table for Raymond by Dr. Sayre's
nurse. To one side, in the changing booth, Raymond's jacket,
shirt, tie, trousers, and shorts could be seen hanging on a
hook. Beyond the table, blowing lightly in the early summer

breeze, the curtains did not quite hide the half-open window through which, a few minutes earlier, a thrashing and struggling Raymond Pierce had been dragged by Kip and K.K.

By nine that night, Raymond's voice was already added to the electronic chorus of children appealing to their parents for help.

The town of Greenport reeled under the repeated disappearances. Kip's "one-a-day" strategy was savagely effective. The latest, Raymond Pierce, particularly affected the township's already shattered parents; there was something sacrosanct about a pediatrician's office, something safe and reassuring—an aura of gentle hands, prewarmed stethoscopes, and unquestioning compassion. Raymond's abduction from Dr. Sayre's office had violated this.

Now Hamish sat staring in disbelief at the man standing in front of him. Lately, Hamish felt, he seemed to spend most of his waking hours staring in disbelief—either at people, papers, or occurrences. And when not staring in wonder, he was listening in shock. Listening to mothers crying as he broke the news to them that their child was the newest victim, hearing hysterical exaggerations, recitals of fact, and opinions of fancy.

"We have, of course, tracked the number back to one source," the man in front of him said, "but it's not a primary point of origin." Miles Laidlaw of New York Telephone, which, through some whim of Ma Bell, provided service to the Connecticut township of Greenport, was trying to explain how a man in New York City (Gilly Axminster's father) could dial a number in Port Chester, first hearing a voice asking him if he was aware yet that his son was missing, and then, redialing the number, receive the New York City time signal. The process was not simple, and Laidlaw was having considerable difficulty making himself understood to these people.

"Not the primary point of origin," repeated Alan Whitemore, a glazed look in his eyes. "The primary point of origin . . ."

Blagden Tyne of the FBI tried to bail Whitemore out. Of all the outside experts involved, Hamish had discovered, Tyne was the brightest; Tyne already knew all about call-forwarding, but realized it would have to be explained to the rest

of them before they could grasp it. "What Mr. Laidlaw means
is—"

But Miles Laidlaw of New York Telephone was not one
to have someone else explain what he meant. To him, telephone company equipment was an intimate part of his life,
something his engineering mind could love, feel close to, and
understand completely, something not to be ineptly described
by outsiders, even ones from the FBI. "The number was not a
primary point of origin in that the terminal number was
reached through a call-forwarder. This is optional subscriber
equipment on certain exchanges that allows calls to be automatically switched by computer from one receiving number to
another. That is to say, the number Mr. Axminster was told to
call was routed through an RB-1000 computer complex which
transferred the call automatically from the number Axminster
dialed to yet a third number which was its terminal point.
This, in turn, also had a call-forwarder, which transferred the
number called in Port Chester to a second number—the one
with the answering machine—in New York City. Then later,
when Mr. Axminster called back, the call-forwarder had been
disconnected from the first number and been programmed to
reroute calls to the New York City time signal."

"And there is no way, I suppose," interjected Tyne, "for the
second number in New York to be traced? It's not on company records anywhere?"

"As a message unit. And as a number on the computer
tapes. But to trace it back—well, it's there, but the number
would take considerable time to locate."

This was too much for Chief Investigator Cummins of the
State Police. "The law clearly states that adequate records—"
he paused, trying to remember precisely what the law did
state—"in Connecticut, anyway . . ."

Laidlaw winced a little, silently wondering what New York
Telephone was doing operating in another state. "A record of
all toll calls is kept, on tape. However, intercity, non-toll calls
show up only as message units. We have the first number, of
course, that Mr. Axminster was told to call. The one in Port
Chester. It is unlisted, but service was installed for—" Laidlaw
studied his notes—"the Peerless Boytoy Factory. The actual
phone, with call-forwarding service, was installed in a warehouse office on Dodge Street, Port Chester. The installer does

not remember too much about the person who ordered the service—it was a month and a half ago—but he does remember thinking it curious that service like call-forwarding should be ordered for such a ramshackle setup. He saw no one, but he did remember that a lot of notes had been left telling him where to put the instrument. There had been no reason to save the notes. Business Office records indicate that the service was originally initiated by phone, although someone—they seem to remember it being a messenger—did drop off an envelope with the three-hundred-dollar deposit required on all such small-business orders."

"Could I have the names of the installer and of the person at the Business Office who 'seems to remember' it being a messenger?"

Hamish watched as Laidlaw pulled a sheaf of Xeroxes from a folder on the table separating him from Hamish and the other men. "I brought a copy of those facts for anyone who wanted one," Laidlaw noted, arranging the Xeroxes with his hands until all of the edges were neatly lined up and even.

"As you can see," he continued, returning to his original explanation, "we can provide the number of the original toll call. It's on the computer tape. However, the intercity calls that were forwarded from that toll call are virtually beyond recovery. We don't even know how many stages of call-forwarding may have been used to complete the call. For instance, the terminal or originating point could have been—" with a sudden sweep of his hand Laidlaw pointed to the phone on the meeting room table—"that instrument right there. Any phone, anywhere."

It was at this point that Hamish began to stare at Laidlaw in disbelief; the implications of what the telephone company engineer was saying had just begun to sink in. "Does that mean, Mr. Laidlaw, that anyone can set up a chain of these phones, each one forwarding the calls to the next, and there would be no practical way to trace where any of them was coming from?"

Laidlaw suddenly looked embarrassed. "The call-forwarder wasn't meant to be used that way, you understand, but yes, that is exactly what it means, I'm afraid."

The men at the table stared at each other helplessly. They could see immediately the problems the call-forwarding device would create in tracking down the Piper—as well as some terrifying possibilities of how the man might choose to operate in the future.

Conversation with Laidlaw continued. When there was no longer anything anyone could think of asking him, Laidlaw left, walking out of the door with a semi-apologetic smile, as if he felt the New York Telephone Company—and perhaps he himself—were somehow responsible for everything that had happened.

In the room, the conversation was suddenly wrenched away from the sophistries of the telephone system back to harsh reality when a note was delivered to Hamish.

"Oh, Christ—another one." Hamish stared at the others, pain etched across his features. "The Stokely girl. She was taken from her car, somewhere up the back road leading to the Stokely house. They found her car; they haven't found her." Hamish paused, bit his lip, and sighed gently. "There was a lot of blood on the front seat." The table exploded.

"This changes everything," announced Alan Whitemore, slapping his hand down hard to get the men's attention.

"Why?" Hamish kept his head lowered, reading and rereading the note he held in his hands.

"For Christ's sake, Hamish. It's the first kid not from Country Day. It's the first girl. It's the first public school student."

"Yes, it's all of those things. And maybe what you're thinking is exactly the way the Piper wants all of us to think. Christine Stokely can be a trick. Something to throw us off the scent."

Alan Whitemore spoke again, letting his mounting impatience show. "I'm getting damned tired of you saying everything is a device to put us off the track."

Blagden Tyne looked at Whitemore with visible distaste. "Things aren't that simple, Mr. Whitemore. Hamish could be dead right."

"In the meantime, Christine Stokely is plain dead."

All the heads at the table turned to stare at Whitemore. His had been a cheap shot. Slowly the heads moved slightly to see what Hamish's reaction would be. He remained calm, making notes on a yellow pad, acting as if Whitemore had not spoken, or if he had, that Hamish hadn't heard what he said.

Suddenly Hamish looked up. "I got some recommendations

on what we do until we can track down this nut—whatever kind of nut the Piper is. First, I want all of the schools shut down. Originally I thought only of Country Day, but this Stokely thing, well, probably we ought to play safe. *All* schools. To be shut immediately. Today. Right now. Secondly, State Police at all the country clubs, yacht clubs, tennis and golf clubs—wherever kids with money gather. Third, a ten o'clock curfew on anyone under eighteen. I also think special buses— each one with an armed private guard—should pick up and deliver the kids between their homes and these clubs. No matter how many times we tell 'em, the kids will head for those clubs, so their families shouldn't mind paying to see they get there and back safely. And no one under eighteen out on the streets—anytime—without an adult. Next, I think—"

The men at the table never got to find out what else Hamish thought. For days now, a simmering fury had been building up inside Alan Whitemore. He had never liked Hamish and had put up with him only because so many of the town's wealthiest and most influential residents appeared to find Hamish about perfect for his job. But ever since the abduction of Gilly Axminster—Whitemore tended to overlook Angel Sanchez as more of an irritant than a tragedy—he had found Hamish impossible to stomach. Hamish's attitudes, plus his challenging of Whitemore in front of outside experts, the Town Manager found intolerable.

"For Christ's sake, Hamish," Whitemore yelled down the table, half-rising from his chair, "why don't you just declare martial law? Close the schools, bus the kids to the clubs . . . curfews . . . Jesus."

Blagden Tyne tried to placate him. "Look, Mr. Whitemore, closing the schools—well, hell. Country Day is almost over for the year. And guards at the clubs? So what? They're sound safety steps." After a quick reading of the other faces, Tyne again turned toward the Town Manager. "Do you really have such a problem with these proposals, Mr. Whitemore?"

"Problem! Jesus, I can't seem to get through to any of you. These 'safety steps,' as you put it, will knock us out of business here. People buy expensive homes in an expensive place like Greenport and pay the very expensive taxes they pay to escape the violence of the city by living here. That's no secret—everybody knows it. So everybody hates a suburb like

Greenport, particularly the urban snobs who work for the press. Goddamn, but the media would have a field day. By the time the papers and television got through with us, we'd be lucky if we could get a welfare family to live here."

Almost without realizing it, Alan Whitemore had, in one long sentence, laid bare his real motives for everything he did. In three long strides, Hamish walked the length of the table and grabbed Whitemore by his jacket, pulling him to his feet and knocking the Town Manager's bifocals cockeyed in the process. "You miserable shit. You pathetic, ass-kissing, miserable shit. You toady up to the people with dough, and then are willing to let their kids get killed. Are you so fucking stupid you don't realize these people don't give a damn about property values if their kids disappear because you're too scared to act? Jesus. The town charter makes the Director of Police—your goddamn fancy name for Police Chief—responsible for public safety, damn it, and in my estimation public safety means closing those schools down. My responsibility. Because there's a nut loose in this town, a psycho called the Piper. And we have to find him. In the meantime, we've got to keep the kids out of circulation. We got some pretty good leads as to the kind of guy this Piper is, but tracking him down is going to take time . . ."

At first, Whitemore's face had worn an expression of fear. Now he had regained his composure, letting his head rock back and forth slightly as Hamish continued to shake him by his coat. Suddenly Whitemore reached up and removed Hamish's hands, brushing his coat and trying to restore his dignity. "It would take one hell of a lot *less* time, Hamish, if you'd spend your days working instead of playing around at the Soundsight Motel. You keep saying that Miss Cobb is helping with the investigation. . . ."

"Shut up!"

"What she's helping isn't the investigation, but you. Nothing but a goddamn easy lay."

The fist pushed into Whitemore's face from nowhere. Falling backward, he grabbed at the table to save his balance and pulled the telephone and a pile of papers off the surface on top of himself, the loose pieces of Xerox and carbon copies drifting downward like errant paper airplanes. Hanging at an angle from one ear, the bifocals finally came off completely and landed softly on Whitemore's lap. One hand went automatically to his mouth, where a thin trickle of blood was already spilling from the left corner. Carefully, he moved his jaw back and forth, gingerly testing to see how much it hurt. All of this time, his eyes remained locked with Hamish's, in fear of a renewed attack. Finally he opened his mouth to speak, but there was so much blood, and what he suspected were broken pieces of teeth, that all he could produce was a hissing, bubbling sound.

For a second, Hamish stood over Whitemore without saying anything. Then: "My resignation will be on your desk in half an hour. God help this town with people like you running it."

Hamish didn't even dare look at the other men in the room. He spun on his heel, turned, and stalked out of the room, slamming the door to the cavernous meeting hall behind him noisily.

He had no idea of what he would do or where he would go. He could still hear Whitemore's whining voice echoing in his ears: "Nothing but a goddamn easy lay." The words seemed to repeat themselves endlessly.

Hamish climbed into his car and headed toward the Soundsight Motel.

Chapter 9_____

Somewhere, Winston Churchill wrote that in winning a war it is important to maneuver other countries—frequently unwilling ones— into joining the fight on your side. The Lusitania, he pointed out, was the result of careful British, not German, planning. Likewise, Pearl Harbor.

Maybe the old guy had something there. Because that's just what I'm beginning to get: allies, unwitting ones or not. The fight between Hamish and Whitemore helps. Hamish's being bounced from his job has to be counted a point for my side. Now, if I could just get Hamish and Jenny Cobb fighting with each other . . .

I wonder: exactly how did Churchill engineer the Japs into Pearl Harbor?

—TAPE-LOG OF THE PIPER,
ENTRY DATED JUNE 5TH.

Saturday, June 5th, was the day Kip came very close to being caught. For Kip, the realization he *could* be caught at all, on top of the suddenness with which the tables were turned on him, was a difficult thing to accept. Particularly in the middle of the "one-a-day" phase of his plan, a phase that was progressing so smoothly and effectively he could hardly believe it himself. Monday had produced the theft of Ramsey Lakewood from the choir loft of Heavenly Redemption; Tuesday had presented Greenport with the grim news of George Lennox and Lyle Pritchard's having been plucked from the *Skipper* in the middle of Long Island Sound; Wednesday, Raymond Pierce had been shanghied, stark naked, from Dr. Sayre's examining room; Thursday had shaken the town with the dragging of Christy Stokely from her car on the very grounds of the Stokely estate; and Friday, the 4th of June, had seen the taking of the youngest prey yet: William Davis III, spirited away in the middle of his own 10th birthday party. The guests had been holding a noisy game of hide and seek, and William had baffled the "it" by hiding himself with great ingenuity. In fact, it was not until nine that night that he was discovered—on the regular broadcast from Kip's mobile transmitter, begging his parents to do whatever they were told to. Some of his birthday presents, William pointed out, had not even been opened yet.

In the face of such easy success, it was possible, Kip thought, that he had become overconfident. (Later, he was to learn, his assumption that Hamish's resignation would be accepted was one facet of this overconfidence. The fact was that the Town Council had no intention of letting Hamish quit, for the Council felt he was doing a good job in an impossible situation. With some reluctance, Hamish had allowed himself to be pressured into staying on, a fact Kip was not aware of on Saturday morning.)

The next victim was to be Peter Parsons, a handsome if poisonous child of 13. To Kip, Peter's arrogance was symbolized by his mop of tow-headed hair. Every morning, the hair was washed in the shower to a gleaming brilliance; every Saturday, Peter slipped into Pelligrini's Barbershop to have the blond locks trimmed and styled.

That Saturday, Kip leaned against the brick wall down the street from Pelligrini's, watching as Peter got out of his father's car and strode purposefully into the barbershop. Kip joined K.K. at the back of the shop, and noiselessly, they slipped in through the rear door. Kip watched through the heavy faded curtains that separated the back of the store from the front, listening to Mr. Pelligrini's whistling through his teeth, observing the leisurely, hedonistic smile on Peter's face as he slumped, half-dozing, hypnotized by the caress of the barber's hands and the mesmerizing snip-snip of his scissors. Kip waited until Mr. Pelligrini had Peter's chair facing away from the mirror. Then he nodded to K.K., who stepped outside and rang the back doorbell of the shop.

As soon as the barber pushed his way through the curtains into the darkness between them and the back door, K.K. hit him over the head with a padded truncheon; together, he and Kip lowered the unconscious Pelligrini soundlessly to the floor. Virtually without missing a beat, Kip slipped behind the chair and took up the snipping where the barber had left off, whistling through his teeth the aria from *Aida* Pelligrini had been humming. Peter, sedated by the sunlight streaming in through the venetian blinds, barely flickered his half-closed eyelids; the switch of barbers went unnoticed, as did K.K.'s slipping into the room to join Kip.

Peter's eyes, in fact, didn't really come fully open again until he felt the chair swing around violently. Facing the mirror now, Peter was stunned to see Kip and K.K. standing behind him. Even more astonishing, he suddenly felt Kip pin his arms behind the chair, while K.K. slipped his wrists into a pair of handcuffs. As Peter watched, he saw Kip advancing toward the chair with the electric clippers, and began to shout. It was a joke, Peter told himself; Kip was too nice a guy, too much a school leader, to go through with shaving his head. But if it was a joke, what little humor was in it for Peter disappeared as the first piles of tow-blond hair began falling into his sheeted lap.

His shouts for help were not yet in fright but in fury; that someone like Kip could be a party to this sort of behavior was hard for Peter to believe. But in the last few seconds, as Peter felt himself being lifted over the back of the barber's chair and dragged toward the heavy green curtain, the full realization that Kip was probably party to something far more frightening than shaving somebody's head finally hit him.

At the threshold of the door to the back, Peter saw K.K. return to the barbershop, scoop up his shorn blond hair, and stuff it into an envelope, Scotch-taping it to the mirror. Then Peter felt them dragging him again, through the curtain, past the still unconscious Mr. Pelligrini, and out into the alley behind the shop.

Outside on the street, Hamish walked up to the window of Pelligrini's wearing a puzzled expression. Beside him stood Ollie, his 12-year-old, looking grim because his father had finally maneuvered him into his monthly haircut. The reason for Hamish's puzzled expression was the venetian blinds on Mr. Pelligrini's window. Usually they were open, but today they were set so that the slats blocked off the interior of the shop completely (K.K. had done this the moment they got into the place). Yet, outside the door, the peppermint-striped cylinder still rotated inside its glass case. Squinting, Hamish finally found one slat of the blind that hadn't turned flat with the rest and peered inside. All he could see was a pair of boy's feet being dragged out through the green curtain. It all came together at once in Hamish's mind. He grabbed the knob but found the door locked. Stepping back, he shielded his eyes and crashed one foot through the bottom of the store window. Gingerly, he slipped himself through the gaping hole in the store window and raced toward the still swaying curtain.

If Mr. Pelligrini had not chosen that exact moment to regain consciousness, Hamish would have tackled Kip just as he and K.K. carried Peter out the back door. But Pelligrini had flung one arm wide as he slowly struggled to a half-sitting, half-lying position, and his arm tripped Hamish, throwing him to the floor. In his semi-conscious state, Mr. Pelligrini thought he was being attacked again, and grappled with Hamish in the dimness. By the time Hamish struggled free and made it to the door, all he could see was a cloud of dust slowly settling back down on the surface of the alley parking area. Swearing, he went back inside to see if Pelligrini had any information to volunteer. The barber had seen and heard nothing. Dreading having to ask the question, Hamish asked whose hair he'd been cutting.

"Peter Parsons. Such nice boy. Such fine hair. You think they . . . ?"

Hamish nodded. Reaching forward, he removed the envelope stuck to the mirror and let the shimmering locks fall into his hand. It was all that remained of Peter Parsons, age 13, of 102 Crooked Lane, Greenport, Connecticut 09360.

"Hell, I should have stayed fired. Or resigned. Or whatever I was." Hamish sat that evening in the stiff little chair with which the Soundsight Motel had equipped the writing tables in its rooms, staring disconsolately at the floor and pulling halfheartedly on his Scotch.

Jenny lay back on the bed, propping herself against a mound of pillows, sympathetic enough, but at a loss as to how Hamish could be shaken out of his depression. He would slump from the desk chair to the easy chair, getting up to mix himself another drink, staying as far away from her as he

could. Jenny felt the emptiness inside her beginning to ache.
"Spill it, Hamish. What's really wrong?"

"Everything's wrong. Hell, I'm the town's chief law enforcement officer and I spend half my days shacked up in a
motel. I go home at night and look at Martha and wonder
what to Christ I was thinking of in the first place."

"Oh, come *on*, Hamish. You wouldn't have married her;
she must have meant something to you once."

"I was bombed."

"You don't marry someone because you're bombed."
Jenny's nervous little habit of running her fingers through her
hair returned abruptly.

"No, but you can get yourself in one hell of a spot. Remember, Jen, that was back in the days when abortions were illegal. So—Russel. I didn't have too much choice, and neither
did Martha. Her plans to go to college, her whole life, the
kind of guy who might have been right for her—well, I'd done
it and there was no way of getting around that. What's sad is
that now she's dried up and miserable. Me? I'm just miserable."

"Okay. But you shouldn't go on feeling guilty about it. It
happened. Period."

"No, what I feel guilty about—really guilty—is those
damned missing kids," continued Hamish, speaking to the wall
somewhere above Jenny's head. "A kidnapping a day. Jesus.
Some Chief of Police."

Jenny's temper flared; if there was one thing she couldn't
stand it was self-pity. "Come off it, Hamish. Stop the self-
flagellation."

Hamish appeared oblivious. "Maybe I *should* go ahead and
quit."

"You're whining like a child, Hamish. For Christ's sake.
The FBI, the State Police experts, the Federal Crime Bureau—all of the best law enforcement brains in the country
have been in on this and haven't gotten anywhere. Are you
supposed to beat all of *them*? Is it some kind of race?" Jenny
had moved from the bed now, and was kneeling in front of his
chair so that she could meet Hamish's eyes.

"Nine kids, for Christ's sake . . ."

Jenny exploded. "Damn it, Hamish, you've played everything but the violin. All those experts I was talking about. Not

one of them came even close. You, at least, came within striking distance. At the barbershop."

"By accident," Hamish noted bitterly. "I came close by accident."

A strange look came across Jenny's face, washing away the
expression of anger Hamish's self-pity had evoked. "By accident," she repeated. "By accident." Something in her voice
had such an infectious sound to it, Hamish suddenly stared at
her. Jenny stood up and, taking him by the hand, led him
quickly over to the bed. "By accident," she said again. "You
know, we can make another accident *happen,* Hamish. Something that will force those men into moving. Only this time
under our control." He was sitting on the bed, his face a
puzzled mask. She drew him to her and, running her fingers
up and down his back, began to paste together the outlines of
a plan.

Suddenly Hamish felt better.

Across town, another plan was being pasted together. Kip
sat in K.K.'s lab, the copy of *Gray's Anatomy* he'd borrowed
from the library on the desk in front of him. Occasionally he'd
stop and cross-reference something with the index of *Burke's
Pathology,* also from the library, which lay open beside it. It
would work. K.K. had told him it would, but there had been a
bright glitter in his eyes when he spoke that had made Kip
wonder if K.K. was really sure of what he was saying or was
merely looking forward to executing the plan.

With a sigh, Kip slapped the books shut and pushed back
his chair. The noise startled the white rats in their cages behind him, a nervousness compounded when the back of Kip's
chair bumped into a corner of one of the cages and jarred the
whole row of them. Inside, most of the rats began scurrying
around in a state of frenzy, giving hurried little cries of panic.

K.K. studied their movements nervously, his eyes checking
to make sure all the cage doors were fastened securely. Kip,
after one desultory glance behind him, ignored the rats and
turned toward K.K. "You're right. Everything you said checks
out."

A look of petulance crossed K.K.'s face. "I don't know
what you expected."

"Hell, K.K., learn to take a compliment without bickering about a guy's motives."

"Some compliment."

"Anyway, K.K., the actual doing of it—well, that will have to be your job. It's just not my bag."

"No problem." K.K. struggled not to appear condescending, but to have Kip admit there was something he, K.K., could do that Kip couldn't was a novel and delicious sensation for him.

"You have that kind of mind."

"I have a strong stomach, is what you mean."

K.K. realized he had gone too far as Kip retorted angrily, "Damn it, you've had the training and the background. My stomach's as strong as the next guy's. Remember what I did to Christy Stokely first?"

"Okay, okay." K.K. bit his lip, wanting to draw some parallel to Paige Rathbin but knowing he'd already pushed Kip further than was safe. The memory of Kip forcing his hand inside the rat cage still haunted him.

Kip seemed to read his mind, swinging around in his chair and studying the still scurrying rats. The pictures evoked by what he had read in *Gray's* kept flying around in Kip's head, exciting him in some way that disturbed him, frightening yet tantalizing, and above all, forbidden. Kip shuddered. Then, as they walked down the row of cages on their way out the door, Kip took the pencil he held in his hand and ran it down the bars of the enclosures like a boy running a stick down a picket fence.

The screams of the rats sounded oddly like Christy's.

Hands in pockets, Kip surveyed the activity outside Town Hall and tried to figure out what was happening. His usually reliable underground had failed him badly; no report of anything unusual scheduled for four o'clock Monday afternoon had been passed on to him. That it had been passed on to a considerable number of other people was obvious, watching them climbing the limestone stairs into the Hall.

Hamish was standing at the foot of the stairs and only moved from this spot to talk to someone on his way in. Earlier, Kip had seen Alan Whitemore arrive, stopping at the base of the steps to hold a heated exchange with Hamish. From the gesticulating and arm waving, it was clear that, as always, they were in disagreement. Finally, Whitemore turned on his heel and stormed up the steps, his jaw thrust angrily in front of him.

Twice, Kip saw Jenny Cobb run down the stairs to say something to Hamish, then dart back inside. Her hair bounced lightly as she ran, and she continually tossed her head to settle it back into position. That Hamish greeted her with a smile each time, that she met his smile with one equally ebullient, and that she allowed him to squeeze her forearm before she returned up the steps, caused the streak of childlike jealousy in Kip to sear his insides. The sight of their mouths moving in some unheard, animated conversation made the burning inside him worse. He only began to feel better when Jenny was safely through the doors of Town Hall again, apparently for good.

With a sigh, Kip returned to studying the crowd, trying to figure why all these people should be here at such an improbable time of day. That the man from the FBI—Tyne, Kip thought his name was—was here was logical enough, but the fact that he didn't join the others and go into the building was not. After a brief but intense talk with Hamish, Tyne clapped him on the shoulder and walked away from the building. On the other hand, Chief Investigator Cummins of the State Police, after holding the same sort of brief talk with Hamish, did not leave but walked firmly up the steps into the building, his gold-braided State Police uniform making him look like a surrealistic Eagle Scout.

There seemed to be an unusually large contingent of cameramen and what Kip supposed were reporters, although at this point he paid them no unusual attention. Kip's first awareness of how intimately these newsmen were involved in what was taking place came with the arrival of George Pritchard and Lanier Pierce, the fathers of Lyle Pritchard and Raymond Pierce. The moment they stepped out of a limousine together onto the curb, the photographers and reporters swept forward and the flashbulbs began popping. Over this intermittent flashing, a sudden glow appeared as two bright floodlights picked them out for the benefit of a mobile TV cameraman Kip had not noticed until now. Following the cable with his eyes, he saw that the camera was attached to a CBS mobile transmitting van parked in the alleyway beside Town Hall; whatever was going on was being taped for transmission. To the newsmen, the two fathers merely shook their heads, then pushed their way through the crowd, swallowed by the two-story doors of Town Hall. A few moments later, Senator Lloyd Blyden stepped onto the curb to another scattering of flashbulbs; the Senator chatted briefly with Hamish, shaking his head the entire time, and then joined Hamish in climbing the steps into the building, the cloud of reporters, photographers, and the mobile television cameraman swarming up the steps behind them. Seeing that Jerry Fisk, a policeman he'd known since childhood, was on the door, Kip seized the opportunity to mount the limestone steps himself, hoping to get inside and find out the reason behind all the excitement. Fisk would not let him past. "Sorry, Kip. Closed to the public. You can watch it tonight on TV."

"What the hell's up?"

"News conference. About this Piper guy and all them kids."

"You can't?—"

Fisk shook his head. "Get my ass chewed real good if I did. Hamish said nobody goes in, and he said it like he meant it."

Walking away, Kip could not shake the sensation that with the news conference—an event so shrouded in secrecy—somebody was up to something. Something he didn't understand, yet something he desperately needed to know about as quickly as possible. He was, of course, right on both points.

What Kip sensed was the platform from which Jenny Cobb's plan of "making a little accident happen" was to be launched. Unknown to Jenny, Kip had a plan of his own for making a little accident happen, something which required a copy of *Gray's Anatomy* and *Burke's Pathology*, and something so psychotic in concept only K.K. was fit to undertake it.

Inside the hall, the audience of reporters, officials, and a handful of plain citizens talked among themselves in hushed tones until a sulky-looking Alan Whitemore advanced to the lectern and called for attention. The expression that he wore indicated that he clearly disapproved of this entire project. Up until this afternoon, he had managed to keep the media at arm's length. But then, about two o'clock, he was telephoned by Hamish, told about the press conference, and told that he was expected, as Town Manager, to lead the proceedings. After all of his efforts to keep the press conference from being held had failed—the members of the Town Council had been individually briefed by Hamish on the reasons behind the meeting and supported Hamish down the line—Whitemore had little, if any, choice but to comply. He sat sandwiched between members of the Council on one side, and Hamish, Jenny Cobb, and Chief Cummins on the other. Mute with rage, Whitemore had said nothing to anyone; as he rose, he nodded briefly toward the fathers of Lyle Pritchard and Raymond Pierce, seated together several feet behind him.

"Gentlemen," Whitemore began. "This meeting is a tragic one indeed . . ." Whitemore was not used to appearing on television, and he suddenly found his mind numbed and his tongue swollen; the smoky red light on top of the camera stared at him like a demon's eye—searching, relentless, and unmerciful. He had been against a press conference from the beginning, he told himself, listening to his own uncertain voice continuing on in its nasal monotone. He suddenly found himself wondering what the hell he, Alan Whitemore, was doing, moderating a press conference he didn't believe in, forced to lead a meeting called by a police chief whom he neither liked nor respected, stripped naked in front of a million eyes, stumbling and losing his way in words he had been told to speak. He could feel his skin prickling beneath his suit, and pondered what would happen if he simply chose to stalk off the stage and out the door.

Whitemore tried to shake these extraneous ideas from his head, but they would not go. Wired to some distant control room by what looked like a telephone operator's headpiece, the floor manager was staring at him curiously, and Whitemore could see him doing something with his hands that seemed to say, "For Christ's sake, Whitemore—start making sense . . ."

George Pritchard, President of ALTEC, was more used to facing cameras and reporters. "I would like to address myself," Pritchard said, staring straight into the center of the camera's omnivorous eye, "directly to the man who kidnapped my son. To the man who calls himself the Piper. My son is 16—only 16. He never hurt anyone. And, were he in a position to do so now, he would not hurt even you, you who have done so much to hurt him."

For a moment, Mr. Pritchard appeared to be the victim of some painful memory that his own sentence evoked in him, for his voice shrank to a whisper until the words stopped coming out of his mouth completely. Squaring himself, he looked back at the lens and began again. "I do not know what you want. None of us do. You take our children, we hear their voices on radio, but nothing so far—no ransom, no price, no requirements—have been given us for their return. Several times you have mentioned an 'ultimate ransom' for our children. I do not know what that ransom is. And while I cannot speak for anyone but myself, I stand here tonight to assure you that whatever this ransom is—whatever the price, however outrageous the demands—that Lyle's mother and I will pay it, if it is humanly within our abilities to do so. All we want is our son back. The price—the 'ultimate ransom' that you keep referring to—is of little concern to us. I only pray to God that you can find it in your heart to tell us what it is you want, so that we can arrange to give it to you, and in return, receive back our most valuable possession: our son."

He finished in complete silence. In this eerie stillness, the sound of his heels striking the bare wood floor as he returned to his chair became magnified, almost funereal in its starkness. The camera's eye never left him, following him back to his seat, watching his head as he raised it to blow his nose soundlessly, then studying him as he looked from the platform and, using his fingertips, gave a small, reassuring wave to someone offstage, probably his wife.

Raymond Pierce's father, Lanier Pierce, unlike George Pritchard, was not as used to the ordeal by camera. He, too, addressed the kidnappers of his son directly, but was far less effective. The message, however, was virtually identical: tell me what you want so that I can give it to you and get my son back. With a relief that was evident, he scurried back to his seat, staring at the floor as if he knew he had failed his son by the inadequacy of his words.

Hamish Hamilton was something else. But later, even he would wonder if he would have been as effective had he known his words would bring an excruciatingly painful death to someone extraordinarily dear to him.

Chapter 10 _____

Every now and then, thinking about the plan, I begin to wonder about my real motives. Most of the time, I'm pretty sure, but then, out of nowhere, I get these nagging doubts.

The plan, I suppose, could be a device to cover up some kind of hidden kick I get watching those kids struggle. I have to admit I sort of enjoy that part. But maybe that's only normal. Maybe I'm just admitting what most people can't see in themselves. Normal or not, sometimes I wish to hell I could stop.

I guess that killing is a little like Mom and her pills. You start with one, which is harmless enough, but you keep on needing more and more. It's cheaper than drugs, but you're just as badly hooked.

—TAPE-LOG OF THE PIPER, ENTRY DATED JUNE 5TH.

Until Hamish took the floor at the press conference, no one suspected how powerful a speaker he could be. His words had the ring of the deeply believed, yet still sounded completely spontaneous and unrehearsed.

The truth was that almost nothing Hamish said that afternoon reflected what he really believed, and that every last syllable had been meticulously rehearsed for hours. That he could deliver the words so effectively was a tribute to Hamish's ability as an actor—and Jenny's power to persuade. For the basic thrust of his speech had been worked out over dinner with Jenny earlier that week; almost everything Hamish said was conceived by her and dedicated to pushing the Piper into what Jenny had earlier described as a "controlled accident."

"You're not going to be wild about the idea, Hamish, but

if you can stomach what I want you to do, I think it might
force him to react. Hopefully, with something stupid. Hell,
you'll have plopped the kid's virility on the line," Jenny said,
outlining her approach while attacking a lobster claw in the
little seafood restaurant, the Seven Points, that had gradually
become as much a part of their lives as breathing. So far
Hamish hadn't been very enthusiastic.

"Kid," Hamish snorted. "The Piper's no kid."

Jenny gave an expressive gesture with her lobster fork just
before popping a morsel in her mouth. "Well, I keep having
this gut feeling that it *could* be a kid or a couple of them
. . . For instance, one of the older kids from Country Day."

Hamish put down his lobster claw, uneaten and still dripping with butter, and stared at Jenny, unbelieving. "Another
student? A student at *Country Day*? That's crazy."

"Maybe yes, maybe no."

Hamish was wiping his mouth with a napkin, taking quick
sips of water in his confusion. "You can't be serious, Jen?"

Jenny shrugged and changed the subject. "Whoever the
Piper is, it's a safe bet he's an almost classic case of overcom-
pensation. The mere rumor you were considering he was homosexual was all it took to produce the Stokely girl. So, the
kid's touchy. His virility. Always a sensitive point with teen-
agers . . . Now think, if you get on television, Hamish, and
say you think the Piper is a homosexual . . ."

"*Me!*"

"You. Say you don't believe any of the kidnappings were
for money, but were some kind of perverted rape. Cite the
Houston mass murders. Picture the Piper as a sexually aber-
rant psycho. Say you think all the crap about an 'ultimate
ransom' is pure fake. The guy will knock himself out to
prove you're wrong. And doing that, he might just make a
mistake—a big one." Jenny turned her head away slightly,
not wanting to look directly at Hamish; she knew she'd
thrown a lot at him at once, and she knew he was having
trouble accepting any of it.

For several minutes, Hamish stared at her with a bewildered expression, looking like someone who thinks he under-
stands the meaning of some long, unfamiliar word, only to
discover he doesn't know what the word means at all. "I don't

know, Jenny. It's bound to hurt the parents terribly. I don't know."

"To flush the Piper out, it's worth it," Jenny explained. "He'll have to prove to the world how wrong you are."

"I don't know, Jenny. What if he just shrugs it off?"

"He'll respond, believe me. And if we set the right bait out for him, we'll catch him."

"Bait?"

"You."

Blinking hard, Hamish stared at her. A smile passed briefly over his face, as if he thought she were joking but that somehow the humor had escaped him. Then, Jenny's intensely serious look told him she wasn't joking. "I see," Hamish said. He looked at her again, waiting for some clue to surface. Finally he gave in. "I *don't* see, but I guess I'm supposed to, and I don't want to look stupid by admitting it."

Hamish had expected Jenny to respond lightly to his admission, but she remained deadly serious. "Think back to what I said earlier, Hamish. About adolescent boys and touchiness about their virility. You challenge his masculinity in front of the world. Call him sick. Deviant. You degrade him. The Piper will *have* to make some public response to prove that you're wrong. That he's not deviant. That the 'ultimate ransom' *is* the real motive. And the most effective way to do all those things is to come after you directly. Only it's a setup to catch him. I'll work with you on what to say. Every trick I can think of to make him loathe you."

"Thanks." Hamish said it dryly, without humor. He could see the possible effectiveness of Jenny's plan, although to him, the whole scheme seemed very much of a long-shot.

And he suspected that it was no moment for long-shots, only sure things.

Giving the speech, saying the words that Jenny had coached him in so carefully, Hamish could not escape the unseen pain he knew he was causing in the chairs behind him. The words about the Houston murders, the torture boards, the depravity, he had known would cause all of the kidnapped children's families terrible anguish; he could almost feel the agony of the parents seated behind him.

Hamish could sense something else happening, too. There

was a sudden nervous rustling of paper as Alan Whitemore began to shift uncomfortably in his seat. Hamish could imagine him exchanging glances with the members of the Town Council seated on the platform with him. Doggedly, though, Hamish continued, his words as unfaltering and powerful when he finished as when he began.

It was not until later, after the rector of Grace Episcopal had asked them to lower their heads and join him in prayer for the children's safe return, that Hamish felt the full brunt of the reaction. Those of the Town Council who had been up on the platform melted away, clearly embarrassed and avoiding him. Whitemore, he knew, he would hear from later. The two fathers of the kidnapped boys stood there, facing him alone.

Swallowing, Hamish marched over to them. Mr. Pritchard stared at him, looking at once both hurt and perplexed. "Hamish, if that's what you thought all along, don't you feel you owed it to us to say so? I realize you were probably trying to spare us the worry, but—"

"Damned right, you should have told us." Mr. Pierce was furious. Furious and frightened, an explosive combination in anyone. "I was worried before—now I'm worried sick. I have to face my wife in a few minutes. What am I supposed to say to her? That Raymond may have been raped and tortured? Not that boy . . . my God, not that boy . . ." Mr. Pierce's anger suddenly drained out of him, replaced by a fit of soft choking.

"I don't know, Hamish. Maybe you couldn't tell us, maybe . . . but, dammit, I think you should have, regardless." Mr. Pritchard's approach continued to be softer, but the reproach, couched in gentler terms, was even more difficult for Hamish to bear.

The promise of silence Hamish had given Jenny seemed cruel and insupportable. She had not taken into account the effect on the boys' parents. Hamish collapsed under the weight of his own feelings of sympathy. "I don't believe it had anything to do with homosexuality. I would have told you—I wanted to—what I was doing, but we felt we had to keep the strategy secret. That, I can see now, was a mistake."

Taking them by the arms, Hamish led the two fathers off to one side of the platform and leveled with them. He

knew Jenny's point on secrecy was technically right, but
he also knew simple humanity demanded the fathers be told.

The conversation was not an easy one, but both fathers
were so relieved to learn that what Hamish said was untrue, it
went far less abrasively than Hamish dared expect. In the
process, though, Hamish realized that from now on neither of
these men would ever believe anything he said again.

The grace note to the press conference was added by Alan
Whitemore. Sidling up to Hamish, who was still deep in conversation with the two fathers, he grabbed him by one elbow.
"You son of a bitch," he hissed, sliding past him. "I'll pay
you back for this."

"That son of a bitch. I'll pay him back for this." It was not
hard to understand why Kip had unwittingly used precisely
the same words as Alan Whitemore. K.K. watched his friend
but said nothing; when Kip lapsed into one of his dark
moods, silence was safer.

They had seen the press conference on a portable television
set, sitting uncomfortably on the hard chairs which were all
K.K.'s lab offered. Staring at the small screen, Kip had appeared thoroughly pleased by what was said initially, even
pretending not to notice that Jenny was seated only a few
feet from Hamish on the platform. Up to that point, everything said helped clarify his plan. And listening, the sense of
power the kidnappings gave Kip was heightened. Leaning
back, Kip allowed himself to relax; it was going well.

The moment Hamish began speaking, however, Kip was
seized by a fit of nervous depression. Even the rats, watching
from their cages behind Kip and K.K., appeared to sense
Kip's mood, and they became quieter; like K.K., they perhaps
felt it was a moment to become as unnoticeable as possible.

But it was when Hamish described the Piper as a homosexual, and began drawing parallels to the Houston affair, that
Kip exploded. Hamish's words not only dismissed the 'ultimate ransom' as a fraud; they struck, as Jenny had intended
them to, at some secret inner fear of Kip's. Shrinking further
into a corner, K.K. watched. Kip had jumped to his feet and
was storming up and down the aisle in front of the cages; he
remained mute when Kip, swearing and yelling, swept a rack
of feeding dishes off the table onto the floor; he still sat mo-

tionless and silent as Kip grabbed one of the cages and began shaking it until the terrified rats inside, screaming their high-pitched little screams of panic, clawed at the meshwork of the cage and began biting each other in their frenzy to escape.

Kip rarely lost his temper, but when he did, the effects were awesome. K.K. was waiting until the right moment when he could, as he had done before during those seizures, adroitly suggest something completely removed from whatever had brought the fit on. "Do you see what they're up to?" Kip suddenly yelled at K.K. "They're trying to get me. Those bastards—Hamish and Jenny Cobb. They want to wreck me. Do you see what they're doing?"

K.K. tried his tangential approach. "How about a Coke, Kip? It's hot in here."

Kip looked at him as if he had never seen him before. Then, grabbing him by the shoulders, he shoved his face to within a couple of inches of K.K.'s. "It's your fault, you prick. You little fag prick. Why do you think they brought up the Houston thing? They know about Paige, that's why. It's all your fault. The plan's falling apart, and it's all your fault."

The charge was so insane, K.K. didn't even bother to acknowledge it. He kept looking squarely at Kip, trying not to notice the sudden sourness of Kip's breath in his face, and tried again. "Hotter than hell in here, matter of fact. Got to get a ventilating fan one of these days. A Coke'll do us both good, Kip. What do you say?"

The fury drained out of Kip as suddenly as it had seized him. Sitting down, fondling the cold Coke bottle K.K. shoved into his hands, he became for a few moments intensely introspective. Some distance away, K.K. watched him silently, waiting for him to emerge further from the mood before speaking.

Then, for the first time K.K. ever remembered, Kip turned to him in contrition. "I'm sorry, K.K."

K.K. nodded. For now, the less said the better. A few minutes later he asked, "Are you okay?"

"Okay."

"Anything you want?"

A small smile crossed Kip's face. "I already have it. It

came to me just as I was coming out of—well, whatever it was."

K.K. did not question what this cryptic statement meant. With Kip, after one of his near-seizures, it was always best not to argue points, raise questions, or volunteer opinions. Behind him he could also hear the rats quieting down in a return to normal. In dealing with Kip, K.K. and the rats shared many things in common.

In the sudden silence, a thousand thoughts raced through Kip's brain. It had been lucky, he thought, that the maneuver involving *Gray's Anatomy* and *Burke's Pathology* was already in the works. Pure luck—he had not planned it that way. At the right time, K.K.—the star of the plan, as it were—would be filled in. For the moment, Kip was satisfied to realize that his upcoming tactic, until a few minutes ago a crime in search of a victim, was now complete. The perfect victim had just presented himself.

The empty Coke was held up. "You have any more, K.K.?"

K.K. did.

Even at noontime on a sunny day, the bar off Cedar Street was dim. The lighting inside was hopelessly inadequate—two lamps hidden behind graying, semi-opaque shades. The only other light source—the two plate-glass windows of the bar— were so dirty that the light of the sun had to battle the grime of years to make its way inside. The unnatural dimness made the people seated at the bar look poorly defined; occasionally, someone would play the pinball machine, which at least gave off brief flashes of intense light, although of a brilliant orange or yellow.

A man—by the tone of his greeting, one familiar to the bartender—dusted some dirt off his threadbare watchman's uniform and, grunting for his "usual," pulled himself up to the bar; the pistol at his side had probably been drawn no more recently than the bar's windows had been washed. Shortly after the guard sat down, the door opened again, and, framed in the bright rectangle of light from the outside, stood Hamish. Looking around, Hamish spotted the guard—he had followed him from the warehouse across the street—and casually drew up a stool beside him. "Getting hot out there," he offered with a sigh. The guard shrugged and said nothing.

"Real hot." Hamish's second offer was met with the same lack of enthusiasm as his first. "Pinball machine work?" The question demanded an answer.

"Yeah. But it's tilt-happy." The guard stopped, realizing he'd been drawn into a conversation he hadn't wanted. But his desire to play the expert overcame his reticence. "If you only use body English on the left lower end, it ain't too much of a rip-off."

In the name of criminal investigation, Hamish sacrificed two quarters. To his surprise, the guard walked over to the machine with him and stood watching each bounce of the po-lished steel ball; he moved his body and hands as though in personal control of the machine, wincing when the ball missed, giving a low sigh of pleasure when the board lit up to register a multiple hit.

"You want a turn?" asked Hamish.

The guard laughed. "Shit, no. The damned thing knows my touch."

Forcing himself, Hamish laughed too. Together they walked back to the bar, and the guard allowed himself to have a boilermaker forced on him. Hamish made a point of letting the guard see him studying his uniform. "Quite a rig," he finally volunteered.

"I'm the watchman across the street at the warehouse. Nothing much to watch these days. I'm there to see no one don't steal the building, I guess."

Hamish feigned surprise. "That old place? Empty, isn't it? Who'd want to break into a place like that?"

The guard had been put on the defensive; his mission in life, his job, had been challenged. It was one thing for *him* to deprecate the warehouse, but it was something else to have this stranger do it. "More stuff in there than it looks," he said mysteriously. "Few small companies still have offices there. Lots of junk in 'em. Electric typewriters. Adding ma-chines. Somebody's got to keep kids out of there at nights. Bums. Rip-off artists."

Hamish suddenly pretended to put his cards on the table. "Well, somebody isn't keeping them out. I'm here for New York Telephone. Some joker's getting at a phone in"—he paused, pulling a scrap of blank paper out of his pocket and pretending to read it—"the Boytoy Company. Calls long distance all over hell and gone. Big joke, I guess."

The guard looked abashed. "Boytoy, Boytoy. Hell, there's nothing in that place *but* a phone. I was there—maybe six weeks ago—and let the phone company guy in to install it. Yeah, and I was there when somebody from Boytoy came to hook up a recorder or something. But making calls from there at night—well . . ."

A surge of excitement coursed through Hamish. For the first time, one of the kidnappers had been seen. And by a reliable witness, too, because the watchman, like most commercial guards, was probably a former cop. "This man you saw. The one from Boytoy . . ."

"What man? Christ, I didn't say it was no man. Crazy-looking old broad. Secretary, or something like that, I guess. Kept talking about her heart. I remember being curious. I got a heart condition myself, see, and this old lady didn't make sense. Why, she—"

None of it made sense to Hamish. His sudden feeling that he'd finally made a breakthrough ended in the discovery that he had once again run up against a stone wall. No little old lady had garroted Angel Sanchez. Or sawed off his hand and mailed it to his family. Or climbed into a wet-suit and dragged Paige Rathbin under the surface of the Sound.

With only the most superficial pretense of politeness, Hamish took down the guard's name, strode out the bar's front door, and stood blinking in the noontime sun. The kidnapper always seemed to be one step ahead of him. Or maybe he was simply brighter.

Bright enough, anyway, to make people believe he was a crazy-looking broad, a little old lady with a heart condition.

Chapter 11 _____

There's more and more talk in Green-
port—and on TV—asking what the 'ultimate
ransom' is going to be. Well, nothing as easy
as money.

People in places like Greenport, you see,
are always yakking about how much they
love their children, pointing out how they
give them everything money can buy, as if
that proved what they were saying. Balls.

So the 'ultimate ransom' was designed to
make them prove just how much. With deeds,
not words. For if they really love their chil-
dren, they should be willing not just to pay
money, but to cheat, steal, lie, kill; to make
any sacrifice to save their children.

And if they don't *love them that much,*
well, hell, their kids are probably better off
dead anyway . . .

—TAPE-LOG OF THE PIPER,
ENTRY DATED JUNE 6TH.

"You're going to wear a path in the rug, walking over to look
out the window."

"I know. Stupid."

"No, not stupid. Just hard on the nerves."

"I keep wanting something to happen. *Anything.*" Jenny
nodded in understanding. She and Hamish had been in his office for about an hour, and he'd gone to stare out the window
half a dozen times, waiting, looking, trying to force action
out of inanimate trees, shrubs, and roads. She searched for an
angle that would release some of his tensions.

"Back in Wyoming, you must have done a lot of hunting
and fishing. So you know the kind of patience it takes. Okay,
it's been twenty-four hours and nothing's happened yet. Any

good hunter knows it takes time to get an animal to walk into a trap." Jenny smiled at Hamish, trying to transfuse reassurance into him.

Hamish smiled grimly. "I've never been the bait before."

The smile she had forced was met by one equally difficult for Hamish to produce. He fussed with his string tie, stretched his long legs out in front of him, and yawned elaborately. "If nothing else, the press conference got a few people shook up."

This was something of an understatement. The effect of the press conference had been extremely valuable to Hamish in dealing with the authorities; they could sense the problems, they could be terrified by them, but until Hamish went on the air, they had been resisting taking steps, as if to do so might make their worst fears come true. Following the conference, this attitude changed dramatically.

After a brief but blunt talk with Chief Investigator Cummins of the State Police, the Connecticut Director of Education pronounced the public schools closed, even though they had been the least affected. Oddly, Greenport Country Day, DeWitte, Reed, and Bryant—the private schools—were less compliant, and there was no state official to force them to be. In the case of Country Day, the only decision made was to end the school year a few days earlier; the headmaster pointed out that what was left of the school year consisted almost entirely of final exams followed by social events such as Glee Club concerts, the school play, and, finally, graduation exercises. All of these, he pointed out, would be well protected.

In the matter of the armed guards, Hamish won a split decision. State Policemen were refused for duty at the country and beach clubs, with the explanation that the private guards already there should be sufficient. But their presence would be mandatory on all school grounds. The idea of busing children to the clubs was also not accepted, but the Town Council agreed that putting guards on the private school buses which took children to and from their homes was probably a good idea; these guards were instructed to escort the children from wherever the bus stopped right to the doors of their homes.

On another front, the armed vigilante groups roaming the reaches of Greenport made Hamish and others considerably nervous—"Some innocent bastard's going to get shot in the name of law and order, but he'll be just as dead as if he'd been shot robbing a bank." There was not much, however, the police could do about men carrying shotguns and hunting rifles in their cars until something—probably something tragic—happened.

At the end of his first day as "bait," Hamish felt more frustrated than ever. "No one bit," he told Tyne. "A guy could get a complex."

"Jesus, I don't know why we couldn't have just gone and bought the stuff." There was what sounded like a thunderous crash as K.K. tripped over a pile of stacked cartons, and both boys stopped dead in their tracks, listening. Actually, the sound was nowhere as loud as their nervous imaginations made it seem. After a pause, they both began breathing again.

"Watch the hell where you're going, dammit," hissed Kip. "And as for buying the stuff," he added, his voice edged with sarcasm, "that would be real smart, wouldn't it? No one, of course, would remember. Kids buy things like that every day. Use your head . . ."

K.K. sighed. This part of the Gray's Anatomy Plan—the name they'd finally attached to the maneuver—was the part he liked least. He considered it not only dangerous but unnecessary. The two of them continued threading their way down the aisles of Gristede's, having a hard time finding what they wanted in the bleak darkness of the store. Both had flashlights, but since any light would be visible from the street, they decided not to use them. About a block and a half further down Greenport Avenue was a single street lamp, and they would have to depend on its light—along with their senses of smell—to locate the area they were looking for.

"Here," said Kip suddenly, his fingers coming in contact with the cold, slippery edges of a glass-fronted freezer. "I found it."

From behind he could hear K.K., still fumbling and running into things. Kip swore underneath his breath. Next time he tackled anything like this, it would be by himself. Then it struck him that only K.K. could possibly know what was needed; his presence was a necessity. This dependence on K.K. only made Kip swear louder.

"Goddammit, I'm coming," grunted K.K. Carefully, he edged himself along an aisle of what appeared to be the freezer for dairy products and very gently began edging himself past it. As he passed the end of the case, a sudden burst of sound terrified him. K.K. had run into some kind of trick display piece sitting beside the dairy case, something with a recorded advertising message inside it, which started to play the moment he bumped into it. A thin recorded voice in the display piece sang:

"Have lots of milk, kids, every day. Milk makes children grow up stronger in every way—Strong teeth, strong bodies, strong eyes, bones, and brains . . ."

"Shut it off, shut the damned thing off," hissed Kip frantically, trying to get down the aisle to K.K.

"I can't find the button. There has to be a button somewhere," K.K. shot back, shaking the display piece in a desperate effort to make the recording stop. By now Kip had reached him, and both of them were tearing apart the cardboard display piece, trying furiously to get at the machine inside and silence the singers.

The recording continued blithely:

"We're all in our places. "With bright, shiny faces, Drinking milk, milk, milk, till we're—"

Finally, with a mechanical groan, the machine's heart was stilled, and the recording ground to a halt. K.K. and Kip stood there panting, holding the shreds of the display in their gloved hands. "Jesus," groaned K.K., "I'll never drink another glass of milk as long as I live."

The sound, Kip slowly realized, had not been really loud; it only seemed deafening because of what they were up to. Suddenly relieved, he snorted, almost giggled. "Their damned little teeth and bodies won't do them much good when we're through with them. Shit. C'mon, K.K., I found what we're after down the aisle to the right. Let's grab the stuff and get our asses out of here before you set off the Philharmonic again."

The actual theft took about ten minutes. To conceal what they were actually after, Kip carefully left jimmy marks on all of the cash register drawers and even sawed through the chains protecting the supply of refrigerated beer. Half an hour after they had broken in, Gristede's last customers of the day had silently departed.

By the following morning, Hamish's new rules for Greenport's children were already causing resentment and bitterness among the kids. With the public schools abruptly shut down, this resentment ran highest among the less wealthy children; with many of them already restricted to home grounds by their families, school had been their last bastion of freedom and social contact with other children. The resulting cloud of boredom was massive.

The boy sat on the front stoop of the modest little house on Evergreen Avenue, picking his nose and expressing his general disgust for the world by occasionally selecting a pebble from the front path and throwing it at nothing and everything. Glancing at the cheap watch on his wrist, he realized it was only ten o'clock and that he had already exhausted the morning's possibilities. In front of him, the day stretched like an empty road, swept of all promises and excitement by the awkward new orders restricting him to the house and immediate surroundings. His friends at Benjamin Franklin High School all lived at some distance from him, and to a 14-year-old, a day without friends is something just short of the end of the world. Twice he had asked his mother if he could leave the property—once to go to the drugstore a block and a half away for a Coke, and once to ask if he could visit a friend of his who lived only a few blocks away. The answer to both requests had been a firm "no"; her husband had made it very clear to her that when he said his son was to go nowhere, he meant *nowhere*.

While in the house, the boy picked up his fungo bat, his catcher's mitt and his baseball cap; considering the available space in the backyard, none of this equipment was really useable, but wearing it made him feel better. Outside again, the 14-year-old tossed the ball into the air for a few minutes before giving up in disgust; with the desperation of boredom he slipped into the small shed at the end of the yard to sneak a cigarette. The boy didn't particularly enjoy smoking, but the pressure of senseless regulations formulated and imposed by grownups made the prospect of such defiance satisfying.

With a sigh, he sat down on a crate and pulled the pack of Chesterfields from their hiding place behind the tackle box. Lighting the cigarette, he coughed as the smoke hit his lungs, and made a sour face; for a moment, he thought he heard a snicker, but he dismissed the idea as imagination. Eyes half-closed, he watched the smoke curl lazily up from the cigarette end. He didn't notice that another pair of eyes was watching him from behind an empty oil drum, or that they were watching him far more intently than he was watching the cigarette end.

Rising to his feet, the fledgling major-leaguer found himself doubled over by a new fit of coughing. Angrily, he ground the cigarette into the dirt under his left foot and started toward the door and the fresh, clean air of the backyard.

As he neared the door, he saw, through his smarting, tear-filled eyes, a dim shape blocking his way; simultaneously, a strong pair of arms seized him by the neck and threw him to the dirt floor. When he began to yell, a hand was clamped over his mouth. He felt his hands and arms pulled behind him and handcuffed; someone was sitting on his back and attaching handcuffs to his ankles as well.

"Anyone out there?" the youngster heard a voice ask and, twisting his head, saw the tall blond boy who was straddling his body. The face was familiar but he couldn't place it; all he was sure of was that the boy was no student at Franklin High. The other boy—also familiar, but similarly unknown to him—peeked out of the door and shook his head.

"Good. Let's go. You've got some—" the blond boy gave a laugh that had such overtones of evil in it, their captive felt a shudder run through his body—"work to do." Struggling, he was dragged into a Volks van parked on a side street behind the family house. Some innate understanding of what was going on swept through him, and he couldn't help wonder if he would ever see that house again.

It was a good question. Jenny had been right in guessing

that the program would compel the kidnapper to get even with Hamish, but she had been wrong in figuring out how he would go about it: the new victim was Russel Hamilton, Hamish's son.

The realization of what had happened came slowly. Martha Hamilton, Hamish's wife, at first kept glancing out the kitchen window to check that Russel was still around, but eventually she stopped, Russel had been a terrible pest this morning. Once she looked up to see Russel's desultory heaves of the baseball into the air; there was something essentially pathetic about his getting all dressed up in a baseball uniform to play catch with himself. But Hamish had been adamant about Russel's staying where she could keep an eye on him. Quickly, Russel slipped out of her mind as she devoted herself to scraping the burned-on patches of grease off a broiling pan.

A little later, when she looked up, the yard was empty. But she saw that the door to the shed was partially open, and she assumed Russel was inside. Doing what, she didn't know. Smoking again, probably. A small flush of anger swept through her. Holding the pan under the running water, she dried it with a paper towel and held it up to the light for inspection. Not good. That, she told herself, was the last time she would let Russel and Hamish try to cook spaghetti. Thinking of Russel made her look out the window again; there was still no sign of him. At first, she didn't really worry about this; he could have had a book in the shed, or be reading a forbidden copy of *Playboy* or *Penthouse*, or simply have surrendered to the warmth of the day and fallen asleep. But when he hadn't reappeared in the yard by eleven o'clock, some inner fear began to nag at her.

Drying her hands, she walked briskly out the back door, across the yard, and knocked loudly on the door of the shed. Silence. Timidly, she pushed the door open—she knew Hamish felt his sons should have all the privacy they wanted—and looked inside. The place was deserted. And everything Russel had been carrying had disappeared along with him: the ball, catcher's mitt, fungo bat and cap. Lying on the floor to one side, she saw the partially empty pack of

Chesterfields, and, sniffing, could still smell the stale smoke. But no Russel.

The worry grew. Perhaps, Martha told herself, in spite of everything Hamish and she had told him, Russel had slipped over to see Bill Yancey, his friend from down the street. She shook her head, partly in disbelief, partly in fury. Martha began calling Russel's name, although since she could see the entire backyard and had just looked inside the shed, she knew this to be useless. Once again, she checked his room upstairs; it was filled with that curious smell of all little boys' rooms, but empty of the little boy who had produced them. The worry began to consume her.

Still, she procrastinated, forcing herself to avoid calling Hamish. For one thing, the climate between them had been steadily worsening for some years now; the more recent rumors about Jenny Cobb and Hamish had not escaped her, and Martha felt more insecure and uncertain of him than ever. She feared his reaction, knowing that she hadn't followed his instructions not to let Russel "one foot out of her sight," meticulously. The yard he couldn't argue with, certainly, but the fact that she could have lost track of him for nearly an hour was stretching a point.

During these early stages, Martha Hamilton could afford the luxury of worrying as much about her problems with Hamish as she did about Russel's safety because the possibility of his becoming a victim of the Piper still seemed impossible. Russel was, after all, the Chief of Police's son; he didn't go to Country Day; and, most important of all, they were obviously too poor to pay a ransom of even the smallest size. Thus, for another half-hour she sat on her fears, expecting any minute now to hear the door slam and Russel's voice bubbling with excuses and apologies for slipping away. Repeated trips to the back door and another look inside the shed had produced nothing. The worry inside her began to get out of control. Twice she had put one hand on the phone, and twice she removed it, suddenly remembering the day that Hamish had met Jenny Cobb—talking excitedly about the woman's competence, her ability, and her professional brilliance.

Finally, one hour and forty minutes after Russel had gone out into the backyard to play catch, Martha surrendered and called Hamish. He was furious. Only a sudden burst of tears from Martha kept him from saying a lot more. He would, he said, be right over.

But, as either Kip or K.K.—or even Russel—could have told him, it was already far too late.

As the day wore on, it became more and more obvious to Hamish that there was no possibility of mistake: Russel had been kidnapped by the Piper. For perhaps half an hour, shouting into the phone, he had tried to operate out of his house, mostly for Martha's benefit. It was obvious that she was on the edge of going to pieces.

"Stop tearing yourself up, dammit," he commanded. "Playing catch in the backyard, where you could see him most of the time—well, that's about all anybody could be expected to do."

Martha looked at him gratefully, but her expression said that she was not really convinced. "Why should this Piper man want to kidnap Russel?" she asked softly. "He must know that we haven't got any money. Look at this place, for God's sake."

"Because whoever he is—or she—or they—is crazy." Hamish ran different ideas around in his head, unable to escape the obvious—if painful one. "Maybe," he finally suggested, "he's trying to get back at me for that broadcast. But hell, who knows why he does *anything* that he does?"

Mention of the broadcast produced the flood of tears that Hamish had tried to avoid. Quietly he took Martha by both shoulders—it was not a loving gesture, but it was the first time that he had so much as even touched her in months— and told her that she had to be brave. To take care of Ollie —two years younger than Russel—and not to let him out of her sight, not for any reason at all. Hamish was going back to the station, to make sure the search had started rolling. The phrase was an empty one; Hamish and Martha knew it, and anyone who heard it would know it, but it at least made it sound as if there were things that could be done. "Phone me if you get any strange calls. Don't tell anybody what's happened. I'll phone every half hour. Okay?"

Numbly, she nodded. With a smile that he hoped looked more encouraging than he felt, Hamish went out the door and climbed into his car to head back to the station. His own belief was that they would hear nothing from Russel until the evening broadcast from the mobile transmitter.

For the second time that day, Hamish was to find himself totally wrong.

Chapter 12 _____

> *Once, when I was about eleven, I guess, I*
> *had a baby hamster. I didn't have anything*
> *against the hamster; I just wanted to see what*
> *would happen. So one day, I put it in a tin*
> *box and held the box over the burner of the*
> *gas stove. Did you know that hamsters could*
> *make a crying sound?—tiny, sure, but like a*
> *baby screaming. And after a lot of clawing*
> *and scratching at the sides of the box, the*
> *hamster began jumping up and down in the*
> *air trying to keep its feet off the hot bottom*
> *of the box. Finally my poor hamster gave a*
> *sad little whimper and fell over dead. It made*
> *me feel terrible; I couldn't get the smell of*
> *burning hair out of my mind for weeks. But I*
> *remember I got a strange thrill out of the*
> *whole thing, and even an erection.*
>
> *Well, I guess that's the way K.K. feels*
> *about what he's doing to Russel; the*
> *thing's giving him some kind of charge. I*
> *wish I didn't suspect it was giving me one,*
> *too.*
>
> —TAPE-LOG OF THE PIPER,
> ENTRY DATED JUNE 6 (P.M.).

At 4:10 that afternoon, Martha Hamilton's phone rang. Even
though she was virtually sitting on top of the instrument,
waiting for someone—anyone—to call, Martha's nerves were
filed to such a fine edge that she jumped a good six inches out
of her chair, spilling the half-finished cup of coffee sitting on
the table in front of her. From the other end of the phone—
clear and unmistakable, but sounding as if he were half-cry-
ing—came Russel's voice.

Martha Hamilton was not ordinarily an effusive woman,
nor one easily given to show her emotions. She was steady,
practical, and enormously predictable—some of the qualities

that had long ago caused Hamish to weary of her. But the strain of the day's events, compounded by her own sense of guilt, caused her to lose control; Martha barely heard what Russel was saying. Her voice rose to a tearful scream, half in relief, half in anger at her son; she tried to find out where he was and why he had disappeared without a word, causing everybody worry and concern. It was only when Martha realized that she was receiving no reaction at all from the other end of the phone that she really began to listen. No matter how she looked at it, the call made no sense: after a pause, his voice—with a curious mechanical cadence to it—repeated exactly the same words and phrases he had just finished saying, almost as if she wasn't there. Before Martha had time to consider the meaning of this new phenomenon, the phone was hung up, abruptly. Only snatches of the conversation remained with her. One phrase in particular stuck in her mind, sending a chill through her whole body: "Oh, Mom. It hurts so much."

Numbly, Martha picked up the phone and called police headquarters. Hamish, she was told, was across town at the First Baptist and there was no way of reaching him. Yes, they understood it was a matter of terrible urgency, but the Chief, they explained, was meeting with Blagden Tyne of the FBI and Miss Cobb, and there was no way of reaching him by phone.

Martha exploded. The mention of Jenny Cobb was the last straw. "I don't give a damn if he's at a meeting with the Pope," she yelled at the startled desk sergeant. "Get a car over there and tell him I've had a call from Russel and to leave his Goddamned whore long enough to come and do something about his son."

The sergeant blinked, listening as the phone was crashed onto the receiver. Then he sent for a squad car. His phrasing of what Hamish was to be told was somewhat different from Martha's.

"He could have just wandered off, I suppose." Tyne didn't believe it when he said it, but accepting the alternative was too painful. The three of them—Jenny, Hamish, and Blagden Tyne—sat uncomfortably in a windowless room of the small headquarters that the FBI had set up in the basement of the

First Baptist Church, trying to assess what the disappearance of Russel Hamilton meant.

"Not like him," said Hamish glumly. "Not like him at all. I told him what the ground rules were; so did his mother. No, I've tried not to accept it, but the hard fact is the Piper's got him."

Blagden Tyne leaned forward, "But why, Hamish, why *him*? With the exception of Angel Sanchez, all the rest of the children have families, well, with—" Tyne's face colored; it was an uncomfortable set of words to say. Hamish spared him the embarrassment.

"With money. Families that could pay to get their kids back. Except for Angel. The Piper must know that I—that no cop—can come up with ransom money. Maybe he's just trying to make me lay off."

"It would only make you want to go after them harder, Hamish." Blagden Tyne rifled some papers in front of him, as if the answer to the problem might lie buried somewhere inside them. "Hell, one way, for instance, for a car thief *not* to get a cop to lay off him, is to steal the cop's car. He must realize that."

"Unless this was his revenge." Jenny Cobb was choosing her words carefully. It was she, after all, who had suggested the speech that Hamish gave at the press conference. It was she who had talked Hamish into becoming the "bait" for the trap. And because he was the bait in the trap, every precaution that could be taken had been taken; every move of his around the town had been discreetly monitored by Tyne's men. How could they have overlooked the obvious?

Now, without warning, the whole operation had gone sour. "*You* were supposed to be the target, Hamish. That he would take this way of hurting you—through your son—well, I guess that I just have to admit to being stupid. The possibility never hit me. Probably it should have. I'm sorry. My God, I'm sorry."

Hamish sighed, shrugged, and waved the apology away. Events in Greenport, ever since the disappearance of the first child, had been so unreasonable, so illogical, that no one should hold themselves responsible for anything. He should have said this—and wanted to say this—but his imagination kept picturing what might be happening to Russ.

Blagden Tyne said it instead. "It was a good plan, Jenny. A sound one. No one could have predicted a crazy turn of things like this."

Jenny smiled gratefully, but remained unconvinced by what Tyne said. A knock on the door was followed by a police sergeant's head, partly stuck through the crack. "Excuse me, Chief. Your wife called. She said it's urgent, real urgent. Something about a telephone call. She wants you to call right away."

For a second, Hamish sat frozen in his chair. A thousand possibilities passed through his mind: Russel had suddenly shown up, sheepish but with a perfectly reasonable excuse; Russel had turned up dead; Russel had slipped away to meet an old friend and spent the last few hours at his house, forgetting to call, unaware of the worry that he had pulled down around his ears. Russel had—Russel was—Russel would— Hamish shot to his feet, sweeping the possibilities out of his head. Two at a time, he raced up the stairs of the church to get to the phone in the sexton's office and call Martha.

Still panting from his run through the woods to the clearing around the cistern, Kip climbed over the edge and lowered himself down the ladder, into the main tunnel. In one of the smaller rooms off this, K.K. was working. Just beyond was the padlocked steel door behind which Paige Rathbin and the other boys were being held captive. Russel Hamilton was not with the rest of the captives but was locked in the room where K.K. had set up his equipment. At the sound of Kip's feet on the stone floor, the door to this room opened and K.K. came out, carefully locking and closing the door behind him.

Kip leaned against the wall. "Well, the first part's taken care of. The box is planted. I hope to hell she heard what the tape on the phone said; she kept talking so much, I'm not sure."

"My end's coming along." K.K. shifted uncomfortably. "But I wish that you had let me set up the job in my lab, like I asked. I can't guarantee much staying power under these conditions."

"Too risky. He might get loose and get out of there. Here, even if he makes it out of the room, he's got nowhere to go."

K.K. shrugged unhappily. "It's your decision."

"When's the next—" Kip reddened, fumbling for words that half-troubled, half-excited him—"the next—well, hell, you know what I mean."

K.K. checked his watch. "Half an hour. If we're sticking to the schedule."

"We are. I just wanted to be sure that I wasn't here for it. The noise . . ."

"Half an hour," K.K. repeated. He made no comment on what he considered to be Kip's squeamishness, but allowed a faint smile to put his message across.

"Perfect. I've got a lot to do. I'm going downtown to pick up some pills for Mom. And then Dee wanted something or other. I'll be back in three-quarters of an hour." Kip paused, staring at K.K. "That will give you enough time, won't it?"

K.K. couldn't control himself and laughed. "All over by then. You'll be safe."

"Dammit it, K.K., it isn't funny. It's just something that has to be done. And done for a reason—not for the kicks."

"Right. Something that has to be done. And will be done. Just relax." Kip didn't even wave as he turned on his heel, walked down the stone hall, and climbed the rusty ladder to the surface. Inside, Kip was doing a slow burn. He was upset; K.K. was enjoying himself too much.

About twenty minutes later, when Blagden Tyne and Jenny Cobb had gone back down to the cellar hall to Tyne's office, the phone rang. It was Hamish, calling from his home. Martha was in such a state, he explained, that he thought that he'd better stay there—for a while, anyway. And no, there was no longer any doubt about it: the Piper had Russel.

"Are you sure, Hamish?" asked Tyne.

"Positive." He told him about the tape. "One other thing, Russel said that he would call back in an hour and give further instructions or orders or explain what was happening— Martha isn't sure which it was. So I'd better hang in here until that call comes. Or maybe it would be better if I came back and we got a tie-line and . . ."

Tyne was back on the ground that he knew how to deal with instinctively: distraught families. "Look, Hamish. Stay where you are. Right there, understand? I'll get some men over with a tape recorder—maybe we can pick up something from the background noises, I don't know. Also, we'll get the telephone company to flag your line so that they can start tracing any calls that come in. Not too much hope there, of course, but there's always a chance. And, oh yeah. What was the kid—what was Russel wearing? Somebody may have seen him picked up or driving away in a car."

There was a pause as Hamish consulted with Martha. Jenny, on an extension phone, could hear them very clearly. "He was wearing *what?*" she heard Hamish ask.

"His baseball suit. The Yankee one, from Sears. He was only playing catch with himself in the backyard, but, well, you remember how he always got all . . ." Martha's voice choked up and she was unable to continue.

"A picture, Hamish, a recent picture. Particularly if there's one of him in that baseball getup," said Tyne very softly to Hamish.

Again, Jenny could hear Hamish talking to Martha. Only this time, the conversation was muffled; Martha was crying, trying to answer but having trouble getting the words out. Finally, from Hamish: "The only one we got in a baseball suit is a couple of years old. I'll try to find that, but there's some in regular clothes, taken about a month ago, I think, that might be useful for I.D. I don't know. The kid's been growing so fast . . ."

Here, Hamish's own voice wavered, and Jenny could hear him cough to cover up the sound. If only she hadn't been so damned smart and set up that phoney press conference . . .

"Look, Hamish," said Tyne, rising to his feet. "We'll be over as soon as we get our equipment together." A slight pause, then Tyne, not realizing the whole situation, made what he thought might be a helpful suggestion. "I thought I might bring Jenny along. Maybe she can pick up something from—"

Hamish exploded. "Jesus Christ, Tyne! Are you crazy or is that your idea of a joke?"

The phone was abruptly hung up, and for a long time, Tyne stared at the receiver, the pieces of the puzzle slowly coming together. Still wearing a perplexed look, he turned to Jenny. "Did I do something wrong?"

"Nothing worse than inviting Adolf Eichmann to a Bar Mitzvah."

Hamish's outburst and Jenny's comment finally came together in Tyne's head. His face reddened. Picking up the phone, he started the FBI teams into action. Within half an hour, Russel Hamilton's face—clear-eyed and smiling—was silently emerging from hundreds of teleprinters in FBI and police offices across the Northeast; an hour later, an FBI artist's composite drawing would follow this with a doctored photograph giving an approximation of what Russel would look like dressed in the cap of his Yankee uniform.

At Hamish's house, now under heavy surveillance, two FBI technicians had installed themselves in the living room. One, wearing earphones, was manning the controls of a high fidelity tape recorder—a special setup designed to pick up the subtlest nuances of background and other nonverbal input. The other agent was also in headphones, but equipped with a talk-back microphone such as telephone operators use, monitoring an open line to another agent at the telephone company's switching center. With this arrangement, any calls from the kidnapper could be shunted onto the "trace-back" pattern the moment it was received.

To Hamish, all of this efficiency, this mass of highly sophisticated equipment and expert knowledge, was impressive and encouraging. His mind, however, couldn't escape how excited and beside himself with questions all of these goings-on would have left Russel. It was a party to which no one had invited the guest of honor.

Chapter 13 _____

*It was interesting, something Lyle Pritchard's
father said during that program. You know,
something like, "Tell us how to get our son
back—money is no object—just tell us what you
want to give us back our most valuable
possession: our son."*

*That way of thinking is one of the biggest
troubles with Greenport. Your kid is a possession, just like the municipals in your safe
or the cars in your garage or the heater in
your pool house. It's not that parents mean
anything bad by it; hell, there's even a
funny side to it.*

*Because, like with all possessions, it follows
that some are worth more than others. Which
leads to relative appraisals. How, for instance, would you like to have K.K., with his
scrawny frame and dirty underwear, as your
most valuable possession? Christ, his mother
ought to pay someone to take him away.*

*That's an idea for a whole new business
right there. "Ugly kids disposed of. Reasonable rates. Free estimates, quick, courteous
service." I don't think I'd have time to handle
all the orders.*

—TAPE-LOG OF THE PIPER,
ENTRY DATED JUNE 7TH.

At 5:12, exactly one hour less three minutes after the first
call received by Martha Hamilton, the phone at Hamish's
house rang. Hamish, Martha, the two FBI men, Cummins of
the State Police, and Hamish's own Deputy Chief Bill Littel,
had been sitting in the living room making nervous conversation. Russel's younger brother, Ollie, had been sent to stay
with neighbors. Martha kept insisting on feeding them all

coffee—and more coffee, and then more coffee, until the men felt in some danger of floating away. Yet, they were all aware of her desperate need to keep busy, so none of them dared to refuse the coffee when offered.

At the sound of the phone, all six of the people jumped simultaneously. To Martha, it was the call that she had been praying for and the call that she had been dreading. For a full two or three seconds, she sat completely motionless, her hands folded in her lap, staring at the phone as if it were the Angel of Death. The two FBI men had already gotten to their feet, and by the second ring, one had already set the tape machine in motion. The second agent was using the tie-line to the phone company, speaking softly into the headpiece microphone. Because everyone else was standing, Chief Investigator Cummins got to his feet too, shifting his body awkwardly back and forth in front of his chair.

Quickly, Hamish strode over to the phone and placed his hand on the receiver, waiting for a signal from the agent indicating that he could pick it up. Martha stood in the middle of the room, her eyes darting from man to man, wanting to scream in protest at a world which could put her in so painful and terrible a position.

The phone had barely given a third shrill ring before Hamish was given the signal to answer it. "Hello," he said tentatively. "Hello?"

"It's Russel," announced a small voice from the other end of the line. "I said it's Russel. They told me to give you a message. You're to look under the shelf of the phone booth on the corner of Greenport and Bleeker. You'll find a package. It's to prove they mean what they say. Dad—maybe you'd better do whatever they tell you. It's going to hurt me a lot if you don't. It already does, but they say it's going to get worse. Please give them anything they want. They'll let you know what and how tonight. I love you. Good-bye."

Even through the small loudspeaker of the tape machine, Russel's sense of terror had quickly communicated itself. Martha shrieked and grabbed the person nearest to her for support—Cummins of the State Police. Almost immediately, the voice on the phone began again. "It's Russel. I said it's Russel. They told me to give you a message. You're to look under the shelf . . ."

The FBI man on the tape machine switched the sound off and the voice stopped, although the reels of the recorder kept turning slowly, as if of their own will. Almost immediately the man on the tie-line shook his head in frustration; the phone company had barely had time to start the tracing process before the connection at the other end was broken.

The phone rang, and once again everybody jumped. Martha knocked her coffee cup over. The process with the tape recorner in his Porsche, and signaled him to follow. They still waited impatiently, hand on the phone, braced for the signal to answer.

"Hamish? I'll pick you up in about five minutes. We've got to get to that phone booth before somebody discovers that package by mistake and louses up the works. I'm on my way." The buzz from the hung-up phone, amplified through the tape machine's speaker, was strident and unpleasant. Outside on the street, he heard Blagden Tyne's car screech to a halt, followed by the short, urgent blast of his horn. Hamish started toward the door, pausing to turn back and reassure Martha; it seemed the least that he owed her. "Everything's going to be all right. Just stick by the phone and do what these men tell you; Bill Littel will stay with you as long as you want him."

Martha said nothing, but the pleading look in her eyes shook Hamish badly. Turning quickly, he walked toward the door, waved behind him confidently, and climbed into Blagden Tyne's waiting car.

When they got to the telephone booth at the corner of Greenport and Bleeker, an FBI man was already sitting in a car beside the booth, trying to look casual. Blagden Tyne had already radioed ahead so that the booth would be covered and some chance stranger wouldn't find and remove the package.

Both Tyne and Hamish quickly hopped out of the car, Tyne tossing a perfunctory nod to the agent in the other vehicle. The man rolled down his window. "No one's been near it."

Tyne nodded again and he and Hamish squeezed into the booth. Taped beneath the small shelf, the package, perhaps five inches square, was easily visible. From what they could make out, paper was fastened around a small box by what looked like ordinary butcher's twine. As Hamish started to reach for it, he felt Tyne's hand grab his arm and stop him. "It could be a bomb, Hamish. Be smarter to call in the squad from—" he searched his mind for an instant—"I think there's one in Bridgeport."

For the briefest moment, Hamish paused and considered. Then: "Fuck it. If it's a bomb, it's a bomb. You can wait across the street if you want."

"I'll stick. But handle the damned thing carefully. Open it slowly and don't do anything sudden."

Without really hearing him, Hamish nodded. Pulling his penknife from his pocket, he cut the string. Tyne winced as the paper fell off the package on one side. "Easy now," he whispered. "There's more paper underneath. If there is a trigger, that's where it'll be attached."

Again, Hamish nodded. Underneath the outer wrapping was more, thinner brown paper, taped instead of tied. Written in Magic Marker, across the top of this, was the word "Bomb." With a frown, Hamish turned and stared at Tyne. "What do you make of this?"

For a long time Tyne stared at the package, taking it and shaking it very, very gently, holding it up to his ear, shifting it back and forth to see if he could make out the sound of anything moving inside. With a shake of his head, he lowered the package to his waist, cradling it between his hands. "What I think is that we should call in that bomb squad from Bridgeport. It couldn't take them more than twenty minutes to get here."

"No."

"Okay, then. I haven't got a clue whether it's a bomb or not. The fact that the label says it is makes me think it isn't. On the other hand, maybe the Piper figures that's just what *we'll* figure. We could still get the guys from Bridgeport."

"No," repeated Hamish, this time more firmly than ever.

Tyne sighed. "I didn't think so." Leaning down, he placed the small package back on the shelf of the telephone booth and studied it. "Chances are there's a wire attached from the trigger to the inside of the wrapper, right where you pull on the paper to open the damned package. Well, with a little luck . . ." With the tip of his tongue showing where his lips were pressed tightly together, Tyne produced the penknife again. Carefully, he made a small incision in the side of the paper. "With a little luck, we can bypass the trigger. If we ... can ... only ... cut ... the ... paper ... not the tape ..."

A sudden blast of sound rocked both Hamish and Tyne. A passing car had not seen the FBI agent's parked car until the last second—the agent turned off his lights as soon as Tyne had arrived—and the passerby blew his horn loud and long as the car's shape loomed into view. "Jesus," hissed Tyne. Angry—as much at himself as anyone—he turned toward the agent's parked car. "Keep your damned lights on, will you? We almost dropped it."

"Look," said Hamish to Tyne suddenly. "Not waiting for the bomb squad—opening this thing here—was my idea. There's no reason for you to stick your neck out. I'll open it."

Tyne never looked up. "Thanks, but if you won't take this personally, I've defused a few more of these mothers than you have, so my chances are better. Just stand back—maybe behind the car would be better—and think kind thoughts. Anything else is a waste of time."

Hamish couldn't tell whether Tyne knew that he did not move back; the FBI man's concentration was so intense, Hamish doubted if he was aware of anything much except the package. "Easy now ... easy, now ... e-a-s-y ..." Tyne's voice was soft as he talked to himself, the penknife moving slowly across the paper.

The device went off after a series of clicks and a buzzing sound. Rudkin, the man in the FBI car, had been eyeing an approaching pedestrian and had taken several steps to the rear of the car, planning to move up the sidewalk and head the man off. "Christ!" screamed Tyne, and dove toward the sidewalk; Hamish flattened himself on the ground, as did Rudkin. For a second, there was complete silence. Then they slowly raised themselves, baffled at what had happened. The bomb now lay on the pavement where Tyne heaved it when it had first become obvious it was about to go. There had not actually been an explosion, but instead the bursting of a fire-cracker-like charge, somewhere beneath the paper.

Cautiously moving closer, they could see that something, indeed, had happened to the package: from inside, raggedly thrust through the paper, was a doll-like figure of a baseball player, a rolled up tube of paper serving as his bat; all of this was suspended in the air on the end of a spring, a little like a jack-in-the-box. Coming through the paper, they could hear the thin sound of a cheap cassette player, its volume turned as high as it could go, playing the Spike Jones version of "Joltin' Joe DiMaggio." The whole arrangement showed that the possibilities of the milk jingle in Gristede's were not lost on Kip.

For a second, the three men stared at each other. They were mad at the "bomb," they were mad at the Piper, but most of all, they were mad at themselves. "Shit," growled Tyne, dusting off his J. Edgar Hoover suit carefully, glaring at the paper and cardboard lying on the street.

It was not until they actually examined the package— Tyne handled it carefully, partly because he feared it might still be booby-trapped, partly because he wanted to preserve every scrap of material for the forensics lab—that they discovered the package was more than an ingenious, if cruel, joke. They found that the rolled up 'paper bat' was a Polaroid shot of Russel, taken since he was kidnapped, wearing the Yankee baseball suit and cap.

Looking at the picture, Hamish felt a sudden stab inside of him. It was harshly lit and you could see that Russel had been squinting in a too-bright sun when the shutter was snapped. His face wore a worried expression, as if more than the sun was bothering him; his hands disappeared behind his back, although whether this was merely his stance or his hands were tied behind him, Hamish could not tell. The background of the picture was in soft focus but you could tell that it had been taken somewhere in the countryside. However, no clue was offered as to whether it was inland, near the water, or somewhere in between.

What totally baffled Hamish, though, was a set of white lines superimposed across the photograph. Holding it up at an angle, studying it closely, Tyne declared that these lines had not been directly drawn on the paper, but on an original print of which this was a copy. Staring at the picture, Hamish tried to make sense of the diagram-like lines; they demarked various areas of Russel's body, forming a series of irregular shapes—some small, some large, and each bearing a hand-lettered number. With a sinking feeling, Hamish was suddenly sure that he'd seen those kind of markings before, but was unable to place where.

"Do you get the lines?" asked Tyne, turning the picture sideways.

"No, I don't," answered Hamish. "They look kind of familiar." But when Tyne threw him a look of disbelief, as if he *must* understand them, Hamish still couldn't put his vague recollection into words. Instead, he denied his irrational feeling of dread. "I just had the crazy notion that I'd seen this type of thing somewhere . . ."

Blagden Tyne, giving a discouraged shrug, had gone back to studying the picture when the phone in the booth behind them rang. Automatically, Hamish lifted the receiver, using his handkerchief to preserve any possible prints (Tyne had already ordered a forensics team to report to the booth—on the double).

The voice was small and distant, but unmistakable. "This is Paige Rathbin. They told me to tell you that if you look at the picture of Russel long enough, you'll probably figure out the meaning. Anyway, what they want from you, and proof that they mean business, is something you'll hear about on the broadcast tonight. Listen carefully to what you hear: it'll be the only time you'll be given the message. If you don't understand it, maybe Jenny Cobb can help; she got you into this mess." There was a pause, then: "This is Paige Rathbin. They told me to tell you that if you look at the picture of Russel long enough—" They heard the phone go dead and the dial tone begin; the receiver at the other end of the phone had been hung up.

Looking at Hamish, Tyne sighed in discouragement. "Well, I guess there's nothing to do until tonight—except maybe for you to try to figure out that diagram."

For a second, Hamish wasn't sure if Tyne might not be suggesting this as "busy work" to occupy the long hours until tonight. There was something in Tyne's voice that made Hamish suspect that Tyne had already guessed what the diagram was, but did not yet want to say. The FBI man changed the subject. "We might get some ideas from Jenny. She's a shrink; that damned diagram might mean something to her."

In silence, they climbed into the car and headed for the FBI setup at First Baptist, where Jenny was spending the day.

Hamish wanted her to be with him tonight, during the broadcast, but the idea of trying to make Martha accept that as a
police necessity was ludicrous. He settled back into the car
seat and tried to put the fears out of his mind as Tyne drove
him through town, down Limslee Avenue, until they pulled
up in front of the brownstone facade of First Baptist.

"*That* much? Too damned expensive."

"It's in good shape," the man said, kicking the tires in the
timeless gesture of the used car salesman. "New rubber.
Clean. Finish pretty fair. Okay, so the interior's a little beat
up. I'll knock off—" the salesman studied Kip for a moment,
trying to figure out how much the kid would go for. Finally he
decided that the denim windbreaker, the cheap pair of dark
glasses, the beat-up Levi's and scuffed shoes might say the kid
wouldn't pop for much, but the boy's manner said something
else: the teen-ager would pay because he wanted this pickup
for something not quite legit. "I'll knock off fifty for the interior work you'll need. It's a steal, but hell, I need the room
for new stuff coming in. Take it or leave it. That's the bottom
line."

"Fifty!" Kip looked outraged and started to walk off the
Bridgeport lot. The pickup was already overpriced by about
two hundred, he figured, but that wasn't the reason for his
performance. He wanted to act like any other kid buying a
car, and he had heard enough about how it was done to
know that this haggling was part of the game. Giving in too
quickly, without a fight, would make him too easy to remember—dark glasses, street-gang clothes, or not.

The salesman watched as Kip walked to the edge of the
lot, turned left, and started to walk down the street. In this
ageless game, it was the man who gave in first who lost, but
the pickup was way overpriced—by much more than the mere
two hundred that Kip was estimating—so the dealer had
plenty of leeway. "Kid—hey, kid." He watched Kip pause,
turn around, and then start slowly sauntering back, but not
all the way onto the lot. "Tell you what, kid," said the dealer.
"I'm not exactly saying that pickup's hot, see, but the papers
aren't quite what they should be. No sweat for you, but, it
could lose me my license. So I tell you. You can have it for
two-fifty less. How's that?"

Kip pretended to consider. He had extra plates, so the legitimacy of the car was no problem to him. "Deal," he said. Fifteen minutes later, he picked up K.K., parked around the corner in his Porsche, and signaled him to follow. They still had a tremendous amount of work to do before the pickup would be in shape for what was needed.

"It doesn't ring a bell at all?"

"Nothing. Except that it makes me feel Goddamned uncomfortable. I can't explain it."

Jenny exchanged a covert glance with Blagden Tyne, as if the meanings on the chart-like Polaroid should be obvious to anyone. From the way that Tyne acted, it was clear to Jenny they were obvious to him, too.

The three of them were sitting in Tyne's office, studying the photograph of Russel. Hamish would turn it this way then that way, look at it close up and then hold it off at a distance, but he seemed to be avoiding what was so clear to the other two.

Jenny tried pushing Hamish a little closer to the reality of the diagram. "It has to mean something. The man went to considerable trouble—the drawing, the numbering—so it's safe to assume that he had a reason. Trying to tell us something, I suppose." Leaning forward, Jenny took the Polaroid from Hamish and, for a minute, pretended to study it herself. "It reminds me a little of a phrenologist's chart. You know—with numbers to show the good parts and the bad parts, what's vital and what isn't." After handing the picture back to Hamish, she carefully watched him, waiting to see if any of her carefully planted clues penetrated his self-imposed blindness.

Shaking his head, Hamish put the picture down on Tyne's desk. "Maybe that's what it looks like to you, Jenny, but damned if I see it. All I've got is an uncomfortable, uneasy ache in my belly, telling me it means something bad."

Jenny wanted desperately to come out with it to Hamish, but she couldn't bring herself to. She pushed this thought one step further and, forcing herself, began. "Hamish, look—"

"So bad an ache in my belly that, in fact," Hamish said, as he was walking toward the door, "I'd like to borrow your can, Blag." Hamish didn't wait for an answer but continued on out the door, without stopping.

Jenny and Tyne stared at each other. "Maybe he honestly doesn't get it," suggested Tyne with a shrug. "He's too damned smart not to, but maybe . . ."

"He gets it. He gets it, but he won't let himself see it. That's why the sudden stomach ache when I began pushing him toward it."

"Shit."

Tyne threw up his hands in defeat.

With his head cocked to one side, Kip twisted the dials and listened. Throwing the switch to "Transmit," he quickly called off an improvised chant. As a "testing, testing" litany, it was curious: "The neck bones connected to the . . . shoulder bones; the shoulder bones connected to the . . . back bones; the back bones connected to the . . . thigh bones; and the Piper's got 'em all."

He was about to begin again when K.K. pulled his earphones off and signaled that he was receiving. On his face was an expression of both worry and impatience. "Dammit, Kip, that was kind of stupid, wasn't it?"

"If the FCC picked it up, they'll just think it was some CB buff playing games. You worry too much." K.K. muttered a reply, but flatly refused to be amused. "Your end all set?" Kip asked him.

"I could use your help."

"You know how to work the tape machine; the rest of it is all up to you, anyway."

"Okay, but I need someone to help hold—"

Kip vigorously shook his head. "Your department. All of it. And one that you'd better get going on right now—we need that tape in less than two hours, and it's going to take some editing. I'll wait here."

"Maybe Hamish was right. Deep down, maybe you *are* a sissy."

K.K. might have carried this line a little further—he felt betrayed because Kip wouldn't help him—but the expression on Kip's face stopped him. He was right.

Kip turned petulant. "Okay, I won't even watch. I'll stay up here."

Turning around sulkily—the hurt struck home—K.K. walked over to the cistern—they were parked in the clearing around it—and began lowering himself, step by step, down the ladder.

After waiting until K.K.'s head disappeared below the cement rim, Kip shut the pickup's door and turned up the radio so that the cab was filled with a burst of rock from a station in Bridgeport. Kip knew that the sounds from the cistern would still be audible in the truck. Perhaps it was his imagination, but Kip kept thinking that he could already hear them, even above the music.

Suddenly looking like a small boy, he covered both of his ears with his hands. But like all small boys, he kept lifting the hands off so that he could hear what both terrified and thrilled him.

Chapter 14 _____

*With kids to ransom you get what you
want pretty damn easily. It's better than
money anytime. Besides, in a place like
Greenport, everybody's got too much money
anyway.*

*Tonight will be tough on Hamish, maybe,
but he kept getting in the way. He got in the
way with Jenny, that broadcast of his got in
the way of people's understanding my plan,
and, hell, that smart cop's nose of his might
just have gotten in the way worst of all.*

*By tomorrow, he should be gone. Nose and
all. So long, Hamish.*

—TAPE-LOG OF THE PIPER,
ENTRY DATED JUNE 8.

"Texaco: 184,800 shares at 25⅝; down ⅜; ASA Limited: 175,400 shares at 20⅝, up 1⅞; and IBM, 143,900
shares: closing at 259⅜ off 2⅞. Total volume, New York
Stock Exchange: 1,859,000. Dow Jones: 685.71, down 9.39
at close. On the Amex, the Piper's reports indicate ..."

Paige Rathbin's voice, coming from Kip's mobile transmitter, had, over the last two weeks, picked up an almost
professional cadence. Only a 12-year-old's timbre labeled it as
a small boy playing announcer.

The special line rang stridently in Hamish's living room;
everyone jumped. Blagden Tyne picked up the phone and listened. "How come?" he suddenly asked. Everyone in the
room stared at Tyne, trying to read his expression. "*No
way?*" The voice on the other end talked some more. "I see,"
he said wearily. "Well, if it's that often, it's tough. Goddamn.
Try to get a fix on both of them, then." He hung up the
special phone and addressed himself to Hamish, ignoring the
rest of the people clustered around the simple pine and maple
furniture.

"This Piper guy must know what I'm thinking." Attacking Hamish's obvious confusion, Tyne explained that, unknown to anyone, the FBI and Federal Crime Bureau had pushed the FCC into sending more tracking units into town. There was, as there had been from the beginning, some question as to whether the additional units would be of any real help. But it was Tyne's idea that given *enough* units, these vans could blanket the town, the electronic direction finders on their roofs crisscrossing the town a square mile at a time. They had always failed in the past because the broadcasts were over before the FCC men could get a fix on the mobile transmitter. But by working small areas with an increased number of units, the FCC men should be able to home in on their vectors two or three times as fast as they had in the past.

"There's no way the Piper could have heard about it," said Tyne to Hamish, in frustration. "Local cops might unwittingly tip off someone, but only the FBI, the FCC, and the Federal Crime Bureau knew about these new units, or that they were starting tonight. Christ, we didn't even tell *you*. Anyway, tonight the guy's transmitting not just from *one* place but at least two. The tape from each spot barely lasts five seconds, then they switch to the alternate transmitter. Not a chance of getting a fix on them. It takes *some* timing to put those programs from two different places together neatly enough to sound so much like one program. Shit."

The people in Hamish's living room watched as Tyne walked over to the window, looking very much as if he might kick the wall in anger and frustration. It was quite a gathering—Chief Investigator Cummins of the State Police, Van Tassel of the Federal Crime Bureau, Hamish's deputy, Bill Littel, Blagden Tyne, of course, and Hamish. Over by the regular phone, two phone specialists from the FBI were also on hand.

Martha Hamilton didn't sit with the rest of them in the living room but had planted a chair in the doorway into the kitchen. Hamish had tried to persuade her not to listen to tonight's broadcast at all; she had been spared the details of the new picture of Russel with its curious lines and the baseball player doll. Still, she was on the edge of collapse. Sitting beside her, on one side, was Dr. Rimbaud, the family physician; earlier he had given her enough Thorazine to deck a horse, but Martha appeared unaffected. If what she would hear tonight on television was bad enough, the doctor knew that he would have to surrender to his first instinct and give her an injection that would completely knock her out. On the other side, sitting upright and prim, a hand clutching one of Martha's tightly, sat Emma Crane, a gaunt Grant Wood of a woman, who was Martha's closest confidante. When Martha told her of her initial suspicions about Jenny Cobb, Emma's reaction had been a simple question. To her, it explained everything: "Went to college, didn't she?"

Paige Rathbin's reading of the stock market leaders halted abruptly. A new voice, someone older but still a boy, took over. "Because of the unusual circumstances of tonight's transmission, the Piper has ordered me to relay a message to Chief of Police Hamish Hamilton. Message: The package you really want is in a booth two blocks further down the street—going south—from where you were instructed to find the phony one. While you're getting it, tapes of earlier broadcasts by other children will be replayed. You have ten minutes."

Hamish and Tyne stared at each other; the message was carefully enough coded so no outsider could get there first. Tyne picked up the special phone and barked his commands. "Unit three, proceed immediately to phone booth, corner of Greenport and Bleeker. Proceed two blocks south to where you will find another booth. Inside is a package; recover and bring to unit "A" command post immediately. Proceed with caution; you will be met by a representative of the explosive devices unit at recovery site." Tyne hung up only briefly, then began trying to reach the men of the explosive devices unit. The other men in the room were electrified, although baffled; the imitation bomb and the curiously chartered picture of Russel had been kept from them, as well as from Martha.

Across town, the same electricity charged the home of Senator Lloyd Blyden. He was already on the phone to Washington, yelling at someone on the other end. His aide was on another line to the Greenport Police Headquarters, trying to find out how he could reach Hamish. "I realize he has a personal crisis," said the aide smoothly, "but so do we. The sec-

ond voice on that broadcast—it was the Senator's son, Kevin.
No one knew that he was even missing."

Piece by piece, Kip's plan was coming together.

At the second phone booth, the package was discovered
hidden above the ventilator in the booth's ceiling. Impatiently, Hamish listened to a word-by-word description by two
men from the explosive devices unit's progress as they
gingerly—and with agonizing slowness—removed the package. Tyne read his mind.

"I know that it seems to take forever, Hamish. But look:
as soon as they get it checked out, they'll bring it back. If
you can, relax; just try to relax."

Only ten minutes later, they learned from the mobile unit
that the package was now being fluoroscoped. This was to see
if any wires or timing devices were inside. Almost simultaneously, Senator Blyden's son Kevin interrupted the
recordings of the other children with a new message for
Hamish. "I am speaking for the Piper . . ." Kevin's voice,
after so many nights of Paige Rathbin's, sounded deep and
mellifluous, even though he was only 17. "The number that
you should consider while you're waiting for the package—
assuming that you haven't gotten it by now—is the number
five. Number five."

Once again, the tapes of the children began. Several times,
earlier recordings of Paige Rathbin's references to the 'ultimate ransom' were played. Hamish and Tyne looked at
each other. The FBI car with the package—the fluoroscope
had pronounced it "clean"—was due momentarily. The phone
rang. "Yes?" Hamish said, after a nod from the FBI man
with the open line to the telephone company. "Yes, this is
Hamish Hamilton."

"This is Paige Rathbin. Do you have the package yet?
Probably not. Remember, the number is *five*." There was a
pause, then Paige returned with another of the Piper's outrageous little jokes. "In New Jersey, the number is 432-1212."
Just before the click of the receiver, Hamish had heard the
tape start to replay.

Numbly, Hamish studied the picture of Russel. The area
marked Number Five was a curious one, encompassing the
left side of Russel's head, part of the torso over his heart, and

running down his body to include a part of his left arm and hand. For no reason, a schooldays representation of a gerrymandered Congressional district ran through Hamish's head. From outside, a squeal of brakes announced the arrival of the explosives disposal unit with the package.

Almost before Hamish could reach out of the front door and take it in, Tyne snatched the package from the agent. "You sure it's clean?" he asked.

"Unless the guy's invented something new. No metal inside at all. Just cloth, I guess. And paper."

"What about plastique?"

"The firing device would show up."

"Dusted?"

"No prints. Outside, anyway."

The two of them, Hamish and Blagden Tyne, returned home. Everyone there turned and stared at them, their eyes automatically riveted on the package in Tyne's hands. Written boldly across the front of the wrapping in Magic Marker was a "#5." From the door to the kitchen, Emma Crane tightened her grip on Martha's hand, unconsciously pressing her lips tighter together as she did.

For a second, no one moved. Then, with a sigh, Tyne pulled the penknife from his pocket and began cutting the paper. Hamish watched as Tyne opened the box inside the wrapping. Slowly he pulled the cover off and lifted the tissue paper beneath. "Oh, Christ . . ." Tyne groaned.

Hamish had only a second to look over Tyne's shoulder before it happened. What he saw was difficult to believe. At the bottom of the box was Russel's baseball cap, cut in half. Wrapped around this was part of his Yankee jersey and the catcher's glove. Inside the hollow formed by these items, were two slips of paper, each with the same elaborately lettered "#5," as on the wrapping paper. Attached to one slip, and apparently glued to the jersey, was a perfect square of Russel's skin, the nipple from his chest a dull, flat red. Attached to the second slip were two fingers of his left hand, neatly and surgically amputated at the first knuckle, and stuck into the glove backward so that the tips projected from the fingers of the mitt.

But Hamish only had a second to study them, fighting the wave of nausea that swept through him. The moment that

Tyne saw what was inside, he had turned his back on the rest of the room. Hamish had automatically turned around with him. Only moments later, a tiny "ping" came from inside, and the contents of the box were violently thrown out, sailing across the room in various directions.

At the sight of Russel's fingers flying across the room, bouncing off a wall, one of them coming to rest on the thick-edged back of an overstuffed chair, Martha screamed a scream that sounded as if Russel's fingers were being pulled from her own hand. Then she fainted. Dr. Rimbaud was prepared for this possibility, but not for its timing. The sight of pieces of Russel flying through the air left the doctor so unnerved he momentarily forgot why he was there. With a limp crash, Martha landed on the floor at the feet of Miss Crane, who was already yelling for someone to help. The entire room was filled with noise, shouting, and confusion. Because of this, no one noticed that the Piper's mobile transmitter was now playing a macabre vocal from Cole Porter's "I Love All of You."

It was doubtful that anyone would have appreciated the humor anyway.

Half an hour later, Martha, given a massive dose of tranquilizers and barbituates, was sleeping the sleep of the dead. In the other bed—Hamish's—a fitful Emma Crane tossed uncomfortably, unsure and disoriented in these new and therefore hostile surroundings. Knowing that Ollie would hear of the matter anyway, Hamish went to see him, told him what he dared to of the situation, and said he thought it would probably be best if he stayed on with his friend, at least for a night or two. Their house, Hamish assured the boy's parents, was already under heavy police surveillance.

"Dad," said Ollie, "what did they mean when they said about—"

"I'm on my way to hear an FCC tape of the program now, Ollie. There was so much confusion at the house that I couldn't before."

"It was terrible, Dad. Those screams . . ."

"May have been faked," Hamish quickly finished. "This man we're dealing with—this Piper—is a nut, a sick-o. Don't take too much of what you hear at face value."

At Blagden Tyne's office, there appeared to be as many people as there had been at Hamish's house earlier. The addition of Senator Blyden's son to the kidnapped children produced an immediate reaction from Washington. Calls to various Senate colleagues resulted in threats of immediate investigations of both the FBI and the Federal Crime Bureau's lack of efficiency, as illustrated in Greenport; the President himself, an old friend of Blyden's, personally called the Senator to say that all Federal agencies available to him under law—as well as some which, strictly legally, were not—would help in finding the Senator's son and "those other poor, unfortunate children of Greenport." On top of this came an awesome nationwide public reaction. Up to this point, people had treated the disappearance, the kidnappings, even the one known killing, as something abstract, an unfortunate event that involved some rich kids in an Eastern suburb, a bizarre situation that was affecting other people and could never possibly happen to them. The press and the networks carried reports, as well as occasional excerpts of the broadcasts from the mobile transmitters, but the coverage had not been consistent or very complete. After tonight, all of this was to change.

"Hamish," said Tyne, holding the FCC reel between the palms of his hands, "these aren't very pretty to hear. We could edit out the worst parts, if you like—"

Hamish set his mouth. "What I'd like is to hear them all. And also the pathologist's opinion whether—"

"It isn't a question of opinion. Two different pathologists have examined the tissue and report that all of it came from a person most likely alive after the 'operations.' And from a person presumably alive at this moment—barring, of course, massive hemorrhaging."

"Which is to be doubted could happen by accident, only design," cut in Dr. Trackman of Greenport Hospital. Trackman, Chief of Medicine at the hospital, had been called in by Dr. Rimbaud, who felt himself in far over his head. "I say this," continued Trackman, "because the person or persons who performed the surgery appears to have a considerable knowledge of medicine and biology."

"The tapes," insisted Hamish. He was developing a

paranoid suspicion that all of the men in the room were trying to keep him from hearing them, a suspicion at least partially rooted in truth.

"Hamish, I think . . ." Jenny said. For the first time, Hamish realized that she was there with the rest of them. She suddenly seemed alien, a stranger, someone that he had once known but a long time ago, and in some different place.

"The tapes," he repeated, staring at Tyne.

"Very well." With a sigh, Tyne walked over to the tape machine and placed the reel on the tape deck, watching it self-thread over the playback head.

It was immediately clear why both Tyne and Jenny had tried to spare Hamish the playing of the total tape. It was enough for a stranger to be exposed to it; for a father, the tape was agony.

"Today, at the second phone booth," said Kevin Blyden, again speaking for the Piper, "you received one section of upper pectoral, and two fingers from the left hand—the midfinger and the first. A portion of Area Number Five. It could have been worse. I assume you have had these tidbits examined and know now they are indeed from your son, as well as verified they were removed from a living person. Having you as a father might not exactly come under the heading of 'living,' but that's another story. Anyway, tonight —and every night hereafter—you'll receive another installment of Russel—we'll let you know ahead of time from which section—unless you follow the orders you are about to receive to the letter. You won't like them, but they are the ground rules. They're not a part of the 'ultimate ransom'; the 'ultimate ransom' wasn't designed for hired help like you. They're just a demand to get you out of the way, because you're a troublemaker. You will probably be tempted to try getting around the order. Don't."

There was a rustle of paper, then Paige Rathbin's voice again took over the reading. "The fingers were removed at approximately five this afternoon. Surprisingly, the operation was not the most painful of the three and, due to quick cauterization, did not cause a significant loss of blood. Before the removal, Russel was adamant about not cooperating." There were sounds of Russel arguing with someone—at one

point, he could be heard telling his captors to "go to Hell"—
followed by a suddenly apprehensive tone in his voice. Apparently, he could not believe what he saw about to happen
to him. The piercing screams that quickly came on top of
this were all mixed up with thrashings, grunts, and panicked
gasps.

"Most painful of all," Paige continued, "was the chest
area, since it involved peeling back a section of skin attached
directly to muscle tissue . . ." A jumble of sobs came from
Russel. Suddenly out of this grisly background rose the voice
of Ramsey Lakewood's fine, thin boy soprano: "Oh, for the
wings, for the wings of a dove . . . ," his singing as pure and as
graceful as ever. Abruptly, in a voice choked with sobs, Russel
could be heard pleading with his father—tearfully apologizing
for his own cowardice as he did—begging him to give his
kidnappers whatever they were demanding. Leaning over, one
eye on Hamish, Tyne stopped the tape.

Hamish sat rooted in his chair. The juxtaposition of Russel's shrieks, with the Piper's sick humor in adding Ramsey
Lakewood's singing, left him not just sickened, but stunned.
Numbly, his head shook slowly back and forth, his eyes
blinking as he tried to find some reason for what he had
heard. "I tried to get you not to listen, Hamish," said Tyne,
softly.

Hamish's voice was flat and expressionless; it was, Jenny
suspected, his way of controlling himself, of keeping the lid
on a set of emotions that were too strong to have shown. "The
rest of it."

"Look, Hamish," said Jenny, shooting a pleading look for
help at Tyne. "Give yourself a breather . . ."

Hamish vigorously shook his head. "No. *Now*. And everybody stop treating me like a cripple."

Tyne sighed and walked back toward the machine. "The
rest isn't so bad, anyway. Just some demands you're not going to like." Once more, from the tape-deck, came the voice
of Kevin Blyden. "If you ever want to see Russel alive again,
I order you—no if's, and's, or but's—to leave Greenport immediately. You can make moving arrangements later. You
can sell your house later. You can bring your wife later. You
can find a job later. But, as long as you stay in town, you will
keep receiving pieces of Russel. Until, well—eventually we'll

run out of things we can cut off without killing him. You have until ten tomorrow morning. The next amputation, disfigurement, and mutilation party is scheduled for eleven A.M., so the smart money says that you better leave before then. You may consider this tough and cruel, but you haven't, after all, been very kind to me. You publicly accused me of being psychotic, of not meaning what I said about the 'ultimate ransom,' and even of being queer. Okay. People like you aren't nice to have around. So, by ten tomorrow morning, clear out of Greenport, or you will receive another early Christmas package. Have fun, wherever you go. Personally, I recommend the West."

The transmission ended with yet another Cole Porter, this one a torchy vocal of "I've Got You Under My Skin." For a long time no one said anything. Hamish stared at the tape machine, as if the answer might somehow lie in the gleaming chromium and softly glowing dials; the loose end of the tape made a strange flapping sound each time the reel revolved and slapped it against the playback head.

His hands clasped together between his knees, Hamish studied the patterns in the concrete floor of the First Baptist, the flapping of the tape as insistent and as illogical as the sudden rush of decisions he had to make.

For a long time, in the chill darkness of the spring night, Kip sat with his back against the cold dampness of the cistern, watching the clouds scud against the stars. Shivering, he pulled his jacket tighter around himself and listened to the soft hum of the wind through the pine trees, the music that had always sounded to him like a feather being brushed across the strings of a harp. Quite suddenly, after coming back from the broadcast in the van, he found himself wondering about his whole plan, how he had gotten so irretrievably far into it, and why he was out here, with a collection of children— many of them personal friends from Country Day—locked deep under the ground beneath him. His first instinct was to blame all of these things on K.K., but for once, even in his own mind, he could not make the accusation stick. The plan was his, the energy behind it was his, the commitment was his—K.K. had only been his instrument.

As if drawn by a magnet, Kip lowered himself down the

ladder and walked softly down the corridor of the underground prison. He paused, silently drawing back the small iron door over the peephole, and peered inside; the children were asleep, making soft, sighing noises as they restlessly tossed on the hard stone floor, wrapped in the thin blankets that were all he could provide them. Moving on, he noiselessly slipped into the room where Russel was. To one side was the "operating table"—actually a raised rolling platform that K.K. bought secondhand from a cutrate supply house in Bridgeport—on which the mutilations took place. On the other side was an iron cot where Russel lay asleep on a thin mattress beneath a collection of heavy blankets. The mattress, the blankets, and the sleep were all at K.K.'s insistence; he had pumped Russel full of Demerol and sleeping capsules to make sure that he drifted into temporary oblivion after the operation. As he had told Kip, "Otherwise, the kid'll slip into shock."

Russel now lay flat on his back with one arm thrown protectively over his head as if to ward off dangers that might attack him while asleep. The heavily bandaged area of his left chest was visible above the top of the blanket; his hand was also swathed in gauze and adhesive tape. For a long time Kip stood beside the bed, staring at the boy, and Russel, as if he could feel the stare, stirred uncomfortably in his sleep. Kip could not explain it, but when K.K. originally proposed the dismemberments, the idea had seemed appalling to Kip, so appalling he insisted he be absent when the operations were performed. Yet, staring at Russel, he felt a surge of excitement; tentatively, one finger reached out and touched the warm, smooth skin inside the boy's upper arm. Perhaps, Kip thought, he owed it to the plan to be present at the next session; maybe he should supervise, even be a part of it. Kip brought himself up shortly. Unknown to K.K., he had slipped back down into the cistern during the first surgery session, standing quietly outside the door while K.K. cut, cauterized, and bandaged, feeling strangely affected by Russel's screams. That was enough. K.K. was sick and enjoyed things like that; he himself could not afford to sink to the same level.

With a snort, Kip spun on his heel and marched from the room, climbed the ladder, and ran the whole distance back to the house, as if pursued by some dark thing that was chasing him and could only be left behind if he ran fast enough.

"What are you going to do? It's one hell of a spot." The three of them—Hamish, Blagden Tyne, and Jenny—were sitting in the small garden behind First Baptist, inhaling the soft but already chill air of early night. All of them had tried, one way or another, to discuss irrelevancies, to shake the pall of Russel's agony from their minds for a few moments. But it was impossible.

Hamish picked up a handful of pebbles and began tossing them into the darkness beyond the church. "I don't know. Easy enough to leave here in a hurry like that Piper bastard demands. The bank will advance me money on the house; the mortgage is all paid up. That's not the real problem. I just got this gut feeling that doing what the guy demands is wrong. That it would be a dumb maneuver."

Tyne quickly picked it up. "I think your hunch is right, Hamish. Stretching out your answer to the Piper's demands is your only real guarantee that Russel will stay alive. It's like any kidnapping: once the kidnappers have the money, there's no great need for the victim anymore. Up until they get what they want, the kid alive is their ace in the hole; then he becomes a threat to them. Kids remember things. Voices. Whispered names. Smells. Sounds. The victim becomes a problem, not an asset. So by giving in to the Piper and leaving town, you may eliminate the one reason they have for not killing Russel."

"I buy all of that. But I can't stay in town and have Russel delivered to me a piece at a time."

Tyne said, "Right now, the important thing is to face what you're going to do."

"I guess the first thing to figure is whether to give in to the Piper and leave town, and maybe get Russel killed because he's no longer of use to them. Or to stay and maybe get Russel killed one piece at a time."

"I don't think that you *could* really leave, Hamish." Jenny raised her head and looked him hard in the eye. "You're too strong a guy to sit in a hotel waiting for someone to call and tell you what's happened."

"Maybe I could just pretend to leave. You know, grab

Martha—*Christ*—and hide out somewhere. Say I was leaving, but stay right here in town."

Tyne shook his head. "Pretty damned risky. Anyway, he'd probably insist on a phone number for you out West—or wherever he expects you to go—so he could call and check that you were there for real. He might also insist on an address to mail you stuff." Tyne blanched. Given the circumstances, this was an unfortunate example.

"Risky, my ass. Not if we do it right. We get a number in, say, Salt Lake City—anyway, someplace with call-forwarding—and use his own gimmick right back on him. The Piper calls me there, I answer here. Or some kind of tie-line. We beat the bastard with his own system. As for the mail, hell, the FBI must be able to set up a dummy mail drop . . ."

Sitting in a stiff, wooden chair, Jenny had been leaning forward, rubbing her temples, thinking. Abruptly, with a toss of her head that sent her golden hair flying, she sat upright, looking first at Hamish, then at Tyne. "There's a lot to be said for the idea. This Piper has been torturing Hamish by torturing Russel. I don't know why. But if you play to his ego by pretending to leave town, and if we can find some way to open a dialogue with him—even an indirect one—then, we'll be that much closer to nailing him. Crawl to him—publicly. Appeal to his hunger for power, his need to be noticed. Try and get some response out of the Piper, even an argument."

"How?" Tyne's voice was cold and skeptical. "It's great to talk about all these things, but how do you reach him? Hamish has until ten in the morning." He glanced down at his wristwatch. "That's only twelve and a half hours from now. So . . . how?"

"I go on the air at seven in the morning. That's how. In the meantime, Blag, we should start setting something up, so it looks like I'm leaving, and someplace where I can hide . . ."

For a brief moment, the three of them stared at one another. They had a sinking feeling that, once again, they might be underestimating the Piper.

And they were right.

Chapter 15 _____

*I keep wondering why Jenny and her thing
for Hamish bugs me like it does. I'm not a
jealous guy. In fact, I don't remember being
jealous since I was six or seven and Carey
was born. Damn, but that got to me.*

*Everybody, even Mom, making a big deal
out of it. Especially Mom. And it wasn't too
long after that that she took up with the pills
and I can remember thinking maybe it was
Carey's fault somehow. Stupid.*

—TAPE-LOG OF THE PIPER,
ENTRY DATED JUNE 8 (P.M.).

"School called," Mr. Grolier said, looking up from his paper.
"Everything's canceled. Except for the final Glee Club
concert at Fairfield." Kip's father lowered the paper and
stared at his son, dressed in his blazer and tie, all set to have
breakfast and head for school. "But, you're not in the Glee
Club, are you, Kip?" Kip, thunderstruck by this sudden
change in events and all that it meant to his plans, shook his
head numbly. "I didn't think so. Anyway, that's the end of
the year, as far as you're concerned. With all this crazy stuff
going on, I think they were stupid not to close weeks ago."

Kip was still having a hard time accepting the news. "They
said *everything's* canceled? Graduation, finals, the works?"

His father's head rose again. "Everything. Only sensible
thing to do." Mr. Grolier smiled grimly. "If things had kept
on, there wouldn't have been anybody left to graduate anyway."

"Daddy!" Dee looked up sharply from her grapefruit, with
a reproachful expression. "All those children. And you make
a crack like that."

"Don't be so damned uppity, young lady. That's the way
things are, and there's no use crying about it. If the school
had had any brains—not just Country Day, *all* of them—

some of this mess would never have happened. Anyway, the net of it is, your school's already closed, Dee, and yours, Kip, just folded on you. Hello, summer." With a stern look at each of them, Mr. Grolier retreated behind his paper once more.

Kip was recovering. Plans were going to have to be switched. He had expected trouble, but thought that, with so few days left to go, Country Day would finish the year out. "Did they say how come the Glee Club thing was still on?"

His father, giving up on the paper momentarily to attack the eggs, searched his memory. "Said something about it being in another town. Fairfield, Greenwich, I don't remember. And that just because of the trouble here, they didn't want to disappoint the other kids by canceling the arrangements made with our Glee Club. Said it was safe enough."

Her father's earlier grim humor returned to haunt Dee, and her mouth twitched sourly. "I don't think anything's safe anymore."

Mr. Grolier stared at her for a second, shrugged, and buried himself back behind his paper. He didn't even look up when the stuttering strains of Chopin drifted down from his wife's retreat upstairs; for a second, Dee appeared to listen, then sighed and ignored it too. Kip looked at both of them, squirming in anger, and finally gulped his coffee down. Unnoticed, unappreciated, ignored, the Chopin struggled bravely on.

Sleepily, Hamish looked out through his living room window and studied the people loading his station wagon. Ollie was helping Patrolmen Larkin and Sturgis of the Greenport Police Department carry out his suitcases, clothes bags, typewriter, linen, sporting equipment, and a small number of books. These were stacked on the two rear sets of seats of the Datsun; Sergeant Fuller stood at the door, appearing to help occasionally. In actuality, he was watching for any cars that slowed down enough to study the loading. For Hamish's instincts told him the Piper would watch his loadup and departure with great care, probably from a car that would come driving by the place to check. Hamish's instincts had been right, even if his assumption of how this surveillance would be accomplished was not.

A yawn racked Hamish and he struggled to stifle it. The day before had been traumatic, and the night even worse, and Hamish was exhausted. Dr. Rimbaud had been successful in bringing Martha out of her stupor the night before. The problem was that once awake again, there was no chance of Martha going back to sleep. She had stayed up all night, mostly, it had seemed to Hamish, badgering, berating, and accusing him. As a result, he had gotten practically no sleep himself. Watching Ollie almost drop his typewriter, Hamish winced; Ollie must have spent a sleepless night too.

Carefully, slowly, Hamish last night tried to explain the situation to Martha. Separating her, even with Dr. Rimbaud's assistance, from Emma Crane was not easy; Emma was a highly inquisitive and suspicious person.

He would be starting at ten in the morning for Salt Lake City, Hamish had told Martha; she would be staying behind to act as conduit for further word from the Piper. Deceiving Martha was something he had finally decided was necessary. He trusted her, and he knew that in anything involving Russel's safety, Martha would do anything that she was told to; but Hamish did *not* trust Martha's ability to withstand pressure. And he was afraid that if she knew that he hadn't really left, she might fall apart the moment the slightest thing went wrong and tell someone like Emma Crane, or try to reach him, or turn to Alan Whitemore in desperation. The game would be over. Her reaction was about what he could have expected.

"You're going? Just leaving? Climbing into your car without any idea of what's happened to Russel? My God, Hamish, you're incredible."

"I don't have much choice. If I don't go, they'll send him—a piece at a time—back to us, until—well, you know. . . ."

"What guarantee do you have that they won't anyway?"

"No guarantee. Just a little bit better chance. You'll have to stay and be the conduit. I'll give the Piper my number in Salt Lake City—it's a motel out there that Blagden Tyne knows about—and the Piper already knows ours here. The Piper guy will call one or the other of us, I guess. First, I have to get on the air and convince them that your staying here is all right; it's me that they want to hurt, so I don't think that should be too much—"

Martha was looking at him strangely; some inner radar had scanned the horizon and sensed a bogie. "What do you mean, it's *you* they want to hurt? They're torturing Russel."

Hamish was tired—exhausted—or he never would have let himself be caught off-guard and answered her question the way that he did, "The plan we had—my broadcast—what I said—was all done to flush the man out, to make him come after me. Instead, he went after Russel. No one's to blame, it's just one of those things the best psychiatrist couldn't anticipate happening."

For a moment, Martha just stared at Hamish. Then the words slowly sank in, were arranged in her mind, and put together in an inevitable conclusion. All of Emma Crane's speculations and dark suspicions formed themselves into an inescapable cloud of dark wind, fanning Martha's own worst fears and hurts. Watching her face, Hamish realized he had said not merely too much, but all of the wrong things; anything that he said now could only make the blunder seem worse. Martha suddenly rose to her feet and threw the coffee in his face. In spite of the shock, he stood silently where he was, wiping the coffee from his shirt and hair with his handkerchief.

"You bastard. You filthy bastard. You gamble with your own son's life. You cost him two fingers and God knows what else with your policeman's games. And why? Because your whore-lady shrink tells you to. You don't even consider her to blame, you say—'it's just one of those things no psychiatrist could anticipate,' you say—you forgive her and make excuses for her and lie for her because you like to stick it in her. That's why. And the reason he took Russel and is doing those incredible things to him is because she 'had a plan,' you say. You goddamned fucking prick—"

Before Hamish had even realized what was happening, Martha had leaped at him, her nightgown and bathrobe wildly flapping behind her, tearing at his face, kicking him, biting him. Hamish staggered backward, his hands frantically trying to protect his face from her fingernails, but the wall behind him prevented him from moving back any further. Finally he was able to get his hands around both of her wrists, and, struggling to hang on to them, began yelling for Dr. Rimbaud, who was still downstairs with Emma Crane.

They seemed to burst through the door almost simultaneously with his shouts. Actually, they had been halfway up the stairs when Hamish first started yelling, for Martha's shrieks and wild screaming had brought them out of their chairs and on their way long before he thought of calling for them. Together, the three of them wrestled Martha back onto the bed, her accusations against Hamish and Jenny punctuated by sobs and cries. Now, standing by the window, Hamish looked back on the scene with wonder. For a few moments, Martha had seemed to be more animal than human.

Rimbaud had slapped her hard, twice, across the face. "Stop it! Stop it, Martha," he had yelled at her. "Stop it, or I'll have to put restraints on you and take you to the sanitarium. Stop it." The mention of the sanitarium seemed to quiet her down quickly; her mother, Hamish remembered, died in a state hospital. But she continued to cry and swear. "That's better, Martha," Dr. Rimbaud said, pulling a syringe from his black bag and sticking the needle through a rubber membrane to draw off a clear fluid. "I can't give her much," he whispered to Hamish. "Part of the problem, I think, is the combination of ups and downs she's getting from all these shots."

Emma Crane snorted. "Shots, baloney. Jenny Cobb up and down is what," she hissed.

Whatever Rimbaud injected seemed to have an immediate effect; the crying continued, but the oaths disappeared, replaced by an uneven moaning. As Emma Crane's remark sank in, Dr. Rimbaud looked curiously at Hamish. His sideways glance took in the blood welling from the fingernail scratches down the left side of Hamish's face. Helping Emma tuck Martha back under the covers, he turned toward Hamish. "You'd better let me do something for that. You're a mess."

Putting his hands to the side of his face, Hamish was aware, for the first time, of how deeply Martha had driven her nails. "Damn."

"This is going to hurt," Rimbaud said, moistening a piece of cotton with something from his bag. "But you'll live."

A sudden deep intake of air came from Hamish. Rimbaud had been right.

Hamish sighed, thinking back as he watched Ollie tying a pair of skis to the ski-carrier on top of the Datsun. The same scene was studied with intense interest from the back of a black Volks van, parked a little up the street. K.K. had been there since early this morning—since about five A.M., in fact—giving the impression that the driverless van had been there all night. Kip realized that a car driven past Hamish's house often enough to get a real idea of whether the packing and departure was genuine or not would be spotted and, after hearing Hamish's first broadcast appeal last night, had worked this plan out with K.K.

"Do you think it's on the up and up?" K.K. asked. "All that pleading and begging. The crawling to you. The decision to leave town. It doesn't sound like Hamish. Maybe it's a trap."

The only answer K.K. got from Kip was a disgusted look.

For without realizing it, Jenny had found the combination to Kip: pride. Hamish's groveling in public, over the air at that, satisfied Kip's need and longing for power. In his own mind, Kip had already won.

At eight that morning, still exhausted from his confrontation with Martha and then his second broadcast, Hamish jumped slightly at the sound of his phone ringing. The two FBI technicians had gone through their routine, and Tyne watched Hamish's face, as he listened to Kevin Blyden's voice coming out of the squawk box. "Your offer to leave town is accepted. I'm feeling generous. Mrs. Hamilton may stay; you are correct in pointing out that she can serve as a conduit for information. In fact, she even looks like a conduit, but who else would marry a guy like you? The telephone number of your hotel in Salt Lake City and its address should be read over the six P.M. news tonight. I am pleased you have taken back so many of the unfair things you said about me during your news conference. But don't attempt any tricks, or Russel will be sent back as a smorgasbord. Have a good time in Salt Lake."

One hour and forty minutes later, at 9:40, twenty minutes short of Hamish's ten o'clock deadline, the pair of eyes watching from the rear of the black Volks van saw Hamish emerge from his house, shake hands with the three policemen on the street, throw his arm around Ollie and hug him, and then, after checking to see that the skis were tightly fastened, climb into the Datsun and drive away. Because Kip was afraid that the street might be watched by the FBI (it was), K.K. didn't climb in behind the driver's seat for another full hour; he remained lying down in the back and listened to the radio reports of their exploits. With a satisfied smile, K.K. listened as the news broadcasts played sections of the tapes from the other children. (Only one station carried Russel Hamilton's screams as he was mutilated; the balance of the news outlets considered them too grisly for airing.)

A little later, out by the cistern, K.K. met with Kip. The closing of Country Day was putting a crimp in their plans, but Kip had used the time alone out there to figure several alternatives. A couple of telephone calls he had made from the house had given him the answers that he was after. "We go today," he told K.K. "It's now or never." Kip paused and cocked his head toward him. "Also, I think we should send another instalment of Russel along to his mother. Just a little one. To make sure that Hamish is gone and really gone for good."

The phone rang at least three times before Hamish even walked over to it; finally, after letting the intercom buzz twice, he picked up the receiver. "Hello?" he said tentatively.

"Just testing, Hamish. I wanted to make sure that everything was working. Obviously, if you left at ten, you couldn't be at an Albany motel until this evening. Even the way *you* drive." Blagden Tyne's voice had an optimistic sound to it, and Hamish wondered if that was the way that he really felt, or whether it was merely an attempt to keep a worried father's spirit up. "Once you're due there, the operator, besides answering with the motel's name, will buzz so that it sounds like she's trying to get your room. We'll do the same thing when you presumably arrive in Salt Lake. It's a pretty convincing setup—we just did a dry-run on it."

"It damned well better be." Hamish, holding onto the phone on its long extension, paced the small room, his feet making a hollow echoing sound on the bare cement floor.

Tyne's voice, still deliberately cheerful, came at Hamish

again through the receiver. "And either you'll have to stop
pacing, or we'd better get you a rug; I can hear the sound of
your feet over the phone. Even in Albany, motel rooms have
carpets."

"This place could use a few other little touches, too."

Hamish was dead right. He was installed in a windowless,
cement vault, one flight below the basement of First Baptist.
No one seemed too sure why the room was even there, since
most of the sub-basement was given over to the two furnaces,
the ventilating ducts, what at one time had been coal bins,
and tanks for the oil burner's supply.

Lighting was provided by two fixtures of incandescent brilliance, and the bathroom—actually a small lavatory further
down the same wall of the sub-basement—had had to be broken into from Hamish's quarters so that he could go to the
bathroom without being visible to the sexton or anyone else
who might be working down in the church's bowels. For air,
the room had had nothing more than a ventilating shaft.

Besides the telephone, the cell contained a stark metal
bed—the kind found in army barracks—four hard wooden
chairs, a table, and a television set. Stacked against one wall,
almost as high as the ceiling, was a pile of electronic gear:
amplifiers, pre-amplifiers, tuners, speakers, oscilloscopes, and
what appeared to be miles of wiring. This was pure sham; the
FBI men, first making sure that the sexton and one of his
helpers was down in the sub-basement, began carrying in all
of this equipment early this morning; the cot had not been
brought in until they were equally sure that there was no one
around. This way, Tyne figured, the sexton, although warned
not to tell anyone what was going on in the basement of his
church, would be sure to spread the word that the FBI had
expanded its operations into his sub-basement and was even
using the church vault for electronic eavesdropping devices.

All of this elaborate subterfuge was to keep word of
Hamish's continued presence in Greenport a secret. The sub-
basement vault had been chosen because it would provide
easy access to Hamish for both Tyne and Jenny; by now everyone in town knew that First Baptist was the FBI's working
headquarters, so their comings and goings from the church
would seem perfectly logical. Hamish himself had arrived at
about the same time as the steel bed; he had driven his car as

far as Interstate 95, followed by an FBI car to make sure that no one was tailing him. No one was. Just short of the ramp to I-95, Hamish slipped out of his car and into a panel truck, which had taken him back to Greenport, backed up to the basement loading area, and unloaded him along with a supply of crates and files. Then, an agent drove Hamish's car on to the Hudson Motel in Ravena, a few miles from Albany, and checked in, using Hamish's name.

The FBI in Albany had decided against using the call-forwarder, describing it as too unreliable; Tyne had agreed, citing the kidnapper's familiarity with the device. Instead, the FBI had installed a special line to take any calls Hamish might receive at the motel; it was an open line from the motel switchboard back to Hamish's phone at First Baptist.

"We're having a small meeting in your room in about an hour," Tyne suddenly said.

"Meeting?"

"Meeting, conference, strategy session—whatever you want to call it."

"Any word from Martha?" Hamish asked.

"Mad as hell about your going. Yelling like crazy. Couldn't be doing any better if we coached her ourselves."

"Ollie?"

"See you in half an hour."

By now, Hamish was so tuned to disaster that his first instinct was to believe that Tyne's sudden obliqueness meant that there had been new trouble. But he felt that he was close enough to Tyne at this point; that the man would have leveled. Listlessly, he switched on the television set, using a set of plug-in earphones. Daytime television, he discovered, was even worse than nighttime. But, not as bad, he decided, as the news broadcast that followed *Let's Make a Deal*. The program included tapes from last night's torture session with Russel, as well as Hamish's own broadcast of early this morning. The first made him shudder; the second made him cringe.

The knock on the door came—first two raps, then three fast ones. When there was no reaction, the same rhythmic pattern of knocks was repeated. Finally came the sound of a key being turned inside the door. The door opened a crack, and the dim face inside saw that it was Kip. "Come in, darling," said a weary voice, and threw the door open far enough to admit him.

As soon as he was inside, the door was closed and locked behind him; Kip blinked, trying to adjust his eyes to the sudden semi-darkness of his mother's room. She once was a vibrantly beautiful woman, but the ravages of time and drugs had taken a heavy toll; her skin was sallow, her cheeks sunken, her eyes hollow. The hair, in which she had taken such pride, hung loosely down around her shoulders; it had been combed, but there was a suggestion of matted snarls in the way its brittle grayness hung around her face.

"Can't we have a little light, Mom? It's a beaut of a day."

"No." His mother spoke sharply and firmly as she moved away from him. Kip had never been sure if she clung to this dimness trying to hide—even from herself—the way she looked, or because strong light had a painful effect on her. Sometimes, when she was on a real high, she would allow him to pull up the blackout curtains and flood the room with sunshine; other times, she would insist on the sort of perpetual twilight she was living in today.

He handed her the bottle of pills that he had gotten her this morning from Dr. Demerest, one of the dozen or so doctors who unwittingly provided her with a continual overdosages. "This is all I had time for this morning, but for God's sake, don't lose the bottle like you did that last one. I had to swipe these from the drugstore last night, and one of these days I'm going to get caught." A thought crossed his mind. "You should have some of the old ones left, anyway. Do you?"

His mother's voice suddenly took on a whining quality, like a little girl caught eating too much ice cream. "I was so nervous, Kip. It was all that waiting. I needed more." She turned away. "No, I don't have any left."

"Damn." On top of all that he had to do right now, the last thing Kip had time for was getting prescriptions from other doctors and taking them to the druggists in other towns to be filled. The cross his mother represented never felt heavier, and with the plan coming to a critical stage, it seemed as if it might cause the whole thing to crumble. The resentment abruptly boiled over. "Why, dammit, why? Why did you ever let yourself get on the stuff? That crazy shrink . . . and you don't have the guts to beat it. You don't even *try* to stop. Jesus, I can do just so much . . ."

His mother began crying softly. "I *have* tried to stop—you sound like—I had some money once—your father got it away from me and put it in some kind of trust—he and the lawyers—they said if they didn't I'd just spend it all on fixes . . . But Kip, darling Kip, I've tried to stop—it's just that—"

Kip was stunned. He had always assumed—in fact, he thought he remembered her telling him—that this was their secret, his mother's and his, and that, no, his father didn't know anything about the drugs. Yet, as he thought about it, that had never really made sense. His father wasn't the kind of passive man to let his wife suddenly resign from the world without a struggle; the psychiatrists had been rebuffed, but his father had never pushed the matter. He had just let her crawl away and hide. Not like his father at all—unless he had a good reason. His father, Kip suddenly realized, had plenty of good reasons. The bastard knew that if she'd been institutionalized, everyone would have found out what was wrong with her, so his father had allowed her to stay as she was, withdrawn into her two rooms upstairs here. She was less of a public liability this way, less of a threat to his business reputation, less of a detractor from his carefully nurtured social standing as "that absent Mrs. Grolier" than as "that junkie Mrs. Grolier."

With a sigh, Kip turned back toward her at the sound of her crying; the sight of her twisting her hanky between her hands and the tears running down her ruined face could always destroy Kip, and something inside him wanted to reach out to her, to hold her and comfort her. Instead, he offered a kind of comfort probably more appreciated: "I'll try to get some more, Mom, I'll try. But I've so much I have to do now . . . today . . . so many things."

His mother had just swallowed one of the pills from the bottle he'd given her and was suddenly relaxed—long, Kip knew, before the pill could have had any effect, or, for that matter, have even dissolved. But the mere fact she now had a new supply and the reassurance of more to come changed her completely. She smiled, traces of the same warm smile that he could remember from early childhood flooding his memory. "I know, Kip darling, I know you do."

Kip looked up sharply, feeling a small shudder run through him. She said those words almost as if she knew what he had to do. Blinking, he dismissed the thought. Leaning over and kissing her, Kip quickly went from the room.

Chapter 16 _____

*All my scheduling got loused up by the
Country Day closing. But with Hamish out of
the way now, I ought to be able to pull it off
anyway.*

*I mean, I think he's out of the way. His
broadcast this morning was certainly convincing; the guy sounded like he was crying. But,
I'll have to check out his story carefully; he's
got a mind like a steel trap.*

*Which reminds me, I've got to tell K.K. to
get some bear traps to set out around the
edge of the clearing. With that many people
inside the cistern, some kid might just make it
out. Maybe they should be called boy traps.*

*K.K. would love that. Clang! And you've
got yourself one boy.*

—TAPE-LOG OF THE PIPER,
ENTRY DATED JUNE 9.

Hamish knew it the moment that Tyne and Jenny walked in
through his door. A foreboding of disaster had been building
in him ever since his earlier talk with Tyne, when he had first
heard about this meeting. The man had struck Hamish as
being evasive in his conversation, a quality unusual for Tyne.
Something, Hamish felt, was not being told to him.

But it was the expressions on their faces that was the give-
away: Tyne looked grim, while Jenny looked deeply troubled.
"Okay," said Hamish, after studying them for a second.
"What's happened? Is he dead? Level with me. What?"

Silently, Tyne pulled a folded piece of brown wrapping paper from his pocket and smoothed it out on the small table in
front of Hamish; across its center, written in the same bold
Magic Marker lettering as the package that had been taped
to the phone booth, was an elaborate "#6."

Tyne said, "Alan Whitemore found it in the glove compartment of his car, a couple of hours ago. Two toes from the right foot. We wanted to run some tests before telling you about it; the pathologist says that the toes, too, were removed from a living person. So Russel's still alive, at least."

A wave of relief, so strong that Hamish found himself on the edge of laughter, swept across him. Ever since Tyne's call, his sudden evasiveness had thoroughly convinced Hamish that Russel had been found dead. "Thank God," Hamish said as he sat down again. The relief was suddenly replaced by anger. A picture of what the loss of two toes— didn't he remember reading somewhere that that could completely cripple you?—would mean to anyone as physically active as Russel, flashed through his brain, followed by a painful confusion as to what was demanded of him. "I did what the bastard told me. Left town. Christ, what does he want?" His eyes opened wide to stare at the creased wrapping paper on the table, then raised themselves to Tyne and Jenny. "Or does he know somehow that I didn't leave town?"

Jenny had seated herself in a hard wooden chair, at right angles to Hamish, and she took both of his hands in hers. "I don't think so, Hamish. That crazy, macabre sense of humor of the Piper's would have put the package somewhere else besides Alan Whitemore's glove compartment, if he wanted to tell you that. Taped to this building. Or to Tyne's car. Or to the police station."

Tyne pulled a small reel of tape from his pocket. "Besides, there's the tape that he sent along. In it, the Piper calls this package his 'insurance.' A reminder of what will happen if you don't follow his instructions."

"Oh, God," groaned Hamish. "What are they doing to that kid?" From out of nowhere, a new fear suddenly seized him. "And how long can he last?"

It was a good question.

> "The Pope
> He leads a jolly life
> And though
> He's not allowed a wife
> He drinks the best of Rhennish wine
> I wish the Pope's gay life were mine!

He drinks the best of Rhennish wine
I wish the Pope's gay life were . . ."

The words and music died slowly, as if the Glee Club had
suddenly lost its way in the score. Scattered snatches of the
old German drinking song continued on for several seconds;
the noise of the bus, roaring back from Fairfield to Greenport, left some unaware the others had stopped. There was
some uneasy, uncertain laughter as everyone in the bus
looked at the scene taking place beside the driver.

"Oh, come on!" someone yelled.

"Hey, Kip. Siddown!"

Kip Grolier was a freeloader on the bus. Although not a
member of the Glee Club, he showed up after the concert at
Fairfield Country Day, announced that his car had broken
down, and asked the faculty adviser, Mr. Blaffin, if he could
hitch a ride back to Greenport on the bus. Always a little in
awe of the Student Body President, Mr. Blaffin was delighted
to offer Kip the ride. It had not yet occurred to Blaffin that
Kip's story of having driven over to Fairfield in his own car
violated just about every possible rule of the school as well as
those of the police.

"Kip, I don't think that's entirely funny . . ." Mr. Blaffin
began.

"No," Kip agreed. "It's not funny at all. It isn't meant to
be."

Kip stood in the cleared area beside the driver of the bus.
The school's Pinkerton man sat in the front row of seats, eyeing him nervously. In one hand, Kip held a .45; with the
other, he held Robert Teal II, youngest member of the Glee
Club, pressing the gun against the squirming boy's head as a
threat to the others to follow his orders and stay where they
were.

Because of who Kip was, the rest of the boys still felt that
it was some kind of a gag. A joke. Only the bus driver and
the Pinkerton man had their doubts, Mr. Blaffin found Kip's
humor, given the circumstances in Greenport, to be surprisingly childish.

Still holding Teal hard against the .45, Kip turned to the
Pinkerton guard. "Slowly. Very slowly. Pull your gun out of
its holster and drop it on the floor."

"Hey look, young fella, look, now—" the guard began.

Kip pulled Teal's head back, pressing his thumb hard into the flesh below the child's left ear as he did. Teal's body arched, Kip's knee pressing his midsection forward, his other hand bending him backward; the sudden pressure of the thumb gave rise to an agonized yelp. The guard and Kip stared at each other. With a ponderous sigh, the guard pulled his 45 from its rarely opened holster and dropped it on the floor.

"Okay, good. Now kick it over toward me." Kip listened to his own voice and was shocked to hear how Western his phraseology sounded. Like Clint Eastwood. Or was it Hamish Hamilton?

The guard complied, trying to give the revolver an extra hard kick so that it would shoot past Kip to where the bus driver could grab it. But the bus driver neither caught the guard's signal, nor did he want to; he was paid to drive a bus. Period.

Pulling Teal down with him, Kip scooped up the revolver and threw it out the window. "Okay, one funny move from anybody and Robert Teal the Second becomes Robert Teal the Last." Kip studied the concerned faces of the children in the bus with mild amusement and a growing sense of confidence. Suddenly twisting his body, Kip glowered again at the driver. "Turn off at Exit Thirty-six. Seven Hills Road. About a mile and a half."

From one side of him, he heard the Pinkerton man try to reason. "Look, kid, I don't know whether this is a gag or what. But disarming me was a state crime. A felony. That's heavy enough. But maybe if you quit now, we can . . ."

"Lock me up," finished Kip for him. "Balls. I'm not stupid. Now, everybody shut up."

The guard shut up. He and the driver had their own secret weapon. Somewhere behind them, in the swimming sea of headlights, was an unmarked State Police car with two plain-clothesmen inside. Hamish, learning of the sole activity left on Country Day's schedule, had suggested this escort after talking with Jenny Cobb; she was concerned that the Piper might try to pluck one final child from the Fairfield auditorium or when the bus left the children off at their homes. Tyne had talked with Cummins of the State Police, and the

escort car was provided. Both the guard and the driver had
chatted with the plainclothesmen briefly in the parking lot at
Fairfield Country Day and knew that the car was somewhere
close behind; when the police saw the bus make an unsched-
uled turn at Exit 36, they would turn with them, probably
boarding the bus when they halted for a stop sign, and then
their private nightmare would be over.

Mr. Blaffin, who did not know of the escort car, rose half
out of his seat. He would make logic work where the guard
had failed. "Kip, I'd like to say that—"

"Shut up is what you'd like to do," Kip yelled, and
jammed the .45 into Teal's stomach so hard that the youngster gave another cry of pain. Mr. Blaffin sat down. Watching
him, Kip smiled a small patronizing smile. He was feeling
good. Up until now, all of his work had been anonymous.
Frequently brilliant, but always anonymous. Now he was
being seen by others in action—the genuine Kip Grolier, not
the papier-mâché confection he usually hid inside. Kip suddenly felt a sense of strength and power that he had never ex-
perienced before.

"Kip," tried Mr. Blaffin again. Other voices in the bus
joined his.

"I said shut up. And *shut up* is what I mean." The sense of
power was overwhelming; he fired his pistol through the roof
of the bus, feeling Teal twitch in terror, watching the eyes of
the boys, the guard, and the driver blink in reaction to the
sound. Then, the eyes recovered, widening in fear as a full realization that there was no element of gag in Kip's words
finally reached them. From the ceiling, a light dusting of
shattered plastic and acoustical stuffing slowly drifted down;
the driver, his mouth open and his body shaking visibly, began pulling the bus over toward the side of I-95.

"Keep it going, keep it going," ordered Kip. "Exit Thirty-
six, I said. I'll guide you from there." The bewildered driver
pulled the bus back into the light traffic, his head constantly
turning back to eye Kip. A squawking sound, distant and incoherent, came from the radio receiver beside the driver.
"Damn." Earlier, Kip remembered that all of the school buses
had recently been equipped with two-way radios, and dispos-
ing of this one had been on his list to take care of when he
climbed aboard in Fairfield. Somehow he'd forgotten. Look-

ing over at it, he could see the microphone hanging from a small hook in front of the driver. With one strong yank, he pulled the microphone from its socket and flung it on the floor. "You didn't want to talk to anyone, anyway," Kip said to the driver with a laugh. Then he allowed his face to turn grim. "Or did you?"

Numb with fright, the driver vigorously shook his head from side to side, so hard that his cap fell off; he started to lean down to retrieve the cap, but thought better of it. With elaborate gentlemanliness, Kip reached down and picked the cap up, placing it on the driver's head and patting it smooth. Out of the corner of one eye, he saw Terry Parmalee slowly coming down the aisle toward him, steadying himself by the seat-backs as he came. Terry was an old friend of Kip's and wore a look of total mystification on his face. Kip spun around. "Dammit, Terry, stay where you are. Sit down. Teal here is already shitting in his pants. Very untidy. You don't want to be responsible for me blowing his brains out and messing up the rest of his clothes, do you?"

Silently, Terry Parmalee slid into a seat a couple of rows from the front of the bus. Terry felt he knew Kip better than anyone and simply would not believe that Kip was the person responsible for the disappearances in Greenport. Like anyone else, Kip had his faults, although in his case, they always seemed buried beneath the exterior of the perfect teen-ager. On this point, Terry knew better. He himself had been involved with Kip in a couple of house break-ins and minor vandalizations; he had dabbled in marijuana with him; he had experimented, when they were about 12, in the usual minor sex play. Didn't everyone? But on the major points, Kip was genuinely different. It had always been the overwhelming goodness of Kip that separated him from the rest of the boys, and even, Terry would admit, from himself: the essential morality, the seemingly total unselfishness, the force for good that Kip appeared to exercise over them all.

Kip was not capable of being what he was pretending to be, standing there a few feet in front of him. Carefully, obliquely, Terry tried to reason with Kip, so that the bus could be set back on its course and the strange presence which had overwhelmed his friend could be exorcized.

"Kip," he began softly. "You know I love a gag as much as anyone . . ."

"It's no gag. Can't you understand that?"

The anger in Kip's voice, so unusual for him, made Terry extra sensitive about provoking him. "Okay. Okay, Kip. But I know damned well you aren't the guy who's been swiping all those kids. You're not the Piper. This is just some—"

"I'm not? Well, let me tell you, Parmalee, I sure as hell am. And I can prove it."

"Oh, c'mon, Kip. I've known you since kindergarten. Longer than anybody. And like a book. This isn't your style at all. You're not the Piper. Why don't we just sit down and talk about—"

Parmalee could see that Kip was growing furious. "I am, dammit, I am." A sudden strange wave of panic struck Kip. What if they—what if nobody believed him? "I am the Piper, I am, I am! I did all of it, everything. Dammit, can't you see that?" he screamed.

Parmalee, on his feet again, swaying in the aisle, stared at Kip with a quizzical look and put his question in a gentle voice. "Why?"

"You'll find that out later. It was all in the broadcasts, but you didn't understand. Well, you will."

Parmalee nodded gravely. The threats had an empty sound to them, but Kip's desperate earnestness sounded real. He was sick. His friend was sick. A collection of half-forgotten, strange stories about Kip's mother suddenly hit him. "Kip, listen to me." He moved a couple of steps down the aisle toward him. Kip grabbed Teal by the waist and lifted him off the floor, squirming. The shirt beneath his blazer rose and Kip's fingers could feel the skin beneath, hot and slightly sweaty from fright, making it slippery and hard to hold onto. He dug his nails into Teal's middle to get a better grip, causing a new whimper of pain to rise from him.

"Stay where you are, Terry. Stay where you are," Kip threatened.

Very slowly, Parmalee advanced, talking soothingly. "I've heard stuff about your mother and I can imagine how tough it is. But this—"

Parmalee had said precisely the wrong thing. Kip fired at him. The bullet struck his friend in the upper thigh and Par-

malee collapsed in the aisle. The boys screamed. The guard
half-rose out of his seat, but Kip fired a second time, into the
air, forcing the guard and the rest of the boys, half of them
now in the aisle, into a sudden silence. Kip once again adjusted his grip on Teal. "Everybody sit down and everybody shut
up." In a detached way, Kip watched as Parmalee thrashed
in the aisle, wondering if he had aimed at Terry's head and
missed, or whether his poor aim had been deliberate.

"Exit Thirty-six in half a mile, sir." The bus driver's voice
had a quaver in it, mixed with a note of subservience that fed
Kip's mushrooming sense of power.

"Slow down when you get close to it, turn off, and wait for
instructions," he commanded. Kip turned from the driver to
the rest of the bus's occupants. "All right. Back in your
places, you guys. Somebody lay Parmalee across a seat and
see if you can stop the bleeding. Anybody here take Red
Cross?"

One small hand timidly raised itself. "Okay, you. If you
need something for a tourniquet, use somebody's shirt. And
the rest of you—shut the hell up."

The boy came down the aisle and, with the help of another
student, pulled off Parmalee's pants to reveal a heavily
bleeding wound in the fleshy part of his upper thigh. Instead
of a shirt, they used one of his trouser legs, tightening it with
a recorder that one of the boys carried with him, instead of
the usual stick. Parmalee was groaning and cursing, muttering in such a garbled way that Kip couldn't make out too
much of what he was saying.

"Exit Thirty-six," called the driver. He had already
switched on his turn indicators to make sure that their secret
weapon, the unmarked police car following them, would see
that he was going to take the wrong exit and realize that
something was wrong. After that—the driver sighed in relief
at the thought—the busload of kids would be their problem.

Kip leaned down to look out through the windshield,
watching as the driver expertly spun the heavy wheel to put
the bus onto the exit ramp. "Drive down Seven Hills Road,
three and five-eighths of a mile. Tell me when we're getting
close and I'll give you instructions from there. And drive
slowly, dammit. No cowboy tricks to attract attention."

Driving slowly suited the driver just fine. It would give the police car plenty of room to keep track of them. Looking in the rear-view mirror, he kept waiting for the lights of the police car to show up. They didn't. As they came to a turn, the driver slowed the bus even further. Maybe they had their headlights off, maybe they were staying even further back than he would have thought. But a small knot of doubt began to grow in his stomach.

Still holding onto Teal, who had started to cry when Kip shot Parmalee and hadn't stopped yet, Kip turned around to address the nervous busload of Glee Clubbers. "Okay now, kids. How about a song?"

The boys shifted uncomfortably in their seats.

The silence was unearthly.

Further back toward Fairfield on 1-95, the silence was equally painful. Plainclothes Sergeant Farleigh Kramer jiggled the toggle switch on the State Police car's transmitter back and forth, but could not get an answer. They could receive but not send. "Damn." He looked at Edwards, seated beside him. "Can't raise a soul. Lots of crap coming in, but our signal's not going anywhere. Crazy. First the motor, then this."

The unmarked police car was pulled over onto the narrow strip of grass beside the turnpike, its hood raised and its tail-light flashers blinking their dull red at timed intervals. About ten miles short of Exit 36, the police car's motor suddenly coughed several times, sputtered once or twice, and then died. They barely had enough power to pull over onto the grass shoulder. In frustration, the two policemen had watched the bus it was their job to follow vanish down the highway. It was at this point that they discovered that their radio had also conked out; the bus was equipped with a powerful transmitter, but although they had checked the system before they left Fairfield and everything was in operating order, the set had died as unnatural a death as their motor.

"I guess we'd better try to get a lift to the nearest phone." Kramer's voice sounded disgusted; for a State policeman to lose both his motor and his communications at the same time was embarrassing.

Getting a lift, it turned out, required some time. It was ten minutes before a trailer truck, on the opposite side of the

turnpike, finally stopped for the two frantically waving plain-
clothesmen; Kramer identified himself and told the driver to
have the next toll gate operator notify the State Police Barracks and send out a tow truck.

Kramer neglected to instruct the driver to have Chief Investigator Cummins notified, an oversight that he realized almost the moment the heavy tractor-trailer truck lumbered
away. Swearing at himself, Kramer drew back his foot and
gave the police car a hard kick on its door. As integral parts
of a secret weapon, plainclothes officers Kramer and Edwards
left something to be desired.

"Sugar." State Police mechanic Ian Leary said the word
with satisfaction, even though his mouth was still slightly
puckered from the bitter taste of gasoline on the tip of his
finger. After turning over the motor with his booster cable
from the tow truck, he'd sensed something more than the
breakdown that he occasionally encountered in his cars.
"Sugar," he repeated. "Sugar in the gas tank will knock out
any car, anytime."

Officer Kramer was less sanguine. "Sugar, my ass. We got
damn near the whole way from Fairfield to here without any
trouble. If somebody's gunked up the gas tank with sugar, we
never would have gotten half that far."

Leary smiled knowingly and took a long, stiff wire from
the tow truck. At one end he fashioned what looked like an
oversized fish hook, then stuck the wire down the police car's
gas tank. For a moment or two he probed the inside of the
tank and finally gave a satisfied sigh, coupled with a smile of
triumph. Slowly and carefully he withdrew the wire; attached
to the end was a small conelike device, with the eaten-away
shreds of a plastic bag still visible. "This is how come you
could get this far. The sugar was in a plastic bag. Soluble in
gasoline, I guess. The bag was hung inside the tank and attached to the rim of the cap; the bag began dissolving and released the bulk of the sugar into the main gasoline reservoir.
As soon as it was mixed with the gas, you stopped. Somebody
sure as hell didn't want you to get where you were going."

Kramer felt his heart skip a beat. Edwards still looked
baffled; the full implications hadn't hit him yet. "But the

radio. Going out at the same time. We tested it back in Fairfield . . ."

As Leary shone a flashlight under the radio console on the dash, his eyes caught sight of something. He reached one hand up underneath and pulled out a fused wire. "Heavy wire replaced by fine wire. Deliberately overloaded. Set worked at first, but after the amplifier was on for a while, the wire melted and broke the circuit. Same principle as a household fuse. Somebody real cute figured this one out."

"The radio," repeated Kramer, and dashed across to the police tow truck. It was now obvious that the simultaneous breakdown of both car and radio was part of some very careful plan. "Car six-twelve reporting, car six-twelve reporting, come in Barracks," he yelled into the mike. A voice crackled on the radio. "Someone deliberately japped our motor and killed our radio. This is six-twelve. We were escorting Country Day bus from Fairfield to Greenport. Bus no longer under surveillance. Suggest immediate all points. Notify Cummins immediately. Repeat. Notify Chief Investigator Cummins immediately. This is an emergency. Car six-twelve . . ."

Hanging the mike back on its hook in the tow truck, Kramer walked back to Edwards and Leary dispiritedly. "We been had. Christ, but we been had. Them poor damned kids."

Chapter 17 _____

*Obnoxious and repulsive as he is, I have to
hand it to K.K. for figuring out a way to
keep that police car from following us back.
While those Smokies were inside the hall listening to the Glee Club bleat its heart out,
K.K. fixed their car, but good. Absolutely
brilliant.*

*If K.K. would just take a bath once in a
while, I might even grow to like him. But
even a brain like his needs an occasional
shower, just to make staying in the same
room with him bearable.*

Thomas Alva Edison didn't stink, did he?

—TAPE-LOG OF THE PIPER,
ENTRY DATED JUNE 10 (P.M.).

"We can't find a trace of them anywhere. It's like the bus fell
off the face of the globe." Cummins threw his hands up and
avoided Tyne's eyes. The story was lame-sounding; he had no
explanation for it, and worse, no reasonable excuse for what
had happened to his surveillance team.

"What do you mean?" roared Tyne. "You can't find a
trace of them? A school bus with twenty-three kids and an
armed guard and being followed by a State Police car and no
one knows where the hell it is? Jesus Christ!"

Cummins struggled to keep control of himself. He knew
that Tyne was right; he knew that one of his men had been
sloppy or careless or worse, in handling the job; he knew that
someone was at fault for not letting him know sooner.

Tyne sat down heavily in his chair; the way that his precautions had been gotten around made him squirm in discomfort. His original hunch—that the bus should be followed by
his own FBI men—had been right.

Cummins sighed heavily. "I said I don't know how to explain it, and I don't. The thing is now, what's the next move?"

"Find the bus. It's out there somewhere. By now it's empty. But we'll call out all the Greenport PD cars, bring in extra FBI field agents, and alert all toll-gate stations. Any extra State Police you can get your hands on would be a help, too. It's just a matter of infinitely careful searching. Crisscrossing every foot of ground. A bus isn't all that easy to hide."

Tyne had made it sound easy because, under ordinary circumstances, it should be easy. But a churning, uncomfortable feeling in his stomach told him that this mystery, as with so many of the rest of them in this case, might not only be difficult but impossible to find an easy solution for.

"They're all painted and precut," Kip noted firmly. "Putting them in ought to be a cinch." The older boys looked at him, then at K.K. and his 30-gauge shotgun, and decided that they had little choice. With whatever energy they had left, the boys started putting the painted sheets of plywood into the windows of the bus, fastening them to the inside of the glass window openings with ropes that were anchored to the plywood itself. As K.K. had planned, this effectively blocked the windows so that there was no way for anyone to either look out or—more importantly—to see in. "Come on, come on," ordered Kip. "Get them up fast. We've got a lot to do."

The bus and its load of singers was pulled up outside what had once been the garage of K.K.'s former family place. Long ago, the house it was built to serve had burned down, and when K.K.'s family put up their new house, they had attached a new garage to it, abandoning this old one as being "too far away from the house." The ancient building was cavernous, it was secluded, it could not be seen from either the new house or the road. Most importantly, access to it was from a little-known back driveway shooting off at right angles to Seven Hills Road. Because of this, Kip was able to order the bus up the road with impunity, sure that there were no other cars or people in sight to see them bounce their way up the old driveway. Once the bus arrived there and had been met by K.K., Kip told the driver to park it in the cracked, overgrown circle of asphalt outside the dilapidated garage; on command, their hands in the air, the driver, the guard, and

Mr. Blaffin were marched inside and the massive doors swung shut. Now armed with a shotgun of his own, Kip remained outside guarding the busload of boys, directing them in the hammering and in the attaching of plywood boards to the bus. The noise of the hammering also served another purpose; it drowned out some unpleasant sounds from inside the old garage.

"Climb down, climb down. Come on, Mr. Blaffin. It shouldn't be that hard, even for a fat old auntie like you." K.K. jiggled the 30-gauge menacingly; Mr. Blaffin got the message and lowered his soft, bulky self, hand-over-hand, down the rope ladder as fast as he could manage. He was the last of the three men to descend into what had once been the lubricating pit, back in the days when the old garage still serviced the family cars. About eight feet deep, the pit was made of solid concrete and had had at one time, a slatted wooden platform across its floor to raise the mechanics to the right level for working on the undersides of a car. Around the edge of the lube pit was a curious construction of fresh, new wood, so new you could still detect the clean smell of recently sawed lumber. Long planks running the length of the pit were nailed to shorter ones at either end; this hollow wood rectangle was bolted to the floor formed by the edge of the concrete. A pile of other short planks, also sawed to size, was stacked beside this odd-looking affair of wood and cement. Forced down the ladder into the pit, the men had looked apprehensively at these preparations when they were first ordered to climb inside, but said little. To the guard and the bus driver, at least, putting them into the pit and then covering it with a crisscrossed network of planks—like bars in a cell—was a perfectly logical way to hold them prisoner while their captors did whatever they were going to do with the passengers from the bus. Only Mr. Blaffin suffered a deeper fear. From teaching at Country Day, he had heard a lot about K.K. While considered extraordinarily bright, K.K. was usually described as an untrustworthy, devious oddball by his other teachers. "I wish the little bastard wasn't so intelligent," Regis Flaherty, K.K.'s physics teacher, once said of him. "Then I could flunk him. There's something about that boy that scares me half to death."

"Comfy?" K.K. inquired, looking down at the three men in

the pit, the shotgun swaying back and forth like a hypnotized cobra. The question was met with silence; the three men, standing in an eight-foot hole that was simultaneously cold, damp, and frightening, could think of nothing to say. K.K. didn't bother to wait for an answer. "Good. Because you'll be in there for quite a spell. Quite a spell."

Carefully positioning himself so that there would be no chance for one of the men to jump high in the air and grab him—the shotgun replaced by a .45 jammed into his belt—K.K. methodically began to hammer the stack of shorter planks across the top of the pit. At first, his captives remained mute, but as they realized that he was nailing the boards close together, not at some distance from each other as they expected, they began to yell. "Hey," shouted the Pinkerton guard. "Leave some room between the boards. We'll suffocate. Dammit, leave some room for air."

Barely responding, K.K. continued to nail the planks down. When he was two-thirds of the way done, he finally answered the shouted protests from below him. "Stop bleating. Plenty of cracks for air. More than you'll need. I couldn't make the damned thing air-tight with this stuff if I wanted to." More hammering from above, more shouting from below. "Besides, I'm putting a ventilating pipe in one of the last planks, just to make sure. Relax."

Inside their cement prison, the guard and the bus driver held a hurried conference. Mr. Blaffin was left out—not out of mistrust or malice, but because his weight and delicacy made any contribution toward escape on his part highly unlikely. A hasty plan, as dangerous as it was desperate, was concocted and immediately put into action. Trying not to grunt enough to be heard, the driver lifted the guard onto his shoulders and pressed him against the concrete wall. On the next fall of the hammer, they had agreed, the guard would reach out and grab K.K. by the arm, hang onto him, and drag him into the pit with them. Once the boy was subdued, they could grab hold of one of the planks and haul themselves out through the small area above them not yet covered over. But their plan would have to be executed immediately; one or two more planks nailed down and they would neither be able to haul K.K. in or themselves out, and none of them relished the prospect of spending several more hours—perhaps even days—in this cold, uncertain prison. "Now!" whispered the guard, and the driver gave him a mighty shove upward.

As the guard's hand—then both hands—grabbed the plank, K.K. brought his hammer down hard on the fingers gripping the plank. The guard howled in pain, still trying to hold on but unable to. K.K. again brought the hammer down on his fingers.

The guard, cursing and yelling, let go and collapsed back on the bus driver, both of them landing in a heap on the hard floor. The guard, almost crying in pain and struggling to appraise the damage to his fingers, looked up to see K.K. smiling benignly and shaking his head back and forth at him, like a parent unwittingly amused by an errant child's behavior.

K.K. quickly nailed the final two planks into place, putting a solid roof over the three men in their cement tomb; only an occasional shaft of dim light filtered through the cracks between the uneven edges of the boards. The hammering above them suddenly took on a new metallic sound; K.K. was forcing a two-inch pipe through a precut hole in the planks. Skeptically, the men looked up at it. As a ventilating shaft, it didn't live up to its billing, yet K.K. had been right in saying that there were enough small cracks and spaces between the uneven edges of the planks to admit more than enough air to breathe. From the airpipe came a new rattling sound, followed by the noise of something smooth being slid into it. The men looked at each other in confusion; they had no way of identifying what this new sound might hold for them. They discovered soon enough. The sound of K.K.'s footsteps as he walked away from the lube pit was followed by the squeak of something being turned. Almost immediately, a rush of frigid tap water began pouring through the pipe into the pit. "Hey," yelled the guard. "Cut it out, dammit. That stuff's freezing."

K.K.'s voice above them sounded serene, almost amused. "You'll be getting enough exercise in a minute to warm you up. Besides, you all need a bath anyway." Walking calmly back to the side of the garage, K.K. stepped over a hose running from a faucet on the wall to the ventilating pipe and turned up the water to maximum strength. The plumbing was

old and leaky, the pipes corroded, but the basic system still
had enough power to deliver a torrent of water. By K.K.'s
figuring, it would take about twenty minutes to fill the pit.
Sitting on the edge of an empty crate, K.K. lit a cigarette and
listened.

In the beginning, the men thought the water was a cruel
joke, another one of the indignities this boy K.K. seemed intent on subjecting them to. But as the water steadily rose in
the lube pit, K.K.'s intentions became increasingly ominous.
The water would rise until they had to swim to keep their
heads above it. Eventually, the water would float them up
against the planks nailed over the pit's top; there they might
expect to survive for a while by throwing their heads back
and pressing their mouths against the cracks to get air. But in
the end, exhaustion would get them. K.K.'s remark that they
would be there "quite a spell" was a gem of understatement.

Simultaneously, all three of the men seemed to realize just
how desperate their situation was, and they all began yelling
and screaming. On his crate, K.K. listened with his head to
one side, then leaned back against the wall, waiting. The
pleading and crying—the crying, he suspected, came from
Mr. Blaffin—grew louder and more desperate, interspersed
with promises of silence, offers of money, and other futile attempts to bargain for their lives. At the first sounds of the
men's fists beginning to pound uselessly against the planking
above them, K.K. rose from his crate and walked over
toward the lube pit at a leisurely pace, carrying something
rolled around a long cardboard tube in one hand. The men
were to be denied even the temporary lease on life that they
had figured the cracks in the planking would afford them.
With elaborate care, K.K. unrolled a large sheet of
transparent plastic from the tube and began nailing it across
the top of the planks, fastening it down tight at each end,
then sealing it to the floor with plastic masking tape. A small
hole was left around the pipe itself, then made air-tight with
more of the same plastic masking tape.

Just before he closed the final opening, K.K. shouted over
the men's yells of panic. "Soon as the water spills out onto
the floor, I'm taking the hose out. Three men, one pipe to
breathe through. Spirit of good old-fashioned American competition. Very democratic."

As he calmly walked out of the garage door into the balmy night air outside, all K.K. could hear was a distant hammering sound on the planks, already weak and growing weaker.

From Tyne's desk came the strident ring of his phone. He picked up the receiver and barked his name into it. "They what? Where?" Jenny watched as a series of expressions, running from disbelief to annoyance, flitted across Tyne's face. "Are they sure?" asked Tyne, the note of incredulity clear in his voice. "Damn, well, tell them to keep at it." He hung up the phone and looked at Jenny helplessly. "My guys have definitely established that the bus was okay when it went through the Stratford Tolls, which gets them by Bridgeport. Also seen at the Norwalk Tolls. And Greenwich. The guys on the gates remembered because it's an unusual hour for a school bus to be going through. And if there was anything wrong, it hadn't shown up yet; one of the toll collectors remembers that it was a busload of kids singing in harmony. So the vanishing act had to be after Greenwich but before Greenport; nobody at the Rye Toll Gate remembers them at all, not that that's definite proof of anything. The armed guard was still aboard; the Norwalk toll-taker noticed him because a guard like that's unusual. So what it boils down to is that somewhere between Greenwich and here, the kidnappers stopped them, got aboard, and took over the bus. How they did it, where they took them, God knows."

"Did the usual broadcast go on air tonight?" Until now, Jenny had sat against one wall saying nothing. Tyne stared at her before picking up the phone again. His conversation with the FCC Field Director told him that no, they were still waiting, but that so far, for the first time in weeks, there had been no broadcast from the kidnappers.

"There's one possibility," began Jenny. "And the Piper's sudden silence ties into it, but hell, I don't know." Hamish's reaction to her basic premise had been so universally negative that she felt disloyal even mentioning the subject. "Forget it."

"No, dammit, I won't forget it. What were you thinking?"

"Well, I've been wondering for some time now whether maybe the Piper couldn't be one of the older boys at Country Day." She looked at Tyne. His eyes widened as the implications of her statement began to sink in more fully. "This new thing—the bus—adds a little more ammunition to my idea. Hell, you have one guard, one bus driver, and one old teacher, none of whom could have done the rest of the stuff. If the radio on the bus was still working, then the bus had to be taken over by someone already on it. The only people on the bus, besides those three adults, were boys from Country Day. And tonight, for the first time, no broadcast. The kidnappers were busy. Singing in Fairfield. Or at least riding on the bus with the singers."

Tyne said nothing. A troubled look had settled across his face, as if a great deal of what Jenny had said made sense. "I don't know, Jenny. It's a startling notion at first. It fits an awful lot of things, though, things that are tough to explain any other way. I just hope we turn up an explanation that isn't as frightening. The idea gives me the creeps." Tyne sat motionless in his chair, the look on his face growing more troubled, the muscles of his jaws working. Part of his mind was trying to dismiss any possibility that Jenny's idea could be right. The effort was unsuccessful.

In the half-light outside the garage, provided by a couple of dim floods set above its double doors, K.K. could see that the bus had been almost completely transformed while he was inside. K.K. was on the verge of saying something to Kip about it, when Kip started cross-examining him. "Taken care of?"

"Done. Completely and finally."

"You're sure?"

"Positive. See, I had them . . ."

"I don't want to hear about it. Just that you're sure."

"I said I was. You can check if you want."

"I don't want." Kip watched the older boys working; the younger ones were still inside the bus. "Dammit," he called. "Careful with that paint." He suddenly handed his shotgun to K.K. "Hold this while I straighten them out. And keep 'em covered every minute. Jerry Widdicomb's already tried once to make a break for it." A thought struck him. "Can we move the bus inside? It'll make keeping track of them much easier."

"Sure."

The whole crew was loaded back into the bus while K.K.

drove it into the garage. The floor of the place was wet and the water still running, but the sound of the hammering had stopped. Kip eyed the planking and the water overflowing from the lube pit and shrugged, while K.K. studied the transformed bus in the stronger light inside. It was an amazing piece of work.

"Okay," shouted Kip. "You two there—" he pointed to two 17-year-olds—"go back to work on the wheels. The tires—everything. One red, one white, one blue. The fourth—well, that silver stuff. And Corky and Jerry—" Kip nodded toward two other boys standing sullenly to one side—"get this up on top." For a moment, neither boy moved; then Kip walked back and took his shotgun from K.K. and waved it at them. "Now, dammit."

With a stare of resentment, the two climbed on the bus's roof, lugging a large, three-horned device with them. Following Kip's instructions, K.K. quickly slipped into a bus driver's uniform. Perhaps fifteen minutes later, the bus drove out of the garage again with K.K. behind the wheel, turning left on Seven Hills Road and heading toward Greenport. Inside sat the entire Glee Club, watching nervously as Kip covered them with his shotgun.

Because of the boarded-over windows, they had no real idea of where they were going, or that Kip was about to unveil the boldest maneuver he had yet to try.

Chapter 18 _____

*Funny, Dee never made me jealous the
way Carey did. Oh, I can remember there
was a time when my old man was really a
pushover for her, but as I grew older and
people began telling him how bright I was,
and what a leader at school, and even how
handsome, my father sort of turned off Dee
and concentrated on me.*

*On the other hand, Carey was a constant
worry to me. He never got the attention I
did, but I always felt he was a threat. I
remember once—maybe he was seven or
eight—pretending to kid around when he was
taking his bath and then holding him under
water until I damned near drowned him.
And if his body hadn't been so slippery with
soap, I probably would have.*

*Nobody said much, but I know they
thought plenty. I had to go win the Harold-
son Trophy to get out of that one.*

      —TAPE-LOG OF THE PIPER,
      ENTRY DATED JUNE 9.

By nine that night, Greenport and the entire surrounding area
was crawling with town police cars, State Police cars, FBI
teams, and a suddenly reinforced contingent from the Federal
Crime Bureau. As Tyne pointed out, a bus is not an easy
thing to hide. The going theory was that, given enough man-
power properly applied, the bus would be quickly flushed
out—and possibly with it, the twenty-three children and three
adults aboard it. From the center of town, where Tyne was
directing operations out of the cellar of First Baptist, these
search teams fanned out like the spokes of a wheel. Another
search zone had been set up to cover the area between Norwalk and Greenport Toll Gates, forming a pattern overlap-

ping the one in Greenport itself. At first, some effort was
made to keep the object of the search a secret; quickly
though, it became obvious that this much activity was impossible to hide. Tyne and Hamish reluctantly decided that some
sort of announcement would have to be made over television,
or the kidnappers' mobile station would break its unusual
silence and do the job for them. "Besides," Hamish pointed out,
pacing his cell-like room in the sub-basement, "the more people
know we are looking for that bus, the more chance somebody
will report having seen it."

Considering Hamish's personal situation, his reaction was a
somewhat curious one. He suddenly appeared resigned, as if
the disappearance of the bus was something he had expected
all along. Slowly Jenny realized that Hamish, by losing himself in all these suggestions to Tyne on finding the bus, was
able to keep his mind off Russel.

At 9:10, the force of newsmen infesting Greenport were
suddenly summoned to a press conference by Blagden Tyne.
The information he gave them was brief, almost telegraphic,
but the basic story was all there: a busload of twenty-three
children—along with the bus driver, an armed guard, and the
Glee Club's faculty advisor, one Gerald Blaffin—had left
Fairfield Country Day at approximately 8:05 P.M. The bus
had last been positively identified by a toll collector on the
Greenwich tolls on I-95, at approximately 8:20. After that, it
was not seen again. The bus and its occupants must be assumed to have fallen victim to the Piper, as the man called
himself. Yes, not only the State and local police, but the FBI,
the Federal Crime Bureau, and other agencies of the Federal
Government were taking part in the search. No, he had no
idea why the man called himself the "Piper." Yes, it was true
that Senator Blyden's son was among those kidnapped earlier.
Well, his disappearance had been kept a secret at the Senator's request. No, there would be no further questions accepted from the floor at the present. Yes, a special news
bureau would be set up—he thought at Town Hall—to
handle any further developments. And those were all, definitely all, the questions he would respond to at this time.

Tyne's news release, brief as it was, hit the air perhaps ten
minutes later at 9:42. NBC, ABC, and CBS programs in
progress were interrupted to present this new development.

As with many places, Thursday was a late-shopping day in Greenport, and the streets were still filled with people. The news swept through the crowds in an undulating buzz of disbelief. It was so unbelievable that little attention was paid to an odd spectacle making its way through the very heart of town: the missing school bus.

The transformation was such it is not surprising no one recognized it. From a standard yellow school bus, the vehicle had been changed into a traveling Fourth of July-Memorial Day-mid-Bicentennial exhibit. Its sides were painted in Calder-like designs of red, white and blue, blending neatly with the similarly painted sheets of plywood which blocked the windows. Down its entire length hung swags of brightly colored cloth, punctuated by strings of red, white and blue Christmas tree lights. From either side, shrouded in bunting, were painted signs reading "Holiday Fair—Spring Shopping Center—Tmmrw." On top of the bus was a large three-horn loudspeaker playing military music; as the bus passed the Town Hall, the speakers burst into "Stars & Stripes Forever."

Inside, K.K., looking fierce in his uniform and a British military mustache, sat behind the wheel. A blue curtain separated him from the bus's other occupants in the rear— twenty-three children glued to their seats and covered by Kip and his shotgun. Kip was enjoying himself. The band music was originally planned to cover any sudden cries for help when they passed through whatever populated areas they might have to, but, at the last moment, Kip changed their route and directed K.K. to drive down the most heavily populated area of all: Greenport Avenue. The notion of the school bus using every possible device to draw attention to itself, moving brazenly through the most densely peopled part of town while every inch of the countryside was being scoured for it, was a touch that Kip could not resist. When K.K. had objected, Kip's answer was succinct: "The last thing anyone sees is what's right under their noses. Who the hell would expect the bus to be right there in the center of town, blinking its lights and shaking up the place with band music? No one. And the cops will all be too busy chasing around the State looking for it to ask for a parade permit or wonder why the hell they weren't notified about a fair. Simple. It'll work because people—most of them, anyway—are pretty damned stupid."

Only a philosopher or a psychologist could have passed judgment on Kip's appraisal of people. The fact was, whatever the reason, the device worked.

The press conference held by Blagden Tyne produced one side effect which, while it should have been anticipated, had not been: a full scale assault on Greenport by every available newsman and every piece of media equipment that could quickly be brought into the area. The streets were jammed with mobile vans from the networks and with major independents from as far away as Boston; there were so many reporters, lighting men, sound technicians, directors, and tape experts in town that all motels and hotels were completely booked solid. Finally, cots were set up in the basement of Town Hall to handle the overflow.

By ten o'clock, the crush in Greenport had grown until media people were literally climbing over each other. The improvised newsroom, upstairs in Town Hall, was filled with men setting up lights, with cameras being aligned, and with a seemingly endless number of men shouting "Testing—one—two—three—four" into dead microphones. Out on the street, the vans and trucks were drawn up in a circle around the building, like covered wagons waiting for Indians; the marble floor of the hallway into the conference area was a spider web of cables—heavy rubber-covered umbilicals connecting cameras to control vans.

There was one major difficulty with this sudden invasion of newsmen and equipment: there was no news to cover. By 11:30 the press was in a state of total frustration. The Town Hall stood empty and deserted, peopled only by media people and a lone guard posted at the door to demand credentials before allowing anyone to enter. The police station had a deserted air about it, too; most of the men were out in patrol cars searching for the bus, while the Police Chief, the newsmen were told, was in upstate New York, en route to Salt Lake City. The Town Manager could not be found. In managing to entice Senator Blyden out onto his front portico for an interview, Barbara Walters at first thought that she had scored a coup, but for once, the outspoken Senator refused to say

much more than that he had very little to say. Forced into a
virtual corner by Ms. Walters, Blyden shook his pretentious
jowls and noted that, with his own son among the missing, he
thought it unwise to answer any questions at the moment.
With that, Senator Blyden turned on his heel and ponderously
lumbered back inside the house.

The boys, their hands folded on top of their heads as Kip
had ordered, filed from the brightly painted bus into the
clearing around the cistern. A bright burst of light from the
bus's headlights fell across the area; after the last boy came
down the steps, the bus's Christmas tree bulbs were extin-
guished. Some time earlier—not far outside of town, in
fact—the music had been silenced.

The shadows the children made on the bare earth seemed
unusually long in the stark harshness of the headlights; each
figure seemed attached to a dark ghost-shape of itself that
shuffled uneasily across the ground. Kip did not want the
bus's lights on any longer than absolutely necessary, but felt
that only illumination of great intensity would allow him and
K.K. to keep track of all the prisoners and make sure that
none of them escaped into the darkness beyond.

"All right," he commanded. "Single file. Two older boys up
front, please." Squinting, Kip indicated two 17-year-olds with
the barrel of his shotgun. "Okay you, Bart. And you,
Wayne."

"Stay close, stay close, the rest of you." K.K.'s voice from
the other side of the circle irritated Kip. Somehow, K.K.'s
giving orders diminished his own feeling of power. Yet he
could see that K.K.'s command was a necessary one; as the
two older boys reluctantly moved to the front of the line, the
rest began churning around, making it hard to keep track of
them in the darkness. K.K.'s order had herded them back
into a tighter formation.

"Bart, Wayne, grab hold of the cover and lift it off the cistern. Now!" The two boys put their hands on the heavy
cover, but exchanged a glance between themselves before
turning back toward Kip with anxious expressions. What was
on their minds was obvious: was the whole bunch of them to
be forced down into the cistern and the cover replaced? Kip
thought of Gilly Axminster and wanted to smile; it was as if

these two boys knew how Gilly was disposed of. Instead, Kip kept his face very solemn. "Don't worry. No one's going to get pushed or forced to jump in." He allowed his smile to surface now, a small one, but sincere and understanding. "Would the President of the Student Body do a thing like that to you?"

The two boys at the cistern traded glances and gave in. Straining, they heaved the cover off, following Kip's instructions to lean it against the side once it was removed. "There's a ladder," Kip noted. "All of you, one by one, climb down the ladder. At the bottom, just about a foot off the water, you'll see a stone doorway. Swing yourself off the ladder into the tunnel through that."

A picture of boys, loose and waiting for him in the labyrinth of corridors suddenly flashed through Kip's mind. It wouldn't do. "Wait a minute," he yelled, over the rising murmur of protests. "K.K., you'd better go down first and line them up as they come through the door. I'll cover them from up here." K.K. looked at him dubiously; the possibility of his own overthrow under this sudden, new arrangement of Kip's bothered him.

"Down you go, K.K. And if any of them give you any trouble"—he patted his own shotgun— "Well . . ." He let the words finish themselves. The younger children looked affected by what he had said, but some of the older ones still appeared unsure, an undercurrent of rebellion growing inside them as they saw their position growing progressively more dangerous. Kip decided the point had to be hammered home. "And if any of them *do* try something, everybody up here and on the ladder . . ." Again, Kip didn't finish the sentence but allowed a firm shaking of his shotgun to speak for him.

Still not comfortable with the arrangement, K.K. threw his leg over the cistern and lowered himself uneasily down the rusted ladder. At the bottom, he swung himself through the stone door and watched the first of the boys begin his way down. Once there, each of them was lined up against the tunnel wall in such a position that K.K. could keep an eye on them as well as each new boy coming down the ladder.

By 10:40, the last of them had descended, been counted, and then marched—or carried, as was the case with Parmalee—down the hallway to the heavy steel door at its end.

After K.K. unlocked it, Kip began herding the file of boys
through the door into the vaultlike room beyond. For the first
few seconds there was a stunned silence as the boys adjusted
their eyes to the light of the thick candles set in the rock
walls; then the new arrivals and the boys already there became aware of each others' presence. Paige Rathbin and
Kevin Blyden flung themselves at the first few boys to come
through the door, assuming it meant that they had been freed
themselves. It took several moments longer—until they saw
Kip and K.K. out in the hall herding everyone in with their
shotguns—for them to realize that the crowd pouring in
through the door was just as captive as they. The new and
old prisoners embraced, but the reaction of the boys from the
bus was considerably less exhilarated than that of Paige and
Kevin. Briefly, Kip watched them through his peephole in the
now closed door, finally turning away to sit down.

"We still got a lot to do tonight. Tapes. The bus. Broadcast. Jesus."

"What about Russel? Not more of him tonight, too?"

Kip screwed up his face before making a decision. "Not
much time, but I guess so. He really ought to have a night
off, but we can't afford it."

"The time, the time," protested K.K.

"Something simple but juicy. Your choice."

K.K. stared at Kip. For the first time in weeks, he made a
statement to Kip that was both frank and accurate. "Christ,
Kip. You're a mean bastard."

"I don't think that I can answer that. I don't think anybody
but you can. The choices are so limited and so personal . . ."
Jenny suddenly found herself backing away from her own
question. When she had asked Hamish, later that same night,
what he was going to do, she had meant the question to be
one that would start him thinking. She hadn't expected his
answer: "I don't know. What do you think I should do?"

They were in Hamish's sub-basement room, having a quick
sandwich. Earlier, she had found him pacing back and forth,
his face gaunt and drawn. The sight bothered her in ways
that she didn't like to admit. For ever since Russel's disappearance, she had shared his pain and worry, his constant
awareness that at any moment the phone could ring and

bring him the news he spent his days and nights dreading. She wanted to take him in her arms and reassure him and comfort him, but could not bring herself to. Hamish, she was afraid, would think she meant something else.

In this area, Kip's hopes of driving a wedge between them had been most successful. Yet in another, perhaps more important one—emotional dependence—Kip had drawn Hamish and Jenny closer together.

Hamish looked up at her. "Nothing—no packages—today, so far," he noted. "Maybe he thinks I really have gone on to Salt Lake. Or stayed in Albany. Damn. Who knows what he thinks?"

"I think the Piper does believe that you've gone somewhere—and if my theories are worth a damn, that probably means he already wants you back here. Maybe that's what the bus was all about."

Hamish looked shocked. "What you're saying is that I'm on the hook for all those kids, too."

"Of course not. It's just strange that he hasn't made a broadcast—crowing about what he's done. Challenging you. Daring you to come back."

"So he can really carve up Russel."

"He probably will anyway."

Hamish stopped his pacing and turned on her. It was a point that they had both considered, but neither had articulated before. Even as she said it, Jenny was aware she was taking a calculated risk, but it was no longer possible to hide from reality.

Hamish's face suddenly went white with fury. All traces of the laconic Westerner vanished before his outburst. "You've got the guts to say that? Shit! It was you, goddamit, who talked me into the whole crazy scheme. If anybody's to blame for Russel, it's you. You, the smart-ass doctor. If anyone's to blame for Russel carved up into as many pieces as a Parcheesi set, Jesus, it's you. You, the big-deal psychiatrist. Shit. Martha was right. I should have listened to her. 'My whore-lady shrink,' she called you. And she . . ." The words rattled on out of Hamish's mouth, but a glazed look came over his eyes, a look of confusion, as if he didn't believe what he was hearing himself say. "I don't know . . . I don't know . . ."

Jenny sat in stunned silence, watching. She knew that

Hamish didn't mean what he was saying—it was only his helpless fury that made him use her as an outlet. Jenny had seen patients go through the same processes, and she knew that the release it provided was necessary. She knew all of these things and much more, and yet, and yet . . . if she knew so much, how could what he said hurt so much? How could this man's entirely excusable fury upset her so much, making her cry, leaving her with her insides shriveling as she sat there?

Hamish stopped, his mind replaying the words he had said. He looked at her unbelievingly. "Oh, Christ, Jenny. I'm sorry. Jesus. I didn't mean that. Any of it. I don't have to tell you that."

It was time. Jenny stood up and smiled widely, as if no one had said anything. "I know, Hamish. I know."

Hamish made a curious gesture with his arms and hands, as if he wanted to open them to Jenny but was embarrassed to after what he'd said, or was afraid that he would be rejected. Jenny Cobb walked the three short steps across the room and put herself inside his tentatively open arms, which suddenly stopped being tentative and wrapped themselves around her. She found she was crying, which she couldn't ever remember having done in anyone's arms before. Hamish's body was shaking, but she couldn't tell if he was crying, too, or was still trembling from the terrible things he had said.

They didn't even hear Blagden Tyne knocking on the door. And after a minute, when Tyne remembered that Jenny was in the sub-basement room with Hamish, he stopped knocking and walked quietly away.

Chapter 19 _____

> *When I undertook this thing, it was simple*
> *because there was a single-minded reason for*
> *every step of the plan.*
>   *Now I don't know. The thing kept growing*
> *so—like some dark weed that gets started in*
> *a garden and finally chokes out everything*
> *else. How come? K.K. says I'm crazy. Well,*
> *he's wrong, of course. But I wish I could find*
> *out what's really going on inside my head.*
>   *Too bad I can't ask Jenny Cobb. I bet she's*
> *a pretty good shrink—for a lady. I keep*
> *reading about women patients who sue their*
> *psychiatrists for shoving them into bed. I*
> *wonder if a lady shrink's ever had a guy pull*
> *the same stunt?*
>   *Don't worry, Jenny. I wouldn't sue.*
>   —TAPE-LOG OF THE PIPER,
>   ENTRY DATED JUNE 10 (EVENING).

At 11:05, Hamish Hamilton threw his legs over the hard, steel-frame cot and went over to pick up the phone. Jenny watched from the bed, dreading what the call might be. It was Tyne, calling from his office upstairs. "Sorry to bother you, Hamish. But you'd better turn on your TV. The Piper's back broadcasting. Late, but back."

For a second they talked, then Hamish hung up. Jenny wrapped herself in a blanket and watched as Hamish, stark naked, turned on the set. Automatically, he slipped into his clothes while his eyes remained glued to the glowing television tube.

Since it was after prime time—at least in the East—the news programs for late evening were manned by the local stations' anchormen rather than those from the network. They had chosen to play the Piper's program in the clear, keeping silent instead of blending their own comments with the Piper's words as they had in the past. For pictures, the cameras picked up scenes of a serene-looking Greenport and its surroundings, Senator Blyden's house, and whatever else they had been able to tape during the day. The effect was eerie.

One after the other, the children from the bus identified themselves and said that they were safe—for the moment. The last of them to speak was Robert Teal, the youngest member of the Glee Club. "This is Robert Teal," his voice piped uncertainly, a quaver very close to tears evident in his inflection. "They used me on the bus to make the other boys stay quiet. A gun, they used a gun. And they've got a boy here all cut up. And it's what they'll do to me, Mummy, if you don't do what they say. Please do what they say."

Jenny saw Hamish wince as Teal talked about the boy who was "all cut up"; quickly she tried to slip back into her clothes as unobtrusively as possible. Over the TV set now, they could hear Paige Rathbin talking. A few minutes later, the station put a picture of Paige on the screen. (The remote directors could by now guess which voices they would probably hear, and they had scurried around town today until they had pictures of them: Paige Rathbin, Senator Blyden's son Kevin, and, possibly—if only as a detached scream—Russel Hamilton.)

The stock reports for the day droned on. The reading had become so ritualized, Kip himself wasn't sure why it was continued; the device no longer contributed anything. Obviously, Paige Rathbin was alive; Kevin Blyden was alive; Russel Hamilton was alive. Their statements were usually artfully woven in with stretches of old tapes of those who weren't, including snippets that hadn't been played the first time around, so that being sure who was alive and who wasn't became largely impossible.

Kevin Blyden's voice suddenly broke in on Paige's reading. After a few seconds' pause, his picture appeared on the screen—the only photograph of him the station had been able to find—looking odd in his sailing clothes, his famous father's message from the Piper. Message: To all parents, including arm thrown protectively over one shoulder. "This is a those whose children were on today's bus. Tomorrow night I

shall demand the 'ultimate ransom' from one of you. Only
one. And it will be done privately. What the ransom is,
you—and only you—will learn at that time. Do not contact
the authorities to tell them either who you are or the nature
of the ransom for your child. If you do, I shall know, and
your child will wind up in more pieces than Russel Hamilton.
If you really love your son, you will pay the Piper in silence,
and your child will be safely returned. I think by now you all
know that the Piper is no politician; he means what he says.
Tomorrow night, then, for one of you, the 'ultimate ransom'
for your child. For the rest of you, out there in radio land,
the 'ultimate ransom' will be explained and demanded
later—and from all of you at the same time." There was a
pause, almost a giggle, then: "Kind of keeps you guessing,
doesn't it?"

Paige Rathbin began speaking again. The picture momentarily went back to the anchor desks of the various stations,
then abruptly returned to the earlier snapshot of Paige. "In
the matter of Russel Hamilton, a package will be received
sometime tomorrow. Area Two. Repeat. Area Two."

The sound from Kip's mobile transmitters went dead. The
camera returned to the anchormen, who immediately began
trying to make some sort of sense of what they had just
heard. As with most such instant analyses, the effort was not
very successful.

Hamish had groaned when Paige Rathbin mentioned that
another package would be arriving, and now he was searching worriedly on the small flat table for the Polaroid snapshot
with the butcher's markings on it. Area Two was a neat rectangle running from Russel's navel to his kneecaps. A terrible
thought swept through Hamish's mind, one so terrible that he
dismissed it immediately. Silently handing the picture to
Jenny, he sank into the hard, wooden chair.

"I'm right back where I was. What the hell do I do?"

Jenny didn't answer.

By morning, the entire country found itself emotionally involved in what was happening in Greenport. What the Piper
was doing to that town's children had always carried with it
the frightening thought that the same thing could happen
anywhere. People across the country were shocked by the

events. But up to now, people not familiar with Greenport had listened with a distant, detached ear. Some stations had broadcast the first tapes of the kidnapped children and then stopped; others had stepped up their coverage until the arrival of the torture tapes, when most viewers found the sound of Russel's screams and a description of the packages' contents too strong to take. However, the disappearance of the bus with twenty-three children and a driver, guard, and faculty advisor—right from under the very noses of the police—left everyone in the country shaken. It was no longer a matter of events happening in some distant place to unfamiliar people; it suddenly felt as if the Piper's crimes were being committed against people they knew intimately.

In broadcasting circles, it was generally agreed that it was the tapes of the children that made the story so terrifying. The voices of these children pleading with their parents gave the incident an immediacy that made the Chowchilla kidnapping seem like an event that had happened on some other planet. The newspapers only had the written word to work with, but even transcripts of the tapes had a ring of immediacy to them that the ordinary ransom note rarely produces. And radio, usually the media stepchild, in this case was on an equal footing with everyone else. The result was as dramatic and detailed a coverage as ever given any crime, short of assassination.

When the early searches set up by Tyne and Cummins produced no sign of the bus, Connecticut's governor called in the National Guard to help comb the area. The Guard was in addition to teams of Boy Scouts, the FBI, a detachment from Andrews Air Force Base, and helicopter teams from both the Coast Guard and the Groton Submarine Base. To simplify the chain of command, the White House, through the Justice Department, ruled that all Federal units involved would be responsible to the FBI, with Blagden Tyne reporting directly back to Justice.

(White House involvement produced one curious sidelight. The bus had disappeared on a Thursday. During one of his every-other-week fireside chats, the President suggested, in a brief aside, that the country pray for the return of the children. Kip had watched this with amusement, wondering if Angel Sanchez, too, would be reborn. If so, would it be with or without his missing hand? He thought of writing the White House a letter on the theology of this point but decided against it. Letters, somehow, were always being tracked back to their senders.)

Kip decided that he didn't have very much time for writing letters, anyway.

After the broadcast, Kip and K.K. made their separate ways back to the cistern, Kip in the Volks van and K.K. in the recently purchased pickup. Quietly letting themselves down the ladder into the labyrinth of tunnels, they silently slipped along the hall and picked up headphones connected to a hidden mike inside the vault. Kip hoped to hear nothing but the restless sleep-sounds of unhappy boys; instead he heard Kevin Blyden making a soft but clearly audible speech to the rest.

"They come in here one at a time," Blyden said. "There's twenty-seven of us in all, and that makes twenty-seven to one. My plan—I've been studying this place pretty carefully—is to hide behind the door. Then when one of them comes in, I'll jump him. Even if he gets one shot off, he can only kill one of us. We get his gun, go knock off whoever's outside, and clear the hell out of here. But the timing's got to—"

"With a shotgun he won't kill just one guy," said another voice, about the same age as Kevin—17—but one that neither Kip nor K.K. could identify. "The pattern spreads out and could nail a whole bunch of us."

Kevin Blyden wasn't used to being contradicted, and his voice sounded irritated. "Okay, sure. If we were dumb enough to be standing close together. I meant for us to be spread out along the walls and back."

The unidentified voice sounded skeptical. "So he only kills two or three. Or, maybe he has time for two shots—both barrels—and gets half a dozen. Jesus. It isn't just grabbing him—what counts is getting that damned shotgun away from him before he can fire. If there was something in here to zonk him on the head with . . ."

"Besides," Paige Rathbin's voice could suddenly be heard, "they don't always come in here one at a time. Sometimes it's both of them. Like when they take Kevin or me out to make the tapes. Quint's right. We've got to get something to hit the first one on the head."

Now that Kip knew the anonymous voice belonged to Quinton Bradley, the voice's expertise in weaponry made more sense; Bradley knew guns the way most boys his age knew their own bodies. Kip turned around to K.K., taking the headphones away from his own ear as he did. "We've got to break this up. They've got too much time to think and too much light to think by. Open the sliding panel."

K.K. reached up on the heavy iron door and noisily slid a small sliding panel open. Through it, he and Kip could see the whole room, the huge candles stuck on the walls burning unevenly in the dimness.

"Okay in there," Kip bellowed. "Time for lights out. Paige, start collecting those candles and hand them out through the panel, one at a time." For a second, no one moved. Kip banged the barrels of the shotgun against the open panel for emphasis and watched Paige collecting the candles. Slowly Paige began handing them out. Kevin Blyden marched over to the door when all but one of the giant candles were gone.

"For Christ's sake, Kip, aren't you at least going to leave us one?"

"Keep you kids up too late. Plotting. Hide behind the door. Fat chance."

Blyden's face wore a mystified expression as he tried to figure out how Kip had heard that conversation through a three-inch, iron door. "You're as much of a prick as I always thought you were, Kip."

"Shut up and go to sleep. All of you."

"Just one candle," pleaded Paige Rathbin. "The younger kids will be terrified in this place if it's all black."

"Sorry, Paige. Give it to me."

The final candle was shoved out and the panel door slammed shut again. Kip and K.K. softly walked away. Behind them, the room full of children began yelling and pounding on the door in panic, but the only answer was the echo of their own cries and the steady drip-drip of water down the solid rock walls of their prison.

At 2:12 A.M., the school bus that half of the State was looking for showed up. It was not found by the Boy Scouts, the Coast Guard, the National Guard, the FBI, the Air Force or the Navy; instead, the bus found *them*.

The planning behind this maneuver was exquisite. Half an hour earlier, Kip and K.K. stood in an alley behind Town Hall. K.K. had driven the bus there, with Kip following a little later in the Volks van. The bus was still in its bright colors, bunting, and Fair signs, although the music from its speakers was no longer playing. K.K. carefully parked the bus in the mouth of the alley, at the top of a small incline overlooking the mostly darkened building. At this hour, virtually no one was on the downtown streets, and the one policeman they encountered had cheerfully waved at K.K. in his disguise, figuring the Fair bus was on its way home. In the alley, the retransformation took place. A hose that Kip had spotted there earlier was turned on and the water color paint was washed off, returning the bus to its original bright yellow. Silently, the loudspeaker was unscrewed from the roof and put in the back of the Volks van. The boards covering the windows and the Fair bunting followed it into the Volks. At the last moment, before climbing into the van and driving away, K.K. switched on the bus's lights, forced the accelerator to the floor with a brick, and then, just before jumping out through the open passenger door, jammed the bus into gear with his gloved hand. Kip and K.K. were gone by the time the bus's motor responded. It careened down the narrow alleyway, bounced off one wall, and roared down the incline into the side of Town Hall. In the two A.M. stillness, the crash seemed tremendous, a sound made even more shattering by the accidental jamming of the bus's horn on impact.

The Town Hall building seemed to explode with people. The lone guard came running out, followed by those of the press corps unable to find a motel or hotel room, and therefore sleeping on cots in the improvised press room. Pouring out in their undershorts, the newsmen gaped in disbelief. Cameras flashed. Later, Alan Whitemore, roused from his bed, was photographed—without realizing it—looking as if he had personally been driving the bus when it crashed into the wall. A man from the company that provided the bus examined it and said that this was indeed the missing one, noting that most of the major damage came from crashing into the side of Town Hall. Three small holes had also been drilled into the roof, he said, but it was otherwise pretty much a badly caved-in version of the bus that left his garage earlier that day.

In spite of the hour—and because he suspected that Hamish wouldn't be asleep anyway—Blagden Tyne went downstairs to Hamish's room when he returned to First Baptist. Behind, he left the teams of forensics experts still swarming over the bus. His suspicion was correct: a narrow slit of light coming from under Hamish's door showed that he was still up. Not sure whether Jenny was with him, Tyne knocked softly. The door flew open.

"The bastard's laughing at us." Tyne walked into Hamish's stark little room and sank into one of the hard wooden chairs. "Making us look like a bunch of Keystones." He explained about the bus and its crash into the side of Town Hall. "It gets worse," he added. "Nobody could figure out how the hell the Piper got that bus around town without someone spotting it. Well, one of the forensic guys noticed some odd colors where the metal sections of the body joined. Water color paint. Bright colors—all over the bus. Splinters, shavings, in all window casings. Apparently, they were covered with plywood. Three strange holes in the roof that nobody could explain at first. Then some of the locals remembered that a bus advertising some fair or other drove down the street earlier tonight. Painted psychedelic-style, with bunting, streamers, light, flags, the whole bit. Music coming out of a loudspeaker on the roof. It turns out there wasn't any fair to advertise. That was *our* bus. Probably with the kids right inside. Smack down in the middle of the main drag. Flashing lights, music and all. One cop remembers seeing the fair bus later tonight. Assumed it was on its way home, but it was probably going to the alley behind Town Hall. Big wet place there and dissolved paint where the Piper washed off the water colors."

Tyne, whom Hamish had rarely seen lose his even temper, suddenly stood up and kicked the hard wooden chair halfway across the room. "I can understand guys who are sick. I can understand guys who are sick and bright. But sick, bright, and *funny*? Some sense of humor. Laughing while he kidnaps kids, kills kids, and carves kids up for kicks. What the hell are we dealing with?"

Hamish could only sigh. For a moment the two men stared at each other in their helplessness. Tyne was the first to turn his eyes away, suddenly aware that if he had problems, they were abstract, while Hamish's were personal and a thousand times more painful. He flicked an imaginary speck of dust from one shoe to hide his embarrassment.

"I'm sorry. That was pretty thoughtless."

"No, you're right. Everything you said. Sick. With a sick sense of humor. It's been there all the way through. Now this. Taking a big chance with the bus just to show how clever he is. Laughing at us. Thumbing his nose." Hamish shrugged.

Tyne abruptly changed the subject. "That ring you got on your phone earlier."

"I thought it was a misdial from upstairs. I picked it up and nobody was there." The implications of Tyne bringing it up hit Hamish, and he stared at him.

"Somebody put in a call to you at the motel in Albany. Collect. Then when you answered, disconnected. Phone company says the call was from a booth in Greenport. Just checking on you, I guess."

Hamish ran the words through in his mind. "Collect. Collect from who?"

Tyne turned away. It was a question that he knew that he could no longer avoid answering. "The operator said the voice told her it was from—" averting his eyes, Tyne spoke very softly—"from the manager of Russel's Prime Meats."

"Shit."

"More of that damned sick humor."

"Did the operator have anything to say about the voice?"

"It sounded like an old woman's, the operator thought. She remembered the call because of the disconnect, and also because she thought it was kind of crazy that a store with a name like Russel's Prime Meats would be run by a woman."

His conversation with the night watchman from the warehouse in Port Chester swam through Hamish's head. "The old lady again."

"Still in business."

"Yup."

"Do you know what you're going to do yet? About staying undercover or coming out."

Hamish walked over to the ventilating shaft and stared at

the grill, as if it were a window that he could see out of. "No, I don't know. As far as I can see, there's no right answer. Leave town or we cut up your kid. So you leave town and they keep cutting him up anyway."

Uncomfortable, Tyne changed the subject. "The 'ultimate kidnapping' isn't what I expected at all. I thought it was going to be a child movie star or the President's kid or something like that. The Secret Service and the FBI had agents crawling all the hell over the place. But a busful from Country Day? It was always a possibility, I guess, which is why we pulled the school closing without any warning and why the bus was presumably covered so well." Tyne considered something a moment, then shook his head and slapped his palm with his fist. "I should have used my own men, dammit."

Hamish acted as if Tyne hadn't spoken. "Hell, I don't know. Maybe Russel would be better off if the Piper did kill him. Cold-blooded thing to think about, but, Jesus, you reach a point somewhere. How much can a fourteen-year-old kid be expected to take?"

Tyne shuddered. He shouldn't be here, talking about the Piper's sick sense of humor, the bus, and protecting movie stars' kids. While Hamish himself was being torn apart. Tyne swore at himself for his own insensitivity, squeezed Hamish's arm, and went out the door, walking slowly and worriedly up the stairs of First Baptist to his makeshift office.

Somehow, someway, the man behind all of this had to be caught before the rest of the children met the same fate as Russel, in the process systematically destroying their parents as Hamish was being destroyed.

"You didn't get home until awfully late."

"Snooping again? I should have figured."

"No, your car driving in woke me and I couldn't get back to sleep. So I looked out the window and saw you. Very, very late. Three in the morning, to be exact."

Kip shrugged, then blew his horn at a dog seemingly unimpressed by his coming. It was 8:30 A.M. and Kip would have liked to sleep a lot longer—his whole body cried out for more rest—but there were a lot of things to be done today. And on top of everything else, his father had told him that he would have to drive Dee to the Racquet Club for her tennis lesson; some friends would then take her to Seven Hills for the rest of the day. This change had required a quick call to K.K. to get him to cover something for him. K.K. was as enthusiastic about his assignment as Kip was about his, but neither directive could be ignored.

Now, just to make the burden heavier, Dee was twitting her brother about when he got home. "Three o'clock. Wow! If Dad knew that—with all the gross stuff happening around here—he'd land on you, Kip. He really would."

"Well, he doesn't know. And I'd like to keep it that way." Kip slightly turned his head to look at Dee and appraise her mood.

Dee shrugged. "You could help me get to know Reggie Bowers."

Something twisted inside Kip. Reggie Bowers wouldn't look twice at Dee, and this conviction existed not just because Dee was his sister. Dee, he would grudgingly admit, was quite attractive for her age. But right there was the problem—age. Too young, too damned young, for Reggie Bowers even to notice. "Deal," he lied. "Not this week, maybe. But for sure, the week after."

"Mellow."

Kip winced. He supposed that when he was 15, his language was filled with the same teen-age argot—words like "gross," and "mellow," and "heavy"—which each year appeared out of nowhere and suddenly became part and parcel of basic self-expression. He could remember wondering how it was that kids from everywhere—not just in the East, but clear across the country—fastened precisely onto the same words at precisely the same time, as if fed by some giant word machine in the Midwest.

The main point was the promise of closer exposure to Reggie Bowers had purchased Dee's silence about his late hours. That was important. So was, he suddenly realized as he was driving between the brick gateposts and up the long drive of the Racquet Club, so was his appearance here. Kip Grolier had to to be seen—functioning in his normal pattern around town, waving confidently, smiling encouragingly.

The Racquet Club appeared only superficially touched by

the crisis that currently kept a number of its members
chained to their phones, waiting for the news about their
missing children. Certainly the conversation on the terrace
was more subdued than usual, with the members talking to
each other about the only subject anyone could think of dis-
cussing. Both a State policeman and a Pinkerton guard were
visible around the grounds—and there were probably more
that weren't so visible. On the club's perimeter, the Anchor
fence back-gates and delivery entrances were locked and
chained, a fact in itself unusual and inconvenient. But on the
courts, the soft *poing*-plop of the tennis balls, the quick thud-
ding of agile feet in sneakers, the subdued cries of victory
and defeat sounded the same as ever. Kip walked around the
entire area, making sure that he was seen by as many people
as possible before climbing back into his car and racing
toward his meeting with K.K.

"Hi, Miss Cobb. Kip Grolier. What a surprise to run into
you here."
"Oh, of course . . . Kip. The interview. Well, running into
me here shouldn't be a surprise. Everyone has to go to a
bank eventually. It's why bankers are so rich."
The two of them stood at the counter of the Greenport
National Bank. Actually, Jenny had been the one surprised,
not Kip. For K.K. had been following her ever since she left
the Soundsight Motel this morning, reporting her every stop
into Kip's phone-answering machine and leaving messages on
the tape. As soon as he got back from the Racquet Club, Kip
had taken this last message and raced over to find K.K. outside the bank. After a curt nod, Kip sent him back to keep
an eye on things at the cistern.
Kip laughed at Jenny's remark because he knew that he
was supposed to. At the same time, the way she tossed her
hair as she spoke, the delicate yet agile expressions that flew
across her face whenever she said anything to be amusing, affected Kip, making him *want* to laugh, to be part of her en-
chanted world, where everything was fresh and clean and
smiling. Jenny studied him as he leaned against the wall, his
face radiant and laughing, the rows of white teeth almost
blinding. His pelvis, as always, was thrown slightly forward.

Inside herself, the same stirrings she had felt the first day she had met him returned, making her angry with herself all over again. She saw his face suddenly go serious.

"It's been terrible, hasn't it?" he asked in a soft voice. "All this crazy stuff around here. The Piper. It makes you sick."

Jenny stepped up to the counter, her place in line automatically moving her forward. She presented a check, but the teller said that he would have to have it authorized by an officer of the bank and disappeared with it.

"Yes, Kip, absolutely unbelievable," Jenny finally replied.

"I heard you were helping the police and the FBI."

Jenny shifted uncomfortably. "Yes. That's right."

The teller returned and counted out some money. Kip's first idea was to cash a check of his own to explain what he was doing here, but decided that would give Jenny too easy an excuse to say good-bye. He patted his madras jacket and feigned annoyance. "Damn. Forgot my wallet. I'll have to come back later. No checks."

The teller shrugged. "You don't have to have your own, Mr. Grolier. I can give you a cashier's check. Your father—"

"No sweat. I don't like to write a check without my book. I could get overdrawn."

The teller laughed, breaking up to show Kip how ridiculous an idea that was. Kip could see Jenny trying to get away, but so far he'd been able to keep his position, shifting slightly so that it was difficult for her to move very far from the window without asking him to move. Now that his business was complete, she could. "Kip," she began. "I have some things—"

He took her by the arm, flashing a smile as he did. "I'll help. Need a ride?"

From a distance, some faint warning bell signaled inside Jenny; she felt the rise of a small panic. "Don't be silly, Kip. I can get around by—"

"My car's just down the street." Still holding onto her lightly by one arm, with his free hand Kip indicated the convertible Porsche, an extravagant 17th birthday present from his father.

"So's mine," said Jenny tartly, withdrawing her elbow from his hand. "Or rather, Mr. Hertz's. Nowhere as fancy as

yours, but everybody knows they don't try as hard. Anyway,
it gets me there."

He was seized with panic. "I wanted to talk to you. I didn't
have anything to do in that bank," he blurted. "I just saw you
go in and I followed you. There's something I have to say."

Jenny stared at him in amazement. Kip's mobile smile, for
once, was gone, replaced by a solemn, tight-lipped expression.
His eyes were wide and pleading. She wasn't entirely sure,
but she thought that she saw trembling movements in the tiny
muscles around his mouth and eyes. "All right." She said it
tentatively, confusion evident in her voice. At the same time,
she stepped toward the small blue Chevy she had rented. Sliding in, she took her seat behind the wheel as Kip followed,
leaving the door open behind him. His legs were stretched out
of the car onto the pavement, as if they were too long or he
too lazy to bring them inside.

Jenny waited for a moment, letting him settle down. She
had done this a thousand times with people in therapy, but
somehow the last person she had ever expected to be using
this device on was Kip. Remembering his sense of humor, she
decided that the best approach was a light one. "Is anything
wrong? Or, given the present circumstances in this town—is
anything right?"

He smiled weakly. "It's those circumstances I wanted to
talk about."

"I see." Jenny didn't exactly congratulate herself but,
rather, felt a glow of professional pride; the "circumstances,"
she had already guessed, probably lay behind what was troubling him.

"You see, some of the guys and I, well, we talk about
things all the time. I pick up a lot that way. And, hell, I'm no
shrink and I'm no detective, but I came to some theories
about the Piper. Maybe, since you're working so close with
the police and the FBI, they might start something ticking in
your head. I know it sounds foolish . . ."

"In my line, things ticking in people's heads pay the rent; I
wouldn't dare consider them foolish." Jenny had forced the
remark and the laugh that followed it, but the gambit had
worked; on Kip's face she caught sight of a smile floating
perilously close to the surface.

"I suppose."

"I *know*. Tell me about those theories of yours. I promise not to laugh. We need all the help we can get." Years of experience had told Jenny that Kip wasn't really interested in telling her his theories; it was something else, something deeper troubling him. But to find out—and to be of any help to him—she had to play along.

He finally brought his legs into the car and closed the door, as if to insure privacy. "The theories. Well, some of the guys and myself, you know, that is—I came, sort of, to a conclusion on one point."

"Anybody with one rational conclusion is one step ahead of us."

Kip winced mentally. The word "us"—Hamish and Jenny?—bothered him. "What I read, what I see on TV, they say you're looking for a youngish guy who knows Greenport. A fag, sort of. Sick in the head, too. But, I think you're missing the boat."

"Oh. How?"

"I don't know how to put this, but you know, it's crossed my mind a couple of times, you're looking for a grownup, an adult. The Piper could just as easily be a kid, couldn't he?" Kip looked at her, feeling his whole insides begin to tremble. Why the hell had he said that? It was asking for trouble.

To Jenny, his question was as if someone had just pushed the plunger and set off a chain reaction of high explosives. This wasn't just Kip's theory; it was her theory. Did he know something? Had he heard something? Guesswork? Intuition? Instinct? She struggled to remain looking noncommittal; too much interest on the surface could easily frighten him off. "A kid. The Piper a kid . . . a boy at Country Day, I suppose. I don't know. I've never thought about that, Kip. These things the man does—they would be so difficult for a youngster."

"That would depend on his age. I mean, the younger kids, sure. Impossible. But some of the older ones, seniors, for instance—Christ, some of them are men, really."

Jenny turned herself around in her seat, resting her back against the corner formed by the seat-back and the side of the door. She sensed the subtle implications that were buried in Kip's last remarks. Automatically, she fought to keep the conversation going; she could not entirely tell why, but Kip's line of reasoning, so like her own, was making her uncomfortable. "It's a possibility," she said. "No one can argue with that. But why? Why would a student—students, probably—be kidnapping other students? Most of the boys don't need money. Not enough to take chances like that."

Jenny looked at Kip, urging him to continue.

"The students. There's this one guy . . ." Kip let his voice trail off and shook his head. "No, that would be a pretty damned bad thing to say . . ."

"Kidnapping kids, killing kids, is more than just 'pretty damned bad,' Kip. If you know something . . ."

"Artie Lansing. He used to come into the locker room after tennis. Always just when I was getting out of my tennis shorts. Follow me right into the shower room and stare. And once, one night, when we were in the back seat of somebody's car, on the way to the beach, he put his hand down, well, sort of down the back of my bathing suit, between my skin and the suit, you know. Kept moving his fingers around, y'know? I had to pretend that I needed to pee and then get into the front seat when I came back. . . . Artie Lansing. Football team, you know? Tackle, I think. Strong enough to do just about anything. Good swimmer, too. Used to skin-dive for kicks."

It struck Jenny the accumulation of facts that Kip was presenting grew a little faster than it should have, but she dismissed the idea as overreaction. Kip seemed to be studying her, and moved restlessly in his seat. "I probably shouldn't have mentioned it. I don't have any proof about Artie's being queer. Just a thing here and a thing there. And besides, being a fruit wouldn't mean he was the Piper and went around killing kids. That's a—stereotype."

"No, Kip, you were right, absolutely right, to tell me . . ." Jenny spoke very slowly, trying to digest this new twist in its entirety, arguing both sides of the concept to set up the rationale that she would present to Hamish and Tyne, an argument which essentially boiled down to: *Even some of the kids think this Piper could be another student.* After a moment, she realized she'd stopped talking and went back to reassuring Kip. "Nothing you brought up really proves Artie is the Piper. Or, that he isn't. And from what you said, it doesn't even mean he's a homosexual. It's all just suspicions. But right now, suspicions are all that any of us have to go on. So I'm glad you told me. Very glad. Anyway, you shouldn't ever feel embarrassed to talk to me about anything, Kip. Please. As for the student thing—it's a new angle we can try on for size." She smiled at him.

"Great." Inside Kip was a growing disbelief that he could really ever have fingered himself so neatly. Probably someone besides Jenny had had the idea already, but what the hell was he doing spreading support for it? Jenny Cobb, after all, was working with the authorities, dedicated to catching a psychopath, and, that psychopath, in the end, was himself. If anybody ever checked out alibis and stories against time, he'd had it.

"You've been a big help, Kip. I'm glad that—"

"I'd like to keep on being one. I'd like to work with you, Miss Cobb." Calling her "Miss Cobb" sounded strangely out of place as he felt his hand creep over to her and suddenly and clumsily fasten around her neck. He leaned his body in closer and put his other arm around her, watching Jenny's eyes widen in disbelief.

"Kip!" She said the word sharply and loudly. Briefly, his hand went motionless, then withdrew itself. Jenny watched him move himself away from her, his whole frame cringing in embarrassment. Worse, she was embarrassed for herself. She had the ridiculous feeling she would have liked to let his hand, so tentative and untried, wander and explore everything and anything it desired. But he was a child. A child, she repeated to herself.

She sat where she was, her mouth slightly open in what was still surprise, trying to think of what she could say to spare him the inevitable apology. She saw Kip's eyes raise themselves to her face, watched his body convulse in a sudden shudder, and was stunned when he abruptly threw himself at her, pinning her into the corner as his hands tore at her dress. "Kip!" This time she said his name in what was more of a shout than a warning. "Kip! Stop it!" Suddenly she could no longer speak because he had forced his mouth against hers, his lips moving savagely against hers in an attempt to force them apart. Both of his hands had grabbed hers, pinioning them so that she could not use them to force him away.

She was never quite sure how she managed it, but some instinct caused her to jerk her knee off the seat, and it caught him squarely between his legs and where they joined his body. Kip gave a sudden yelp of pain as his body doubled over. When he straightened himself up again, his eyes wore a glazed look, as if he was as mystified by his sudden attack as Jenny was.

For a moment he said nothing. Then, wincing, he appeared to remember everything that he had done and shook his head with the agony of remembering. "I don't know . . . I don't know. My God, what was I thinking? You. Of all people, you."

Summoning every last bit of strength she had, Jenny laughed and tried to put a light face on the incident. "Oh, come on, Kip— Me of all people, indeed! I'm not *that* old." Kip ignored her remark and kept staring ahead of himself.

"I'm sorry, Christ, I'm sorry. I don't know what—it's all the uncertainty—the pressure—the terrible things here in town—Jesus, I don't know what happened."

Once again, Jenny forced a laugh. "Nothing to worry about, Kip. Tension makes everybody lose their heads a little. And, when you think of it, it's really a great compliment." He was already half out the car door, but she touched his near arm lightly, giving him her warmest smile so that he wouldn't feel rejected or foolish or put-down, as a child. "I'd love to have you help me. Anything else you run across, please, Kip, please just call me. I appreciate it. I really do."

He smiled back shyly, closed the door, and quickly walked away. Jenny noticed that he had kept himself slightly bent over until he could jam his hands into his pockets; it didn't require a psychiatrist to figure out why. The person who needed a shrink, she decided as she put the car into gear, was herself. She had asked for it. Jennifer Cobb: lover of boys.

On his way to the Porsche, Kip cursed at himself. He had played with fire, openly courting disaster. For what? He couldn't answer his own question. But for the first time since the disappearance of Gilly Axminster, one of the authorities, at least, had been given a rich clue as to the identity of the

Piper. Finally the shadow of guilt had been cast across the right group, if not yet across the right person. And given the peculiar way he was acting, Kip knew, the narrowing down of focus could come at any time

Chapter 20 _____

Only two things about my talk with Jenny
Cobb really bother me: that half-assed pass
of mine (Robert Teal II could have done
better, and he's only 10), and, that I got
myself talking about how maybe the Piper
was a student.

Jenny seemed to have already thought of
that anyway, but talking about it was still
stupid. Like issuing an invitation to my own
funeral. Of course, she issued her own kind
of invitation when she said, "Come talk to
me about things, anytime. Please, Kip."
Goddamn, I haven't stopped shaking yet.

Sometimes I wonder whether I don't have
a death wish. If the police were bright, what I
theorized to Jenny could get me caught, tried
and fried. Or, hell, if Artie heard the
whopper I made up about him, he'd come
kill me on the spot. If I do have a death wish,
he'd be happy to oblige.

          —TAPE-LOG OF THE PIPER,
          ENTRY DATED JUNE 11.

Above Greenport, the usually pristine skies aquired a new—
and slightly threatening—appearance. Usually, you could
gaze upwards into the Heavens without fear of anything
more hazardous than an occasional chickadee or cardinal.
But as the search for the children's hiding place intensified,
the skies were suddenly filled with an armarda of Army,
Navy, and Coast Guard light observor aircraft and helicop-
ters, buzzing thick as flies around a beached cod. From there,
men with field-glasses leaned out and scanned the country below, holding the glasses in one hand and keeping a precarious
grip on the plane's door-frame with the other. As Kip, looking up uncertainly, put it to K.K.: "It's only a matter of time

before one of those guys falls out of the sky onto someone's head. They're more dangerous than we are."

Up to this point, the only danger the spotter-aircraft had presented was to themselves: at eleven that morning, a National Guard Piper Cherokee coming in low over the Sound, was caught by a sudden downdraft over the Leafpoint Harbor clubhouse, crashing into the Wesley Brothers Boatyard beyond. No one was injured.

In the sub-basement of First Baptist, Hamish, unlike the rest of Greenport, ignored both the growing flotilla of aircraft and the Piper Cherokee's crash. He lay on his bunk, hands behind his head, staring blankly at the ceiling, tracing imaginary patterns on the ceiling, and feeling depressed and lonely. He had tried watching television, but the daytime soapers, usually good for at least a laugh, had left him unsmiling; he had tried reading the paperbacks that Jenny left for him, but after a few pages, discovered he had already read them. Usually, Tyne would be popping in and out of his room, or he could count on Jenny to put in an appearance or two. But this morning they were all over at Town Hall at a hastily summoned meeting of the Town Council. The Council was looking for reassurance, and neither Tyne, nor Jenny, nor Chief Inspector Cummins had very much to give.

At around 11:30, Hamish, half-dozing, was startled by the sound of his phone ringing. Picking it up, he heard the voice of Ellery White, the man closest to Tyne at the FBI. "Mr. Hamilton?" the voice asked. "Another package was just delivered. To your home. Our men there picked it up and it's been fluoroscoped and tested and it's okay. I guess you'll want to wait for Mr. Tyne before opening it. But I knew that you would want to hear about it."

"Can you bring it down?"

"Well, yes. But I know Mr. Tyne usually—"

"He's going to be tied up in that meeting for quite a while. It's important I find out what's inside. If you'd come down with it . . ."

Ellery White's voice sounded uncertain. He wasn't sure he knew what Tyne would want him to do. "I could open it up here and tell you," he suggested.

"Goddammit, bring it down!"

White sighed. After a few minutes during which neither

man spoke—they could hear each other breathing quite
clearly—Ellery White capitulated. "Okay."

Taking the usual care not to destroy any part of the wrap-
pings, the box was forlornly centered on the stark wooden
table and slowly unwrapped. The cover on the Spaulding
Brothers box had been Scotch-taped shut, but once the pieces
of transparent plastic were cut, Hamish was free to open the
package. Taking a deep breath, he tugged on the cover until
he could feel it loosen from the box, and finally pulled it
completely off.

White saw him turn ashen, then grab the table to steady
himself. White stepped in closer, partly to see for himself
what the box contained and partly to grab Hamish if he
keeled over. What he confronted inside the box made White
gasp. Too late, he realized that he had made a serious blunder; he should never have let Hamish know that the box had
even been delivered.

With an animal roar, Hamish seized the package and raced
out of the room, up the stairs, and out of the door of First
Baptist. The sexton, Mr. Rawlins, watched him in silent surprise; he had heard, both from Mr. Tyne and on television,
that Hamish had left town to satisfy one of the kidnapper's
demands, and it stunned him to see the man come bounding
out of his own church basement. Hamish's agonized expression also left Rawlins baffled; the Chief of Police was ordinarily such a laconic, self-controlled Westerner, it had
never occurred to the sexton that he could cry, just like anyone else. Most of all, as he later told FBI Agent White, it
struck him that Hamish didn't really know where he was going; his breath was coming in gasps and his eyes had a wild
look, and his tires gave a terrible screech as he raced his borrowed FBI car up Captains's Avenue toward Charter Street
and the access road.

At Town Hall, as Area Representative for the FBI and the
man Washington had put in charge of the case, Blagden
Tyne, was just finishing his explanation to the Town Council
as to where he thought things stood. Around him, sharing his
side of the table, sat Jenny Cobb, Senator Blyden, Brigadier-
General Hastings of the Connecticut National Guard, Chief
Inspector Cummins of the State Police, Town Manager Alan
Whitemore, and a Naval Commander who was struggling to

coordinate the efforts of various service branches. As Tyne
sat down, he could sense his reassurance that everything possible was being done had not convinced anyone. Whitemore's
summary hadn't helped either; he clearly wasn't overly convinced himself.

Senator Blyden, in his deep-voiced, ponderous sentences,
added further to this feeling of uncertainty. "I'm sure, Mr.
Tyne," he said, "that you are doing your professional best under very trying conditions and in very difficult circumstances.
Certainly, no one could fault you on your efforts to find the
children; there must be a small army of service personnel as
well as other Federal forces visible every time you turn
around in Greenport. No one wishes you better in this effort
than I—for obvious reasons. However, it occurs to me that
the most positive way to insure that no further incidents take
place would be to apprehend the perpetrator with the same
zeal you are demonstrating in your search for the children
. . ." There was such a pompous, circular quality to what the
Senator said that Tyne almost gagged.

"Do you have any specific information, Mr. Tyne, to help
you track down the kidnapper?" The Council member who
asked this, Gordon Laidlaw, fastened his eyes stonily on
Tyne; earlier, Hamish had warned Tyne about Laidlaw,
pointing out that as a close friend of Alan Whitemore's, he
was sure to try and make points for the Town Manager at
Hamish's expense.

"We have several leads, possibilities, areas," explained
Tyne, one hand nervously adjusting his breast-pocket handkerchief. "It would be dishonest, however, to pretend any arrest was imminent."

Laidlaw leaned forward heavily with his arms on the table,
one fist massaging the palm of his other hand. "Don't you
feel, Mr. Tyne, that some kind of gap in the town's own police workings are making your job more difficult? For instance . . ."

Laidlaw found himself interrupted. Robert Grieves, another Council member, had seen where the drift of Laidlaw's
question was heading and, as a strong supporter of Hamish's,
wanted to cut off this line of questioning quickly. He allowed
his voice to override Laidlaw's, which so surprised the man
that he didn't resist.

"I was wondering, Mr. Tyne," said Grieves in a loud voice, so loud that Laidlaw would have no chance to break back in. "I was wondering—and I know other people in Greenport have asked themselves the same question—if you have any idea of what the 'ultimate ransom'—I think that's what this damned Piper calls it—what the 'ultimate ransom' may turn out to be. Any idea? Any guess?"

"None."

Alan Whitemore could contain himself no longer. Where Laidlaw had failed, he would succeed. "I wonder how you feel, Mr. Tyne, about Greenport not having an active Chief of Police during a time of crisis?" The heads at the table turned first toward Whitemore, then toward Tyne. They were concentrating so deeply, waiting for Tyne's answer, that no one heard the door to their left open and close with a soft thud.

"You do, Alan." Hamish, completely collected by now, strode across the room to the table, the box still beneath his arm. A few feet behind him, trying to get to Tyne before Hamish did, was a breathless Ellery White. Tyne and Jenny Cobb stared at Hamish in disbelief, trying to figure out what could have happened to make Hamish show himself. Hurriedly, White began whispering in Tyne's ear.

Hamish firmly planted the box on the top of the table and faced the group seated around it. "Giving in doesn't work. Some things you have to face. All of us. Or, maybe you don't realize what you're really up against." His lips pressed together, Hamish began struggling with the top of the box. Tyne angrily pushed Ellery White away and tried to put a restraining hand on Hamish's arm.

"Hamish . . ."

With a grunt, Hamish pulled the top off the box. Inside, cradled in the palm of Russel's baseball glove, frozen stiff by the dry ice the glove was surrounded by, were Russel's genitals.

"You fucked it up. But good."

"Maybe. But you were supposed to help. Instead, you walk off in a goddamn huff."

"It was my job."

"You weren't there. You were off sulking."

"It was still my job."

"Crap."

K.K. and Kip were standing outside of K.K.'s "operating room" next to the cistern's main holding chamber. K.K. was on the verge of walking off in a huff again, and Kip was alternately trying to calm him or to shift the blame from himself to K.K.

"No reason for it, Kip. No reason, dammit."

"It had to be done. You didn't stick around. So, I did it."

"Swell job, too. You're lucky he didn't croak on the table. Pruning shears, for Christ's sake. I told you I was going to do it, only I'd have done it right."

Kip gave K.K. his most acid smile. "You'd have liked that, wouldn't you, K.K.? Playing around with it. The same way you liked playing around with Paige Rathbin's."

A long-stifled resentment in K.K. suddenly burst into the open. It was a flash fire, ignited by the situation and fed by years of careful observation of his only friend's motives.

Shaking with fury, K.K. thrust his face into Kip's, who blinked in surprise. "Listen, goddammit, listen. Okay, so I'm a homosexual. In your vocabulary—a fag, a fruit, a queer. I'm not pretending I'm anything else. But listen, and listen good. What the hell makes you think you're so fucking immune? Because you're not. Why do you think you so suddenly take over the surgery when it becomes castration? Tell me. Christ, you wouldn't touch a knife before; you even had to leave the room when I cut off unexciting things like fingers and toes and hunks of tissue. But all of a sudden, when it's time to slice off Russel's balls, *wham!* You got to do it yourself. What do you think that means, Kip?

"Why do you guess all the kids we kidnap are boys—well, okay, one girl, and you had to rape her to prove how virile you were. To prove it to me? Or to yourself? And don't tell me you didn't get some kind of thrill when all those other kids were thrashing around, trying to get away. Because you told me you did. Sadism? Sure. But a certain kind, the queer kind. And then there's Jenny Cobb. The sweet and brilliant lady shrink. I have to follow her around town so you can 'run into her.' You tell me how much she sends you. Over and over again. Why tell me? To convince yourself? To hide

from the real reason? What the hell is the real reason behind
any of this?

"Shit, forget all that crap about teaching their parents
something. Forget all that stuff about the 'ultimate ransom'
and face reality—you're probably just as much of a fag as I
am, only I've got the guts to accept it and you don't. I'm
sick, but you're sicker because you don't know you're sick.
You're probably just as—"

Kip's fist crunching into his face made the finishing of
K.K.'s sentence impossible. K.K. staggered back and crashed
into the wall, slipping to the floor with one hand to his mouth
and the other still groping wildly to save his balance. For a
second or two, Kip and K.K. remained motionless, K.K.
studying Kip, his eyes wide with fear. In Kip, the longing to
go at K.K. again was strong; the urge to wipe him and his
painful accusations forever from his mind was overwhelming.
But Kip's strong sense of purpose stopped him; there was so
much to do, and eliminating K.K. would only make it that
much harder. Suddenly he reached down with one hand and
helped K.K. to his feet.

At first K.K. looked at Kip with suspicion, but, confused
as he was, he gradually began to accept Kip's new attitude as
genuine. Perhaps, he told himself, his straight talk had
reached Kip; perhaps Kip already recognized in himself what
he'd just told him, but had been unwilling to talk about it
in front of anybody, even him. Perhaps, perhaps . . . no,
never. It didn't make sense. But K.K.'s devotion, his feelings,
his need for Kip were so strong that he let what he wanted to
think overcome what he really believed.

Finally straightening himself up, K.K. looked Kip in the
eye. "I'm sorry," he said. "But, what the hell, you know—"

"We've got a lot to do. Let's get to it." Kip's face held no
reaction at all. Slowly, K.K. realized that whatever was going
on inside Kip's head was not going to be explained, now or in
the future. The subject would never be mentioned again.
With a small sigh, K.K. shrugged.

Leaning hard, they swung open the door to K.K.'s operating room, inside which Russel lay waiting. The door
slammed shut behind them, the echoes booming heavily back
and forth along the stone corridor outside.

The brief meeting between Hamish and Martha was painful and awkward. Hamish had gone more out of a sense of duty than anything else, but discovered it impossible not to feel a strong pity for her as well. It was probably the *only* strong emotion that he had felt for her in years. Upstairs in the house, she waited for him, as she had ever since his call at noontime telling her he was coming. She was, as he expected, lying in bed, nursing her self-pity, something that she had done, in matters small and large, for years.

As he came into the room, Miss Crane eyed him belligerently and, when Hamish pulled a chair up beside Martha's bed to talk, she showed every intention of staying. Quite curtly, Hamish suggested that she "must have things to do downstairs." Sniffing, Miss Crane left.

Slowly Martha allowed her red-rimmed eyes to rise from the covers to Hamish's face; she looked, Hamish thought, tired and old and anguished; she had every reason to be the last, but that she appeared so tired and old was something she'd done to herself over a period of years. "I thought you were in Salt Lake City," she said unsteadily.

"I had to come back." Hamish's reply edited out a great deal, and was even, on the surface, a direct lie. At first, Martha seemed to accept his answer, although, screwing up her eyes, she squinted at him as a new worry quickly crossed her mind.

"Won't that make the kidnapper kill Russel? Isn't that why you went away? Wasn't that what that Piper monster told you to do?"

Hamish sighed. There was no point in avoiding the issue any longer. Sitting on the edge of the bed, he took her hand lightly. "I think they will anyway. I've thought a lot about it, and that's where I keep coming out. Anyway, Martha—and this is a tough thing for me to say—the kind of stuff they're doing to him—hell, maybe he's better off dead."

"Oh, Jesus." Martha suddenly sat up in bed and grabbed Hamish around the neck with both arms, letting her weight, moist and hot, sag against him. Hamish was made uncomfortable by this sudden, unexpected closeness, but could not bring himself to push Martha away; it seemed too cruel. For some minutes she hung there in misery, while Hamish squirmed. Finally, he withdrew a small distance.

Sitting on the far edge of the bed, he tried to be frank. "I'm sorry I had to tell you that. I'm sorry for a lot of things. I know I've made you unhappy. But I can't do anything about any of it." Hamish felt his tongue grow fat in his mouth, helpless to articulate what he meant while pinned under Martha's painful accusative stare.

"You're killing my son. That's what you're doing. You run off with some floozie, and now you're killing my little boy. My baby."

"Martha, this isn't going to—"

"Dead. Just like you stuck a knife into him. You're killing him dead." As Hamish strode toward the door, he paused and looked back at her, shaking his head from side to side in discouragement—or pity, or defeat, he wasn't sure which himself. She stared at him with hatred, her jaw trembling and her voice rising from an accusing chant to a scream. "Russel. You're killing my Russel. Murdering him. Butchering him. To kiss the ass of this terrible town. To please that whore-lady shrink. You're killing my son, you're killing my son . . ."

The screaming and sobbing half-strangled her, making her words mercifully hard to understand. Hamish spun and walked out the door, calling for Emma Crane as he went.

Emma must have been waiting just outside the door the entire time. She watched Hamish leave with undisguised contempt. "You bastard," she called after him.

Hamish fled down the stairs and out the front door, trying to shut the sound of Martha's words from his ears, but hearing them long after he went inside the FBI offices at First Baptist.

The broadcast from Kip's mobile transmitters came early that night. The FCC had totally failed in getting a fix on them because of K.K.'s ingenious system of cutting back and forth between the two different broadcasting points, leaving Fleming, the FCC's Field Director, helpless. But tonight the Signal Corps, working with some communications specialists from the FBI, thought they would be able to pinpoint the locations much faster, giving the police at least a chance of getting to one of the transmission points before the broadcast switched to the other. Almost as if the kidnappers could read their minds, the system was changed again.

"Shit," said Fleming to Hamish and Tyne. "One point's due East. Out on the water." Through his single earphone, he again listened to the talk back and forth between two field supervisers. "And that point's in motion, too. If we'd known, we could have had the Coast Guard out there and guided them to it. But we didn't know."

Out on the Sound, his running lights doused, Kip glided along in the *Coupon*. There was no special reason he had chosen tonight to use the boat for one of his transmission points; actually, he planned to use this idea later, but he wanted to try it out first. From behind him on the launch he could hear Paige Rathbin's voice piping its way through the nightly ritual of the stock market averages for the day; at the end of this two-minute recital, the broadcast would switch over to K.K. in the van, and would not return to Kip's launch for three minutes. During this silent period, Kip would gun the twin Grays and shoot around to the far side of the Point, slipping along as far as he could down its coast. By reaching a spot on the Point's eastern shoreline further south than the main body of land, the trackers would not know if his broadcast was still coming from the water or from land further to the West.

"This is an announcement from the Piper . . ." Kevin Blyden's voice had the nasal, uncertain sound of any 17-year-old's, but it caused the heads of those gathered in Tyne's office to snap upright. There was an unusual fervor to the way the boy spoke, something that telegraphed that what he had to say would be of particular importance. "Announcement to parents of kidnapped children," Kevin read. "Within the next two days, I'll be outlining for you the 'ultimate ransom.' Pretty damned expensive, too. But . . . once you have paid the ransom, you can go back to your martinis, safe in the knowledge that your kids will be safe. Don't believe me? Don't blame you. But to check me out, call Hamish Hamilton in Salt Lake City, Area Code 801, 434-8500. He was given instructions about his son Russel, and he followed them. He will tell you that he has received a package every day proving his son is still alive. What better word could you have than that of your former Police Chief? And because he followed my demands, Russel will soon be set free. **Free at last, free at last,** as the man said. Parents of the swiped kids are to watch their television sets and be near a phone tomorrow night. To get their marching orders. One final demand for one individual tomorrow night, then, the 'ultimate ransom' for all the children the next night. Your kids are counting on you. End of announcement."

For a few seconds, the people in the room heard a recording of "Good Night, Sweetheart," and then, abruptly, the broadcast from the mobile transmitter ceased. Hamish slumped in his chair.

No one spoke. Finally from Jenny: "That 'Free at last, free at last . . .' It's a Martin Luther King quote from a Negro spiritual. If the Piper was using it correctly, it means being free because you're dead . . ."

Chapter 21 _____

*At school, I've always been looked up to as
one damned big wheel. "A natural-born
leader" is the way Country Day's report cards
described me.*

*There's nothing so surprising, then, in my
running this operation; a real leader can
make people follow him when he's doing
something evil just as easily as when he's
doing something good. It's a special power
all real leaders are born with. Like Lenin
or Stalin or Nixon or Mao.*

*Part of it's being brighter; part of it's
making others feel like a jerk if they don't
do what you tell them. Or that they're not
good enough for you.*

*I wonder if Lenin or Stalin or Nixon or
Mao worried about what made people follow
them. I guess they only had time to worry
about keeping their power. I do that too—
me, Mao Tse Grolier.*

— TAPE-LOG OF THE PIPER,
ENTRY DATED JUNE 11 (EVENING).

Farther down the Sound—perhaps ten miles from Greenport—is the township of Rye, and in Rye, Playland. Playland
is an aging amusement park, complete with boardwalk, roller
coaster, endless rides, and an apparently unlimited supply of
concessionaires.

Usually at noon, close to the opening hour, the place was
frequented mostly by young children trying to slip into the
rides free or counting out their meager supply of quarters
and dimes. Today, for reasons no one could explain, a sprin-
kling of teen-agers were mixed in with the younger kids.
Tommy Agee and Foodles Brown, each 13, were two of
these. For some time they watched the children, and when a

couple of the younger children headed for the fun house, Tommy and Foodles followed. Watching the kids get scared during the ride could be a gas, and they might be able to add a little to the scaring themselves.

Whispering to each other, they climbed into the boat directly behind the younger children and waited. Propelled by a cable hidden beneath the murky surface of its artificial canal, the small, flat-bottomed boat disappeared, creaking and groaning, into the cavernous mouth of the fun house itself. The two children immediately became nervous; the howls of maniacal laughter, audible but innocent-sounding enough outside, were suddenly chilling inside the tunnel.

From the ceiling, almost invisible in the dark interior of the tunnel, rubber spiders and tarantulas brushed against the children's faces; as soon as the craft rounded the first bend, a series of gauze and papier-mâché demons began swinging directly out toward the boat as it passed, turning aside only at the last possible moment. Tommy and Foodles stood up and began trying to catch each dummy as it popped up at them, rocking the boat dangerously.

They had just passed a pair of dummies—a waxen executioner beheading a papier-mâché Anne Boleyn, then swinging his ax menacingly at the passing boat—when the canal took a sudden bend. There, hanging from the ceiling, was a dummy of a child swinging by its neck from a scaffold. Its supporting machinery appeared to be old; it swung out too slowly and remained suspended over the boat too long. With a lunge, Tommy and Foodles were able to catch it, getting their hands around the dummy and yanking it directly toward the boat. The younger children in front screamed, partly in fear, partly in delight, as the dummy tore loose from its gallows and crashed down into the boat itself. The heavy crash that the dummy made landing in the boat surprised Tommy. So did a realization that the dummy was naked, something he had never seen in any fun house before. Filled with a sudden fear, Tommy turned the dummy over on its back. His eyes took in the dummy's too realistic stare and sagging jaw, the patches of thick, dried blood that had crusted over its body, and pasted to its forehead, a curious collection of Polaroid prints. All of what he saw confirmed what Tommy could no longer avoid admitting: this was no dummy of a murdered child; it was real. He stood up, shaking and terrified, trying to get as far away as he could from this creature that had suddenly invaded his life, gripping the edges of the boat and hollering at the top of his lungs. It took Foodles only a moment longer to reach the same conclusion as Tommy; then he, too, stood up and jumped out of the boat. With a great splash, he began wading through the waist-high water as fast as he could, tripping and stumbling over the underwater cable, shrieking in a kind of terror the fun house's architect had never imagined in his most optimistic dreams.

At first, the two younger children were simply confused. But terror is infectious, and when Tommy followed Foodles over the side, they did, too. The four of them, yelling at the top of their lungs, splashed their way out the exit of the fun house into the bright sunlight, screaming of some nameless terror inside. The operator, waiting for the day's first boatload of passengers to reemerge, at first thought that a boat had sunk, or that someone had fallen overboard and was drowning. But, as he stared, he saw the boat sail gracefully out the exit, its gruesome cargo lying with head partially raised against the high stern-board. Then he, too, began yelling.

Russel Hamilton, of 121 Cedar Street, Greenport, Connecticut, the Polaroids fluttering from his forehead, was the only one to remain silent.

If Kip expected the grisly return of his son to debilitate Hamish and put him out of operation, he had badly misjudged his man. A renewed fury and determination to capture and punish the Piper swept over Hamish as he hardened his search into a personal vendetta; the strain of Indian blood in him cried out for vengeance. Even Jenny, who had expected Hamish's latent sense of guilt about Russel and his bereavement to at least slow him down, was amazed, almost terrified, to see ice-cold anger push Hamish into a twenty-four hour working day. She knew the deep grief Hamish must be suffering, and feared what repressing it could do to him.

Word had been received in Greenport almost immediately after discovery of Russel's body; positive identification from fingerprints took only a brief time longer, although the mutilations made it largely unnecessary. Hamish sat in Tyne's office and stared at the small pile of Polaroids. The pictures were of poor quality—the light had been poor—but the subjects could be made out. One showed Hamish arriving at his house on yesterday's visit to Martha. Another showed him driving away. Two final ones showed him walking up the path and then entering First Baptist for his meeting with Tyne and Jenny Cobb.

"He's a lousy photographer," was Hamish's only comment as he threw the pile back down on Tyne's desk. (It was an opinion shared by Kip. "Christ," he had berated K.K. the night before, "couldn't you do better than that?")

If Hamish and Jenny and Tyne had a growing idea of what the pictures might mean, it became crystal clear to them that night during the broadcast. "Attention to all parents of kidnapped children. Important announcement from the Piper," said Kevin Blyden's voice. "I was wrong in believing that Director of Police Hamish Hamilton had obeyed my orders and left town for good. He returned, and therefore did not obey me. As by now you all know, his son's body was left early this morning at Playland. He was executed by way of a warning to the rest of you: do what I say or your children will be dealt with accordingly."

Tyne snorted; Hamish shook his head. From Jenny came a sudden suggestion. "We could make the fact public. That Russel had already"—Jenny stumbled, not wanting to use so specific a term in front of Hamish—"bled to death long before Hamish resurfaced. It would make the point."

No one commented on her idea; there were too many variables to consider. But Jenny's idea had a solid background. The pathologists—one from the State, one brought in by the FBI—both fixed the time of Russel's death as early morning of the day before, and agreed that the cause of death was massive hemorrhaging and shock. This timing proved that Russel's death had not been brought about as an answer to Hamish's reentry, but before. The Polaroids at Hamish's house were apparently taken after the fact. Jenny felt that this fact might show families of the other children that no amount of dealing with the kidnappers guaranteed anything.

The voice on the loudspeaker, gone dead for reasons unknown, suddenly returned. (The FCC's Mr. Fleming later reported that during this interval the location of Transmitter Λ had changed dramatically.)

"Continuation of announcement to the parents of kidnapped children," Kevin's voice began. Hamish and Tyne exchanged a quick look; this interruption, then, had been planned. "I told you all last night that one final demand would be made of one specific parent before the 'ultimate ransom' for all the children is spelled out. To confuse the fuzz, even that parent's name is in code. So he'll know who he is, it's a father with a brother named Henry. Okay, brother of Henry, you are to call the following number, also coded, immediately: First digit: half of your son's age. Second digit: the month of his birthday minus two. Third digit: the last number of your street address. That is the exchange. The fourth digit: the last number of your age plus one. Fifth digit: the first number of your street address plus three. Sixth digit: the number two. Seventh digit: the number of letters in your first name."

As Kevin Blyden's voice painstakingly repeated the code for the telephone number, the three of them in Tyne's office stared at one another. They had a list of some perhaps twenty-nine parents, their home addresses and telephone numbers. But the name of whomever this message was intended for was too cleverly masked to get at easily.

"We'll just have to call each of them," Tyne sighed, "until we find one who has a brother named Henry. If this Piper's up to his usual games, we'll probably find that at least three of them do." Tyne appeared about to say more, but the voice of Kevin Blyden, gone silent after repeating the coded telephone number twice more, returned as suddenly as it had disappeared.

"One final reminder, brother of Henry. Don't tell anyone who you are, or what you're being told to do. If you do, buddy-o, your son will wind up in as many pieces as Lizzie Borden's mom. To impress you how much that hurts, here's a little tape made during Russel Hamilton's farewell surgery. You will not hear from me again, except by telephone. Follow instructions."

Abruptly, Hamish got up and left the room. His steel veneer of calm was strong, but not strong enough to listen to any more of his son's cries. Not looking at each other, Tyne and Jenny listened to Russel's voice, frantic with fear, as he saw Kip's pruning shears. You could hear his terrified stream of questions, followed by a gasp as the blanket, or whatever it was that covered him, was thrown back. The rest was screaming. It stopped suddenly, replaced by a moaning sigh—and silence. Tyne and Jenny could only guess that Russel had, mercifully, passed out.

A few seconds later, it became clear that Hamish hadn't gone very far away; he walked back into the room the moment the sound of his son's voice disappeared. Tyne had already split the list of parents into three sections, and an agent was calling the number of each to discover who had a brother named Henry. Some of the numbers were busy, one did not answer, and no one they *did* reach would acknowledge a brother of that name.

Surreptitiously, Tyne studied Hamish. His hands were steady and his eyes clear. How he felt was well disguised. Watching him, Tyne detected one device he was using to keep his mind off Russel: keep busy. When one of the FBI agents left to go to the men's room before his list was run down, Hamish grabbed his phone and began making the calls himself. The sound in the room of all the people talking at once, busy trying to track down the "brother of Henry"—and with him, hopefully, a chance of catching the Piper—seemed to pacify Hamish, to lull him, to free him of some of his personal agony.

"Damn," Hamish said suddenly. "I thought for a moment we had it. Mrs. Teal—Robert's mother—said she had a brother Henry, but it can't be her. The first number of her street address is eight. Add three and you'd have eleven, which would give the phone number one digit too many. Damn."

The place was filled with the sounds of Hamish and the agents talking to the unseen parents on their lists, the whirl of phone dials being spun, the scratching of pencils on paper as one name after the other was eliminated. It was like a bookmaking parlor in hell.

Colonel Rathbin—the "Colonel" was now honorary, since he long ago retired from the Army Reserve—sat in his chair staring at the phone. He had just hung up after dialing the number given on the broadcast, and was mystified by the process. The telephone company would have been less baffled. For when Colonel Rathbin dialed 673-7125—the number produced when he had unscrambled the broadcast code—what followed was a seemingly interminable number of small, sharp, clicks. In actuality, his dialing first caused a phone in Stamford, sitting on the floor of a dingy, unfurnished apartment, to ring briefly—so briefly that even if there had been anyone in the place they could not have answered it. The call-forwarding device, with which the phone was equipped, quickly shunted the call to a number in Greenwich, where the phone rang in a two flight walk-up, also empty. Transferred back to a phone in Stamford, the phone there rang in an unfurnished office loft, and then, in turn, was forwarded to a number in Bridgeport. At this final number, a phone answering machine lit up and answered the call by playing its long, prerecorded message. From it, the Colonel heard Kevin Blyden's voice giving him instructions of what he must do to free his son Paige. The message concluded with a firm warning to the Colonel not to notify the FBI or the police of either what the demand was or that he had been the person referred to in the broadcast. In fact, the message added, if he ever wanted to see Paige again, he was to firmly deny he had a brother named Henry.

Staring at the phone, weighing the terrible price of the Piper's demands, Colonel Rathbin jumped when his own phone rang. "Hello?" he said tentatively. "I see. Yes, I heard the broadcast. Of course, I heard the broadcast." With some effort, the Colonel forced a small laugh. "No, it's not me. My brother's name is William—terrible bore—but, he's the only one I have. No Henry . . . Yes, of course I would. I certainly would. But there's nothing to tell you; I'm not the person you're looking for. I wish I was. If they would just tell me what they want from me, I could pay it and get Paige back. Yes, I will. Yes. Thank you."

For a long time, he sat completely motionless, only his eyes moving. Slowly, they wandered across the library walls to the clutter of objects ranged below them; he knew every book, every article of furniture, every piece of *vertu*, every engraving and photograph, as well as he did his own hand. He and Dorothy had spent a lifetime putting together not

only this room but the entire house. There were signed photos
of Presidents, kings, and heroes, some faded, some still bright.
Over the mantelpiece hung an oil of Dorothy; he could sit
and stare at it for hours, and even Dorothy had had to admit
the painting captured her likeness better than any photograph
ever taken. "Too flattering, of course," she would always add,
loving the fact that it was. Wonderful, adorable Dorothy.

Stacked on the lower, wider shelves of the bookcase lining
one wall, were the family photograph albums. He and
Dorothy when they first met, he and Dorothy when they were
first married—she was twelve years younger than he was, but
she married him anyway—he and Dorothy in Marakeech,
Cannes, Copenhagen, on safari in Kenya, in the Bois de Bol-
ogne, Dorothy as a child. And then the little family suddenly
expanded—quite late in their lives—to include Paige. There
were pictures of the Colonel and Dorothy holding him as a
baby in Zurich and Sameden, in New York and in Greenport. Pictures of Paige at 4, 7, 10. Abruptly, the family was
smaller; just he and Paige and, in the background, a new figure in their lives: the nanny to try to replace Dorothy, who
had died while sailing off Leafpoint Harbor.

All of the love the Colonel once lavished on Dorothy had
been given unquestioningly to Paige. And, unlike most only
children of lone parents—who tend to be spoiled—Paige had
grown up into a sweet child, a gentle child, a wonderful boy.

Suddenly, a small shiver ran through the Colonel. For the
first time that he could remember, he was glad that Dorothy
wasn't here, to suffer, as he was, through Paige's disappearance. Here to hear the children screaming to their parents on
television. Here to share the terrible decision he had to make.
Rising, the Colonel moved from room to room, touching the
familiar objects, running his hands over the softly glowing
furniture. Of course, it could be replaced. The house, all of
it. But not really. Never. In everyone's life, there are some
things that can't be. This house and everything in it represented twenty-five years of memories, and no amount of insurance in the world could replace a memory.

Standing behind his favorite chair, letting his eyes continue
their moving inventory of the room, the Colonel blinked as
he found he kept asking himself "why?" Why had Paige been
kidnapped in the first place? Well, a lot of children had.

Something about some crazy 'ultimate ransom.' Why had it been Paige's voice reading the nightly stock market reports? But most important, why had he himself been signaled out for this special demand he'd just received on the phone? The choice made no sense. He had hurt no one. Certainly Paige hadn't. Why, then, had he and Paige been chosen for this special side-torture?

It was a question a lot of people would shortly be asking themselves. In the Colonel's case, the answer was simple. The Colonel wouldn't remember—and no one else knew—but his house had been one of the ones broken into by Kip and Terry Parmalee two years before. Parmalee had escaped, but Kip hadn't been so lucky. The Colonel cornered a shadow with his shotgun, and was stunned when that shadow turned out to be Kip, a boy of whom he was genuinely fond. Caught red-handed, stealing small silver objects, writing filth on the walls with spray paint, peeing on the Orientals. And because he was a kind man and liked Kip so much, he had given the boy a choice: exposure and the police, or a sound thrashing. Naturally, Kip chose the thrashing.

The pain was one thing. But bending over, his pants down, each whirring stroke of the Colonel's riding crop on his bare skin cost Kip dearly in humiliation.

The Colonel's kindness was now being repaid. The incident would not occur to him because he felt that he had done Kip a favor. It would not occur to anyone else because no one else knew of it—except Parmalee, and he was safely locked away in the cistern.

For a brief instant, the Colonel also wondered if any of what was asked would really result in the release of Paige, or whether it was just a cruel device. Quickly, he dismissed his own growing rationalization. He couldn't gamble with Paige's life. Even if there was the smallest chance that Paige would be set free—and the Colonel, fuzzy and vague as his mind seemed to be these days, was not a stupid man; he was aware that the chance of release was a very small one—the demand, he knew, had to be met. As with the body of memories this house and its contents represented to him, Paige could not be replaced either. For in the fuzzy, not entirely rational world of dim patterns and amorphous shapes in which the Colonel now existed, Paige was the last proof he had that Dorothy had ever even existed.

Hamish—once into the job he had insisted on continuing even when the FBI man who had started the phoning returned—had just completed the calls to the remainder of the list, when a call came in for Jenny. Leaning back, Hamish watched her as she walked across the room to take it, then turned to Tyne.

"Nobody on my list has a brother named Henry. The one DA number belongs to the Calhouns, and Mr. Calhoun's sister swears there's no brother by that name in the family."

"*Nobody* will admit to having a brother Henry," Tyne corrected him. "Whoever that call was intended for was told to deny it."

"Hello," said Jenny into the phone, aware that both Tyne and Hamish were watching her face. "Oh yes, Kip. No, I don't mind at all. Who? Well, I don't know, Kip. Just a minute." She put her hand over the receiver and looked at Tyne and Hamish blankly. "Were you able to reach a Colonel Rathbin? He's one of the kids' fathers—the kid who reads the Dow Jones and stuff every night."

The agent who had done the other half of the calling spoke from the far side of the room. "I talked to him. Crazy old guy. But he said he didn't have any brother named Henry." The man looked down at his pad, checking something. "Said his brother was named William."

Annoyed, Jenny took her hand off the receiver to speak. "Are you sure, Kip?"

In an aside to Tyne, Hamish supplied an alternate possibility to an outright lie, which, knowing the Colonel, sounded out of character. "The Colonel's pretty damned vague these days. Been half off his rocker ever since his wife died. A couple of belts and he probably doesn't know whether he even has a brother."

"Who's she talking to?"

"Kip Grolier. Good kid. Saw off his arm for you."

The macabre irony of Hamish's appraisal would have caused Kip to fall off his chair laughing. "Kip," said Jenny. "We don't have any record here of it—his having a brother named Henry—but, we could be wrong. Someone will check it out, although I think there's probably been an error some-where. But thanks very much, Kip, for being thoughtful enough to call. It was nice of you. Yes, I will. Good-bye.

"It was Kip Grolier," she announced unnecessarily. "He says that Colonel Rathbin has—"

"We heard. And we'll go check it out. But why was he calling you?" To Hamish, it didn't make sense, and anything that didn't make sense was something to explore.

"Maybe he's an admirer. A couple of days ago, he— Well, never mind. Anyway, he's trying to help, that's all."

Hamish was already on his feet and Tyne was halfway to his. Silently, one of the agents fell in behind them. "Let's go, Jenny." With a small bow, Tyne took Jenny's arm and the three of them walked to the door. Behind them, they could hear the telephone begin ringing again, but after glancing at each other, kept on walking.

Kip had gotten there long before anyone else showed up. In fact, his call to Jenny had been made from a phone booth a short distance down the street. Although the timing of his arrival was accidental, it was perfect. Upstairs, flames could already be seen leaping up inside the windows and beginning to curl outside the one or two already open. Across the street, the fire began bathing the sheer cliff wall in a reddish glow, although it would take some time before any house down the street or behind the Colonel's was aware the place was in flames. On the ground floor, the Colonel could be seen through the windows near the front door, a large jerry-can in each hand, pouring gasoline over the rugs and tapestries in the front hall and splashing it on the heavy curtains that flanked the glass windows on either side.

Unsurprised to discover jerry-can after jerry-can of gaso-line in his garage—he seemed to remember dimly the voice on the phone telling him to be careful with it. It was, the voice said, not ordinary gasoline, but special high-octane avi-ation fuel—the Colonel poured the gasoline around the house as instructed. A glitter grew in his eyes as he saw the pinkish liquid making dark, ugly stains on Dorothy's curtains and Orientals and antiques. God, but he was glad that she wasn't here; he never thought that he would hear himself repeat that twice in one day. But, she would have approved of what he was doing; any chance, however slim, to save Paige must be taken.

Slopping the last of the gasoline in one great puddle on the Aubusson in the front hall, Colonel Rathbin calmly drew his gold Zippo from his pants pocket, lit it, and dropped it on the floor. In seconds the entire area was engulfed in flames. Choking on the acrid fumes, he raced for the front door, pausing only to pick up something that he had carefully left leaning beside it.

Kip watched fascinated, then pulled back into the shrubbery to watch as he saw the blinking lights on top of Hamish's car careening down Cedar Swamp Road. With a screech, it halted in front of the house. Blagden Tyne and Jenny Cobb jumped out and stood on the sidewalk a moment, transfixed; Hamish was speaking rapidly into his car radio.

Sirens wailing, police cars could be heard racing through the night into the area; the fire trucks would not be far behind. As Kip watched, Colonel Rathbin staggered out through the front door, coughing. Hamish and Tyne began running up the steps toward him.

"Halt!" commanded the Colonel, and for the first time they saw that he was cradling a thirty-gauge shotgun in his arms; as they moved up the path toward the front door, he lowered it to the ready. "Halt!" he repeated. "This house is being burned down on my own responsibility." He pulled an envelope from his pocket, crumbled it up, and threw it at Hamish. "There's a letter indemnifying the insurance company. Chubb, I believe. The most you can do to me is arrest me for disturbing the peace. Or, malicious mischief, I suppose." He gestured with his gun. "What I can do to you, is blow you up. And I will. The first man who tries to stop me, or to put the fire out, or makes any movement I consider to be against me." Colonel Rathbin paused, lowering his voice and suddenly sounding plaintive. "I'm doing it to save Paige, you see. It's the only way. If she were here, Dorothy would approve. But she's not, thank God."

"Colonel," began Hamish. "There'll be policemen and firemen here soon—you can already hear them—let them in. You don't want to go threatening people. It isn't worth it."

Colonel Rathbin appeared to stagger from another sudden fit of coughing; the smoke was billowing out through the door behind him, and he moved further out on the brick terrace, his body silhouetted against the angry red glow that had rapidly filled the house.

"Mr. Rathbin, sir," began Tyne. "Why don't you come out here, further away from the house? You'll get hurt, dammit."

Rathbin stared unbelievingly at the fire equipment grinding to a halt on the street, the sirens in a groaning, decelerating whine. Men jumped off the trucks, unwrapping hoses, moving up the wide path toward him. "Isn't worth it," he mimicked Hamish emptily. "It *is* worth it, all of you. Hear me. The house, the memories. Dorothy is inside with them. But it *is* worth it. Paige . . . Paige . . ."

The Fire Chief looked at Hamish questioningly. "What's the gun for?"

A loud shot rocked them both; the Colonel had fired one barrel into the air, quickly reloading with a shell from his pocket. "That's what it's for," he said. "I'll shoot anyone who comes near this house. Do you all understand me? Shoot."

The police and firemen gathered around Hamish, milling in confusion. The Greenport police knew old Colonel Rathbin, knew his crotchets, and also knew he would probably shoot himself rather than shoot one of them. The firemen and the State Police—two carloads of them arrived almost simultaneously—did not. Their revolvers half-drawn, they huddled around Hamish and Tyne.

One of the State Policemen returned to his car and came back with a rifle, eyeing Rathbin nervously. "With those flames behind him, he's a lead-pipe cinch." He turned to Hamish. "Does he mean what he says or is he crazy?" He began checking the chamber of the rifle, waving it around as he did.

Brusquely, Hamish seized the muzzle of the gun. "Put that goddamned thing down. He's not going to shoot, for Christ's sake. The old guy's tired, frightened, and a little bit nuts."

Angrily, the trooper twisted the muzzle to get it away from Hamish's hand—Hamish had pushed it down so that it was aimed at the ground—and glared at him. "Keep your hands off. Crazy or not, he can't go burning up houses."

"It's his to burn."

"We couldn't save that one now anyway," noted the Fire Chief glumly. Then, pointing upwards, he waved at the drifting shreds of glowing ash climbing into the sky. "But one of those things could land on a roof and set somebody else's house on fire. We got to put the damned thing out. Now."

"Mr. Rathbin. Colonel . . ." Hamish took several steps up the path toward the Colonel as he spoke, gambling on what he figured was the reason behind Rathbin's behavior. "You've done what the Piper demanded. Now let these men keep the fire from destroying other people's property."

The Colonel's answer was another shotgun blast into the air. Watching them carefully, Rathbin reloaded. "We can't just stand here," the State Trooper in charge said, waving to some men in two more newly arrived cars to get out of the cars but stay back where they were. "I suppose we can wing him in the arm with the rifle."

"No." The voice startled everyone around Hamish. Kip had emerged from his hiding place in the shrubbery, slipped around, and came running up the lawn as if he'd just climbed out of his car down the street. As soon as she saw him, Jenny, who had been in conversation with one of the FBI men, joined the crowd around Hamish. "No," repeated Kip. "I know him. I know him very well. Let me talk to him."

Hamish paused for a second, then made his decision. "I don't think so, Kip. It's too dangerous for a civilian. I can't let you."

"Stop me." With his broadest grin, the dazzling smile of an irrepressible boy taking a dare, Kip sprinted up the path and walked directly up into the barrel of Mr. Rathbin's shotgun. "It's Kip Grolier, Colonel Rathbin, sir. You remember me. I'm a friend of Paige's."

Hamish signaled the policemen and troopers, who had started forward the moment Kip did, to freeze. No one could hear what Kip was saying, but they saw him and Mr. Rathbin in deep conversation, with Kip soothing him, smiling at him, holding onto his arm.

Turning, Hamish looked at Jenny in bewilderment. "Where the hell did he come from?"

Looking back toward the house, they watched Kip. Gently Kip took the shotgun from Mr. Rathbin, without any protest. Then, still holding onto his arm, Kip slowly walked him down the path, helping the Colonel negotiate the steps toward the road. There were tears streaming down the old man's face now. Passing the police, Kip shoved the shotgun into Hamish's hand and kept on walking with Mr. Rathbin. The Colonel suddenly stopped and turned around, as if he wanted one final farewell. From the house came a sudden and terrible noise as the center section of the roof caved in, sending a torrent of sparks and blazing embers skyward. Like Roman candles, the glowing pieces of flame in the air would suddenly blaze up or die down, as if by whim.

The Colonel gasped at the sight. "Dorothy. Dorothy, I hope I did the right thing, Dorothy." He turned on his heel, and Kip helped him into his car and drove him away.

Racing up to the house, the firemen had already uncoiled their hoses and were pouring streams of heavy water onto the house. There was another sickening crash, and the entire top floor collapsed inwards on itself.

Hamish had watched Mr. Rathbin climb into Kip's car, and looked now at Jenny. "That's some kid . . ."

Jenny said nothing. For a long time she stood staring at the spot where Kip's car had been, a terrible suspicion beginning to grow inside her that was at first so improbable she wanted to laugh. But she didn't. She couldn't.

Chapter 22 _____

*The old Colonel was a pretty sad sight. I
took him home with me and Dad asked him
to stay until he got himself settled. He
wouldn't, thank God.*

*Just his being around was depressing. He'd
talk a bit, then suddenly choke up and look
like he was going to cry. Funny thing,
though, he seemed to have his wife and Paige
all mixed up.*

*Maybe that's K.K.'s problem, too. His head
doesn't keep the girls separated from the
boys.*

*After all that crap K.K. fed me, I suppose
K.K. is due to become a victim himself. I
wonder if anybody will be a "pretty sad
sight" when he goes. I doubt it. Even his
mother would probably feel relieved. And
when you come right down to it, the only
real mourners for K.K. will be his white
rats—and I'm not too sure they're going to be
all that broken up either.*

                —TAPE-LOG OF THE PIPER,
                ENTRY DATED JUNE 12.

When K.K. saw the first of them, over by the large spruce at
the edge of the clearing, he was so terrified that he almost
lost his grip on the ladder and dropped straight down into the
water below. A few minutes earlier, he'd thought he heard
people calling to each other from the thick woods, but had
dismissed the sounds as imagination. Now K.K. wished he
hadn't. For one thing, the heavy cement cover was still off
the cistern—as it always was when one of them was inside—
and he couldn't climb back out and replace it; one of them
would be sure to spot him.

For a moment, K.K. watched them move forward, just his

eyes showing above the rim. They advanced like a tribe of
natives beating the bush on a Kenya shoot, probing the
ground in front of them with sticks. In all, K.K. guessed,
there must be over fifty of them ranged out across this strip
of the Grolier property; they were a strange-looking collection of people, in all different kinds of uniforms, their heads
fixed downward like guests at a party searching for a dia-
mond ring that someone has dropped. Even with his weak
eyes, K.K. could recognize sailors in blue denim—Coast
Guard, he supposed—soldiers in fatigues, Senior and Eagle
scouts from every town in the area, State Troopers, and, a
scattering of local police.

A shout from the far left, strident and urgent, caused the
line to stop and all heads to turn in its direction. Much as
K.K. would have liked to know what was causing the excitement, he realized that it was only a matter of time before the
line began advancing toward him again. Quickly and soundlessly K.K. lowered himself down the rungs of the ladder,
swung clumsily through the archway just above the water,
and stepped inside. After catching his breath, he found the
swivel on the rock and swung the heavy stone shut. Panting
from the effort, he stood there, worried. The rock would
probably fool anyone who looked down inside the cistern, became curious, and climbed down the ladder. On the other
hand, if he and Kip had discovered the stone that opened the
door, anyone else who spent enough time on the ladder could
probably do the same. K.K. only hoped they would not be
that curious, or would be in too much of a hurry to explore
the cistern very carefully. With luck, they might not even
bother to explore it at all.

Aboveground, the line resumed its forward progress once
more; the shouting on the left had come from a man stung
by a yellowjacket. Seaman 2nd/Class Ramlarson of the Coast
Guard Academy in New London smiled inwardly when word
of this was passed from the end of the line to the middle,
where he was positioned; he hoped it was one of the Middies
or at least a Chief. Looking up, Ramlarson found the cistern
directly in his path, and began edging left to avoid it. But instead of simply passing it by, he paused to look inside. It
struck him as odd that the cover had been removed and left

leaning against the side; some kid, for Christ's sake, could climb up on the cistern and fall in.

Ramlarson tried to move ahead, but the cistern drew him toward it with a strange power. Looking inside, his eyes took in the ladder and the dark glint from the water far below. Ignoring the fact that the line was advancing without him, he pulled the flashlight from his belt and shone it downward. This was a place that deserved more exploration. If they were looking for thirty-two children held captive somewhere, what better place to hide them than underground? Possibly, this damp, dripping cistern had a door on its side . . . perhaps the ladder was there for a reason (why would anyone build a ladder into a cistern anyway?) . . . perhaps . . . perhaps . . .

Ramlarson's musings ended abruptly when a pain of incredible intensity suddenly struck the back of his neck. A man slightly ahead of him had blundered into a small bush in his path and, in the process, knocked down a grayish conical formation hanging off one of its upper branches. Out of this swarmed a whole nestful more of angry yellowjackets, bent on revenge. The man ahead of Ramlarson was screaming, and, almost before Ramlarson could grasp what had happened, the yellowjackets reached him, too. Swinging his arms wildly, yelling, slapping, and running, Ramlarson—along with most of the men on either side of him—headed back for the woods as fast as they could run, stumbling and tripping over roots and vines in their frenzy to escape the cloud of angry buzzing creatures spinning over everyone's heads.

If Kip or K.K. had loosed the creatures themselves, they couldn't have planned the operation more successfully. Half an hour later, when the line was once again formed to carry on with the search, Ramlarson was not with them but at a First Aid Station at Greenport Hospital, being treated for multiple stings. All thoughts of the cistern had been wiped from his brain by the painful encounter. And when the line did begin moving forward once more, it started on the far side of the cistern. No one else bothered to look inside.

Kip, who hated insects of any kind, never knew that his entire plan had been saved from disaster only by the instinctive reactions of a nestful of social insects seeking to protect their home.

Russel Hamilton's funeral was held in front of a crowd so
large that he would have been totally mystified. But his was
the first body to emerge from the whole terrible chain of
events, and many of the people attended the service as if it
were a memorial to all of the missing children. As a result,
the graystone Episcopal church, St. Andrews, could not
handle the crowd, and it overflowed onto the church's well-
kept lawns; hastily set up loudspeakers brought the service to
those outside.

Inside, in the first few pews, the atmosphere was electric.
Martha was no longer speaking to Hamish at all, holding him
personally responsible for Russel's death. Beside her was
planted the inevitable Miss Crane. Ollie sat on the other side,
between Martha and Hamish. In the row behind was the
Town Council, along with Blagden Tyne, Chief Investigator
Cummins, and the Connecticut Attorney General (represent-
ing the Governor). Originally, Jenny Cobb was supposed to
attend the funeral with Tyne, but when she discovered that
this would put her only one row behind Martha, she decided
that she'd better come by herself, and took a pew in the very
rear of the church. In their own pew, Senator Blyden and his
wife, with four of the missing Kevin's brothers and sisters, sat
in lonely splendor. Scattered throughout the church were virtually all of the parents of the kidnapped children, their
families, and many of their family friends. The man acting as
spotter for the FBI—their agents seemed to be everywhere—
also pointed out Russel's classmates from Bryant Junior High,
Ollie's classmates, and delegations from high schools in Rye,
Greenwich, Stamford, Darien, and Fairfield. Even Mr. and
Mrs. Sanchez and their cousin Rosa were in attendance; the
latter felt particularly bad for having spoken so rudely to
Hamish about her cousin Angel.

At Hamish's request, the service was brief. A short eulogy
was read by the principal of the junior high school, followed
by a closing prayer read by the Reverend Ainslee, beseeching
God not only to receive His child, Russel, but also to protect
and preserve the lives of the other of His Children held for
ransom. The organ swelled and the pallbearers carried the
small casket down the aisle, followed by Martha, walking
with Ollie, and with Miss Crane and Hamish a few steps behind them.

As they reached the outer door of the church, Hamish attempted to comfort Martha, taking her by one elbow. "Martha," he began.

The elbow was snatched away. "You son of a bitch," she hissed at him, striding toward a car waiting at the foot of St. Andrews' granite steps.

Ollie shot his father a look that was both bewildered and compassionate, then turned to follow his mother. For a moment, Hamish stood where he was. As he saw the people beginning to pour out of the church and start down the long row of steps toward him, he turned and began going down the steps himself. Behind him, the loudspeakers used to pipe the service to the overflow crowd outside were now playing the mournful organ music of the recessional. In mid-phrase, the organ stopped abruptly. Over the loudspeakers, the crowd suddenly heard, distant and fragile, the small, high-pitched voice of Paige Rathbin.

"Fingers, shaved a fraction. Toes, down three. Testicles, off two. Penis, up at the opening, slashed at the close . . ."

Someone inside the church could be heard swearing violently as he ripped out the wires of the P.A. system to silence it. On the steps, the mourners stood frozen; that someone had contrived to play a tape parodying Paige Rathbin's nightly stock market quotes was so incredible that no one at first knew how to react.

The unearthly silence was shattered by Martha. She was half in, half out of the car that was to take her to the cemetery; now, staring at the loudspeakers in disbelief, she threw back her head and gave a scream that curdled the blood of everyone there. Incoherent, she collapsed into Ollie's arms. Hamish too found that the steps were beginning to spin below him.

Coming up from behind, Blagden Tyne grabbed Hamish's arm and squeezed it as hard as he could. "Come on, Hamish. Don't let those bastards get to you. Not now." Silently, the two men walked down the steps and climbed into Tyne's car.

"Okay. Everything's got to be moved up. Collapsed into a shorter time frame. It'll be tricky, but there's no other way."

K.K. stared at Kip and nodded numbly. The two of them were in K.K.'s laboratory, where they had been talking about the stunned expressions on the crowd coming down St. Andrews' steps. "You did one hell of a job, K.K.," Kip had said. "Those people's faces!" Then they had both laughed, Kip because he really did think it was funny—something which made K.K. look at him strangely—and K.K. because he had been complimented on his work. The master had appraised his efforts and found him not wanting.

Now, they were reviewing the accelerated schedule of the plan's final stages.

"I don't see how we can do all of that," K.K. said, sitting down heavily. He was not complaining exactly, just being realistic. "My God, Kip, you can't squeeze what was planned for a week into a couple of days. Something'll go haywire. We'll get caught."

"Balls. If you don't think you can do it, I'll find somebody who can."

It was an empty threat and K.K. knew it. Nonetheless, the hurt of what Kip was threatening cut deep with K.K. In spite of all logic, he found himself backpedaling. "I guess we can try."

"I guess we'd damn well better."

Remembering the line of men advancing across the clearing near the cistern suddenly sent a wave of cold fear sweeping through K.K. "I don't know, I don't know," he said in a semi-whisper, his fear open and obvious. Haltingly, he told Kip about the incident, trying to make his own flight down the ladder into the tunnel sound as competently handled as he could.

"And you left the cover *off?*" Kip asked.

"I was inside. Nobody—nobody—can put that cover back on once they're inside."

Kip grimaced, kicking at a chair with his foot. K.K. was right, he supposed, but Kip was angry that the incident had taken place at all, and the nearest thing to vent his fury on was K.K. "Well, anybody could have looked into the cistern, noticed the ladder, and gotten curious. You should have slipped out and put the cover on, then beaten it into the woods."

"They'd have seen me."

"Did they look into the cistern?"

"Don't know. How the hell would I? I was twelve feet underground with the stone door swiveled shut."

"It shows I was right in speeding up the schedule. I guess they're really going to tear this town apart looking for those kids."

The nervous tone of K.K.'s voice told Kip that he'd better find something reassuring to say. There wasn't much that sounded right. "Anyway, one good thing, now that they've combed the area, we're probably safer than ever. If anybody'd gotten curious, we'd certainly have known about it by now."

"Sure." The nervousness was gone, replaced by sarcasm, but K.K.'s reaction showed that he was less than convinced. Keeping him busy would take his mind off the fire that they were playing with. Quickly, Kip opened the drawer of the table K.K. had in the lab and withdrew two small packages. "Okay. Start with these. You know what to do."

Staring at the two parcels, wrapped in plain brown paper, K.K. felt a surge of apprehension course through him. "Yeah, I know what to do."

"C'mon, Kong, get your ass moving."

K.K. could still hear Kip's laughter as he walked out through the door and slipped behind the wheel of the pickup.

"I left the note with the number inside the house. No, how could I possibly remember it?"

Colonel Rathbin sat in a chair in Tyne's office, looking miserable. His face showed that he hadn't slept well, if at all. Sitting through Russel Hamilton's funeral had been an additional ordeal for him, one compounded by having to stand on the church steps and hear Paige's voice recite its grisly parody. Gently, Hamish produced a transcript of the message Kevin Blyden had read over the air to Mr. Rathbin; by using this device, the old man would at least be spared having to hear any more tapes.

"Colonel, if you'll help us, we can reconstruct that number easily. First, half of your son's age would be—"

"Six."

Obviously Hamish already knew this, as he did all the rest of the numbers; they were easy to come by, once you knew to whom they applied. But Jenny wanted him to get Colonel

Rathbin involved, to get his mind replaying the phone call, in the hope that through free association the man would produce the precise wording of the message he'd been given.

"The first number of your street address plus three," Hamish went on.

"Six."

"Plus three is—"

"Nine." Colonel Rathbin's face colored. "I don't know why you're pestering me with all of this. The school could give you the same information. I'm tired, very tired. Please, just leave me alone."

"The voice on the tape machine when you called the number—"

"I've already told you. Flat. Undistinguished. Young-sounding. Told me what to do and hung up." Pausing, the Colonel's pale blue eyes burned into Hamish's. "What makes you think it was a tape?"

"Because they all have been. Like Paige's voice this morning at the church."

Rathbin winced. "Who made the call to me? Do you know?"

Hamish shook his head. "Not yet. We know from where, but not by whom. But we hope to." God, but they hoped to. As soon as they had been able to get someone to open up the Bureau of Records, they had reconstructed the number and traced it to the address the telephone company had for that listing. All they'd found was an empty apartment in Bridgeport, and a frightened black landlord who said the place was rented by, "An old white lady. Name of Braun. Said she had a bad heart. She said that twice, understan'? Looked it, I tell you. But, man, that old lady couldn't be in no trouble like you talking about. Kidnap a rich kid? Hell, man, she be lucky if she lives out the month. More chance some kid kidnap her, you know?"

The forensics team had spent most of the night dusting the place but came up with nothing. The landlord had thought he remembered—yes, he was sure he remembered—she was wearing gloves. "We don't have no trouble in this place, understan'? Ever. You must got the wrong address," he added.

Hamish, sitting with the stricken Colonel Rathbin, swore under his breath now, as he had sworn then. The damned old lady again. Trying to tie her into the picture made no sense. Yet the same old lady who had rented the office in the warehouse had also rented this apartment in Stamford, along with a phone that had a call-forwarding machine. With the call-forwarder now disconnected, there was no way to trace what other numbers the Colonel's call might have gone through before reaching the tape machine answering device the Colonel finally heard the voice on. What Hamish had only imagined in his session with the technical expert from New York Telephone had come true.

"I'm so very tired. If you don't need me any further . . ."

Hamish did need the Colonel, but something inside him went out to the old man, so visibly defeated. In a relatively short period of time, Colonel Rathbin had had his only son kidnapped, had had to burn down his beloved house by his own hand—and along with it, a lifetime of memories that were most of what kept him alive. Then, attending Hamish's son's funeral this morning, he had had to listen to Paige's voice reciting an obscene parody, while his friends stood by uncomfortably on the church's steps and tried to pretend they didn't know whose voice it was. Colonel Rathbin should be tired. Much as Hamish wanted to press him further about what the Piper said on the telephone tape, he could not bring himself to inflict more pain on this already deeply hurt human.

"Of course, Colonel." Hamish stood up and guided the man to the door, waving to him as he left to go home. To go home where, Hamish wondered?

Tyne looked at Hamish in surprise. "He must have more information than that," Tyne said, rearranging some papers on his desk, sounding irritated with either Hamish or himself. "What was on the tape—there must have been more in there we don't have yet." His eyes met Hamish's, in an unspoken question.

"I know. Should have tried to get more out of him. But the old man's about to keel over from all of this. And Jenny wants to do some talking to him, too—she thinks she can get most of the tape back verbatim if she has a clear shot at him. If I'd asked him to stay here until she showed up, I think he'd have been out like a light."

"Jenny?" Tyne looked as if he'd just realized she wasn't in

the room with them. "Where is she? What's she doing anyway?"

"Working on a chart. Lining up all the names of kids that were kidnapped before the bus thing, collecting the names and facts about them to see if they had anything in common. Beside going to Country Day. People in common. Things, hobbies, activities in common."

"But why just the kids?" Tyne already knew the answer to his own question, but wanted to see Hamish's reaction.

"She's got this crazy theory, that this whole thing is the brainchild of a student—or masterminded by one anyway."

Tyne shrugged and sat down, an unhappy expression on his face. "What the hell, I suppose it makes as much sense as anything else we're doing."

To Hamish, Tyne's reaction seemed less skeptical than his own had been. Out of Tyne's window, he watched Colonel Rathbin climb painfully into a waiting police car to be driven home. Again, Hamish found himself wondering, where was home now? And was he really asking the question about the Colonel, or was he asking it about himself?

That night, Thursday, June 13th, the effects of Kip's suddenly accelerated operation began falling on Greenport like the blows of a hammer. The town, although partially conditioned by the events of the previous few weeks, was not prepared for the firestorm that began. Even Kevin Blyden's voice, usually firm and very much in control, seemed awed by what it was required to say.

The first shock came during the six o'clock news; the fact that the Piper's mobile transmitter went into operation early this night was in itself ominous. By 6:08, it became obvious that the Piper, either because of pressure or by design, had moved up his date for the 'ultimate ranson.'

"Attention, attention," barked Kevin Blyden. "This is a message from the Piper. U.R. Time is tonight. Sorry, but the day had to be moved up. The first step will be spelled out shortly. Stay glued to your set. Sticky, but necessary. Remember, U.R. Time is My Time . . ." The mobile transmitter cut off after a brief playing of the original cast recording for *West Side Story,* singing, "Tonight . . . tonight . . ."

The next blow fell at 6:23. Kip's father, Ramsey Grolier, called Hamish, yelling almost incoherently that his younger son, Carey, had just been kidnapped. Hamish was thunderstruck, so thrown that he suggested—feeling silly and helpless as he did—that perhaps Mr. Grolier was mistaken, and Carey, only 12, was being driven somewhere by Kip. No, Mr. Grolier said, it was only when Kip had arrived home a few minutes before that he first realized something was wrong. Kip had been supposed to pick Carey up at some friends named Stuart, but discovered that the Stuarts had just seen Carey leave—presumably with Kip. Then, just before Mr. Grolier called Hamish, he'd gotten a phone call with a tape of Kevin Blyden's voice telling him Carey was the Piper's newest victim.

Putting what he had together, it was not hard for Hamish to figure how the latest kidnapping was pulled off. Someone with a car like Kip's had driven into the end of the driveway and tooted for Carey. According to the Stuarts, this was about 6:15. They paid little attention to the car—they had seen Kip's car many times before, and the dark green Porsche was not unusual in the area—and had only half-watched as Carey ran down the driveway, hesitated a moment, and then climbed in. A few minutes later, they were stunned when another identical green Porsche drove up to their front door and Kip stepped out to pick up his younger brother.

Presumably, whoever was inside the first car had had a gun and forced Carey to go with him; this probably accounted for the hesitation the Stuarts reported seeing before the boy climbed in.

"There's something really crazy about this one," said Tyne, after Mr. Grolier hung up. "With the bus gone, somehow I thought we'd seen the last of the kidnappings."

"And instead of Carey, why didn't the Piper just wait and grab Kip?" Jenny's face ran the gamut of puzzled expressions. A small shudder passed through her when she heard that Carey had been kidnapped; it ran through her again as she asked her rhetorical question. "Kip would have been a much bigger catch."

"Attention again, you parents," Kevin Blyden's voice said during the seven o'clock network news. "There will be a very important broadcast at eight o'clock. You may be taking a lIttle trip right after it, so I suggest you eat first. Because tonight, the 'ultimate ransom' gets explained and demanded, and you'll want to be ready, right? 'Be Prepared' and all that crap." The broadcast ended abruptly with an audible click.

"A 'little trip'?" asked Tyne. "What the hell's he mean by that?"

"Maybe nothing," suggested Hamish. "But we must be worrying him, because something's making him move awful fast. Like he was panicked." Hamish flipped through his stack of notes, trying to find an answer to his own question.

Like Jenny, he had a terrible suspicion that the Piper would provide the answer himself, tonight at eight o'clock.

Chapter 23 _____

*When I first had the idea of grabbing
Carey, I worried a lot that the idea might not
be so much for the plan as for settling some
long-time scores. After all, the little bastard
did come along and louse up things in my
life.*

*But in the end, the decision to kidnap him
was determined by one very simple fact: I
had to be inside that hall.*

*Jesus, but he screamed when I pulled that
gun on him. I felt good all night.*

—TAPE-LOG OF THE PIPER,
ENTRY DATED JUNE 13.

At 7:10, the hot line rang in Tyne's office. The makeshift
switchboard had set this line up at Tyne's direction, with its
own peculiar ring and red flasher. Both Hamish and Jenny
looked up at the sound, dreading what news it might bring.

In Jenny's hands was the chart she had been working
on—trying, frantically now, to pinpoint some common element in the lives of the kidnapped children. At the sound of
the phone, she unconsciously beat the air with the chart,
showing how disturbed she was. With much the same sense of
desperation, Hamish was sorting his notes into small piles,
each one containing a different category of information; now
a number of sheets flew off the table and sailed lazily to the
floor.

As shaken as Hamish was by the hot line's ring, his immediate attention was focused on trying to recapture as many
papers as he could. In the process, he knocked over another
pile. Inside, he had a sudden urge to sweep everything off the
table and curse violently.

"Yes? Tyne here."

Through the squawk-box attachment on the phone, Jenny
and Hamish could hear what Tyne heard, another tape made

by Kevin Blyden: "This is a message from the Piper. At eight
tonight, I'll be telling all parents of kidnapped children to as-
semble in the main seating area of St. Andrews Episcopal.
They have to be inside by nine. No stragglers. That gives you
guys plenty of time to search the building ahead of time,
something you suspicious types will undoubtedly want to do.
No police, FBI, or other fuzz at the meeting, please; I'll
know. And by now, you probably get the idea I can be pretty
nasty.

"There are two points I'm going to make on my eight
o'clock announcement, but they should be repeated to the
parents by you people in person. One of them is that once
the parents are inside, you are to lock the front doors so that
no one can go out. If anyone tries to leave, his kid buys it.
The other point is that if any parent doesn't show up, his kid
will get it instead. The parents will be nervous about this
meeting, but you're to tell them it's simply another test of
their love. Another part of the 'ultimate ransom,' and certainly
the least they can do. You can reassure them you have searched
the place for explosives. The rest will be up to them . . .

"Oh, yes. I'll need a pair of loudspeakers hooked up to a
radio tuner that can receive CB broadcasts." There was a
pause, and then, "Any questions? Silly comment. Because I
have no way of hearing even if you did. Get cracking, kids."

There was consternation in Tyne's office. Of all the things
they'd speculated on, going after the parents—perhaps holding them for ransom, too—was something no one had even
toyed with. "What does this creep want, for Christ's sake?"
Defeated, Tyne sank heavily into the chair, staring mournfully at his highly polished shoes.

"Could one of your men—the Piper might recognize any
of mine, but he can't know all the FBI agents—be slipped inside?" Hamish asked. "I don't know if he'll be able to do a
damned thing, but if he could go in with the rest of the
people, it would at least give us one guy we could count on."

"More than one. We'll use as many men as we dare."

"Dangerous," interjected Jenny. "He knows all the parents.
I'd hold it to one. Even one's taking a chance."

The regular phone rang. From the agent on the switchboard came the report that the call had been too short to

trace. "Shit," Tyne said, as much to himself as them. "It would only have been traced back to one of those banks of call-forwarding machines anyway." He paused for a moment. Finally he shook his head. "This damned thing in the church worries me.

"I'll start rounding up the troops. That church is going to be searched—but good. Security men on the rooftops across the street, the works." He turned toward Hamish. "You'll want to have all your men and as many State Troopers as we can coax out of Cummins. The whole area should be sealed off; the broadcast will bring out every thrill freak for miles around. And do you know the sexton at St. Andrews? We ought to talk with him—fast." He jotted something on a pad and looked at Hamish quizzically. "Anyway, Hamish, the Piper's demand that no police be inside the church means you're free to work outside during the time the parents are locked up inside. It's a good chance to do a little hunting—remember, the Piper will have to be on the outside, too."

For the last few minutes, Hamish had been staring at a piece of paper he held in his hand. It was covered with scrawled notes he'd taken during an early interview with some of the boys at Country Day, and had been buried at the bottom of the pile on his desk. When the pile got knocked over, this page was one of those that slid to the floor. In retrieving it, Hamish had unintentionally put the page on top of the pile; now, for the first time in weeks, Hamish reread his own observations. He felt an almost electrical shock course through his system. "How much time do we have?" he asked Tyne suddenly.

"Until the parents go inside? Little less than an hour and a half."

"Jenny, you and I. Once they're in. We've got some fast business to do." Hamish squeezed her arm with excitement. "Your pet theory may have something to it after all."

"Are you sure it will work?"

Kip smiled grimly and stood up. He and K.K. were in K.K.'s lab, the small, frail boy watching as Kip slipped into a light Madras jacket that almost, but not quite, covered the two thin packages wrapped in brown paper he had strapped around his chest.

"Let's see. The wires come out of the floor . . ."

"Right where I said they did. I checked. Four along the sides, lined up with the pews. The rest in the rear, behind the font. Hell, you were in the choir—you ought to know the place backwards and forwards, Kip."

"Rehearsals twice a week, performance every Sunday. I didn't really sing very well but the choirmaster liked my smile." He leered at K.K. "Or something."

K.K. felt uncomfortable. Kip's remark was no slip, but intended to taunt him. Mean bastard, Kip. K.K. watched as Kip leaned down and pulled what looked like a small book-bag or rucksack over his jacket. After thinking a moment, Kip slipped the bag off his shoulders again and experimented with holding it loosely in one hand. "Looks more natural this way, right?"

"Right."

"Okay. Wish me luck."

"Luck."

K.K. was baffled. This should have been Kip's clue to leave, only he stood there, smiling at him, an enigmatic smile that K.K. couldn't understand. The eyes above the smile made K.K. squirm uncomfortably. A real mean bastard, that Kip.

"So long, K.K."

Too late, K.K. realized just how mean Kip really was.

"Over there on the left."

"They're okay. The Sanchezes. I don't know why they showed up, but they're legit," Hamish said.

Tyne sighed and glanced at his watch. It was 8:25, and the last of the parents were climbing the stone stairs and filing into St. Andrews. Gray sawhorses blocked off all streets leading to the church, and the roadway was lined with Greenport police and State Troopers, there to hold back the surging crowds. Those in the front of the mob craned their necks to see the faces of misery now entering the small Episcopal church. Hamish held a clipboard in his hand, waving on the parents, all of whom were known to him by sight.

Senator Blyden paused at the pool of TV cameras and reporters, leaning forward to say something neither Hamish nor anyone except the newsmen could hear. Clapping the nearest reporter on the shoulder solemnly, the Senator nodded toward his wife and began climbing the stairs. Only Blyden could make his entrance appear so much like the arrival of royalty.

Among the last to arrive were Kip and Mr. Grolier. Kip had smiled and waved at Hamish, raising the bag he held in one hand to him in a salute; even given the circumstances, Kip's smile did not strike Hamish as cold or uncaring. The smile, Hamish thought, was so much a part of Kip's personality that even in direst times he would have seemed naked without it.

Hamish's pencil marked a final "X" on the clipboard as the last two people, Mr. and Mrs. Ramsey, entered the door. With a nod toward Tyne, Hamish climbed the stairs himself and stood just inside with each hand touching one of the heavy double doors, addressing the parents in the church. "If I can have your attention for a moment, please. As you know, I am required to lock these doors once you are all inside, and no one is to leave. Experts from the FBI have been through the church, from top to bottom, for your protection. But I still cannot guarantee your safety. For the good of everyone, then, any person who feels he might rather leave should do so now—immediately." Hamish studied the faces turned toward him from the pews; no one made a move. "Very well. And good luck. I and my men, and Mr. Tyne of the FBI and his, will be just outside." With a final nod, Hamish swung the doors shut, took the key provided him by the sexton, and locked the great main entrance. Just before the doors closed, he had seen Charlie Goodenaugh, Tyne's "inside" man, sitting alongside the Senator near one of the aisles. Stuffing his hands in his pockets, Hamish slowly went down the long flight of steps to the street and walked into the gathering darkness without speaking to anyone.

The *Coupon* slipped smoothly along through the waves, the only sound the muffled roar of its twin Gray's and the hissing sibilance of the water racing under its sleek hull. This sound was magnified by the sound of the water slapping against the bow of the dinghy *Coupon* was towing from its stern; turning around to look at it for a moment, Kip couldn't remember the launch ever towing one before.

As they reached a point in the Sound approximately opposite the Long's Bay Beach Club—he thought he could see the lights on the porch of the club burning brightly and leaving a glistening trail of reflections on the water—Kip put the *Coupon* into a shallow circle, marked the degree of turn on the autocompass, and settled back to make sure the automatic pilot was functioning properly. For a boat as small as the *Coupon* to have an automatic pilot was unusual; this one had been rigged up by K.K. from equipment he'd bought at Du rand's Boatworks.

Kip felt good. Tonight, he decided, was the final test of his skill. And so far this evening, his skill had more than met all tests. Getting away unnoticed from St. Andrews, for instance, had been handled artfully. Hanging back a few paces as his father had slipped into a pew, Kip allowed some other parents to get in front of him and go down the pew between him and his father. When his father turned to look at Kip questioningly, indicating with his hands for him to come join him in the pew anyway, Kip had smiled and shrugged his shoulders, indicating that he would stay standing, leaning against the church's outer wall instead. His father was so lost in thought he had merely sighed and let the matter pass. Slowly, Kip backed sideways along the wall, leaving the rucksack on the floor behind him. In the sacristy, he located the concealed wires behind the baptismal font and, pretending to tie a shoelace, quickly connected the hidden wires to those sticking out from the two packages he had slipped from under his jacket. These he left on the floor.

The trickiest part was getting over to the partly concealed and little-known side door of the vestibule. But Kip had spent two hours every week, as well as Sundays, in this church, and knew every inch of it. No one saw him slip behind the baffle and out through the side door of the vestibule; no one even knew that below this, in the church's cellar, was another door leading to the foundation of the original St. Andrews, which had burned to the ground some thirty years earlier. Kip made his way there and left the church, not through the front doors but through the old church's ruined basement. Unseen.

He knew that his father would miss him; he had seen him look over at him while he was still standing along the side wall. But later, when he would look again and notice Kip was no longer there, he would probably assume his son had joined someone in the rear of the church. It would not be until much later, sometime after the broadcast, that he would realize that Kip had gone entirely—and, if he were clever, all that that implied.

Slowing the *Coupon*, Kip was unable to suppress a grin at his own cleverness. On top of the professional pride he felt in his work, he could still tell himself that the reasons he had done all this were sound, even noble. On this point, however, an uncertainty—an unsureness that began after his fight with K.K. a week ago—continued to plague him. He knew that he was running out of time; he was due to withdraw. The action scheduled to take place in a few minutes, he was convinced, would be his crowning glory. In spite of all the damned nonsense K.K. had spouted.

Leaning over the side, Kip began pulling in the dinghy closer to the stern of the *Coupon*. One final check of the autopilot convinced him he was ready for the next step. Steadying himself, he switched on what looked like a small radio, waited a second for it to warm up, and then threw several toggle switches on a box beside it. Quickly, Kip uncleated the lines and stepped into the wobbling dinghy.

Seated in the stern, he started up the outboard and zoomed away. A few minutes later, he looked back and saw the *Coupon* moving gracefully in a large circle, set on an endless, futile course to nowhere.

Beautiful, Kip whispered to himself, and pointed the dinghy toward the Grolier slip on the far side of Long's Bay Point.

Far to the north of Greenport, almost all the way to the Merritt Parkway, the unmarked van moved slowly up Seven Hills Road, the saucer-shaped scanner on its roof rotating at about the speed of a radar antenna. Inside, one of the technicians on the FCC team adjusted his earphones, suddenly straightening up as the sound hit him. "Freeze it!" he yelled, and the van pulled to a halt. Reaching above him, the technician began to fine-tune the precise direction of the signal by rotating a wheel over his head that moved the antenna manually. When the inner cup of the direction-finder was aimed directly at the signal, the sound reached an intensity that made the technician shake his head from the pain in his ears.

He pushed his chair back, scribbling something on a pad. Grabbing a microphone, he radioed his chief, Griff Fleming of the FCC, whose headquarters were down the hall from Tyne's in First Baptist. "One transmitter located. Direction TWO-ZERO-NINER-POINT-SIX. Repeat: TWO-ZERO-NINER-POINT-SIX. Signal strong; we are in rough vicinity. Transmitter not cutting in and out as in past. When alternate transmitter takes up program content, transmitter now continues broadcasting. Hiss of blank leader-tape identifiable until program content from this transmitter begins again. Please advise. Please advise. Over."

Fleming's answer was short but direct. "Stay where you are. We'll send FBI and police. If transmitter stops, or is moved, notify me immediately. Well done. Out." Fleming got up and started to hurry down toward Tyne's office, when his transmitter began crackling again. The second message was from the Coast Guard.

Using the vectors provided by the FCC, as well as their own tracking gear, the cutter *Langley* was slowly moving across the Sound and zeroing in on an area near Long's Bay Point. Further adjustments in direction headed the *Langley* in toward the beach off Long's Bay Beach Club.

"Hard left!" yelled the deck officer, suddenly seeing a boat dead ahead of them. The launch was circling slowly, but not showing any running lights; it was so close beneath the *Langley's* bow, they came close to ramming her. For a moment, the Coast Guard team studied the launch. Then, the Captain radioed Fleming for instructions. *"Langley* reporting. Transmitter Number Two appears to be aboard a launch circling inner bay of Long's Bay. Nobody aboard. Name of boat painted out. Ditto registration numbers on bow—painted over or removed entirely. Do you want us to board her?"

"Put one man aboard, but don't disturb anything. Do not stop transmission. Repeat: do not stop transmission. Out." Clutching his scribbled notes, Fleming ran down the hall toward Tyne's office.

Tyne was sitting on a hard wooden chair, listlessly watching the broadcast from outside the church. So far the Piper had been transmitting "filler," a rehash of past tapes with nothing new added. On the television screen, the cameras outside St. Andrews showed the crowd gathered further down the street, the people jammed behind the police barricades, tense and waiting. Occasionally they would cut to a camera trained on the great doors of St. Andrews, behind which, the announcer told his viewers, the parents of the kidnapped children were held in a prison of their own making.

Suddenly Fleming burst through Tyne's door. Quickly, the leader of the FCC team explained that they had located both transmitters and were standing by for further instructions. Tyne didn't even wait for the man to finish his explanation, but was already racing down the hall toward the communications room and his own radio transmitter. His only words to him, as Fleming was to recall later, were, "For Christ's sake, Griff, don't let anyone try to stop those broadcasts. If we do, God only knows what happens to the people in the church. Or the children." Then he grabbed the microphone and began trying to raise Hamish.

"Where are we going, Hamish?"

"To the Blakeslee place. Out on Seven Hills Road." Jenny turned her head and looked at Hamish curiously. His jaw was set and his eyes, always steely, now appeared barely open as he pushed the police car to its limit. His driving was causing her to run her fingers through the ends of her hair even more than usual; the trip was enough to make anyone nervous.

"I see." Jenny winced as the car squealed around a curve, narrowly missing another one coming out of a partly hidden driveway. "No, I don't see," she added sullenly.

"Your theory. A kid from Country Day. At least as the mastermind. That Blakeslee kid—what do they call him?—K.K. I went through my old notes from the very first interviews we did with those boys. K.K. was mentioned by a couple of them. Words like 'spooky, scary, evil, dirty, a mean loner.' I never saw a kid so universally hated. I'd meant to get back to him, but we got thrown off when things started happening so fast. Tonight, earlier, I turned up the note to myself on him. I feel like a jerk. We should have followed up that lead weeks ago. And listen—get this—his record at school: he's an expert on science stuff. Electronics, biology, the works. It runs through everything."

"So does something else. From my notes, Hamish." Jenny continued, "The one thing in common those first kidnapped boys had was that, at one time or another, they'd all served on the Student Council. Regular or junior version. And just guess, Hamish, who's been president of that the whole time?"

"Not K.K., for Christ's sake."

"No. Kip Grolier. The school's—the town's—fair-haired boy. He's—"

"Not Kip."

"Listen, Hamish. Something about him has been giving me the creeps lately. And he's not quite the angelic, clean-living young child everyone thinks. It wasn't much of anything, but about a week ago, he made a pass at me, in the car. Okay, kid stuff. But Kip's also—"

The police radio crackled Hamish's name. As soon as he acknowledged the call, he heard Tyne's voice. "The FCC guys tracked down both transmitters. We're letting them keep on broadcasting because we don't have any choice—those people in St. Andrews. But something you ought to know. One transmitter was found aboard an empty boat circling around in the Sound, off Long's Bay Harbor. The other—stationary this time—is somewhere off Seven Hills Road. To the left. The FCC's van's parked along the road directly opposite where they think it is. You're out near there, aren't you, Hamish? I've got backup cars coming, but—"

"On my way!"

Leaning forward abruptly, Hamish turned on the siren and flashers. Jenny found her feet instantly bracing themselves against the floor as the car roared up Seven Hills Road at an even more reckless speed than before. At the same time, she remembered she had something terribly important to tell Hamish. "Hamish . . . about Kip Grolier . . ."

His head turned toward her, and Jenny, seeing his eyes leave the road, shook her head vigorously. "Never mind, Hamish. The road, Hamish, for God's sake, the road!"

In St. Andrews, the crowd was growing restless. From the beginning it had been an eerie sensation to sit in the church with two giant speakers up on the pulpit talking to them instead of the minister. The parents shifted in their seats. It was clear that, for the moment at least, the Piper was marking time by playing old tapes, and the parents, their nerves already worn thin, began to look around impatiently and talk to one another. Then there was a pause in the transmission.

Abruptly, the long pause ended. "Now to business," said Kevin Blyden over the speakers. In his seat, Senator Blyden stiffened at the sound of his son's voice. "The newspaper and television people have kept asking themselves why I call myself the Piper. Simple. As they guessed, it goes back to the old Pied Piper of Hamelin yarn. But the analogy's a lot deeper than it looks. The original Piper, remember, made a deal with the fat cats of Hamelin to chase out the rats in return for loot. He got rid of 'em, okay, but when he came to collect, the fat cats reneged. So the Piper ran off with all the town's kids.

"That sounds like a long haul from Greenport and your children. Not so. Every parent, when he conceives a child, makes an implicit contract with that child to love it, to take care of it, to put it above all other things. In a place like Greenport, there has never been much question that the kids are well cared for. All the best money can buy. But love? The putting of your children above everything else? I don't think so.

"You may not even realize this yourself, but I suspect you think of your kids as possessions. Things to show off, things to be proud of, just like you do your house and your boat and your pool. I think you've broken your implied contract with your kids—and you know how we Pipers feel about that. It's the reason I've been taking your kids. The 'ultimate ransom' is your one chance to prove you really do love them, that you would sacrifice anything for them, would do anything—steal, cheat, kill—to save their lives. If you really love them, you'll pay the 'ultimate ransom' and I'll set them free. If you don't, well, they're probably better off dead anyway.

"Before this final ransom is put to you, there's a few small points you ought to know. This room was searched—and damned well, too—by the FBI, to uncover any explosives and stuff. All right. But come on. Do you really think a brain like the Piper's can't run circles around the FBI? Hasn't it so far? Watch . . ."

From the loudspeakers came a sudden burst of electronic tone, a short but intense high-pitched whine. With a sound that made everyone in the church jump, a frequency-activated device inside Kip's rucksack, still leaning against the side wall, caused the rucksack to burst into flames. Simultaneously, a canister of confetti shot up toward the ceiling. Like a display of fireworks exploding in midair, a rapid series of small explosions showered puffs of confetti above the pews, drifting down on the startled parents below.

"Pretty neat, right? You only know the half of it. Because, if I could engineer that little stunt, I could just as easily have hidden a bomb somewhere in this place, right? Then your kids would become orphans just before they become corpses . . .

"Okay, down to business. Your children are being held in a place with very limited air. Perhaps an hour's worth, maybe less. I have shut off the supply of new air. Very mean of me. The point is, if you don't love your kids enough to pay the 'ultimate ransom,' well, I shall simply leave the air turned off. Simple: your kids will suffocate. It's not a nice way to go, but there you are. All very businesslike, all very fair. The choice is yours.

"Now then . . . for the particulars of what you have to come up with for the 'ultimate ransom' . . ."

Chapter 24 _____

Looking back at everything that happened, I'm pretty sure my objectives were accomplished. At least, I think they were my objectives; that damned K.K. raised a lot of questions I'll never forgive him for. Of course, there's one thing he probably won't forgive me for, either.

Now, though, it's time to haul ass; things are getting too hot here. I have one more delivery of drugs which'll help Mom for a little while, I guess. I'll miss her, which is more than anyone else in my family can say. And there's the rest of my tapes to pick up; I wouldn't want anyone to find them.

So long, Jenny. So long, Greenport. So long, America. I wish I could say I enjoyed knowing you all.

—TAPE-LOG OF THE PIPER,
ENTRY DATED JUNE 14.

Pulled over to one side of Seven Hills Roads, Hamish saw the FCC truck and brought the police car with himself and Jenny to a halt behind it. The man in charge walked over and introduced himself. "I'm Jarret. The transmission point isn't in the main house—" he pointed up the long driveway to where you could see the lights of a large house burning brightly in the darkness—"but a little to the left. Maybe a hundred, hundred and fifty yards."

Hamish nodded and climbed back into his car, dousing the flashers as he did. Through the open window he spoke to Jarret. "Some backup cars should be here in a minute. Tell them where we are, but don't let them move in until my signal." He turned his head toward Jenny. "You probably ought to get out here, too."

"Not on your life."

Hamish shrugged and slowly drove up the driveway. As they passed the entrance gates, he felt Jenny's fingers tighten on his arm. "Hamish, did you see the name on that sign? 'Blakeslee.' This is K.K.'s place."

"I know."

"But he couldn't do it, Hamish. He's such a frail little kid ..."

"He could have friends. One, anyway."

The car stopped at the front door and Hamish rang the bell. To the large Irish housekeeper who opened the door, Hamish nodded and produced a badge from his jacket pocket. "Is K.K.—" Hamish caught himself—"is Timothy Blakeslee here?"

The Irish face studied him warily. "Is he being in trouble?"

"No. I just want to talk with him."

"Down in the lab. Always down there, he is."

"Lab?"

"Where he raises thim bloody rats. Frightful creatures they is, too. Been down there all day, it seems."

Jenny blinked, wondering how much symbolism was involved in what K.K. had chosen as pets. The original Pied Piper had ridded Hamelin of the rats, and then tried to keep the children; apparently, K.K. wanted to keep the rats and get rid of the children.

"Is his mother home?" asked Hamish.

"In Greenwich. With her sister."

"Do you have any objections if I go visit him in his lab?"

"K.K.? You can do anything you like with him. He's a bleedin' monster, that boy."

Hamish, followed by Jenny, walked quickly toward the one-story building the housekeeper had pointed out. Hamish reached it first and knocked at the door. There was no answer. To one side was a lighted window, and Hamish slipped along the wall of the building to look in. Behind him, he could hear Jenny coming up to join him. The window was partially steamed over and hard to see through, but he could make out enough to know the sight was not for Jenny. It was not for anyone.

"Hold it. Jesus. Don't look."

But his order came too late. Jenny was already at the window, and gasped in shock. The children in Greenport reportedly hated K.K., but with someone, it was a good deal more than hate. Difficult as it was to see through the cloudy window, it was possible to make out K.K.'s body lying on the floor, his arms outstretched as if crucified. There was no way to know how he had been killed, since not that much of him was visible; the doors to the cages holding the rats were open, and swarming knots of animals crawled back and forth across K.K.'s body.

For the first time in years, they didn't look hungry.

"Dad, Dad . . . you'd better do what he says . . . he's going to shut off the air . . . Dad . . ."

One after another, the voices of the children poured from the two giant speakers on either side of the pulpit of St. Andrews. "I don't know what he wants, Father . . . but he means what he says . . ."

"Mom, I'm cold . . . now he says he's going to shut off the air or something . . . can't you do anything, Mom?"

"Do what he says. Please, do what he says. I'm frightened. So frightened. Please come get me—" This voice, belonging to one of the younger children, stopped abruptly, overcome by sobbing. As parents recognized their own child—the voices were unidentified—a soft crying rose from some of them in the church, particularly the mothers; others sat in stony-faced silence, determined not to surrender to their emotions.

"Dad. Dad, listen . . ." said an urgent voice, one that anyone in the church—and the people across the country watching on television—could instantly recognize: it belonged to Paige Rathbin and was familiar to everyone because of his nightly stock market reports. "Dad, listen. I know, Dad, that he made you burn down the house, and I know how that must make you feel. But, Dad—whatever it is he wants, well—he's talking about doing what he did to Russel Hamilton to me, and . . . please, Dad . . ."

Kevin Blyden's voice, speaking as himself, not the Piper, rose over the crying and hammering from the vault. "I don't know what he's asking you to do, and I know you've got your position in the Senate to think about. So I won't try to influence you; you have to do what you think is right. But I can tell you—by now, I guess I really don't have to—that anything this Piper bastard says he'll do, he'll do. So there we are. I'll understand it, whatever decision you make . . ." There was a long moment of silence.

Then the voice of Kevin Blyden returned, once more speaking for the Piper. "The details of the 'ultimate ransom' are simple. You have always *claimed* you loved your kids. But—I've said it before—if you really loved your children, you'd be ready to lie, cheat, steal, kill, or destroy,—anything to save their lives. Very well, I now put that love to the test—in deeds, not words. The FBI and the police have put a man in here with you. I don't know what they thought he could do, but he's there . . ."

Sitting beside Senator Blyden, Charles Goodenaugh, Tyne's agent planted among the parents, struggled to conceal his surprise. Senator Blyden, who had been told of Goodenaugh's presence, tried to hide his own chagrin that the Piper knew about the man; he also discovered himself instinctively drawing away from the agent.

In his office, Tyne was confounded by the Piper's announcement. "How the hell did he know about Goodenaugh? God damn." The truth was Kip *didn't* know; he had guessed. In fact, he was so unsure that he had made an auxiliary tape—not discovered until later—in the event there was no planted agent. This tape ordered the parents to demand someone in authority join them in the church; the Piper suggested Hamish. Obviously, this tape was never needed.

"If you don't believe me," continued the Piper, "look around you, study the faces in the pews behind you. The stranger in your midst, the face you don't recognize, was put there by the FBI and the police." Automatically, all heads turned around to study the faces behind and around them; some of the people in the front pews stood up so they could see better.

Charlie Goodenaugh stuck out like a black trying to hide among whites, struggling to appear as much like the rest as he could, but aware even as he tried that his effort was doomed to failure. He blinked at the staring parents and shifted uneasily, feeling a rash of sweat well beneath his clothes. Senator Blyden continued looking straight ahead, as if Goodenaugh didn't exist; the stares from the other parents grew stronger and increasingly accusing, and a subdued angry murmur began filling the church.

"Do you see him? You will probably discover he is armed. Ask the nice man to give you his gun. Quickly. Before he can do something that will cost your children their lives."

The murmur grew, and the people in the church milled in confusion, some beginning to move toward Goodenaugh, then hesitating, then stopping where they were. "Take away his gun," the Piper demanded again. "Now!"

"Here," said Goodenaugh, pulling his revolver from inside his jacket and handing it, butt first, to Senator Blyden. The Senator nodded as he took the weapon, trying to avoid Goodenaugh's eyes as they searched his face, looking for help, silently pleading with the Senator to say something, do something.

"Very well," the tape continued. "In the rear of the church, there are two packages, just in front of the baptismal font. Take the package on the left; inside is some equipment you'll need."

The man nearest the font looked around himself self-consciously. Finally, with a shrug, he walked back and retrieved Kip's package at the base of the stone font. From the wrapping, the man drew a strange assortment of objects: several lengths of heavy rope, two large kitchen knives, some pieces of lighter rope, a short length of wood, a roll of adhesive tape, and a heavy hammer of the kind you use to drive a spike into a beam.

"In the package you will find all the necessary equipment to execute a man. You have your choice of hanging, garrotting, knifing, or using the traditional blunt instrument. You have no choice of victim: it is to be the man that the FBI planted among you. *Quid pro quo.* Nor do you have much time. You are to knock on the outer doors and then deposit the agent's body on the church steps, within one hour. *One hour.* I can easily see whether you do this or not. Unless I see the agent's body on those steps by the end of that hour, your kids will be allowed to suffocate. Don't feel any sympathy for your prospective victim; he is paid to take little risks like getting himself killed.

"I realize that the idea of such an execution will at first repel you; I had the same trouble myself when I began this project. But it grows on you. From time to time, as an added stimulus, I shall let you hear the voices of your children—slowly running out of air. I'll sign off for now, so you can decide how—and by whose hand—you plan to meet my demands."

As the parents looked at each other, no one so much as moved a finger. What they were faced with was too frightening. From the loudspeakers came the first installment of their children's voices, locked in their prison, beginning to panic as the air ran out. (Actually, this was a tape that had been made the day before and was pure fiction. But, as spliced together and edited by K.K., just before Kip killed him, anyone would have been hard-pressed to distinguish it from the real thing.) From the loudspeakers came a shuffling, moaning sound, interrupted by hammerings on the steel door and punctuated by anguished pleadings for air. Occasionally, a cry or scream would soar above the noise and confusion. To their mothers and fathers, clutching the edges of the pews in St. Andrews, the sounds dramatized the plight of their children as nothing else could.

The parents looked at each other, then at Goodenaugh. Helplessly, the agent again turned toward Senator Blyden, apparently expecting help. But the Senator only shook his head. "I'm sorry," he said softly, and moved further away.

At first, no one in the church could quite believe what had been proposed to them by the Piper. If anyone had told them they would ever even consider willfully killing a stranger—even to save their children's lives—they would have laughed. Yet they found themselves pushed toward Goodenaugh, as if propelled by invisible hands.

"I'm sorry," repeated the Senator, and turned his eyes away, as if not looking relieved him of the responsibility to act.

"That does it," swore Hamish, as the police car roared on down Seven Hills Road toward Greenport. "That goddamn Piper found out about Goodenaugh—how, I don't know—and he's putting the blocks to those parents. God only knows what they'll do. Damn, damn, damn." He turned his head to stare at Jenny in his helplessness; with her eyes, she told him to look at the road, not at her.

Hamish's radio crackled again. It was Tyne. "One new piece of information. The Coast Guard was able to piece together the registration number on the launch. It had been painted over, but they discovered the boat belonged to Mr. Grolier. Probably stolen. But since both the kid and his father are locked up in St. Andrews, we can't ask them about it now. Do you want me to send someone to their house, or—"

"No. On my way there. Almost at Long's Bay right now. Let me handle it."

"My notes," added Jenny. "That was what I was trying to tell you on the way to the Blakeslees, but you were too busy. They show that everybody hated K.K. so much they couldn't understand how Kip could be a friend of his. And Kip was a friend of K.K.'s, a very good friend. They said Kip tried to hide it, but everybody knew."

"Kip? I don't believe any of this. I don't believe he was a friend of K.K.'s. I don't think he's involved with this thing at all. I don't believe he did it. Some adult must have gotten K.K. to work with him. Then, when the situation got tight, the man killed him. Kip just doesn't make sense. That's why I didn't want Tyne sending a lot of people out to the Groliers, getting everybody all upset over nothing. There's some simple explanation to how Kip is concerned."

On her side of the car, Jenny sighed and kept quiet. Sometimes Hamish could be infuriating. With a squeal, the police car turned into the driveway of the Groliers and pulled up in front of the door, scattering a small shower of bluestone on either side of it. Silently, Hamish identified himself to Mrs. Braun, who answered the door. She looked at him in confusion.

"No one is home. Except Dee. Mr. Grolier and Kip, they are—"

"I know where they are. Is Mrs. Grolier at home?"

Mrs. Braun hesitated. From somewhere upstairs came a snatch of Chopin. For the first time that Mrs. Braun could remember, the playing didn't stop and begin repeating itself after the first few notes, but continued all the way through to the end of the piece. Her eyes widened slightly and she looked upwards, a small expression but one that Hamish didn't miss.

"I asked if Mrs. Grolier was at home."

Mrs. Braun sighed heavily, ushering Hamish and Jenny Cobb into the great front hall. *"Ja,* Mrs. Grolier is home. But Mrs. Grolier see no one. Ever. Please to understand, she is not well." Twirling one finger beside her forehead, Mrs. Braun grimaced.

"Could we go up anyway. It is urgent we talk to her. This is an official call."

"Oh, I don't know about that, sir. Mrs. Grolier is not well. I repeat. I am not sure—that is, I have my orders from Mr. Grolier. You see, I—"

"If she won't come down to see me," said Hamish firmly, "I am going up to see *her.* Understand?"

"That won't be necessary, officer."

Mrs. Braun spun around in amazement. Slowly descending the stairs, Mrs. Grolier walked with an almost regal carriage, carrying something in her hands. Only when she had reached the landing and advanced toward them did Hamish realize how unsteady her walk was. As soon as she came closer, Jenny immediately guessed, from the look of Mrs. Grolier's eyes and the trembling of her hands, that her problem was drug-related.

"I am Hamish Hamilton, ma'am. Thank you for coming down."

"I'm glad you are here. These. You should have these. I found them in Kip's drawer when I was looking for some— some medicine. You'll want them." Wordlessly, she handed Hamish a stack of recording cassettes, Kip's tapes.

Looking at her curiously, Hamish nodded in acknowledgment. "Thank you. But Kip isn't here, of course, is he? He's at . . ."

"Upstairs. Dead. I haven't been much of a mother, but that was one thing I could do for him." Staggering slightly, Mrs. Grolier sank into a hard wooden chair against the wall of the circular staircase, and Jenny rushed to help her. Hamish stood there, baffled—this strange lady telling them she had killed Kip. It didn't make sense.

Embarrassed, Hamish stood off at a distance watching as Jenny and Mrs. Braun tended to Mrs. Grolier, who was now shaking and trembling. His eyes, searching in embarrassment for anything to look at except this pathetic woman, wandered down to the cassettes she had handed him.

And suddenly, it all did make sense. On the cover of one of the boxes, in what he assumed was Kip's handwriting (actually, it was K.K.'s), was a list of what was on the tape inside, carefully numbered and coded: "5A—children screaming," "7d—R.H., yells, fingers," "7e—R.H., toes," "7f—R.H., emasc.," "10b—Paige Exchng anncmt, Jun 9." Hamish felt his knees turn weak. "R.H." could only be Russel. His own fingers shaking, Hamish looked at the covers of the other boxes. They were similar, although one carried the notation: "Tape-Log of the Piper." All of the tapes played on the air were there. Hidden, she said, beneath the clothes in Kip's bureau drawer. Found in his mother's search for "some—some medicine."

"God." Hamish dropped the whole stack of boxes, his own grief suddenly overwhelming him. To Jenny's stunned surprise, Hamish strode firmly over to Mrs. Grolier and began shouting at her, shaking her violently by the shoulders, demanding to know if she had any idea where the children were now. It was vital, he yelled at her.

Even more to Jenny's surprise was Mrs. Grolier's answer. Already on the edge of tears, she began to sob openly, the effects of drug withdrawal, along with her emotional state, coming together with explosive force. "I don't know where the children are. The tapes don't say. Kip didn't have any tapes that said anything about that. I don't know, oh, God, I'd tell you if I did, but I don't know."

To Dee, drawn from her room by the noise, and peering over the banister, the picture was bizarre. She had rarely seen her mother downstairs—in fact, she had seldom seen her mother at all—and now she was there, crumpled into a chair, being yelled at and shaken by an angry man she knew to be Greenport's Director of Police. Bewildered, she shot down the stairs, listening to Hamish's repeated demands.

Her mother kept denying that she knew where the children were, and Hamish kept insisting that if Kip knew, she must know. Abruptly, her mother dissolved into incoherent crying. Hamish suddenly spun on Dee and began shouting at her. Dee was confused and angry, not knowing what the shouting was about or why her mother was there. It all had something to do with the kidnapped children and the Piper, but what in God's name did that have to do with Kip or her mother? Ig-

noring Hamish, she began helping Mrs. Braun get her mother
to her feet. But when Dee, quite logically, began leading her
mother back upstairs, the mystery suddenly grew deeper.

"No, child. Not upstairs," warned Mrs. Braun, without explaining. "The library. The dining room. Anyplace, but not
back to her room." Dee was so baffled by everything that,
rather than question Mrs. Braun's statement, she helped her
to get her mother into the library. By now her mother was
shaking violently, becoming increasingly disjointed, her attempts to speak punctuated by periods of sobbing—something
about Kip that Dee couldn't understand—and moaning desperately in a way that shook Dee badly. Outside of the house,
Dee was dimly aware of the sounds of sirens and the arrival
of many people; through the window, she thought she saw
more police arriving, as well as an ambulance.

When she tried to question Mrs. Braun, the only response
she got was a firm shake of the head. Bewildered, confused,
and upset, Dee found the room suffocating, and was relieved
when a knock came on the door. A woman, whom she would
later learn was named Jenny Cobb, asked her to step into the
hall with her. Further down the same hall, in the living room,
Dee could see Hamish Hamilton and a circle of police officers, as well as some men in plain gray suits, gathered
around a machine playing the tapes which had seemed to be
such a matter of dispute between her mother and Hamish.
Seeing Dee, the men grew briefly silent.

"Dee," said Jenny softly. "A lot has happened, and I know
it's very tough for you to absorb all of it at once. And I'm
afraid I have even worse news for you." Quickly, Jenny told
her of Kip's involvement with the kidnappings, and that he
was the Piper she had undoubtedly been reading about. Dee
was stunned, so stunned that Jenny decided for the moment
against adding that Kip was dead. "Can you think—I know
that it's hard for you to concentrate on something like this
now—but, can you think of any place where your brother
might have hidden the children, someplace they could be held
captive?"

"Why don't you ask Kip? I don't believe what you said
about him and the children, or him being the Piper or anything else like that. Kip's the greatest brother anyone could
have. Everybody knows that."

"Fair enough, Dee. But those children's lives—your brother Carey's too—depend on finding them soon, very soon. Their air's been turned off and they'll suffocate if we don't. So without saying anything more about Kip—remember, I know him and I'm very fond of Kip myself—could you tell me if there's any special place where he hangs around, anyplace where he might help someone else hide a whole group of children?" Jenny felt cheap using such a primitive brand of psychology—helping Dee shift the blame away from her brother to someone else. Still, it was necessary.

Dee shook her head, turned away, and started back into the library—anything to escape this woman and her hateful accusations about Kip. "I'm sorry, Dee," Jenny called after her. "But it's true. You can't avoid the truth by running away."

"It's not true, it's not, it's not, it's not!" screamed Dee suddenly. It all caught up with her at once, and she sagged against the door. Jenny tried to put one arm protectively around her, but Dee shook herself loose and began to run away, then abruptly stopped, spinning around to face Jenny, speaking through her tears. "You're all after him. You're all after him because he's too good, too perfect, that's what bugs everybody. Why can't you leave us alone?" Turning, she raced up the stairs to her room, her sobs drifting back to Jenny below.

The hammering in the stone-walled chamber was deafening; three of the older boys were beating their fists against the steel in concert, clinging to the slender hope that someone aboveground might hear them. Kevin Blyden and Paige knew better. Unlike the others, they had had considerable dealings with both K.K. and Kip since their capture; it had been necessary because of their role as tape-spokesmen for the Piper. To make the tapes, they had both been taken from the chamber many times, and therefore knew the layout better than the rest.

Kip, they were sure, would have put the cover back on the cistern when he left; the rest of them could hammer until they were blue in the face and not be heard. Their faces were almost blue anyway. Inside the vault, the air was stale and growing staler; with every minute, it became harder to breathe. You would draw in a mouthful of what you thought was air, yet it had an unsatisfying, unfilling feel to it that meant you had to take another breath almost immediately. Most of the younger boys were crying, some calling for their mothers, but a few were curled up in a semi-fetal position on the hard floor, making no sound at all. Henry Cabot, an enormously fat boy for his 13 years, had already collapsed, resisting all attempts to revive him.

Wearily, Kevin Blyden turned to Paige. "It's just a matter of time. Son of a bitch. I was going to be in politics like my old man."

Paige shrugged. He was about to say something, but when he tried, he broke into a fit of coughing so violent that Kevin had to put out an arm to support him. For some reason unclear to Kevin, his arm was almost immediately pushed away. Kevin did not know that Paige, since the incident with K.K., could not bear to be touched by another human, or that the one thing in the world that Paige wanted right now was to be left alone, by himself, to die in the dignity of solitude.

"Could I have your attention, please? Please, would you listen to me?" Senator Blyden had listened, hoping the angry arguments between the different factions of the parents would die down on their own. When they didn't, the Senator climbed up onto a pew-seat and bellowed for silence. The din slowly subsided and the eyes of the parents turned towards him. He nodded in appreciation, trying not to let the careful scrutiny of his wristwatch show. They had, by his figuring, only half an hour left before the Piper's deadline. Then the children . . .

"It's my feeling, since there is so little time to make this decision and it's a very complicated one, that we should take a vote. I would add, for myself, that it is impossible for me to conceive of our killing this man . . . that would be murder . . . in its own way as bad as anything the Piper has done. Yet, on the other hand, I must confess I have an equally hard time trying to picture us sentencing our own children to death by not meeting the ransom demands."

For a second, the Senator stared at Goodenaugh. "However, in any case—and no matter how justified we might feel—killing this man would still be an act of murder."

Senator Blyden was reasonably sure that the vote, however
it came out, would be meaningless. Let them vote. He was
convinced that these people were incapable of killing someone in cold blood. He was unprepared for the reaction that
he got.

"We can vote until Hell freezes over. And if it'll make
anybody feel better, maybe we should. But it's not the kind
of thing you can run by majority vote, the way you can run
Congress, Senator. I'll be goddamned if I'm going to let my
boy die because we decided it by vote." This impassioned
voice came from Everett Quinn, one of New York's most
persuasive criminal lawyers. He stood glaring at the Senator,
apparently prepared to do battle.

Quinn picked up support almost immediately; Ray Pierce's
father came and stood at his elbow. "It has to be done in a
way that allows no single one of us to be guilty. They can't
put the whole body of us in jail. Extenuating circumstances . . ."

"Extenuating circumstances, my ass," said someone else.
"Who's going to do the actual killing? Who shoves in the
knife, or tightens the noose, or uses the sledgehammer? Who?"

Quinn's fine legal mind had been exploring the same area.
"The thing, I think, would never be decided on simple evidence, anyway. Too many people involved. They probably
wouldn't even charge anyone with murder but with something
more like second-degree manslaughter . . ."

Suddenly, one of the few mothers who was against meeting
the Piper's demands spoke up. "Tell that to the man sitting
back there. Or to his widow or children. I want my boy res-
cued, God knows, but . . ."

"Try telling yourself you let your child die because you
didn't have the guts to do what had to be done," said another
mother, and burst into tears.

Goodenaugh listened, feeling increasingly frightened. He
had no instructions on this situation, because none of the
men who had sent him here could possibly have known what
would happen. He had surrendered his gun without a qualm;
certainly, these people were far too respectable to do anything as crazy as what they were talking about. But as he
watched the parents divide into two groups, one of which actually seemed intent on killing him as demanded, he had first

been stunned, then apprehensive. The unidentified voice's questions about who was going to "shove in the knife or use the sledgehammer" had finally unnerved him completely. Studying them, he decided these people were middle-aged, soft, and out of condition; he was young, lithe, and in excellent shape. Without having any particular plan, Goodenaugh suddenly darted out of the pew and raced toward the church's doors. Beyond them lay sanity and safety. For a second, he wrestled with the lock, forced it open, and was able to get one arm and one leg through the partially opened door. But from what seemed out of nowhere, two men suddenly grabbed him from behind and sent him crashing to the floor, where he lay, stunned by his fall.

When he came to, he lay in the center aisle of St. Andrews, his hands and feet tightly trussed together. The floor was of stone and felt hard beneath him, made only marginally more comfortable by a pew cushion one of the mothers was stuffing beneath his head. "You don't have to take it out on him. Give him something to lie on, anyway. He was only doing his job."

Some of the sympathy for Goodenaugh from the undecided group evaporated during his escape attempt. "Sending him in here was playing with our kids' lives. So was trying to escape," said a sudden voice from the rear.

Looking at his watch again, Senator Blyden could see their time was evaporating. He again began pushing for a vote, although he still believed it would have little effect on the outcome; some strong individual was going to emerge from the two groups and get everyone in line behind him. By rights that person should be him, but he had no stomach for the job.

When counted, the vote stood at twenty-six to twenty-four in favor of sacrificing Goodenaugh in favor of the children. But, as Blyden expected, almost as soon as the vote was taken, the arguments began all over again. Exhausted, the Senator sank into a seat. A decision had been reached, but he doubted if they would ever actually go through with it. Suddenly thinking of his son Kevin, Senator Blyden couldn't make up his mind whether he hoped they would or they wouldn't. It was all such a waste.

Hamish, still listening to the tapes, had come to the conclusion that Mrs. Grolier was telling the truth. There was no location mentioned, even on the tapes never broadcast. Wearily, he looked at Jenny. "You can't get anything out of the sister?"

"I don't think that she knows anything. Terribly upset and not making much sense. I can try again, but . . ."

The telephone was handed to Hamish. It was Tyne. "I think they're about to pole-ax Goodenaugh, the crazy bastards. I lied and told them we've found the kids—I think now we will—but they won't believe me. Christ, try pumping the sister again. I don't want Goodenaugh killed for what I ordered him to do. Besides, if we don't find those kids soon, they're goners."

Hamish looked at Jenny blankly. "Give the sister another crack."

Jenny knocked and walked into Dee's room. The girl was lying on her bed crying. "Get out," screamed Dee as soon as she saw who it was. Jenny winced, but walked into the room anyway. This was no time for psychology; this was no time for gentleness. It was time for the truth—brutal or not.

Jenny quickly strode over to the bed. "Dee," she began. The girl jumped off the bed and ran to the far side of the room, flattening herself against the wall and staring at Jenny like a trapped animal. Taking a deep breath, Jenny said what had to be said. "It was Kip, Dee. I knew it, your mother knew it. That's why she killed Kip. Because she knew it."

Another scream burst out of Dee. Jenny walked over and shook the girl, as hard as she could. Telling Dee this way about Kip was probably cruel; telling her that her mother had killed him was even crueler.

"Listen, Dee, listen. I know that all of this is horrible to hear. And you have every right to hate me, because I'm the person you're hearing it from. But Dee, out of hearing it can come some good. Out of all the dreadful things that have come out of this house this afternoon, something good can really come. Please, for Heaven's sake, if you have the faintest idea of where Kip might be hiding those children, tell me, and tell me now. Their lives depend on it. Your brother's life. And a lot of other children's. Tell me, Dee, tell me."

Tearing herself away, Dee threw herself on the bed again, crying uncontrollably. But finally, between the wracking sobs, came the words Jenny had been waiting for—blurred, semi-incoherent, hard to understand. "I'm not sure, but the cistern," Dee said, between convulsions of crying. "It *might* be the cistern. Kip always called it his private place. Ever since I can remember. And there's a hidden tunnel or something."

Jenny began racing to the door but stopped to hug Dee, who, she could guess, was probably feeling guilty for having said so much. For what Dee would consider treachery.

"It's murder, plain murder." Frank Parmalee, father of the boy Kip shot on the bus, said the words softly, shaking his head in wonder as he listened to the discussion in St. Andrews. "I've lived here twenty years and I know all of you. You're my friends. And it's just damned hard to believe you'd even consider killing this, this—" with his head, Parmalee indicated Goodenaugh, as he struggled for the right word to use in describing the FBI man—"this stranger. At the whim of a psychopath. Impossible to believe." He shook his head again, looking reproachfully at the other parents, and then at Goodenaugh.

For a moment, his words had an effect. Greenport was Greenport, after all, and the members of this curious lynch mob were mostly well-educated, all affluent, and, under normal conditions, reasonably civilized. But the strain of the last few weeks had created a lot of exposed nerves, and now that the parents held—if they were to take the Piper's word—the fate of their children in their own hands, the strain rendered them less than rational. Parmalee would ordinarily have represented the voice of calm and reason; in these circumstances, he represented just another stumbling block to what the parents desperately wanted to believe: that they could make a deal and save their children.

Everett Quinn broke the silence, championing the opposite viewpoint, even if retreating to a point that was pretty weak: "We took a vote."

Parmalee's over-large head swung toward him. "Votes can be changed. For God's sake, we have absolutely no assurance this Piper whatever-he-is will release the children. Sure, we can do what he says and lynch this man, but it still doesn't mean the children will be set free. Or hell, they could be dead already."

Everett Quinn used the same patronizing, derisive tone that he used in court to demolish unfriendly witnesses. "Or they could *become* dead because we don't meet the deadline. For Christ's sake, don't other people here at least want to take a chance the children will be freed if we play this nut-case's game?"

The discussion quickly dissolved into everyone talking at once. Each group now had a leader—Quinn for meeting the Piper's demand, Parmalee against a murder he suspected would produce nothing—and the two men were in the forefront of the argument. But the others were also splintering into groups of two and three, and tempers rapidly went from frayed to violent. With a few exceptions, most of the mothers there were willing to stand behind Quinn and the lynching; the maternal instinct had not diminished. But the men, by and large, faced the thought of killing Goodenaugh with reluctance, clinging to the logic that it might easily make them all murderers without saving the children.

Their heightened tempers soon led to angry yelling and near-skirmishes between individuals on opposite sides; the shouting and arguing grew deafening in the vaulted, echoing interior of St. Andrews. From outside was added the hammering on the door, produced by Blagden Tyne. But by now they all knew by heart what Tyne was yelling, and ignored him; the Piper's tape had warned them to watch out for tricks that the FBI might use to protect its man inside.

"I mean it," yelled Tyne. "It's true. Okay, I lied the first time. But we know where the children are now—Christ, believe me, we do—and they'll be here any minute. Don't harm that man you have in there. The children are all right." When there was no answer again, Tyne and two policemen tried to force the doors open, but the parents had locked them from the inside to prevent any such maneuver. The hammering continued, and the arguments grew louder and angrier; everyone appeared to be yelling at once. Standing on one of the pew-seats, Senator Blyden roared at the shouting, pushing mob, trying to make them realize how little time they had left before the deadline.

Parmalee saw his chance. Blyden still held the revolver which Goodenaugh had surrendered earlier, but by now it had become so much a part of him that he held it loosely in his right hand, waving it aimlessly as he yelled at the parents. With a sudden lunge, Parmalee grabbed the revolver out of the Senator's hand and stepped back the four paces to where Goodenaugh lay in the aisle. Standing over him, Parmalee fired the gun into the air. The sound was so loud and unexpected that the parents were stunned, staring at Parmalee in unearthly silence.

Unblinking, Parmalee stared back. "I'll be goddamned if this thing is going to go any further. The first person—I don't care who it is—that takes one single step toward this poor guy here can figure on getting himself shot. Just because the Piper's crazy doesn't mean we have to be crazy, too."

"You son of a bitch, Parmalee." Except for a long troubled sigh from Senator Blyden, still standing on the pew-seat, Everett Quinn's voice was the only sound inside the church. But in spite of the silence, Parmalee did not hear from behind him the soft closing of the door that led to the basement of St. Andrews, swinging gently to and fro as someone returned from the men's room.

Senator Blyden stared once again at his wristwatch; the Piper's deadline was eight minutes and thirty seconds away.

The children returned to Greenport at 10:02 P.M. They arrived in fire trucks, sirens screaming, children shouting, the crowd outside of St. Andrews exploding into wild cheers. From nowhere, the Greenport High School Band materialized and was playing "Happy Days Are Here Again," over and over.

When Hamish and the State Troopers had first broken into the cistern's vault, they were sure they were too late. But oxygen tanks, blankets, and liberally administered shots of cognac brought the children around very quickly. Only Henry Cabot, the fat, likable Henry, seemed to be in real trouble, and a hastily summoned ambulance had already taken him to Greenport Hospital. All of the children should probably have gone to the hospital right away for examination—a doctor who lived further down Long's Bay Harbor from the Groliers made this point endlessly—but because Hamish kept hearing Tyne's pleadings over his radio—that only the children themselves could now convince their parents to open the church doors and save Goodenaugh—he snapped at the doctor: "Later, you can examine them later."

The scene at St. Andrews was bedlam. The television lights, all turned on at once, made the steps as brilliant as noon; there seemed to be children everywhere, with the blankets their rescuers had wrapped them in flapping behind them like enormous cloaks. On their way up the steps, they were hugged by friends, by other relatives not inside St. Andrews, and by total strangers. Tears ran down the children's faces, down the faces of the onlookers, and even down some of the newsmen's.

Prodded by Hamish, the children joined Tyne in hammering on the great doors, yelling to their parents inside that they were free. Free! With a noisy sliding of bolts, the doors were unlocked on the inside and their parents stood there, blinking in the sudden brightness of the television lights.

With shouts of joy, the children hurled themselves into their parents' arms, sobbing, crying, touching, feeling—as if to make sure that the experience was real. The parents whose children hadn't survived—the Sanchezes, the Axminsters, the Stokleys, all of the early victims—stood to one side, happy for the others but unwilling to accept what had happened to themselves, their eyes devouring the children as if they expected some miracle to make their own children suddenly materialize.

It was Kevin Blyden who noticed it first. The Senator could tell immediately from the shock he saw cross the boy's face. "Let's go, son," he said quickly. "Your mother and I want to get you back to your brothers and sisters. And the reporters outside will want me to make a statement. Then we can—"

"Jesus Christ . . ."

The Senator grabbed his wife by one hand and Kevin with the other, and began pushing his way through the crowd. But some mysterious current of electricity had been set off by Kevin, and the other children suddenly stopped talking, their heads turning to see what Kevin had seen.

Hanging from a cross-rafter of St. Andrews, swaying gently in the soft night breeze blowing off Long Island Sound, was the body of Charles F. Goodenaugh, Civil Service Classification 4, assigned to the Federal Bureau of Investigation, and late of Garden City, New York. His eyes were wide, his mouth hung open, and his body was limp. Goodenaugh's personal nightmare was over, and his head kept nodding, as if to acknowledge the cheering still audible from the street.

But the parents could no longer hear the sound.

For them, the nightmare was just beginning.

> *A lot of people are going to say that I was crazy for what I did. But if my guess is right, what will happen at St. Andrews will show I'm no crazier than the next guy, and that when it's necessary, anyone puts the end before the means.*
>
> *Most important of all, I think I'll have made my point. For I suspect the ultimate ransom will be paid by those mothers and fathers, proving what I guess I suspected all along; they really do love their kids. They just make it damned hard for anyone—even themselves—to believe.*
>
> *And, in a crazy kind of way, I suppose that maybe right there was my whole problem—and the problem of most kids in a place like Greenport. The need for proof. Because maybe love is something that shouldn't have to be proved—just accepted.*
>
> —TAPE-LOG OF THE PIPER,
> ENTRY DATED JUNE 3RD.

Coda _____

She had never meant it to happen, but it had. A wave of resentment swept over her and she decided her first assessment had been right—"a cop, for Christ's sake." No, that was unfair. But the progression of events still mystified Jenny. Little by little, Hamish crept into her life. First, it had only been physical—and that mostly on sudden whim. But Jenny was a very physical person, and gradually, insidiously, unnoticed, strong emotions and deep feelings invaded her way of thinking of Hamish. Damn. Watching him and Ollie load up the Datsun that morning, Jenny felt unreal.

"I'm taking Ollie back to Wyoming. Hell, you probably guessed that anyway. We're leaving in the morning." He had said it late the night before, sitting with her at the Seven Points bar, exhausted but relieved that the children were finally found.

"Wyoming," Jenny repeated, as if the word was the springing of a trapdoor. "Wyoming," she said again, trying to hide the hurt and bewilderment and shock. A couple of times in the last few days, Hamish mentioned something about taking Ollie away, but Jenny had paid little attention. She hadn't dared to.

"It's home—Wyoming. Ollie's never seen it. The doctor says Martha will be 'away' for a long time—maybe forever—and the kid just has to get away from here and everything it stands for. Christ, what he's been through . . ."

"That's it, isn't it? Ollie."

"Ollie."

"I can't fight that."

Hamish had looked at her strangely, not seeming to understand what she felt. Now, this morning, watching them struggle to get things onto and into the Datsun, all of Jenny's feelings came together with a rush, and Jenny wasn't sure she understood what she felt herself. Twice, Hamish turned from shoving things into the car to stare straight at her, his mouth half open, as if he were on the edge of saying something, but then he bit his lip and went back, his work with the boxes and crates and bags. Their conversation was sparse and on meaningless subjects, devoid of any sense of focus. Jenny didn't even try; she knew Hamish well enough to know what in him could be changed and what couldn't.

They promised each other, of course, that they would write, and maybe someday see one another, but their words had that hollow sound you hear in people saying good-bye at the end of a ship's cruise. Before Hamish climbed into the car, they kissed and held each other for a moment, but the embrace had the same tentative, awkward feeling as their words.

For a long time after Hamish drove away, Jenny stared at the street where the car had been, half expecting him to come back, sweep her off her feet, and carry her away to Casper, Wyoming. But this, she knew, was fantasy.

Unlike Kip Grolier, Jenny Cobb knew precisely how love was and was not proven.